Ernest Hamilton

The Perils of Josephine

Ernest Hamilton

The Perils of Josephine

ISBN/EAN: 9783337423094

Printed in Europe, USA, Canada, Australia, Japan

Cover: Foto ©Andreas Hilbeck / pixelio.de

More available books at **www.hansebooks.com**

The
Perils *of* Josephine

BY

LORD ERNEST HAMILTON
AUTHOR OF
"THE OUTLAWS OF THE MARCHES," "THE MAWKIN OF THE FLOW"

HERBERT S. STONE & COMPANY
CHICAGO & NEW YORK
MDCCCXCIX

CONTENTS

CONTENTS

THE PERILS OF JOSEPHINE

CHAPTER I

THE DAYS OF AULD LANG SYNE

THREE dull maids sat in a dull room, in the dull, dull town of Chelmsford. Two of these maids were old, and one young. For ten long grey years had these three lived together in that same little house, and during all these years there had happened nothing—absolutely nothing—that would in the very least degree repay recording. Twice in every week the coaches to and from London would rattle past the windows with a great to-do, the guard tooting on his long polished horn, and the driver cutting strange patterns in the air with his whip. And twice in every day, with the first clatter of hoofs on the bald cobbles, would the three of us rush to the window and flatten our noses against the glass, and this without fail and with a zest that never waned. Now and again the great coach would race past with double clatter and double speed; and when that was so, it was as sure as anything could be that it was not the red-faced driver that was on the box, but some dandy buck, with broad-brimmed beaver, and big white buttons staring from his coat like eyes. Very fine and elegant were some of these young men, and one there was one day that, seeing my face pressed against the glass, took off

his hat and bowed to me very low and gracefully, at
which my two dear aunts, as with one accord, must
needs lift up their hands and eyes in a very agony of
horror.   Dear, sweet souls!   It was many a year before
that young man's bow was wiped from their simple
memories.   It may be, it was more than a day before it
was wiped from mine; he was such a *very* elegant young
man, with long yellow whiskers, as I remember, and a
glass screwed into his eye!   And then the honour of it!
For I was no great beauty in those days, nor, goodness
knows, at any other time; but least of all, I think, then.
I can see myself as I write—a memory brushed up in
some part by a mournful old daguerreotype, in red and
gold setting—a tall, rather big girl, with brown hair
held in a net, a very short skirt supported by a hoop,
and an ample show of white cotton stocking!   And yet
he bowed to me!   Mercifully the stocking was hidden,
or it might have been otherwise, but he *did* bow.

Later on, alas! after the world had lived down its
terror of the snorting, rushing, rattling trains, the running of the coaches dwindled down to once a week only,
and half the joy of life was gone.

Ah! those early days in dear, sleepy, dull, stupid little Chelmsford!   They were wearisome enough at the
time, I take it, for all the golden glamour with which
time has clothed them.   But *now*, as a set-off to the
existing, the ever-abused, but really enjoyable and here-
after-very-much-to-be-regretted existing, they seem to
me like glimpses of far-off fairyland itself, just as *then*
the old half-forgotten days at Selworth stood out as
misty dreams of Paradise.

But, in honest truth, poor Chelmsford must have
been a very sink of dulness.   Old Bob Sellar, the milk-

man, in his embroidered smock, the occasional town-crier, the coaches as long as they lasted, and the winter fox-hunters galloping down to the Roothens on their hacks, or else ambling through soberly on their square-tailed hunters—these, with once in a blue moon the hounds themselves trotting meekly through the town, were all that we poor maids, young and old, had to bring us to the window. There was church, it is true, the old Parish Church, with good Mr. Baggally droning peace-fully from the pulpit, and the endless Merridew family staring at us from the pew opposite from under their poke bonnets (there were two without poke bonnets, and these, perhaps, stared hardest of any), and the Hallets, and the Hay-Brownes, and the Calverlies—the dull, dull Calverlies—whom we *knew*, and who would walk back with us as far as their stiff, square house, that was so like their dear, dowdy selves. There were others whom I forget (it matters little), and others whom I remember (which matters equally little), they were not of a stimu-lating kind. All the inhabitants of Chelmsford were women, or seemed to be—women and girls, girls and women. They swarmed everywhere, in church, in the street, at the archery meetings that all the world was mad about, and at the flower shows down in the tent by the river; everywhere, in short, except on the coaches and in the "Saracen's Head."

We always passed the "Saracen's Head" in those days with quickened pace and averted eye, and on the far side of the street. Goodness knows what scenes of wild riot and debauchery our simple minds did not pic-ture within those walls! Poor, innocent, reputable hos-telry! furnisher, too, of many a sober, welcome haven to weary wayfarer! The origin of this grim investment is hard to fix. I think it may have found its birth one winter's night, some two years after the date of my coming. We were walking home from tea-taking with Mrs. Baggally, my two aunts and I, and under cover of the dark, on the near pavement! There were brilliant lights in the windows of the first floor, and as we passed we could hear (and in truth without strain) shouts of laughter, and the bawling of a strong, rollicking chorus. A hunting chorus I took it to be, but of that I am not sure; but whatever it was, from that day on, the "Saracen's Head" was a place to be passed hurriedly and with averted eye.

However, all this is twaddly and inconsequent, and of no interest at all; nor was it of any interest to me at the time, only afterwards, in the light of retrospective sentiment which means nothing.

The Great Event, which I meant to start away with at the beginning, came when I had been at Chelmsford ten years, all but two months; and it came as we sat at tea—the silent, contemplative tea, with which we sustained vitality before bed. We never wasted words at meals; we had worn bare all recognised topics exactly seven years before. Both my aunts were of anecdotal rather than discursive habit; and oh! what dull little anecdotes they were!—dull the first time of hearing, but things of misery and dread at the end of ten long years! Heaven forgive me if I turned at times the cold ear of inattention.

But to the Event. We were at tea, when enter Jane with a letter—a letter for *me!* It was the first and only letter, to the best of my belief, I had ever received in my life. Think of that, ye maidens of busy pen and breakfast-table budgets!

Aunt Maria gasped; Aunt Emily became amiably suspicious, her thoughts flying back six weeks to the young
beau on the box of the London coach, and his never-to-
be-forgotten bow.

My thoughts, it must be owned, ran mildly in the
same direction, and vague visions of titles and coronets,
hurled recklessly at my white-stockinged feet, rose pleasantly before my eyes. But it was nothing of this kind;
it was something far more wonderful—so wonderful,
indeed, that it deserves to be set down in full:

SELWORTH, *22nd September.*

MY DEAR JOSEPHINE,—It would give your uncle and myself
great pleasure if you could manage to pay us a visit here. If
your dear aunts can spare you, we would like you to come at once,
and stay with us till the end of April, when we shall be going to
town for the season. You will doubtless be as glad to see the old
place again as we shall be to see you. Your cousins send their
best love.—With kindest regards to your dear Aunts Fielding,
believe me, dear Josephine, your very affectionate Aunt,

HARRIET DE METRIER.

P. S.—I would advise you to avoid the railroad, which, though
it might bring you somewhat quicker, is terribly unsafe, and, Dr.
Watson assures me, highly injurious to the health.

What are poor words to express the effect of this
missive on our little party? For ten years, mind, my
grand relations at Selworth Abbey had ignored my very
being. During ten years, out of their boundless wealth,
they had not been able to spare one penny for the pleasure or maintenance of poor, penniless, homeless me.
And now this invitation! and for eight months, too! It
was bewildering. The magnitude of the event positively
stunned us for a time. We felt much as Cinderella must
have felt when the pumpkin and the mice swelled into a

coach and four, or was it a coach and six? Aunt Maria was the first to recover herself.

"It is a great honour," she said, reflectively.

"And a great chance," added Aunt Emily, sugges-tively.

And then they both said, "Ah!" and pursed their lips.

"How old is Norman now?" Aunt Maria asked after a pause.　·

"Twenty-six, I think, and Claud two years younger. Sophie must be about your own age, Josephine. Let me see, how old *are* you, child?"

"Eighteen," I said.

"Well, I think Sophie must be a year older; anyhow, there's no great difference."

We all drank more tea; we were agitated, one and all.

"Isn't it ext*raor*dinary?" I said for the tenth time.

"Yes, my dear, most extraordinary, even more ex-traordinary perhaps than you think." This from Aunt Maria.

"Why?"

"Well, you see, Norman is a very great *parti*, and eight months is a long time, and—well, you are attrac-tive, you know, my dear."

Was I? It was the first I had heard of it.

"Well?" I said.

My two aunts coughed simultaneously—thin, genteel coughs—behind their mittens. I saw them exchange a quick glance.

"Well, you see, Josephine, it is possible that Norman, or even Claud, might—ahem—grow attached to you."

"Do you mean fall in love?"

My aunt frowned slightly, and puckered up her mouth. I think she considered the expression immoral.

"Well, yes."

"What fun! I hope they do."

"They!" This from both at once. "My dear child!"

"Oh, well, one would do. Are they handsome?"

"All the De Metriers, my dear, are handsome. Your poor, dear father was the only one that in any way fell short of the standard. And indeed, there is no doubt he fell very far short."

"Poor papa! was he so *very* ugly?"

"Yes, my dear, he was very ugly. He was misshapen, you know, and then his eyes were not straight. We never could imagine what poor Lucy saw in him."

I gave a little sigh for my poor dead parents. It was only a little one, for I had never known them. My mother was only a name, and my father a misty memory.

"But tell me about my cousins," I said. "What are they like? I used to hate them all, if I remember."

"Norman is very handsome, like all his race; not very tall, and dark as a foreigner. He is said to be rather wild."

"Wild?" I said. "What's wild? How is a man *wild?* It sounds like a cat or a bullfinch."

"I fancy it means," said Aunt Emily, doubtfully, "that they spend most of their time at their club."

Aunt Maria shook her head mournfully.

"More than that, Emily—more than that."

"Well," said I, "I like the sound of it. I think it sounds rather fascinating. I think I shall like Norman."

I half expected an outburst of horror. I think that was half the reason why I said it; it was such fun shocking those dear old things. But they were not shocked.

"He will be very wealthy," sighed Maria.

"Perhaps he will like *you*," suggested Emily, roguishly.

I looked down at my white cotton stockings and clump-soled boots, and doubted it.

"Well, I don't care if he doesn't," I said. "Who wants him to?"

The evening meal had been extended half an hour beyond the prescribed time. We always sat down at six and rose at six-forty by the clock. It was now twenty minutes past seven.

"Maria," said Aunt Emily, with sudden decision, across the table, "Josephine must have clothes.".

Aunt Maria screwed up her mouth and nodded emphatic assent.

"It must be managed," she said.

Aunt Maria was the treasurer.

CHAPTER II

I ENTER THE GOLDEN GATES

THREE weeks later I took the coach to London, the one weekly coach that still ran, in defiance of the ceaseless rush of trains. Oh! that parting at the "Saracen's Head!" How we cried, and laughed, and blubbered, and kissed! How we see-sawed from one shoulder to the other as though tired of kissing the same cheek! How we clawed and clutched at one another's backs! I don't know which cried the most. I think I did. Young tears come the readier. And the driver, and the guard, and the grinning 'ostlers, and the two young men going back to Oxford, and the thin commercial traveller, and the apoplectic female on the box-seat, we minded no more than if they had been moles. Emotion such as ours is blind to surroundings. Why do we ever say good-bye? It is so much better not, which is bad grammar, but what I mean.

I tumbled up somehow on to the seat behind the driver. The commercial traveller and the two Oxford men were there already. They were very kind; I don't know what they said, but they were very kind. I turned round and waved my handkerchief wildly. I think I waved long after we were out of sight, but I was quite blind with tears; I could see nothing. The Oxford men made me change my place and sit between them; they said it was less dusty. Ah! dear old Chelmsford! per-

haps not *really* dear, but dear because of associations; if
I had known it was good-bye for ever, I might have shed
more abundant tears than I did.   And dear old aunts!
really dear old aunts; if I had known I was never again to
sit in the front parlour drinking cheap tea out of the
cracked blue "chaney" cups, and listening, or pretending to listen, to those old, old anecdotes that I knew as
well as the Lord's Prayer, I would have died, died a
dozen deaths, before I would have been dragged off to
London and Selworth, and the misty uncertainty that
there lay hidden.

Both are long since dead—dead and forgotten—two
of the many little grey lives that go out quietly and
leave no mark behind.   But for me they will always
stand out as the best thing I have chanced upon in this
world—always excepting one other.   I used to laugh at
them, I used to be rude to them, I used to snub them.
I thought them ignorant and stupid and prim, and—
Heaven forgive me!—even vulgar and affected.   And
it may be they were all this.   Even now, sober and sensible as I am, and full of the grey wisdom of years, I
think they *were*.   But what is the weight of such things
when pitted against the simple sweetness of true tender
hearts?   And with it all, I loved them, thank *le bon Dieu*
for that—loved them all the time I was turning up my
silly young nose at their little old-world tricks and man-
nerisms; not, indeed, because of their good-Samaritan-
ism towards myself, which, childlike, I took as a matter
of course, but because I was not quite the fool in heart
that I was in head.   Peace be to them and to all such!
There is a gospel in their very memory.

My fellow-travellers were very kind.   They pointed
out the many points of interest for which I had so little

present appetite, and saw to my wraps and packages, and to the many needs that I should never have known of but for their showing. They brought me tea and cake at Brentwood, and cake and tea again at Romford, where, indeed, I had no stomach for it, and made the young man that brought it give it to the lady on the box-seat, at which the others all laughed till we were half-way to Stratford. What they saw to laugh at I don't know, for the poor woman was red and hot and puffing, and I am sure in far greater need of refreshment than I was.

London that night, where I was met and housed and fed and comforted by one Mrs. Jedkins, a kindly soul, and a friend of my aunts. She kept a lodging-house in Moorgate Street.

The next day on to Selworth by the train, with a high beating heart and expectation on tip-toe. At Greystoke my uncle's carriage met me. Such a carriage! roomy, well-padded in drab-coloured cloth, and ponderous as a waggon; but with all this, sufficiently comfortable, and with a certain musty smell of its own that I liked, and that hangs in my memory still, pleasantly.

What a fine touch of borrowed glory there is in another man's carriage—when one is inside it! I felt quite an inch taller (though there was little need for that) when the dear fat old man on the box touched his hat to me.

"Miss de Metrier?" he asked, beaming on me with a fatherly air, and a kind of "Welcome-to-Selworth" smile.

"Yes," I said, beaming back, "are you from Sel-worth?" A truly idiotic question! but I felt the need for words.

So my baggage was piled into the rumble, and I my-self, full of dignity, climbed into the cavernous coach, which, after the obsolete manner of its kind, swayed with my weight till the step all but touched the ground. An elderly gentleman, whom I took to be the rector, handed me in, hat in hand. I afterwards learnt he was mine host of the "Red Lion." He stood bowing and smirking as though I had been the Queen herself, while we rumbled away over the stones. The De Metrier carriage brought men's hats off their heads in those days, and pretty quick, too. *Mais nous avons changé tout cela.*

Oh, that drive! No one will ever feel again as I did during that drive. It needs a ten-years' training at Chelmsford to produce the sensations I felt. The mem-ory of Selworth was as a far-off dream, seen through a golden haze. I hardly could bring myself to believe that the place really existed except in my imagination. It seemed too glorious, too heavenly a thing to be an actual part of the same world that contained Chelmsford!

I knew that there *had* been such a place, for I had been there—been there for a whole delirious year, in those misty bygone ages that in childhood lie at the back end of ten years. But I felt somehow that when I left it the place had been turned out like a lamp, or rather put away like a toy to prevent its getting spoilt. It seemed impossible that it should have wasted its sweet-ness all these years without my being there to do it hom-age—a selfish idea, I suppose, and a very hard one to put in words, but I have always had it. I have had it, too, about people that I worshipped passionately, an idea that they are not really a living part of the world except when I am with them. But there—these things concern no one but myself. One might as well try and make a water-colour drawing of one's soul as put such things on paper.

We rumbled on past farms and cottages, through deep-cut lanes and open fields, up hill and down hill, and twisting about round bends and corners in the ridiculous way country roads have; past woods, and ponds, and windmills, and other landmarks that had been far beyond the radius of my eight-year-old rambles, and that I passed unmoved, except by impatience to be on, and within sight of Selworth—the real Selworth of my dreams, my longings, and my imaginings.

There seemed a kind of magic in the very name.

"Selworth! Selworth! Selworth!" I kept saying over to myself. "Can this really be Selworth itself? Is it possible that I am actually *there?* actually within reach of it this very minute?"

I thought at times I was dreaming. I had so often dreamt of it during the past ten years—real, night dreams—and never, curiously enough, was the Selworth of my dreams in the slightest degree like the Selworth of my waking recollection. Never, in fact, was it twice the same. Each individual dream had house and park of its own particular fashioning, as different in size, structure, design, shape, and style from those of the last night's dream as each and every one of these dream-palaces was from the original. And yet in my dreams they were all Selworth—all absolutely and unmistakably Selworth; and all, in whatever guise they came, the one enchanted spot beside which all the rest of the world was a howling desert. I was happier in those dreams than I have ever been in life; happy with the happiness of Heaven, because imagination labelled a fancy-built park, "Selworth!"

But here in very truth was the real thing at last—Selworth in the very flesh! I let down the window, and pushed my eager face out into the cool night air. Things were beginning to look familiar, and I knew we must be near the Greystoke Lodge.

There was a tree in the park in which I am sure a full third of my life had been spent when I was there before. Sophie (pronounced Sophy by all except Aunt Harriet) Sophie and I had made a cave, a fortress, a sanctuary, and a fastness of this tree, especially a fastness, whatever that may be; we were very fond of that word. Claud used at times to come with us, and christened it Inversnaid—he had read Rob Roy, which we had not. But we liked the name, and it stuck. It was the biggest tree in the world, by *far* the biggest, not so much in height, as in rotundity—a pollard beech, lopped off somewhere in the days of Adam, about ten feet from the ground. As a result, five main branches shot out from the seat of pollardism, each branch as big as an adult forest oak. The spaces between these main branches were completely choked up (in their lower parts) by a dense mass of brushwood, among which were any number of big spiky knobs, looking for all the world like hedgehogs stuck on the end of rolling-pins. I think these knobs were a specialty of Inversnaid; at least I have never seen them in any other tree, and they gave it an immensity of character. And in the middle of the branches and brushwood was an earthen floor quite five feet square, free from all growth and encumbrance, and on which half a dozen of us could have stood upright and yet been invisible (even in midwinter) to any below. This was the Banqueting Hall. Then there were little ponds of water dotted here and

there about the lower part of the tree, the largest of
which was Lake Superior, and other smaller plateaux,
where we sowed mustard and cress and potatoes and
onions; and what's more, they grew.   Each of us had a
branch to ourselves, even Norman (we gave him the
worst), but the Banqueting Hall was common to all.

And at the root of the fifth branch, which had no
owner, was the fireplace.   Without the fireplace all the
rest would have been as nothing.   We lit vast fires
there, summer and winter; not little, sputtering, smoul-
dering make-believes, but real red-hot fires, with flames
a yard high.   And the tree never seemed a ha'porth the
worse!   Nor is it any the worse to this day, and it is
still the biggest tree in the world, and that not merely
for old sake's sake.   It stands in a big wood, just below
a shelving bank, and one long straggling feeler shoots out
to within reach of the top of this bank.   This was the
Drawbridge, and our only means, at that age, of getting up.   We wriggled up on our middles; it was probably not graceful, and it was a very slow process, and
bad for sashes and belts, and at times it hurt a good
deal, but it was the only way we could manage, and we
liked it.   It gave an idea of inaccessibility.   Blessed
Inversnaid!

All the way from Greystoke I had been thinking of
this tree, and indeed for many a day before that.   I made
up my mind it was the very first thing I would go and
see in the morning.   I wondered whether Sophie had
grown too old and sober to care for such things, and
whether we should still have to wriggle up the drawbridge on our sashes.

I was still wondering when we pulled up at the Lodge.
After a good deal of shouting and clanging and banging

of bolts and bars, the great iron gates swung ponder-
ously back, and we lumbered on our way. I was just
wild with excitement. I had both windows down the
whole way, and my neck stretched to its limit out of one
or other of the two, searching for old friends. The
night was clear and starry, and showed up the park to
right and left in a kind of dim, ghostly fashion. Old
friends crowded on my memory at every turn. The
marsh at the foot of the lake—"Marigold Marsh," as
we used to call it—then the sluice, and the pump, and
the big, druidical stones that were planted edgeways
between the road and the water—stones full of odd little
cavities and hollows that caught and held the rain.
Then a stretch of open park, with an uncertain glimpse
of the clump that hid the boat-house—two gates, first a
wooden and then an iron one, and, directly after, the
winding climb that ends in the House itself. My frame
of mind was a curious one. I found it hard to say
whether I had really remembered all these things before
I saw them, or whether the sight of them had wakened
my memory with such a jerk that I felt as though I had
never forgotten them. Anyhow, the impression on my
mind was that I had never left the place, and that all
these half-forgotten landmarks were as familiar and
every-dayish as my own face in the glass. It was an odd
feeling, and rather disappointing.

We clattered up under the great portico, the double
doors flew open, and the red glow of hospitality flooded
the night.

I passed in the wake of the butler through the little
stone entrance-hall into the Great Hall beyond. How
well I remembered that Great Hall! and the strange
echo of one's footsteps as one crossed it! It was as big

as a cathedral, a full two stories higher than the rest of the house, and a hundred and twenty feet long. At one end was an immense stained glass window showing St. George killing a lovely blue and red dragon, and at the other end two galleries, one above the other, corresponding with the first and second floors of the house. It was a folly, if you will! Perfectly useless for anything except music, for which it was glorious, and in cold weather like an ice-house; but I loved it; I had loved it as a child, and I loved it now, even more, I think, as I clattered across the polished wood floor to face the ordeal of welcome. The Great Hall was always three parts dark at night. It was impossible to light it, and the thing was not attempted. There was a lamp in each of the galleries, and two standard lamps on little tables that stood by the fireplace, and beyond this nothing but the light of the huge log fire that sent red and black shadows dancing up into the hidden hollows of the rafters. A glorious place for ghosts, and "hide-and-seek," and "bear"! but always a little terrifying with its vastness and gloom and hollow echoes.

The drawing-room beyond was a blaze of light—almost dazzling to my unaccustomed eyes. They were all there, and they all rose and kissed me, first Aunt Harriet and Sophie, then Uncle Guy, Norman, and Claud—Claud a little shyly.

"Goodness!" I thought, "what a kissing family!"

Aunt Harriet held me at arm's length with stock-taking eyes.

"You are not pretty, child," she said by way of welcome.

"Pooh!" said uncle, with his back to the fire. "I think she's very well; and, by Gad! a fine upstanding chit! What say you, Norman, my boy? No fault with that build, eh? Good back and shoulders—clean and straight of limb?"

"I was not talking of dear Josephine as a horse," said my aunt, icily. "She would possibly make an excellent horse, but she is not pretty, not even *distingue*-looking. However, when one thinks of what poor dear Gerard was, and her mother a mere *bourgeoise*, and all, we must make allowances."

As if *any* allowances were any good! I felt humbled and shy and very red. I knew I was not pretty, but it is not nice to be told it before a roomful of strangers.

"I am very sorry," I said, laughing, I think a little awkwardly. "I hope I am not a disgrace to the family name."

"Nonsense, child," said my uncle, patting my cheek, "you'll do very nicely, never fear. Egad! some of our stock would be none the worse of a little of your bone and blood."

He was a splendidly handsome man, this uncle of mine, about fifty, tall and big, with a jolly genial face and big bushy whiskers. I took a liking to him from the first. His wife was very different, thin, small, and sharp-featured, with iron-grey ringlets falling on her shoulders. She looked like an icicle, and she frightened me with the chill stare of her faded blue eyes.

"God bless my soul!" cried my uncle, suddenly, clapping his hand on my shoulder. "Here we are, talking and jabbering like a pack of fools, and this poor little girl starving, as like as not. Here, Norman, you young dog, take your cousin to the breakfast room; you'll find supper there. And give her a good glass of port, or half a bottle of burgundy, or some tea, if she likes it;

or coffee perhaps, or some negus.   Send down for some negus—nothing like it after a journey.''

This last was shouted after us, across the darkness of the hall, as we dipped into the long passage beyond.

Norman was very kind—very attentive.   He talked a great deal, and made me laugh, chiefly, if I remember, at the expense of my uncle and aunt.   He was very handsome, built on a smaller scale than his father, but very handsome, dark, with a high colour, and altogether rather foreign-looking.

It was ten o'clock by the time we finished supper and got back to the drawing-room.   They were all yawning; my uncle, I think, asleep.

"God bless my soul!" he cried, jumping up, "back already?   That's no kind of a supper—no kind of a supper."

"Sophie, my love," chimed in my aunt, taking no manner of notice of poor Uncle Guy, "will you save my old legs, and show dear Josephine her room?   You know, the panelled room in the east turret.   Good-night, my dear child; sleep well, and be careful of fire."

She pecked my cheek frigidly, and I smiled and nodded myself hurriedly out of the room, rather dreading the embraces of the whole family.

We passed down a long carpeted corridor, then turned to the right, up a very narrow spiral stone staircase, then once more to the right along another passage, and we were at the east turret.   The whole house was very dimly lit—I had a recollection of this from old days; lit by yellow japanned lamps hung from the walls at long intervals, generally at a corner.   Some of the offshoots and by-passages had no lamps at all.   Oh! the terror of those dark silent passages in the old days!

They were, as we all knew as children, the chosen haunts of robbers and bears, and of little hunchbacked men, who pounced out and pursued one with noiseless footfall. These little hunchbacks had pursued me time without end in my dreams, and often enough, waking, I would hear their quick breathing behind me, and race like a coursed rabbit down the long winding passages and stairs, till I reached the drawing-room, or the library, or the morning-room, or any other place where prosy protective people sat in spectacles, and read or wrote by the light of many lamps. And just before I reached the door I would slow down to a walk, and turn the handle quite quietly, and walk in with the most composed manner in the world, as though long, dim, shadowy passages were a thing to be left almost with reluctance.

All this, of course, was at eight, not at eighteen. At eighteen I would walk past the black mouths of those passages very stiff and brave, humming or whistling (no particular tune), and never once break into a run from start to finish. However, this is by the way.

My room filled the entire turret—that is, a small staircase ran up to the door of the room, and there ended. Sophie told me Norman slept in the room above mine, in case I might be frightened at being so isolated, but that his room was got at from the passage above, and to get to one room from the other you had to go half-way round the house; so, as I told her laughingly, he would not be of much help to me in case of attack by robbers or bears or hunchbacks. For we had been discussing these old bogies on the way up.

It was a lovely room, all panelled in dark oak, and hung with bright, shiny chintz—little pink roses separated from each other by crinkly blue ribbons. There was a splendid marble chimney-piece, and over it the only picture in the room, the portrait of a singularly handsome young man in the court dress of George the First. It was evidently, even to my eye, a picture of great value and beauty.

"Who is it?" I asked.

"My great-grandfather," Sophie said. "Maurice de Metrier, who married the Flemish heiress, and brought all the money into the family. Isn't he handsome? He built this end of the house, you know; added it on to the old part, and my grandfather Mordaunt, 'the old Squire,' as we call him, built the west wing at the other end. I believe this was Maurice's room."

"And what was Mordaunt like?" I asked, looking with interest at the splendid features of the man before me.

"Mordaunt was better looking even than Maurice. You'll see him all over the place—one in the drawing-room, another over the fireplace in the dining-room, a Sir Joshua, and two heads by Lawrence in papa's sitting-room. He was very wicked, they say." This in a tone of pride.

"Wicked! Why, what did he do?"

"Oh, I don't know what he did, but he was a desperate rake. They were, you know, in those days."

"Isn't it wonderful you should be such a handsome family? and for so long, too?"

"Yes," said Sophie, looking at herself with much complacency in the glass. "We have always been famous for our looks. You know our motto, *Virtus et venustas*. You see the heads of the family have always made it a point of honour to marry beautiful women."

"But—" I said, and then stopped short in confusion.

"Yes," she said, laughing, "I know what you are
thinking of; you are thinking of mamma. But she was
a *great* beauty when she married; she has been very ill,
which makes her look worn and wizen, but she used to
be a famous beauty. I believe she was the image of
what I am."

I made no answer, and shortly afterwards my cousin
rose and yawned.

"Good-night," she said. "I must be getting to my
room before they put the lights out."

I am afraid I made a face at her as she went, behind
her back, of course. It was very silly and childish, but
I was disgusted at her calm vanity; and also, there is no
doubt about it, I was jealous of her looks—yes, horridly
jealous. I think I felt aggrieved in a fashion that it
should be my fate to fall so far short of the family standard in appearance. Sophie had a high forehead and delicately arched eyebrows, beautiful big pensive eyes, a
slightly aquiline nose, and the regular Cupid's-bow
mouth. Her neck was long and swan-like, and she wore
long fair ringlets, that fell almost to her shoulders. I
went and stood before my glass, and what I saw there
was very different, and all wrong, as I knew from the portraits in Heath's "Book of Beauty" and the "Picturesque
Annual." The hair grew much too low on my forehead,
my eyebrows were too straight and thick, my nose
turned up, and my mouth was much too wide, and generally grinning. I felt that I might as well try and fly as
affect the languishing air that sat so naturally on Sophie.
"Pooh!" I thought, "who cares? I'll run her a race
to-morrow."

CHAPTER III

INVERSNAID

IS there in the whole wide world any more heavenly
and glorious feeling than that of waking up for the
first time in the place one has been looking forward to
for days and weeks—a place, too, that for years one has
dreamt of lovingly as a kind of inaccessible heaven? At
cock-crow I was out of bed, with my dishevelled head a
yard out of the window, drinking in the sweet, damp air,
and all the other smells and sights and sounds of early
morning. It was a bright sunny morning at the end of
September. The grass between the beds was grey with
a soaking dew, in which three cock-pheasants, in the
full glory of their winter plumage, were wading about
seraphically. A couple of robins were warbling *pianis-
simo* among the bushes, and just beyond the end of the
garden a long procession of rooks was sailing over the
treetops, cawing ecstatically at thought of the early worm.

It was a particular little garden of its own that lay
under my window, and not a very little one either, only
when compared to the others. It stretched away for
about a hundred yards to the big trees beyond, and was
bounded to the right and to the front by a fine big stone
balustrade. On the left side it tumbled down by ter-
races to a greater garden below, but with that part I
never concerned myself greatly. The part under my window I got to look on as my own particular property.

"Selworth! Selworth!" I kept saying to myself. "Is this really you at last, or am I dreaming?"

A gardener came suddenly round the corner, and nearly had a fit, I think, at seeing me. I took a run and landed in the middle of my big bed with one bound. Presently there came to my ear two of the most soothing sounds in the whole wide world—the gentle raking of gravel paths, and the big musical hum of a mowing-machine. Oh! how I got to love that mowing-machine, and the little piebald pony that pulled it, and the pauses at the corners, or where the tin was emptied! It was always going—every morning in some part or other of the garden.

Ten minutes to seven by my clock, and breakfast not till nine! I kicked about restlessly, and wished it was two hours later. Could an able-bodied girl possibly be quiet for so long, and on such a morning? I thought of going to pull Sophie out of bed and getting her to come out, and then I remembered with a groan that I didn't know her room. How *maddening!* I felt I positively *must* go out. Inversnaid! Heavenly inspiration, I would go and see Inversnaid! Of course; why had I not thought of it before?

In one second I was out of bed, and twenty minutes after I was stealing on tip-toe down my circular staircase. I met a housemaid sweeping the passage, and a girl scrubbing the stairs, and a footman collecting the yellow japanned lamps off the walls, and they all stared at me as if I had no business at all to be about at such hours. I had no idea of how to get out of the house, but thinking to avoid the main thoroughfares, scurried down the little spiral staircase that joined the first and second floors. At the bottom of this, by luck, I found a glass door opening to the garden—not *my* garden, but round the corner. It was locked, but the key was in it, and next minute I was outside, feeling rather guilty.

I came plump upon three gardeners, who pretended not to see me till I was past, when they straightened their backs and stared at me till I vanished round the corner of the turret. I looked up at my own open window, and at the many other closed ones. "Stuffy old things!" I thought. The three cock-pheasants went skimming away over the balustrade into the trees, and I—seeing no better way out, and thinking the shortest way was the quickest—followed them with a vault, a long scramble, and a still longer drop.

Inversnaid was not close. It lay a good mile and a half away across "the Plain." I wondered if they still called it "the Plain," that huge stretch of open park between the house and the Flexham Woods beyond. It was a terrible deceiver, that Plain. One started out full of the expectation of getting across in ten minutes or so; but when the ten minutes were gone, the woods on the hill were as far away as ever, and the house still quite close! It was a shocking place to walk, so dull, and featureless, and monotonous; and the worst of it was, almost all the glories of glades and glens, and woods and water, lay on the far side of it—*all*, in fact, except "Marigold Marsh," and the lake, and the old boat-house, and the chalk-pit at the other end by the Wellham Lodge. But in old days there had been one huge compensation in the fact that the Plain was an insurmountable hindrance to the "grown-ups" coming and poking about in our own particular haunts; this made up for everything.

It took me some little hunting to find Inversnaid. It

was never *quite* easy to find—too many other big trees round it, and no track or anything. But when it was found, it stood out at once unchallenged as the king of all other trees that were and had been or ever would be. It was just as big as ever. Here, at least, there had been no exaggeration of infant fancy; the Plain, perhaps, was not *quite* so long as it used to be, but the tree was still the biggest tree in the world, mathematically round, vast, impenetrable, and awe-inspiring in its majestic silence. No gales ever swayed the branches or ruffled the serenity of Inversnaid; it was too solid and compact. Well, of course, I got up it, and in the old way, by the same old branch (there was no one looking), and I sat there for half an hour, divinely happy, and full of a mad longing for matches wherewith to light a fire. Then I went home, a little late for breakfast.

"God bless my soul!" cried uncle. "What a fine colour! Where have you been, little Joe? You look as fresh as a June rose at sunrise."

"I have been for a walk," I said; "I couldn't stay in bed."

"What! a walk, and all alone? Norman, you lazy young rascal, what were you about not to escort your cousin? and her first day, too, at Selworth! Gad! sir, in my young days, I wouldn't have needed bidding; but chivalry's dead nowadays, damme! yes, dead as Nebuchadnezzar. No such thing, little Joe; no such thing."

"Oh, but I like going alone," I said, laughing at his earnestness.

"Like going alone!" he cried, "like going alone! Nonsense, nonsense; mustn't be allowed, mustn't be allowed, not so long as these two young boobies are in the house kicking their heels. See to it, Norman, another day, or I'll disinherit you, damme if I don't."

All this in the jolliest manner possible, so that we all laughed; but for my own part I thought that Norman, with his airs and affectations, and little languid graces, would be a nuisance so insufferable that I would sooner keep my bed. Claud would be better, but best of all, of course, Sophie, for I was not afraid of her. So, after breakfast, I got her alone.

"Where do you think I was this morning?" I said.

"I don't know. I know where you ought to have been."

"Where?"

"In chapel, of course."

"Oh, nonsense," I said; "I am a Protestant. Didn't you know that? No, I was at Inversnaid."

"Inversnaid! What on earth do you mean?"

"Sophie, you don't mean to say you have forgotten?"

"Forgotten what?"

"Why, Inversnaid; our tree, of course. Don't you remember?"

"Oh! that stupid old tree. I had forgotten all about it."

"O Sophie, how *could* you? Will you come there with me now, and we'll light a fire?"

"My dear Josephine! we are grown-up young ladies, and young ladies don't climb up trees. Besides, where's the fun of it?"

"Well, I climbed up it, and I thought it very good fun, though I was alone, and hadn't any matches. I went right up to the top of my branch, and sat there half an hour. Of course, I didn't go on to any of your branches. You know that always was trespassing, unless one had an invitation."

"You *baby!*"

"Well, I like being a baby. So you won't come?"

"No, my dear girl; of course not. Think of one's clothes!"

"Well, what *do* you do?"

"Oh! we ride, and we drive, and we walk, and go to the archery meetings. But, of course, it *is* shockingly dull here, except when there are visitors staying in the house."

I felt a little chilled, and a good deal disappointed. Was life at Selworth going to fall short of my dreams after all? Of course, every one knows things always do fall short of the dreams of anticipation; but I thought otherwise then, and the first teaching of the lesson hurt me so that for a little more I could have cried. I thought Sophie stiff and stupid and stuck-up. I had learnt enough in that short five minutes' talk to tell me once and for all that we could never be the close bosom friends and confidants that I had pictured. She was a smart young lady, and I—well, I suppose she was right— I was a baby, a big baby, and with no wish to be anything else. But when one *is* a baby, it is nice to have another baby of about the same age to play with, otherwise one's babyhood falls flat. But here at Selworth it was quite clear to me before luncheon on that first day that there were no babies of any age. They were one and all smart, amiably conceited, and *stupid*—yes, emphatically stupid; people who can no longer be babies because they happen to have done growing, *must* be stupid. Not that I took a dislike to my Selworth relations; on the contrary, I liked them all in their way, but

I saw at once that there was no actual kindred spirit among them. They were all kind to me, and even affectionate, and Uncle Guy especially was so amazingly generous at times I was quite ashamed of taking the presents he showered upon me.

"Bless my soul!" he would say, "we must dress little Joe up a bit. Send for Hèloise, Harriet."

"My dear Guy," my aunt remonstrated, "surely you are not serious? The child does very well as she is. What does she want with smart clothes in a place like this, where there is no one to see her?"

"What does Sophie want with her smart clothes, then?" retorted my uncle, with a chuckle. "No, no, Harriet; give the child a chance. Gad! with a figure like that, old Hèloise ought to dress her for nothing; damme but she ought!"

My aunt was not pleased, I could see, and I thought Sophie cocked her nose and sniffed a little. But Hèloise came.

One of the first things I noticed at Selworth Abbey was that my uncle had his way in everything. At first sight he appeared easy-going and good-natured—as indeed he was, when things went right; and on the other hand, Aunt Harriet seemed determined and strong-willed to the verge of obstinacy. But whenever those two wills came into conflict, my aunt's went down like corn before the wind. I noticed it a score of times. I noticed, too, that on occasions Uncle Guy could fly into such passions as shook the whole house. No one would have guessed it to see him; he looked so sleek and jolly and comfortable.

However, as I say, Hèloise came, all the way from Bond Street, and I was fitted for frocks and mantles and a riding-habit, and evening dresses cut below the shoulder, and goodness knows what else besides. And Hèloise came all the way a second time to try them on, and lifted up her eyes to heaven, and raved about *la belle taille de Mademoiselle*—all of which I took for what it was worth; and in due course the result of all this came, and the wardrobes in the Panelled Room were packed to overflowing, and a silly little fool spent half the day attitudinising and cutting capers before the long cheval-glass, to her own complete satisfaction.

This, however, was not till I had been two months at Selworth. The first night the things came, I put on one of the evening dresses, a yellow satin one, I think, for dinner; and Norman, I remember, hardly took his eyes off me the whole evening; and as to Uncle Guy, he paid me such compliments, and was in such tearing spirits, and cracked such jokes, and told such stories, and rapped out so many of his funny old obsolete oaths, that the whole table was in a roar, even Aunt Harriet! Goodness! how pleased I was with myself in my new fine feathers! and the thought of what I would wear next day pleased me even more. But that is a different matter, and needs a little explaining.

I hardly know how to tell it satisfactorily, but the way of it was this. Sophie, as I have said, was no *real* companion for me. She was too smart and grown-up, though in reality only a year older than me—too much of the fashionable young lady, in fact. She rode beautifully, but hated walking, and wore very tight high-heeled shoes. When she did walk, she would never go off the paths unless the grass was as dry as cinders, and as to climbing trees, or messing about in "Marigold Marsh," she simply wouldn't do it; so I soon gave up asking her. Besides, nothing would induce her to go out before luncheon; and at no time, either before or after luncheon, was she ever *ready* to go out. She always had to go to her room first, where she stayed three-quarters of an hour, changing boots and stockings and skirts and things, till one really forgot what one wanted to go out for.

Norman and Claud were generally shooting partridges, or hunting; besides, I knew it would bore them to come with me, so I never asked them. So the end of it was, I used to slink out quietly after breakfast and prowl about by myself, generally in the Flexham Woods, and stay there till luncheon time, when I would come back with such an appetite as made the rest of them stare, and caused Sophie to cock her pretty nose and sniff rather disdainfully.

One morning, a little more than a week after my arrival, I had lit a fine fire in Inversnaid (more as a matter of duty and tradition than for any other reason), and I was thinking what a dull matter-of-fact lot my cousins were not to come and help me, when I saw a man walking through the wood straight for my tree. He was sauntering along, leisurely swinging a stick and whistling, and had evidently seen nothing of me or of my fire as yet. But the fire was a good one, and was smoking magnificently, so there was no possibility that he could pass it without seeing, unless he was blind. I dropped quietly down into the Banqueting Hall, and awaited events with a high-beating heart. I even tried to subdue the fire a little with the long stake that did duty as poker, but it only made the thing smoke the more. I could see the man plainly enough, though I knew that I myself was invisible. He walked right along the top of the bank to which "the drawbridge" stretched. I think he was dreaming, or making poetry or something, for he never noticed anything till he was almost past the tree. "What an old stupid!" I thought.

Then suddenly he stopped short and began staring up. I never saw any one look so astonished. The fire wasn't flaming any more, only smoking like forty factories, and he couldn't make it out at all. He walked round and round the tree several times, trying to see into the middle of it (he might as well have tried to see into the ground), and then finally came back to the top of the bank, where he had started. I thought he was going to pass on and leave me in peace, when, to my horror, he swung himself on to the drawbridge and began coming up! I thought for a moment of dropping down on the far side and running—it was not a very tremendous drop; but while I was thinking, the chance was lost, for the man, who came up twice as quick as I did, caught hold of some branches overhead and swung himself lightly into the Banqueting Hall, within a yard of where I stood! I shall never forget the poor man's face. He looked so absolutely aghast that I burst out laughing then and there. I couldn't help it. And then he laughed, too, and took off his hat, and said he must apologise for disturbing me in the way he had, but he had no idea the tree was tenanted by a hamadryad.

"What's that?" I said.

"A young lady who lights fires in trees," he answered, smiling so nicely that I forgot to be frightened of him any more.

"You nearly made me put it out," I said. "I tried to smother it when I saw you coming. Please get some sticks, quick."

We both scrambled about for fuel, and he began breaking off some of the smaller twigs and branches.

"No, no," I said severely, "nothing that's *growing*, please. There's any amount of dead stuff lying about, if you only look. Get round behind Sophie's branch; you'll find the woodstack there, with fuel enough for a week."

He went round. It wasn't quite easy, I knew. One had to tread on one of the hedgehogs, and make a long stretch to catch another with one's left hand. But he did it, and very neatly, too, and came back with a scratched face and an armful of sticks—small, big, and medium. And we made the biggest fire that ever was seen, and climbed up my branch—which was to windward—to be out of the smoke and heat, and sat there very comfortably for half an hour. And then I showed him "the Moat," and "Lake Superior," and the "ten-acre field," and the "look-out station," three parts of the way up Claud's branch; and the "potato patch," and the "secret chamber," which was a sort of cave under two of the branches, just beyond the woodstack. And he seemed to take it all in, and liked it very much, and said it was quite the most wonderful tree he had ever seen, and altogether made a very fair baby, though he *was* about three inches over six foot, and quite ten years older than me.

"Do you often come here?" he asked.

"Yes," I said, "almost every day; but it is dull work, as none of the others will come with me."

At this he raised his eyebrows and laughed, and said something half to himself which I didn't quite catch. We sat in silence for a time, and then he said:

"If I was to be passing this way again, and you

happened to be here, would you let me act stoker
again?"

"Of course," I said. "I should be delighted. A
stoker's just what I want."

At which he laughed—laughed till the tears came, as
though I had said one of the wittiest things in the world.

"Very well," he said, "I shall remember that."

"Are you likely to be passing, do you think?" I asked.

"Oh, I think very likely indeed," he answered, with
his eyes smiling rather nicely. He seemed very much
amused at something. "You know I am the Duke's
agent, and I live just outside the Slade Lodge," he
added, by way of explanation.

"Oh!" I said.

"And you, I suppose, are Miss de Metrier, the
Squire's niece?"

"Yes."

The wind was blowing stiffly from the southwest, and
brought the sound of the servants' dinner-bell, ringing
down at the house.

"Good gracious!" I cried, "I must be off. I shall
be late for luncheon."

"Shall I help you down?" he asked.

"No!" I said, decidedly; "stay where you are till I
am down. Then you can come."

I dropped down from the two hedgehogs that sprout
just beside the moat. I thought it more dignified, and
perhaps prettier than the drawbridge. He followed me,
and we shook hands and parted.

After luncheon I asked Sophie:

"Who is the Duke's agent?"

"Sydney Grayle," she said; "he is a sort of cousin
of his, you know. Why do you ask?"

"Oh, just curiosity," I said.

CHAPTER IV

THE OLD MANOR HOUSE

CLAUD went back to his regiment very soon, which I was sorry for. He was a nice boy. He was a cornet in the 13th Hussars, then quartered at Shorncliffe. Norman stayed on, and was very kind and attentive. Sometimes I used to feel positively ashamed at letting him fag for me in the way he insisted on doing. I was not used to it. All my life it had been rather the other way. And then, apart from the question of fagging, he was so embarrassingly courteous and attentive and deferential. I didn't quite like it. It oppressed me.

We used to ride every afternoon—that is, Sophie and I did; I in a borrowed habit of Sophie's, and most days Norman would come with us. He was very kind about teaching me to ride, for though the little horse I rode was as quiet as any cow, I was as great a John Gilpin as ever was, and knew no more about riding than a guardsman. Sophie used to be rather cross, I thought, when Norman came. I suppose she felt out of it to a certain extent, for of course the poor fellow, in his capacity of riding-master, had to give most of his attention to me; and I don't think she liked it. So silly!

One day Sophie and I were riding alone, with a groom, of course—we were never allowed to move a yard without a stupid, pompous groom behind. We had had a splendid gallop across the plain, and were riding slowly up the green ride that runs to the Slade Lodge—the most beautiful ride in the world it is—up a deep glade, with giant trees on either side, and bracken underneath. The trees were in their most glorious autumn colours, for we had had several sharp frosts, and the bracken was also dying in great splendour, and the little rabbits scurried about in multitudes, and seemed to be enjoying the beauty of it all as much as we were. Suddenly it began to rain, softly at first, but presently in much bigger drops, and heavier. We turned round and started to trot homewards, and as we did so the rain, as though angry at our turning tail, began to come down in perfect sheets.

"Drat it!" said Sophie, "we shall be wet through before we get home."

However, we bent our heads, and pushed through it as best we could, the poor horses seeming to hate it as much as we did.

Presently Sam, the groom, came pounding up alongside.

"Beg pardon, miss," he said, touching his hat; "but hadn't we best take shelter in the old Manor House? The storm'll pass in half an hour or so."

"Of course," said Sophie. "Come on, Josephine."

She spurted along for another hundred yards or so, then, turning sharply to the left, galloped up a kind of cart track till we came to a house. The most beautiful little old house it was that ever was seen, though I took little enough note of it at the time, being only too glad to jump off my horse and get inside out of the rain; but later on, I got to know the look of it by heart. It was long and low, built of yellow sandstone, with mullioned diamond-paned windows, and a long sloping, red-tiled roof. There was a lovely little garden round it, with an antediluvian sun-dial, and a fountain, and numberless yew-trees, cut into peacocks and pheasants, and things. However, all this I saw later on. At the time I just jumped off, and followed Sophie in, glad enough for once that fat old Sam was there to look after the horses. An old woman came bustling out of the parlour.

"Miss Sophie!" she cried, with hands held up in horror; "poor dear! you must be drowned! come in quick and let me dry you a bit. Sure, you'll catch your death of cold. And this is your cousin?"

"Yes, Susan; this is Josephine."

We were well rubbed down with many towels, and our wet state groaned over with a world of commiseration, and finally we were put before the fire, like bits of toast, to dry.

In the meanwhile the storm gathered round blacker than ever, and it rained as though it meant lasting through the night. The interior of the house was no less perfect in its way than the outside—not that there was any attempt at smart furnishing; the chairs and tables were of the commonest, but the rooms and the staircase were panelled with old oak up to the very moulded ceilings, and the chimney-piece had clearly been carved by a master hand. A wonderful old house! I thought; and I had never dreamt even of its existence in the park! but then there was room enough in Selworth Park for many hidden things.

But the most wonderful thing of all was the old woman herself. She was a handsome old lady, almost beautiful, with her snow-white hair and dark soft eyes. I found myself staring at her perpetually, and every time

I looked up, there were those dark grey eyes fixed upon me so immovably, and with such open enquiry, that I grew quite fidgety and uncomfortable.

"So you are Miss Josephine?" she said at length.

"Yes," I said, laughing; "I am Josephine."

"Do you know, my dear, that I was your father's nurse?"

"*You* were!" I cried. "Why, you are not old enough." For father would have been fifty if he had lived.

"Oh, yes, I am," she said, looking quite pleased. "You see I was only seventeen or so when I took him up."

"Oh! how exciting!" I cried. "Do tell me about him. What was he like?"

"Well, poor dear, he never was much to look at, as you know—a little, white, spiritless thing, and crippled with that shrunken leg from the day he was born. And then there were his eyes, of course."

"Yes, I know," I said. Even I could remember his eyes.

"But a little angel from first to last, and through everything," she said. "God bless him, poor soul, and forgive us all our trespasses."

I had nothing to say; she seemed deeply moved.

"And to think of your being his daughter! Well, well, it does seem strange."

"Why?" I asked.

"Well, he was so small and shrunken, poor thing; but your mother, of course, was a splendid creature."

"Tell me about her," I said.

"I only saw her once—a month or so after they were married. She was the most splendid creature I ever saw, taller even than you, and as full of life as a young race-horse. And then to think of her going off the way she did."

"But she was not *pretty*, was she?" I asked.

"Perhaps not pretty in the way some folks talk of it—not one of your rule-of-thumb hair-dresser-shop beauties, you know; but a woman to send men clean off their heads, if *I* know anything of the world."

I saw Sophie go very red; I think she thought the old woman was talking at her.

"Mamma always says she was common-looking," she said, with a little toss of her head.

It was my turn to go red then. I was speechless with rage. But the old woman broke in:

"No, no, Miss Sophie, anything but common-looking; indeed, it was a most uncommon face; not aristocratic-looking, of course, like the De Metriers—who is? but a sweet face, and a lovable, as ever I saw."

There was an awkward silence for a time. Sophie, I could see, was very angry, and so was I—furious. What right had she to say such things about my mother? I could have said things about hers if I had liked—finniky old mummy! We both looked out of the window. It was pelting. There was no chance of moving yet.

It was our hostess who came to the rescue.

"Is Mr. Norman at the Abbey now?" she asked. They always called it the Abbey—the people about. But my cousins themselves called it just Selworth House.

"Yes, he's there," Sophie answered, sulkily.

"Ah, he's a true De Metrier, from top to toe; that he is. The handsomest young man I ever clapped eyes on—better looking even than the 'old Squire,' and he was hard to beat. No wonder half the girls in London are mad about him, and such a fortune, too! such an inheritance! The girl that catches him'll be a lucky one."

She fixed her eyes rigidly on my face. I was staring into the red embers of the fire, but I felt the magnetism of her fixed gaze, and looked up.

"Yes," she added, reflectively, "the girl that catches Norman de Metrier will be the luckiest girl in all the world; and when Susan Beddington says that, she knows what she is talking about." Then the next moment, and in the same breath, "God forgive us all for our sins!"

"I suppose you mean that Josephine ought to try and catch him," Sophie cried, with a high-pitched laugh.

"I mean what I say," said the old woman, "neither more nor less. Whoever gets Mr. Norman will be a lucky girl. He is a gallant young fellow, and would make a good husband."

"I think we had better be going," Sophie said. "It is not going to stop, and there is no use in waiting any longer."

I agreed thoroughly. It was not raining heavily, and the situation was uncomfortable.

As Sam was putting Sophie on to her horse, I felt my arm clutched from behind, and a voice whispered in my ear, "If ever you want a *friend*, come to Susan Beddington."

We trotted along briskly home, the rain beating in our faces. Not a word was spoken between us till we were close to the house. Then Sophie pushed up close alongside of me, and said: "I am so sorry, Josephine, for saying what I did. It was *horrid* of me."

I hardly knew what to say. If we had been on foot I should have kissed her; as it was, I laughed rather awkwardly, and said, "Oh, it was nothing."

"But it *was*," she said, "and I was a pig and a beast to say it."

I said nothing, but when we were in the house, and in the long passage at the top of the stairs, I flung my sopping arms round her, and laid my dripping, draggled head against hers, and mumbled forgiveness and everlasting affection in her ear. And whether there was any crying or not, it is hard to say, for both our faces were already wet and glistening with the rain. However, in any case, everything was all right.

CHAPTER V

FATHER BOYLE

THE De Metriers had always been Catholics. I myself had been brought up a strict Catholic as long as my father was alive. When, however, his sudden death left me an eight-year-old orphan, absolutely destitute, there had been much debate in the family as to what was to be done with my poor little lanky body. One wanted one thing, and one another, after the manner of mankind, and while they were disputing, and I was starving, my mother's two maiden sisters stepped in and very quietly carried me off to Chelmsford. At first this had caused a good deal of correspondence, and, I believe, some unpleasantness, but in the end it was accepted by all parties as the most comfortable solution, and I was left in peace where I was. But the objections of the Selworth faction were very quickly justified, for within one short twelve months I had left the Church of Rome, and was a regular attendant at Mr. Baggally's mournful ministrations in the parish church. I think it was partly this that made my uncle and aunt wipe me out of their lives for ten long years. Apostasy is a thing beyond the pale.

Shortly after my conversion, I remember a fat gentleman, in a black coat, arriving one day to see me. He asked for a private interview, but this my aunts sternly declined. They were both trembling with agitation, I remember, very pale, but with tight mouths, and battle blazing in their eyes. So we all gathered in the little front parlour, and my two aunts sat bolt upright on stiff-backed chairs, and I sat on the very edge of mine, with my long white stockings tucked under me, and my feet twisted round the front legs. The fat gentleman stared hard at me for some minutes, and then said in an odd, rolling kind of voice:

"Child, is it true that you have been seduced from the arms of the Church?"

"Yes, sir," I said, frankly.

"Am I to understand," he went on, with his voice swelling like distant thunder, "that you have renounced the faith of your father, and your father's father—the sweet, pure faith in which you yourself were brought up from infancy?"

"Yes, sir." This very low.

"Josephine de Metrier," he said, and now his voice sank to a great round whisper, "have you realised that this step means ruin for you in this world and eternal damnation in the next?"

"Mr. Boyle," said Aunt Maria, in a high, shaky voice, and deathly pale, "if you talk in that strain I shall have to take the child away, and request you to leave the house."

"Very well, madam," said the priest. "I am in your hands, and may God forgive you for the wreck of this child's soul. I have but one more question to ask her. How old are you, Josephine?"

"Ten, sir."

"Then you are old enough to understand. You have sinned greatly, but the Church is merciful, and is always ready to receive the penitent with open arms. If you

will repent of your sins, and come back to the faith of
your fathers, I am authorised by your dear uncle to offer
you a permanent home at Selworth, and all the unlimited pleasures that go with such a home—ponies and carriages and dogs, smart little frocks and beautiful rooms,
and such food and wines—such food I should say [this
with a hasty cough], such exquisite food, as seldom falls
to the lot of man or woman in this poor sinful world.''

He spoke with great feeling, especially towards the
end of his speech. Then suddenly, quick as ʻthought,
his brow lowered, and his voice grew very stern.

"And if you refuse, if you persist in your evil, wicked
courses, you shall live and die a beggar, and among beggarly surroundings.''

He shut his mouth with a snap, and glared at me
across the table. I saw Aunt Maria's mouth open and
shut three or four times, as though she were struggling
to speak, but no sound came. Aunt Emily just sat and
mopped her brow feebly. There was a dead silence for
some minutes. I sat fidgeting my feet on the floor, and
twisting the corner of my frock.

"Well, child?" he said, "think well before you answer;
think of the ponies and the clothes—and the food.''

I felt very much inclined to cry. The priest never
took his eyes from my face, but my aunts looked straight
and fixedly before them.

"Please, sir," I said, "I don't want anything but to
be left here with Aunt Maria and Aunt Emily.''

"You are sure, child?" The voice once more was
growing thunderous.

"Quite sure, sir.'' I felt braver now I had said it.

"You hear, sir?" said Aunt Maria, pushing back her
chair.

"Yes, I hear," thundered the priest, rising to his feet. "You have indeed thrown the meshes of Satan tight around this poor castaway. Her perdition be on your heads. I shake the dust of this house from my feet."

He stalked out of the room with great dignity, and next moment we saw him pass slowly up the street.

"Thank God! thank God!" cried Aunt Maria, and then these two dear, kind souls must needs break at one and the same moment into floods of tears, and fall upon my neck and hug me, and half smother me with kisses, till, from sheer sympathy, and without in the least knowing why, I, too, cried as I had never cried before. So we were all very happy that evening.

But for eight years there came from Selworth Abbey neither letter nor message nor any more acknowledgment than if I had been dead. Then in a flash came the invitation to stay for the greater part of a year! No wonder we gasped when we read it.

"Be strong, my darling child, and faithful," were Aunt Maria's last words. "They will try hard to pervert you."

But they did not. Never, directly or indirectly, was the slightest pressure brought to bear on me. They even offered me a carriage on wet days to take me to Benton Church. Father Boyle, or Father Terence as they called him—my old friend of Chelmsford memory—was still chaplain at Selworth; and every morning at half-past eight, and three times every Sunday, would he hold service in the private chapel beyond the Long Gallery. He was fatter than ever, and had little pig-eyes, and an endless fund of humourous anecdote. I never quite liked him. Perhaps the memory of that terrible interview in the front parlour still haunted me a little—

I don't know; but whatever it was, I always felt uneasy in the man's presence. And then he used to call me Miss Joe—from the very first day—which I hated. My uncle always called me Joe, and from him it was all right; and after a time the others, too, got into the way of it, finding my full patronymic rather cumbersome, but Father Terence started it the first day—such impertinence! Aunt Harriet, by the way, could never bring herself to call me anything but Josephine, pronounced French fashion, and at first would even wrinkle her brows and pretend to look the picture of perplexity when my uncle referred in any way to "Joe."

Well, to go back to Father Terence. He had one good point, for which I almost forgave him everything— even the damnation to which he had assigned me eight years before. He could make the most heavenly music. Whether with hands or voice, it was the same, but the voice it was, of course, that moved one. He had what Aunt Harriet called *les larmes dans la voix.* Where he got it from was the strangest thing in the world, for there was no more music in his face than in a soup-plate. But his voice in that Great Hall was like a thing from heaven! I liked to crouch down behind the balustrade of the Upper Gallery and listen to him from there. It spoilt the illusion so if one saw him. He could sing anything—Handel's oratorios, scraps from operas, or the simplest ballads. That was the time of Mrs. Popham's lovely little unpublished songs. He was very fond of these—women's songs though they were.

> "For though the wild fir-trees were creaking,
>   And ghosts were in every part,
> I found what I long had been seeking—
>   A heart I could take to my heart."

The pathos of his voice would pierce my very soul, and I would shiver like a leaf behind the gallery rails, brimful of the emotion that turns all of us to fools, and then by chance I would catch sight of the singer's puffy white face through the rails, and simply shake with laughter for pity of the poor heart that he had found.

Such was Father Terence when I first knew him—a man of about forty, I suppose, and a king in Selworth Abbey if ever there was one. He was the only one in the house that could make Uncle Guy do as he chose. How he did it nobody knew. The methods were not flaunted in public, but whatever he decreed came to pass; there was no doubt of that.

He had all his meals with us, and was excellent company, and ate and drank as much as any other two; and indeed there were times when the effect of this was very plain in his manner. But none of the others saw it; or, if they did, saw in it nothing beyond the prescriptive *droit de prêtre.* For at Selworth Abbey Father Boyle, like the king, could do no wrong. My uncle would growl at my aunt, and my aunt would snap back acid rejoinders, and Sophie, Norman, and Claud would spar with all the frank vocabulary of youth; but no one ever questioned Father Boyle's doings, either to his face or behind his back. The king could do no wrong!

Even the glaring vulgarity of the man never seemed to grate on them, not even on the starched gentility of Aunt Harriet, who would shut her eyes and shiver every time my uncle swore, which was pretty often. But for my own part, I am afraid I never did like the man, only when he was sitting at the organ in the chapel, or at the piano in the Great Hall.

CHAPTER VI

CONCERNING THE APPOINTMENT OF A STOKER

THE day after our ducking, Sophie had a slight cold and stayed in bed. She was "delicate," and had to be taken great care of, at least so I was always told. Aunt Harriet even seemed quite put out with me because it had rained while we were out riding; as if I could have helped it!

"Of course, it matters nothing to you, Josephine," she said, fretfully. "I should imagine you had never had a cold in your life, but you should bear in mind that your cousin is not so strong."

I believe she thought health a sign of low breeding and vulgarity; she always talked as if she did.

So the doctor came, and stayed half an hour, and spoke comforting words, and went away, leaving an atmosphere of hope behind him, and a promise to come next day, and to send up a bottle of medicine in the course of the afternoon. And then, as a sop to his conscience, he drove round three miles to Sillingham and saw Mrs. Black's consumptive daughter, and left a blanket and a bottle of port behind him. I heard of this afterwards from Tom Beddington.

So, all that morning I stayed in Sophie's room, reading and talking. She looked very well, and remarkably pretty, with pink ribbons in her hair, and in the sleeves and throat of her night-dress. When Doctor Watson arrived, I left her and went to the schoolroom, where I amused myself strumming on the piano. Sophie and I had this room to ourselves. It was a huge, bare room on the first floor, over the billiard-room, and so far away from everything that we could make as much noise as we liked—or rather I could; Sophie never made a noise.

Well, as I say, I was trying to play a waltz, with the pedal down, and was producing horrible sounds, when Norman came in.

"I thought it must be you," he said. "I was down in the billiard-room knocking the balls about."

"I suppose you recognised my delicate touch?" I said, laughing.

"I like to hear people play with confidence," he said.

"False confidence," I suggested.

"Nonsense, you play very well. Are you going to ride this afternoon, Josephine?"

"I don't suppose so," I said. "Sophie's in bed with a cold."

"But you and I could go."

"Yes, I suppose so."

"Well, then, I'll order the horses for three o'clock, shall I?"

"All right."

I was still sitting on the music-stool, half slewed round towards the door. Norman came forward a few steps, and produced something from behind his back—a long thing done up in tissue paper, or silver paper, as we used to call it then.

"What's that?" I said.

"A little present I've got for you."

"Oh, how nice! Let me look at it!"

It was a tortoise shell whip—such a beauty!—with a gold mounting, on which he had engraved, "Josephine from Norman."

"How lovely!" I said. "It *is* good of you, Norman."

"Do you like it?" he said.

"Of course I do. Why, it's *lovely!*"

"I'm so glad," he said, coming nearer, and smiling. "I think you might give me a kiss for it, Joe."

He had never called me Joe before. I made a mental note of the fact.

"Of course I will," I said, "naturally."

So he took it—freely. It was a new experience, as I had long since knocked off the family embrace that had taken me so by surprise on my first arrival. Such things are easily done, when one has to do with gentlemen— and the De Metriers, whatever else they may have been, were all gentlemen. But it is not so easily done without comment, especially from a man like Uncle Guy. He noticed the omission from the moment I introduced it, and commented on it loudly and frankly, after his manner.

"Damme! little Joe," he would say, "you may shy and back and rear from the boys as much as you will, but you mustn't try such tricks with your old uncle. I'm the irreducible minimum, you know."

"What does that mean?" I said.

"Well, in this case it means an old fool," he answered, chuckling, "a doddering old fool!"

However, this is all by the way.

Norman took his embrace, liberally, as I say, and then we both stood apart and felt, and I am sure looked, rather idiotic.

I took refuge in the whip.

"It *is* a beauty!" I said.

"Yes, it is pretty," he said, "but not nearly pretty enough for you, little Joe."

Little Joe, indeed! I am sure I was as tall as he was.

"What do you mean?" I asked, trying to look imbecile, and, I expect, succeeding.

"I mean," he said, "that nothing is pretty enough for you."

"My goodness!" I cried, "there goes the luncheon bell. I had no idea it was so late. I must go and wash my hands."

"Then I'll order the horses for three?" he said.

"Yes!" I shouted from half-way down the passage.

We had a delightful ride. Norman was charming. Coming home, we rode almost under the very branches of Inversnaid, and I was so grateful to him for giving me the whip, that I all but told him all about it, and was on the point of asking him to come there with me next day. However, I did not. I think I was half afraid to; I thought he might laugh at me. In fact, I had kept Inversnaid a deep, dark secret from every one at Selworth ever since I found that Sophie was inclined to turn up her little nose at it. There was another reason, too, why I didn't ask Norman.

The truth is—the honest, plain, downright, rather-to-be-ashamed-of truth—that Mr. Grayle had already been five times to Inversnaid. He said the Duke's estate business was always taking him that way. I suppose there must have been some outlying bit of the Duke's property lying the other side of Selworth, for Ashby lay, of course, quite the other way. However, that was his business. He had come five times, as I say, and offered himself as stoker; and a splendid stoker he made, flying about all over the tree like a lamplighter, and I honestly confess I was always a little bit disappointed when he did not come; it was so dull all alone. So I used to look rather anxiously for the tall figure striding through the beech trees. And when he did come, the talk, and the whole talk, would be of the fire and the "Moat" and the other treasures of the tree, including our own respective branches (for I had given him a temporary lease of Claud's, who was away); and if the wood happened to be wet, and the fire showed symptoms of collapse, we would scurry about all over the tree looking for dry twigs as though the keeping alight of that fire was the only thing worth considering in the whole world. And, wet or dry, whether the fire burned willingly or not, our talk was never other than the talk of five-year-old children, honestly.

So, all these things considered, I saw no reason to say anything about my stoker at Selworth. Even before he had found me that first day, I had kept my own counsel about the old tree and my ridiculous leaning towards it. It is such a bore being laughed at. And now, of course, if they learnt about Mr. Grayle, they would be perfectly certain to laugh at both of us as two of the biggest babies that had ever left school. So I said nothing. I couldn't give the poor man away; it would have been *too* mean. And I did *not* invite Norman to accompany me next morning. I came to the conclusion the duties of stoker would not sit comfortably upon him.

All the same, we had a splendid ride, and came back in a fine glow, having raced home for a mile across "the Plain."

"Well, young people," said Uncle Guy at dinner, "what sort of a ride did you have, eh?"

"Glorious!" I said. "We went pretty near to the far end of the park at Ashby."

"And how did the old Pasha behave?'

"Like an angel! He only shied six times the whole while."

· "We must find you something better to ride soon. He's too heavy and slow for you."

"Oh, no! he's an old dear! I love him!"

"By the way," said Uncle Guy, across the table to my aunt, "talking of Ashby, I have had a letter from young Grayle about the Mill Hanger Farm. The Duke wants to buy it."

"Well, I should let nim want," she said. "Why should we sell land?"

"No reason at all, my dear, of course—no reason at all, except to oblige the Duke. It's about the shooting, you know—cuts into one of their beats in an awkward way. Grayle says he would either buy or exchange for one of his farms on the Benton side."

"Well, I should tell Mr. Grayle it is impossible. Why should you lose a good farm, and a good tenant, and get goodness knows what in its place? What do you say, Father?"

"Faith, I entirely agree with your ladyship," said his Reverence, draining a glass of port, and smacking his lips loudly. "If it's only a shooting question, the matter could surely be arranged some other way."

"Of course it could," said uncle, "of course it could. I don't want to sell anything. Gad! no—not come to that yet, thank God! I'll write and tell Grayle."

"Who is Mr. Grayle?" I asked, with great innocence. (Sophie was not there.)

"Grayle?" said uncle. "Why, he's the agent at

Ashby. Capital chap, too—good shot—good man to hounds—no better in the country."

"Oh!" I said.

"He is Lord Delamaine's youngest son," Aunt Harriet explained. She had the whole peerage at her fingers' ends, and was fond of the subject. "They are absolutely ruined, you know, and the Duke took on young Grayle as a kind of charity. They are connected, you know—distantly; the Duchess was first cousin to Lady Delamaine. He has not a farthing in the world, poor fellow, beyond what the Duke gives him; but, I believe, he does very well."

"Oh, yes," said uncle, "first-rate agent—wish I'd got as good a one—damme, yes—old Quayle's as slow as a church—too long in the tooth, poor chap!"

CHAPTER VII

WHAT times those were in the autumn of that year! The days were always too short, and the nights too long, and as to bed, it was a sheer waste of life. The moment the grey dawn began to glimmer round the edges of my blinds, I would be out of bed, and in my blue flannel dressing-gown would sit at the open window, and form plans for the day. Not that any great plans were needed. The mere joy of existing at Selworth was enough. But I liked to sit in my window and drink in the cool, damp air, and watch my old friends, the cock-pheasants, strutting about among the beds, and listen to the blackbirds and the robins piping their autumn songs. I always wondered if they could sing before their first worm. Father Terence couldn't sing a note before breakfast; he would tell you so frankly.

I got to love my little panelled room—not that it was particularly little, rather the reverse—and everything in it; the old-fashioned rosebud chintz, and the jugs and basins with the blue crinkly ribbon round the edge, and Maurice over the chimney-piece—wicked Maurice, with his haughty clear-cut features, and cold, supercilious smile, and the dark eyes that followed one about the room. I never saw a more *living* picture than that; it was really quite embarrassing at times; it was so appallingly human. I could never believe Maurice was so bad

55

as they made out. There was nothing bad about the face; it was rather a kind face, in fact. Then there was a big armchair, and a sofa at the foot of the bed, both covered with chintz, and an oak screen, with a pleated chintz centre, and a funny little shelf at the top of it that one could hook up, I suppose to put one's candle on.

My room faced east, and when the mornings were clear—as they so often are, whatever happens afterwards—the first straight rays of the sun would come shooting in, lighting up Maurice's legs, below the knee, and bringing the rosebuds on the chintz to life. And outside, the same sun would paint the red dropping leaves of the beeches and the chestnuts behind the balustrade such gorgeous colours, and would make the dew glisten so enchantingly upon the grass, that there was nothing for it but to have my bath cold, and to get into my clothes as quick as could be, and down the little turret stair into the garden. This happened most mornings, except when it rained.

Then, after breakfast, as often as not, I would go to Inversnaid—beloved Inversnaid! They used often to ask me where I went, and I would say: "Oh, I go as a rule to the Flexham Woods; I like the trees there."

Then, after a time, Norman used to offer to come with me, which was tiresome, but I couldn't well refuse. However, I always took him the other way, down towards the Greystoke Lodge, or round the lake, and sometimes I made him row me about on the lake while I trolled for pike, which, I am thankful to say, I never caught. And once I even initiated him into the mysteries of Marigold Marsh, with its sluices, and hydraulic pump, and entrancing little water cuts, *and*, chiefest of all, the entrance to Dante's Inferno, which, as every well-

informed person knows, is to be found in Marigold Marsh
and nowhere else, under a brick and mortar arch that
burrows into the embankment that keeps the lake in its
place.

> "In the midway of this our mortal life
> I found me in a lonely wood astray."

That wood was in Selworth Park. Norman had never
heard of it—never heard that this was the place, I
mean—but he quite understood when I told him. I was
surprised. He even "abandoned hope" and went in,
and got very wet feet.

Norman, however, just about that time was nearly
always shooting, either on their own ground or with the
Duke, so I was left pretty well to myself.

There is one incident I cannot help mentioning. It
happened a few days after Norman had given me the
whip. It was a wet day, and Father Terence was singing in the Great Hall—singing "Puritani," and singing
it divinely—and I was listening in the upper gallery, as
I generally did, sitting on the floor, and leaning my
back against the door of the state bedroom, as it was
called, which opened from the end of the gallery. Well,
Uncle Guy happened to come in from the entrance
hall. I heard the *clack* of his shooting boots as he
walked across the polished floor, and guessed it was him,
but didn't trouble to look. Father Terence stopped
singing, and began playing soft, aimless sort of chords.
"Well," he said, still playing, "how does it work?"
"Splendidly—couldn't be better."
"Nothing definite been done yet, I suppose?"
"No; we mustn't be precipitate. There's no hurry."
"Certainly not."
They were hardly talking above a whisper, and the

piano never stopped for a moment, but I heard every word. It was a marvellous place for sound—that big hall.

"The extraordinary thing is," my uncle went on, "the boy's perfectly infatuated."

"Devil blame him!" said the priest.

"But whether it's the same the other way, I don't know. I have my doubts."

"Pshaw! Squire, never bother yourself—

> " 'There's never a maid from pole to pole
>   In valley or hill or town,
>   But would drop in the mud her lily-white soul
>   To pick up a diamond crown.' "

sang Father Terence Boyle.

"Mud!" said my uncle, angrily. "Nonsense, man; where's the mud, I should like to know? There's no mud in the question."

"Well, well, Squire, put it as you will, so long as the end's the same."

"And if not?"

"If not! There'll be no 'if not'; but if there is, well, then, God's will be done."

My uncle passed on into the drawing-room, and the priest started singing again.

> "Se il mio nome saper voi bramate
>   Dal mio labbro il mio nome ascoltate."

But I had heard enough. I was more than exercised over the conversation I had heard. What in the world could they have been talking about? Three or four wild explanations came tumbling into my head, one on the top of the other, but I dismissed them one and all as too extravagantly impossible to be thought of for a moment. The most likely thing seemed to be that they were talking about Sophie and Lord Barham, the Duke's eldest son. I had gathered from one or two little things I had heard that more than one person at Selworth would have found no fault with fate if the heir of Ashby had laid his coronet at Sophie's feet. However, it was not my business, and I can't say I troubled my head very long over it. Good luck to Sophie! was all I thought. What a good duchess she would make!

It was about this time that I began to have a series of what Uncle Guy would have called blank days at Inversnaid—that is to say, that for five days Mr. Grayle did not come. Of course, he might have passed during the days when I was out with Norman down by the lake; or, again, the Duke might have settled the business that took him across Selworth Park, so that he would not have to come any more that way. That was probably it, I thought. The business had no doubt had something to do with that farm that the Duke wanted to buy from Uncle Guy, and that was all settled now.

So I should have to stoke for myself for the future. It was rather a bore; one got so hot and dirty scrambling about all over the tree, and for the last week I had had on my new frocks from Hèloise. I began to wish I hadn't put them on. I began to think that sitting up in a tree all the morning was rather an idiotic occupation after all. Sophie was right; it was only fit for children. And though it was all very well to light a fire now and again, it palled dreadfully after a bit; there was such a sameness about it. "It is a dreadful thing to be old and *blasée*," I thought, "but there is no doubt I am. I am sick of this stupid old tree! I don't think I shall come any more."

Poor, dear Inversnaid! There was never a more brutal, ungrateful speech; but I don't think I was quite well at the time. I was cross and irritable—every one noticed it, even Norman.

One day when my fire had gone out—entirely from neglect, poor thing!—it suddenly flashed across me that I would go and see old Mrs. Beddington. I wanted to hear lots more about father and mother, and it would be something to do till luncheon. So I dropped down with a "flump" into the thick carpet of copper-coloured leaves, and turned down the hill to the right. It was only about half a mile off, the old Manor House, down the hill, and across the broad open valley, and then a couple of hundred yards up a cart track through the dead red bracken. The old lady was delighted; she saw me walking up the gravel path, and came to the door herself.

"I thought perhaps you'd come, Miss Josephine."

"Yes, I want so to hear more about father, if you don't mind."

"My dear, of course I don't mind. Come in and sit down, and warm yourself by the fire. Winter's beginning early this year, I think."

"Yes, it is pretty cold to-day."

"So they've dressed you up, I see." She was looking at my new clothes.

"Yes," I said, laughing, "lots of new clothes."

"And how do you like Selworth?"

"Oh, I *love* it!" I said; "there never was such a heavenly place since the beginning of the world!"

The old lady smiled one of her inscrutable smiles.

"It is a beautiful old place!" she said; "and have they given you a nice room?"

"Oh, yes, a lovely room in the east wing; what they call the panelled room."

"Ah!"

"You know it, do you?"

"My dear, I know every room in the Abbey. You forget I was housekeeper there for several years."

"Oh! I didn't know. Well, isn't it a lovely room, Mrs. Beddington?"

"Yes, a very pretty room, but noisy sometimes if there's any one in the room overhead."

"Noisy!" I cried. "Why, I never hear a sound!"

"Perhaps there's no one above you?"

"Oh, yes, there is; Norman sleeps in the room above."

She got up and put some fresh logs on the fire.

"And how do you like Mr. Norman?"

"Oh, I like him tremendously, of course. He's awfully nice!"

"And how does he like you?"

"I don't know, I'm sure," I said, laughing; "I think he likes me pretty well."

She was staring hard into my face, as though she would read my very soul.

"He's a splendid young fellow!" she said, turning away, "a splendid young fellow!"

"But, Mrs. Beddington, " I cried, "you are not telling me anything about my father. It seems to me that I am telling you all the news."

"Well, well," she said, sitting down, "where shall we begin?"

"At the beginning," I said. "Tell me everything."

"Everything is a good deal," she said, wagging her head at me.

"Never mind," I said, "there's lots of time."

"Well, then, I was a mere child, you must know, when I first took up your father—seventeen only, and as ignorant and silly and vain—Lord forgive me!—as a magpie. I shall never forget when the groom came riding down with a note asking would I go as nurse to the new baby up at the Abbey.

"Father had Croft's Farm, you know, this side of Benton. Well, it took us clean off our feet—such an honour as that, and me a mere chit of a girl and all! But I did know something about children, of course, having looked after the two boys. Well, I put on my Sunday clothes—a lilac print dress, I remember, with a waist under the arms, and a long flat straw bonnet with big ribbons—and walked up to the Abbey, and they sent down a farm cart to fetch up my traps. The 'old Squire'—Mordaunt that is, you know—was sitting in his room, and I was shown straight in. He wasn't old, then—about thirty, I suppose.

" 'Miss Crossly,' he says, as polite as though I was a duchess, 'do you think you can undertake the care of this baby?'

" 'I'll do my best, sir,' says I, dropping a courtesy, and I am sure simpering like the silly I was.

" 'Very well, then, you can enter upon your duties at once; and whatever happens, remember, I shall always feel quite sure that you have done your best.'

" 'I hadn't an idea what he meant at the time, but I dropped another courtesy, and followed the housekeeper upstairs. The baby was in the west wing, or the new wing, as it was called then, and right at the top of the house. You never did see such a poor little misery of a thing! It looked three parts dead; and then that left

leg was all shrunken and short even then, and the cast
in the eyes was something awful. You can remember
that cast, I suppose, Miss Josephine, though it got better, poor fellow, as he grew up. Well, I all but
screamed when I saw the little mite. You see, I remembered what George and Harry, our babies at home, had
been like, and the sight of your poor dear father gave
me quite a turn. How it came to be so, I can't say.
Folks did say something about bad blood on the mother's
side—she was one of the O'Donnells, you know—but
whether that was so or not, I don't know. To be sure,
the Squire, your uncle, never had a little finger to his
left hand, though perfect in every other way. But there
it was; the child was hardly human. However, thank
God for this, that whatever my other sins may have
been, I nursed that little thing as though it had been
my own, and the bonniest child on earth. And it grew,
and fattened, and flourished, and I got to love it better
than anything in the world."

"But, Mrs. Beddington," I said, "I don't understand.
Where was Uncle Guy all this time, and why didn't his
nurse take charge of father as well?"

"Guy?" she said, "Guy?—oh, yes. Well, you see
the old Squire had a fancy for keeping them apart.
Your uncle was always in what we called the old
nursery—the room over yours that Mr. Norman sleeps
in—and your father and I were right at the opposite end
of the house. And the two babies never met. I had
orders always to take mine out down the long walk,
and round about the shrubbery there; and your uncle
and his nurse used always to go through the Italian garden towards the old abbey. We never met, either in the
house or out."

"Do you mean to say you *never* met?" I asked.

"Well, my dear, we were never supposed to meet, and it was very, very difficult, and if your grandfather had heard of it, we should both have been bundled out of the door that very day. He was a bad man to cross, was the old Squire. But as a matter of fact, we did meet once or twice—not more."

"Then, I suppose, you took the baby to see my grandmother sometimes?"

"Never. It was not allowed. Mordaunt wouldn't have the children seen about the house. But she, poor dear, used to come up to the nursery three or four times a day. She just worshipped the little thing."

"But, Mrs. Beddington, I thought she died?"

"Died! Lord bless you, no; not till after—ah! well she did die, poor thing, of course; I was forgetting, but not so quick as all that. She had time to see the baby many times."

"I always understood she never left her bed."

"Oh, no, my dear. She did die, of course, but not so quick as all that."

"Then, did my grandfather ever see the child? I suppose not."

"Oh, yes, he used to come pretty often; but he never could bear the sight of your poor father. You see, Mordaunt was a splendidly handsome man, as his father Maurice had been before him—the De Metriers always had been famed for their beauty, even then—and I think it was a kind of point of honour with him that his children should be fine and large and straight and handsome, as the race always had been; and it drove him wild, I think, to see this little crooked, wizened misery that he had brought into the world. The other child, your uncle, he always worshipped. He was a splendid boy from the first, barring the finger, of course; but that was nothing.''

''But why did he come so often to see my father if he hated the sight of him so?''

''Well, I suppose he wanted to see that things were as they should be, and clean, and kept in proper order. He was wonderfully particular about little things, was Mordaunt—hated dirty clothes, or soiled linen, or speck or spot on anything.''

''Did you like him?''

''Who? Mordaunt? Oh, yes; I was bound to like him. You see he was my master, and a very kind master, too, as long as things went straight.''

''Well, tell me some more.''

''More? Let me see, my dear, what more is there to tell? Oh, I forgot to tell you about the veils. That was another crank of the old Squire's. He would never have the children leave the nurseries to go out without veils—white veils—and so thick that their own mother couldn't have told one from t'other, or either of them from cats or monkeys. A curious craze you may well say, but so it was.''

''But what on earth was the object of it?'' I said. ''I think my grandfather must have been mad!''

''No more mad than you or me, my dear; he had some good reason, you may be pretty sure. Well, this went on—the veil business, I mean—till your father was two and a half or so, and then I married Beddington, and both the children were put under Mrs. Grace, in the new nurseries in the west wing.''

''But you and father were in the west wing nurseries, you told me, Mrs. Beddington.''

"Did I, my dear? Well, and so we were; but you see your uncle's first nurse, Mrs. Graham, died—was found dead in her bed in the old nursery."

"That's where Norman is?"

"Yes; failure of the heart they said it was. Well, after this, your father and I were moved into the old nursery, and your uncle and Mrs. Grace—his new nurse that is—went to the new nurseries. It's rather confusing, isn't it?"

"Very," I said, laughing. "And then you went and married Beddington. Why did you do that? Were you very fond of him?"

"Well, no, my dear, I wasn't fond of him, and that's the truth—never cared a snap of my fingers for him. He was a poor little slip of a fellow as ever you saw, and consumptive, and fit for nothing much except making stools and tables and such like. And I don't think any girl *could* have cared for him, least of all a giddy, silly thing such as I was."

"Then, why did you marry him?" I cried aghast. "I think it was *horrible* of you!"

"Well, you see, my dear, poor folks can't always pick and choose; they have most ways to take what they can get, and be thankful for that. And then Mordaunt gave us this house, and pretty well everything we could want besides, so that it would have been flying in the face of Providence, so to speak, to have refused."

"And you have been here ever since?"

"Ever since, except during the four years I was housekeeper at the Abbey. That was the last four years of the old Squire's life. When he died your uncle sent me back here, and I was pretty glad to come, I can tell you; housekeeping isn't in my line. And here I hope

to be till I die, which will not be very long now, my
dear, for my heart is mighty bad at times, and that's the
truth. Beddington, poor fellow, he went off sudden
when we had been married four years. He was always
weakly.''

"And how many children have you got?''

"Four—all boys. George, the eldest, is head keeper
to Squire, as you know. Bill and John are out in India;
the old Squire gave them a good start in life, and they're
doing well. And Henry, the youngest, lives here with
me. You have never seen him? No, likely not. You
see he's house-carpenter up at the Abbey—brought up
to his father's trade—and he's there in his shop all day,
and just comes home of nights.''

"I must be going now or I shall be late,'' I said, getting up. "You can't think how interesting it has been
to me to hear all this, Mrs. Beddington.''

"Why does it interest you?''

"Well, of *course*, it interests me to hear all about my
father when he was a baby. It seems so wonderful to
think that you should have been his nurse. You look
so young somehow, in spite of your white hair. Were
you very pretty when you were young? I suppose you
were.''

"I believe I was, my dear,'' she said, "and I know
very well I thought I was. May the Lord forgive me
for all my vanity and wickedness, and guide me aright
now at the last!''

"Well, there's nothing very dreadful in thinking
you're pretty,'' I said, laughing, for her manner was
quite tragic. "I wish I could think *I* was. I should
be vain enough, I know.''

She looked at me hard for a minute, but said nothing.

Then suddenly she rose, and putting her two hands on my shoulders, said: "Miss Josephine, my dear, remember ;that whatever may happen, you have always got a friend in Susan Beddington."

"But you said that to me the last time I was here," I exclaimed. "Why should I want a friend? Nobody's going to attack me; I'm not worth it."

"My dear," she said, "we're none of us the worse for having a friend who will stick through good and ill, even though it's only a poor old rickety woman. And now you must run away quick, or you'll be late, and I know her ladyship doesn't like that."

I shook her hand, and then stood for a moment in doubt. I was wondering whether she would mind very much if I kissed her. I felt rather shy about it, but longed to, all the same—she looked such an old dear.

Suddenly I made a plunge, and feeling rather hot, kissed her on the cheek. To my amazement, her eyes filled with tears, and for a moment she could say nothing, but just stood there, holding my hand. Then very low she said, "God bless you, my dear!" and turned quickly away.

CHAPTER VIII

AN EXPLOSION, A JUSTIFICATION, AND A PRAYER

I *WAS* late. And Aunt Harriet *did* raise her eyebrows, and pucker up her mouth, and say, "Wherever have you been, my dear Josephine?"

I was always being late for luncheon, and she hated it, I knew. Sophie was never late; but then, of course, it is easy to be in time for things if you never go out.

And I used often to come in, hot and panting, and with a scarlet face, having run most of the way back across "the Plain," and with my hair all untidy and dropping right down over my eyes, in the way it would do unless I did it up afresh every two hours. And there would be Sophie, opposite, as fresh and cool and spick-and-span as a newly-clipped hedge. And Aunt Harriet would stare at me with that calm look of hers that always frightened me so, and say: "My dear child, you do look hot! I declare you are quite in a *transpiration*. What have you been doing—digging potatoes?" And once, with a little genteel laugh, she said: "Goodness, Josephine, you look just like a Skye terrier! You really should brush your hair a little more carefully. I am afraid you are not very *soignée*."

"I can't help it, Aunt Harriet," I said, hopelessly. "My hair *will* not keep up. I think I shall cut it all off."

But my uncle was delighted when he heard this speech of Aunt Harriet's.

"Ho! ho! ho!" he laughed, "a Skye terrier! That's just what the little minx is—a long-haired Skye terrier (he called it tarrier). Damme! if I don't call her that!"

And he did for a time.

"But you mustn't cut your hair, Joe, you know, or you'll go blind. Tarriers always go blind if you cut the hair that falls over their eyes. Gad! I wish I'd a little more to fall over my eyes."

All this, however, was not on the day that I went to see Mrs. Beddington. On that day something rather dreadful happened at luncheon. I was late, as I have said—only about ten minutes or so—and when I went into the dining-room I was very hot, and, I suppose, a little dishevelled.

It was a great big room, and looked all the bigger when there was only a small party and a small table to fit them. Norman was shooting with the Duke, but the other four were there. Father Terence, as usual, was telling one of his anecdotes, but he stopped short when I made my rather shamefaced appearance.

And my aunt as usual said:

"Wherever *have* you been, Josephine?" as if one was bound to have been to the North Pole, or somewhere, because one happened to be a few minutes late.

There were no servants in the room. My uncle couldn't stand them at luncheon, "prowling about," as he called it, "and handing you everything you don't want, and nothing you do."

Well, my aunt said, "Wherever have you been?"

And I quite innocently said: "Oh, I have been having a long talk with that dear old Mrs. Beddington.'

"With who?" said Uncle Guy, looking up.

"With Mrs. Beddington."

"Oh, yes, the keeper's wife?"

"No, I don't think so. I mean the old lady who lives at the Manor House."

"Oh, you have been talking to her, have you?"

I looked at my uncle in amazement. His face was twitching all over, and great veins stood out on his forehead.

"Yes," I said.

"Well, let me tell you that you had no business to. It was a liberty—a damned liberty!"

"I am very sorry," I said, humbly; "I didn't know. I only wanted to ask her about father; she was his nurse, you know."

I was not in the least afraid of my uncle, in the same way that I was of my aunt; I looked upon him as a sort of easy-going, overgrown boy. He had never been anything but kindness itself to me till this moment; and even now I was not in the least appalled, only astonished.

But after my speech I was more astonished still, and appalled as well. I have never seen such a change in a man; I should scarcely have known him. The whole expression of his face was changed. His skin grew purple, and the eyes seemed to contract and disappear under his thick, bushy brows.

"And what business have you, pray," he said, in a thick, choky voice, "what business have you to go sneaking about in this underhand fashion among the people living on my property? I won't have it, Josephine—won't have it, d'you hear? You're never again under any pretext to speak to that woman. If you do, out of my house you go the very same day—out of my house, and back to your beggarly lodgings at Chelmsford."

His voice rose almost to a shout. There was a dead silence when he had finished. Every one looked hard at his plate. For my own part, I thought my poor uncle had gone clean mad. I don't know what the others thought.

Uncle Guy himself was the first to break the silence.

"Jabbering old witch!" he said. "She never had the brains of a goat, and now what little wits she ever had are gone—gone along with her memory. Nothing those old harridans love so much as tittling and tattling about things they know nothing about. Well, you understand me, Josephine? I forbid you absolutely to speak to her again, or you either, Sophie."

"Yes," I said, very low, and feeling hot all over.

"Very well, then, don't forget."

We sat for another five minutes in one of the most awkward silences I have ever felt. Aunt Harriet and Father Terence tried to get up a conversation about the Christmas festivities, but it all sounded dreadfully forced and sham.

Then at last there was a move. Sophie and I flew out of the room the back way, by the serving-door, and scuttled like rabbits down the long passage, till we came to the little staircase that led to our schoolroom. Never once did we pause or draw breath till the door was closed behind us, and we had flung ourselves, panting and breathless, into two of the many big chairs that littered the room. Even then it was some time before we could find our voices. Sophie giggled feebly, but I was far too staggered.

"What on earth does it mean?" I gasped at length.

"Goodness knows!" she said. "I haven't the very faintest idea. I expect it's the gout."

"But have you ever seen him like it before?"

"Oh, yes; he's got an awful temper, but it isn't often it shows itself. And all about such a silly thing, too."

"I *wish* I knew what it was made him so angry. I think I'll go and ask Father Terence. He's sure to be in the chapel."

"All right. Only don't ask me to go, too. Wild horses wouldn't drag me from this room for the next half hour. It isn't safe."

"Oh, I'll sneak down by the stone turret. There's not a ghost of a chance of meeting him there. But I simply *must* find out."

So I fluttered out of tne room, with my heart in my mouth I am bound to own, and ran down the passage to the left, to the stone turret. From the foot of this to the chapel there was practically no danger, for my uncle's room lay miles away. However, I ran on tip-toe with a slight feeling of being hunted, and was glad enough to hear the organ booming dully through the closed doors. I entered the chapel, still on tip-toe, and shut the doors behind me. This chapel was one of the most beautiful things I have ever seen; rather in a florid style, perhaps, with a great deal of marble and gilding, but wonderfully beautiful.

The ceiling was flat, and in square panels, separated by little gold beams, each panel painted in some Scriptural subject. The windows, too, were very fine, but so small that in mere daylight the place was almost dark.

Father Terence was sitting with his back to me, playing softly to himself. When I was quite close to him he turned round with a start.

"Ah! Miss Joe," he said, "what can I do for you now? Will I sing to you?"

"No," I said, "not now, thanks. I want to ask you a question."

"You're not come to confess, surely?" he said, with a laugh.

"No; I want to ask you something. What was it made Uncle Guy so furious at luncheon?"

The priest was still playing softly, looking round and talking over his shoulder. It was a way he had if one caught him at the organ or piano. Now, however, he dropped his hands from the keys, and faced bodily round. His face, too, assumed a solemn, fatherly look.

"My dear Miss Joe," he said, pawing my shoulder heavily, "my dear Miss Joe, your uncle was very naturally annoyed. This Mrs. Beddington was a legacy of the old Squire's, and not a very respectable legacy, either. He would naturally not wish you to associate with her."

"But you can't *know* her, Father Terence," I cried. "There never was a more respectable old lady. She is beautifully neat and clean, and talks like a lady, and, altogether, she's the greatest old duck I've ever seen."

"Mrs. Beddington in her old age no doubt presents a decent exterior," said the priest, gravely, "but Mrs. Beddington was once Susan Crossly."

"Yes, I know she was," I said; "she told me. But what has that got to do with it?"

"It has this to do with it, Miss Joe, that any one who was once Susan Crossly is no fit companion for you."

"What do you mean?" I said; "I don't understand."

"Well, how shall I put it? This Mrs. Beddington, whom you admire so much, in the days when she was Susan Crossly was a very wicked woman."

"I don't believe a word of it!" I said. "What did she do wicked?"

"Faith! as much as she could, from all accounts," said the priest, with a chuckle.

"I think it's perfectly *horrid* of you to say such things!" I said, furiously. "I don't believe she was wicked a bit. Is it likely my uncle would let her live in the park, and in that lovely old house, if she was wicked? Of course not."

"My dear young lady," he said, in his most solemn voice, blinking his little eyes at me, "there are some things in this world that men are bound to respect, and one of them is the wishes of their dead parents. It was the dying wish of the old Squire that Mrs. Beddington should be left in undisturbed possession of the old Manor House in the park, and that her children should be carefully provided for. A solemn charge like this is a thing that cannot be put aside—and your uncle has respected it, all honour to him! But it is not to be wondered at that he objects strongly to you or Miss Sophie associating with the woman."

He shut his mouth tight, and glared at me from under his brows.

Suddenly a thought struck me—a brilliant thought.

"Then, why, if she was so wicked, did the old Squire leave such a charge to my uncle?" I said, triumphantly. "Is it likely he would want to provide for such a dreadfully wicked woman? I never heard a more improbable story in my life, and I don't believe a word of it."

I saw this was a staggerer for the priest. He hadn't a word to say. He just looked at me fixedly for a minute or so, and then burst out laughing.

"Well, upon my word, Miss Joe, you have me there," he said. "And we will allow, if you like, that Mrs. Beddington has always been a model of every virtue under the sun; but, you see, the fact remains, that this good woman and her numerous family have been left a legacy to the estate; and it is not surprising that your uncle is a little sore about it.   There are half a dozen Beddingtons living in the park this day, and two more out in India, and all this is a serious tax on an estate— well, perhaps not a *serious* tax exactly to so wealthy a man as your uncle, but a distinct annoyance.''

He paused, as though to mark the effect of his words.

''Yes, I suppose it would be,'' I admitted.

''And you'll respect his wishes in the matter, I am sure,'' he said, laying his hand on my head.   He was standing at the top of the altar steps, and I at the bottom.   On the level we were about the same height.

''Well, it seems rather absurd, doesn't it?'' I said, doubtfully.

''It may seem absurd from your point of view, but you must remember this: you are a guest in your uncle's house; he has loaded you with kindnesses; and the least you can do in return is to fall in with his wishes, even though they may seem absurd to you.   Besides, you are little more than a child in years, and an absolute child in understanding, and he *must* know best.''

One of the most remarkable things about this man was the extraordinary way in which his manner would chop and change about.   One minute he would be acting a kind of buffoon, and the next he would put on a manner so sublime and impassioned that it awed one in spite of the sudden change.   Just now his voice was low, but rolling so solemnly and portentously that I was more impressed than I can describe.   I felt that this must be a good man and a wise, and that I was a poor, silly fool. And strangely enough, the whole time my memory was jumping back eight years to the day when he had talked to me in the same deep, musical voice in the little front parlour at Chelmsford. I remembered well the end of that interview—the everlasting perdition to which he had consigned me—but the present effect on my senses was stronger even than memory. I suppose the dimly-lighted chapel, with all its impressive surroundings, was not without its effect on me. Anyhow, for the time, my will was subject to the man's.

"You will do this, I am sure?" he said, in a voice little above a whisper.

"Yes," I murmured.

I think he must have seen the effect he had produced, and determined to improve upon it.

"That is right," he said, with his hand still on my head; "be strong and brave, and put your trust There."

He half turned round, and with the hand that was free pointed to the beautiful ivory crucifix that hung over the altar.

"Kneel, my child," he said. He pressed me down with his hand, and I did kneel—on the steps. Why I did it I can't think to this day. It seems an extraordinary thing to have done; but at the time it seemed quite natural and proper. I bowed my head, and clasped my hands in front of me, waiting. After a slight pause, the priest's voice swelled slowly through the chapel—

"*O Mater Sanctissima Christi, protege hanc filiam ab omnibus periclis, et serva fortem impavidamque ad finem, te precamur in nomine Patri, et Filii, et Spiritus Sancti.*"

I rose slowly to my feet and made my way out, leaving Father Terence standing on the steps.

CHAPTER IX

A SHOOTING PARTY

IT was towards the end of November, and there was a
shooting party at Selworth. Such a gathering of
antediluvians! I never saw anything like it. Old generals, and still older baronets, and Members of Parliament older than either. The Duke was there, and was
very nice and cheery, but the rest were *dreadful!* They
talked nothing but politics and taxation and turnips from
morning to night.

"Do they *never* have a man in the house under fifty?"
I asked Sophie.

"Oh, yes," she said; "as a rule they're quite different. Papa likes young men, you know. I suppose it's
just an accident having all these old fogies."

General Borrodaile had a wife who must have been at
least forty years younger than he was. She was very
pretty, with masses of golden hair, but rather stupid and
silent, I thought. None of the women in the house
cared for her, but she seemed to get on very well with
the men, especially with Norman and the Duke. Sophie
swore she painted her face, but I don't think so. She
had an immense mouth, armed with immense white
teeth, which ought to have spoilt her looks, but somehow did not; it seemed to suit her style of face. The
reason I remember her so well is this: One day, when
they were out shooting, we were all sitting at luncheon—

a dull party of women, kept going by Father Terence. Mrs. Borrodaile was out with the shooters, and the occasion was seized upon by the rest of the party to run her down. They had been discussing her for some time, when Father Terence suddenly turned to me—Sophie and I had naturally left the rending of her to the elder women. "Well, Miss Joe," he said, "and what's your opinion of the lady?"

"She's wonderfully pretty," I said, "but I think she looks carnivorous."

I was thinking of her mouth and teeth. I thought Father Terence would have fallen from his chair. I never saw a man laugh so. He rolled from side to side, and smacked his legs, and got so purple in the face I thought he would have a fit.

"Carnivorous!" he cried, in a high, shrill voice, with the tears streaming down his cheeks, "carnivorous! Oh, dear! oh, dear! I shall die!"

The rest of the women laughed, too—roared, in fact—all except Aunt Harriet, who tightened her mouth, and looked acid.

"My dear Josephine," she said, "you must really be more careful what you say. I cannot say I consider your remark at all *bon ton.*"

"Ah, now, Lady Harriet, let the child be. She has tied the right label on this time, and without her we might never have found it."

They all laughed again—for about five minutes.

"Well," I said, "I'm glad I'm so amusing. Somebody else make a joke now."

"Faith! there'll be none to beat that," said the priest. "The Squire'll have a fit when he hears it."

As a matter of fact, I don't believe the Squire did; I

believe he was more or less angry. However, as to that I never asked, nor indeed troubled myself any more one way or the other about my extraordinary good joke.

Mrs. Borrodaile used to sing after dinner, and sing wonderfully well, too. She had not much voice, but knew how to use it, and sang with immense feeling. She quite took the wind out of poor Father Terence. The funny thing is, too, she sang Mrs. Popham's songs, and a great deal better than he did. Of course, they were meant for a woman, and she looked very pretty and pathetic as she sang them, which, of course, he, poor man, couldn't. I shall never forget his face that first night when she told us, "Why she looked so pale." I think it was a revelation even to him. The songs were just made for a voice like her's, and she made us all cry—at least most of us—I know I did.

> "In the winter years ago,
>   Long before you can remember,
> All the world was white with snow
>   In the month of cold December."

The hall was very dimly lighted, as it always was; the light of the huge log fire flickered up into the black shadows of the rafters, and the effect was immense. In the drawing-room we could hear the General and Sir Henry Huthbert talking at the top of their voices about divisions in the House of Commons on the army estimates.

> "Never since that winter's day
>   Has my heart been free from sorrow."

sang pretty Mrs. Borrodaile, and with such feeling that we all felt choky. I wondered if she was thinking of the General.

She followed this with the song of Littlecote and its ghost of wild Dayrell, and then, when we pressed her, she sang "The Old House by the Lindens," and we all cried again.

Father Terence fidgeted on his chair, and kept coughing the whole time. He was as vain as a gander, and hated any one except himself being at the piano. Afterwards he sang himself, at the top of his big voice, to show, I think, by contrast, what a small thing Mrs. Borrodaile's was. But it didn't do. We had to look at him, you see, which spoilt it all. In the chapel he had his back to one when he sang, and when he sang in the hall, one could get into one of the galleries which answered the same purpose; but to sit within a dozen yards and watch his great mouth twisting round under his left ear was enough to take the music out of anything. Still, he sang very well—he always did—but somehow, it grated after Mrs. Borrodaile.

Oh, that shooting party! It was a deadly affair. Sophie and I had to try and entertain the wives and daughters. We pretended to play croquet every morning, but it was not exciting. Nobody ever knew when it was their turn to play, or what ball they were playing with. Of course, we should have liked to have gone out with the shooters, but the ladies were afraid of getting their feet wet, so we had to stay with them. Mrs. Borrodaile always went.

On Saturday morning the generals and the Members of Parliament and the baronets went off with their dull, dull wives and daughters.

Sophie and I danced a jig in the schoolroom, after which we lay back in two big chairs, and said "Thank goodness!" for ten minutes.

That day at luncheon we heard that Tom Beddington had had his head broken by poachers the night before. Selworth was always a bad place for poachers.
There was a family called Morris that were the worst of
any—a lame father and two villainous-looking sons.
I had met them all at different times in the park. That
was the worst of Selworth—at least I used to think so—
there were so many rights-of-way through it; one met
all sorts of people, which was a bore.

It appears that the last night of a shooting week was
a favourite time for poachers. The idea was that the
keepers would be too tired to be on the *qui vive*. However, as a matter of fact, they had learned that it was a
good thing to be very much on the *qui vive* that night;
so poor Tom had been out watching in Barnard's Copse,
and had fallen in with half a dozen poachers, and got his
head broken. This was not where they had been shooting, but on the other side of the park, on the head-keeper's beat. George Beddington, the head-keeper, lived
within a quarter of a mile of the house, on the way to
the Welham Lodge. The second keeper, a man named
Challen, lived the other side of the lake, just inside the
park wall.

Well, there was a great talk about this at luncheon;
and in the end I got leave to take some jelly and some
port down to the wounded man. Sophie couldn't come,
as she was wanted to drive with Aunt Harriet. They
had some things at Selworth, like big jam-pots, covered
with basket-work, in which we used to take jelly and
soup and things to the poor people. So I armed myself
with one of these, full of strong jelly, and a bottle of
port, and started off. In those days port was looked
upon as a universal remedy for all ailments, especially

the ailments of the lower order. As a matter of fact, it was probably rank poison to poor Tom, and the wonder is it didn't kill him.

I found the whole family in—father, mother, Jack, - the second son, a boy of seventeen, and Minnie, the daughter. Tom was in bed, but fairly cheerful, and immensely grateful for my remedies; I asked him about the affair, but there was not much to tell. He had come upon a party of six poachers, and tried to take their guns and the game they had. Whereupon they had clubbed him with the butt end of their guns, and made off. They were all masked, so he could swear to none of them, but he was pretty sure he had recognised old Ned Morris's limp.

After this I used to go down every day, and never empty-handed. I took a great liking to this family, they were all so honest-looking and so grateful, and so *English*. Tom was a fine-looking young fellow—about one-and-twenty—and picked up again wonderfully quick, though I suspect he made the worst of his head whenever I came. I suppose he was afraid the port and jelly would stop if he got well *too* quick. I liked the girl, too. Jack was rather shy and awkward, and seemed frightened of me, but he had a good open face.

It struck me as odd that Uncle Guy never raised any objections to my going to see these people, even though they were a part of the objectionable legacy.

Sophie thought it must be because George Beddington was such a good keeper. He was not a mere charity pensioner, she said, like his mother in the Manor House. That may have been it; but, whatever the reason was, he actually encouraged my going, and used to ask me every evening for news of my patient, as he called Tom.

CHAPTER X

STOKER AND HAMADRYAD

ABOUT a week after that awful shooting-party, I suddenly took it into my head one morning to go and have a look at Inversnaid. It was more than a month since I had been there, and I felt rather ashamed of myself. The morning was splendid—one of those still, sunny, crisp December days that for beauty and enjoyment beat any summer day that ever was made. The old tree hadn't a leaf left on it, and looked all the more huge and majestic for its nakedness. I felt so glad I had come. It was like meeting an old friend again. I pulled off my jacket and hat, and threw them on the ground, and wriggled up "the drawbridge" in the old graceful fashion—new clothes and all!—and lighted a fire, and enjoyed myself thoroughly. From the very tip-top of my branch, now that the leaves were off, I could just get a glimpse of the lake, two miles away, and far away beyond that again I could see the steeple of Greystoke church sticking up into the haze of the horizon. I was in great spirits that morning; nobody could have helped it on such a day as that. I got my head entangled among a thick bunch of twigs, and they pulled all my hairpins out, but I only laughed. I could hear them tinkling down from one branch to another till they buried themselves at last in the soft carpet of leaves below. I laughed again, but made a

84

mental note that I must get into the house by way of the garden, and by my own little turret door, for fear of meeting Aunt Harriet. For the rest, I didn't care a rap; I rather liked having my hair down.

From my perch at the top of the tree one couldn't see the fireplace; it was hidden by the thick growth of stuff below. I began to think it might want looking to, so scrambled down leisurely towards the lower regions. My branch did not form one of the actual walls of the banqueting hall; there was a smaller branch between, round the base of which one had to dodge in order to get in or out. I ducked my head, and swung myself round this branch, and then stood still, and gasped; for there, sitting on Arthur's Seat, and quietly smoking a cigarette, was Mr. Grayle!

I grabbed at my hair, in a feeble, spasmodic attempt to fasten it up, but of course it was utterly futile—no pins. I am sure I got very red, and looked generally idiotic; I know I felt it.

"How on earth did you get here?" I asked at length, for he did nothing but sit there grinning.

"I came up by a new way," he said. "I will show you afterwards; it's not very difficult. You see it was on the other side of the tree to where you were, so you never noticed me."

"Did you see me up there?" I asked.

"Yes, I saw you; but I saw your hat and jacket first; it was that that attracted me."

"Well, I don't think you have any business to come without being asked; this is *my* tree."

I was rather angry at being caught with my hair down.

"You forget," he said, laughing—he was always

laughing, and generally at me, I think—"you forget, you gave me a branch all to myself."

"Did I?" I said. "Well, you had better go there, then."

"But," he said, "I remember you carefully explaining to me that all tenants of branches had a common right to the use of the banqueting hall."

"Very well, then, you can stay here, and I'll go to my branch again."

"And who's going to keep up the fire?"

"You can, if you like; I shan't!"

"I shall be delighted," he said; "you see, I *am* stoker by appointment to the Queen Dryad."

"All right," I said, "good-bye."

I went right up my branch again, and sat there. I could see Mr. Grayle climbing about, getting sticks. He worked very hard, and I began to feel slightly ashamed of myself for being so cross. I also wanted rather to come down and help.

"I say, stoker!" I shouted.

"Yes."

"Just get down and see if you can find my hairpins; they're somewhere among the leaves under the tree."

"Oh," he said, "in that case they're as good as found. The leaves are only two feet deep, and a hair-pin's a thing one can't possibly miss."

However, he went down and poked about, and actually did find one.

"Well done!" I cried, "now for the others."

"Oh, the others are gone," he said, lazily; "you will have to do with this one."

He swung himself up into the tree, and began coming up my branch.

"What are you doing?" I cried. "How dare you come into a lady's branch like this? Go away!"

"I was bringing you your hairpin," he said, coolly.

"Oh, bother the hairpin! What's the use of one?"

"I don't know, I'm sure," he said. "Better than nothing, I suppose."

"No, that's just what it isn't. You can keep it! I don't want it."

"Thanks," he said, "I will."

He put it very slowly into his waistcoat pocket, and began climbing up the branch.

"Where are you coming?" I cried. "Do you know you're trespassing? Go away! It's most ungentlemanly!"

"I want to have a talk with you, Miss Dryad," he said, laughing in the most irritating manner.

"Do you? Well, you can go to your own branch and talk."

"Oh, no; that would make us hoarse. This is much more comfortable."

"I think you are perfectly *odious!*" I said. "I don't think I ever met any one quite so horrid!"

He laughed again, and came up a branch or two higher. I was like a rat in a trap; there was no escape. I was already as high as I could get.

"Well?" he said, looking up at me.

I took no notice whatever. I turned my back as much as I could without falling off, and stared across in the direction of Greystoke. We must have sat like this in dead silence for about ten minutes. Then, for no reason at all, I suddenly burst out laughing. It was perfectly idiotic, of course, and goodness knows why I did it, except that it was so silly sitting there like a couple of owls. He laughed, too, of course, and after that it was no use pretending to be angry, so I gave it up.

"Where have you been all this time, Miss Dryad?" he asked.

"Where have I been! Where have *you* been, you mean. I haven't been anywhere."

"Five times have I had occasion to pass this tree during the last month, but never once has there been any sign of a hamadryad sporting about among the branches."

"Oh, I haven't been here much for the last month or so. I have had other things to do; but before that I was here pretty often."

"That must have been when I was in Norfolk. I went there for a fortnight's shooting about then."

"Oh!"

"And during the rest of this month, are you likely to have—other things to do, do you suppose?"

"Oh, *I* don't know; how can I tell?"

"Because I have every reason to believe that the Duke's business will necessitate my coming this way pretty near every day."

"Stoker, the fire's going out; I can tell by the smoke."

"Bother the fire!" said the stoker.

"If you abuse my fire, I shall have to discharge you."

"Oh, I am sure you wouldn't do that," he said. "If you did, it would make me very, very unhappy."

"Well, then, go down and stoke. I think you are rather dull to-day."

He went like a lamb.

"I am coming down, too," I called out after him. "It's time for me to go home."

Now, I have already explained that in order to get from the base of my branch to the central platform, known as the banqueting hall, it was necessary to swing round a smaller branch that stood in the way—a miserable thing, no bigger than a full-grown birch-tree, and not considered worthy of either a name or a tenant—it was merely a supplier of fuel. There was nothing the least difficult in this performance; the only thing was, one had to hold on with the left hand and swing round with a jerk. Whether what now took place was entirely accidental or not, I don't know; I have my suspicions that it was not; but however that may be, what happened was that I swung myself with a tremendous bang right round into Mr. Grayle's very arms. He was standing, of course, on the platform, out of sight of me, till I came with a bump up against him. The worst of it was, that instead of getting out of the way and apologising, and hoping I was not hurt, and all the rest of it, he held me tight in his arms, and kissed me half a dozen times before I could get away. I was furious.

"You *brute!*" I cried, "you *pig!* I shall never speak to you again!"

He fell back, and looked perfectly miserable. I have never seen any one look quite so ashamed; I shouldn't have thought Mr. Grayle *could* have looked so ashamed.

"Miss de Metrier," he said, slowly, "I deserve all the names you have called me, and more; but it *was* an accident. I give you my word it was a pure accident. I am very sorry; I can say nothing more."

As if any one could kiss one half a dozen times by accident!

"Mr. Grayle," I said, "you have behaved perfectly disgracefully, and I shall never speak to you again."

"I don't deserve that you should," he said, humbly. "Still, if you knew all that it would mean to me if you didn't, you might not be quite so hard on me."

Poor fellow! he did look so wretched. I felt sorry I had called him a pig.

"Do you really mean that my offence has been so great that you can never speak to me again?" he asked.

"Yes, I do," I said, hotly, and holding myself very stiff; I didn't mean it, of course, but I felt I must keep up my dignity.

"Then I will go," he said, meekly. "But before I go, I must tell you this." He paused as though he had a difficulty in finding words. "What I did, unpardonable though it was, I only did because—what I mean is, I would sooner have died than deliberately do anything to hurt or annoy you. Will you believe this?"

"Yes," I said, very low, and looking away.

I felt pretty wretched myself. I longed to tell him that I hadn't really minded *very* much, but of course I couldn't do that. So I stiffened my back, and frowned hard at the red embers in the fireplace.

"I would sooner die than hurt you," he went on, in an odd sort of voice, "because, you know, you are dearer to me than any one else in the world. Good-bye."

He dropped down into the thick leaves below, and strode away without once looking back. The look on his face made me feel perfectly miserable. I stood thinking for a minute or two, and then I dropped down after him, and followed—yes, actually followed him! I could not let him go like that. He had gone a good way, and I had to run to catch him up. He never turned till I was close upon him, hot, and red, and panting. I felt myself going scarlet, and wished I had stayed in the tree, but it was too late now.

"Mr. Grayle," I said, looking at his boots, "I am sorry I—called you a pig."

There was a dead silence for what seemed an age. I knew his eyes were on my face, but I kept on looking at his boots as long as I could. At last—almost in spite of myself—I looked up, and there he was smiling at me with the old look I knew so well. I was so glad to see it again that I suppose I smiled, too. Anyhow, he caught me by the two hands, and looking straight into my eyes, said: "Little Dryad, if you are sorry, you must care a little; do you?"

"I don't know," I said, "perhaps I do; I have never thought about it."

Which, I am sorry to say, was not quite true, for I had thought about it a good deal, and I knew that I did care very much.

"Little Dryad," he said, still holding my hands, "do you think you could ever care enough to marry a poor, penniless land-agent?"

"I don't know," I said; "please let me go."

I tugged at my hands, but he held them fast, and drew me closer.

"Say yes," he whispered, "and I will let you go."

I don't think I did say yes, but he took it for granted, and he certainly did not let me go—at least not for another ten minutes.

"Wherever *have* you been, Josephine," said my aunt, when I arrived half an hour late for luncheon.

"I have been in Flexham Wood, Aunt Harriet," I said, "and I am afraid I quite forgot all about luncheon." Which was strictly true.

CHAPTER XI

MORE EXPLOSIONS

WHAT words can describe the glory of the days that followed? If Selworth was Paradise before, what was it now? If Inversnaid before had been a thing to dream of, what was to be said of it now? The joy of it all was so immense that it positively *hurt*. I hardly knew what to do to prevent going mad from sheer happiness. That I should have gained the love of such a man as Sydney Grayle seemed a thing so utterly incredible that I had to go to Inversnaid every morning to make sure if it was true. While I was there, there was no further room for doubt about it; but no sooner had I got home again than the thing seemed too impossibly good to be true. It was the doubt about my own attractions that made me so unbelieving. What in the world could he see in a girl like me? It must be the new clothes, I thought. I felt positive he would never have proposed to me in my old white stockings. I asked him about this once, about a week afterwards, and he laughed so that he nearly fell off the tree. I saw nothing to laugh at; I was perfectly serious. I didn't believe he would have, and I told him so. *No* man would propose to a girl in white cotton stockings. Sydney said—when he had done laughing 'for five minutes—that it would have made no difference if I had been in striped stockings and buff clothes, marked with a broad arrow. I asked him what it was he liked in me, and he smiled in the old mocking way, and said it was the way my hair fell over my eyes. I told him Uncle Guy called me a Skye terrier, and he seemed rather to like the idea, and said he would tie a blue ribbon round my neck and lead me about! Such drivel!

I used to go to the tree every morning now, but we lit no more fires, the smoke showed too much. Norman was away somewhere shooting; he was always in great request, and was asked about all over the place. So no one troubled himself about what I did in the morning, which was a blessing. We agreed to say nothing about our engagement—engagement! how grand it sounded!—at least not for the present. We thought people might try and stop our meeting in the tree, or come with us and watch us, or drag us about to places, and make a sort of show of us, and spoil everything.

"We'll tell them all about it presently," Sydney said, "there's no hurry."

I was in no hurry. There was an enormous sweetness in our secret being a secret; and to tell the truth, I was just the least bit afraid of what the others might say, especially Aunt Harriet. I had a sort of idea it was not usual to get engaged to men you had only met at the top of a tree; a man, too, that you had never been introduced to, or anything.

Sydney said we could get married in the spring. He asked who my guardians were, and I said I didn't think I had any, but that my aunts at Chelmsford were the only people whose opinion I should bother about. I should have loved to have taken him off straight away, and shown him to *them*, but not the Selworth people.

Then I told him very seriously that I was absolutely

without a penny in the world—and, what was more, that I never could by any possibility have one. And then, for about two minutes, he too was very serious, and told me that he, too, had absolutely nothing but what he got from his agency; and that any day he might be turned off, or the Duke might die, and Lord Barham not care about keeping him on, in which case he would be little better than a beggar. And then he said, almost solemnly, that he thought it was almost a sin to ask any girl to marry a man in such a position, and that if I were not quite sure of myself he would set me free, and go away and never see me again. And I got very angry and offended, and told him he was at perfect liberty to back out of it if he wanted to, and that I should not care tuppence if he did; and we very near had a bad quarrel, but in the end things came right again, as they have a way of doing—at the beginning.

I suppose no one since the beginning of the world has ever been *quite* so happy as we were. They *couldn't* have been. As to me, my spirits were so ridiculous— so idiotic, I might almost say—that every one noticed it. I am not surprised. I should have been very much surprised if they had not noticed it. I was never given to doleful dumps—not even in Chelmsford Church—but now it was with the greatest difficulty I could sit still in a chair. Whenever I walked I ran—which sounds Irish, but is quite true—and whenever I rode I galloped; and when I was doing neither I sang—songs without words (or tune).

" 'Pon my soul, Joe," said Uncle Guy, "we shall have to do something to you soon if you go on like this— put you on bread and water, or make you smoke opium or something. What right have you, or any one else, to look so ridiculously well, and have such ridiculously high spirits? How do you manage it?"

"I don't know," I said, laughing. "I can't help it. I suppose it's being at Selworth."

"You like Selworth, then, eh?"

"Like it! I *love* it!"

I saw my uncle shoot a quick glance at Father Terence, and I also saw Father Terence smile back an answering glance at my uncle. I wondered what their private joke was.

"Well, I hardly call it decent—'pon my word, I don't—with poor gouty old crocks like me about. You ought to have some consideration for our feelings."

"Yes, Josephine, and for our poor nerves," chimed in Aunt Harriet, taking him *au pied de la lettre*, as she would have called it; "there are times when I really feel quite *accablée* by your excessive vigour."

She spoke almost contemptuously. I really believe she thought nerves were as necessary to a well-bred person as a hair-brush.

"I am very sorry," I said; "I shall take to strong tea and strong cigars. Perhaps that will do me good."

"I believe you are quite capable of it, my dear," said my aunt, icily.

If we had only known, there was no need of any of these things to blot out my spirits, and bring me down to a proper state of nervous gentility. Mercifully, however, we are not prophets. There was not a single cloud in my sky just then. How could I tell of the black storm gathering below the horizon? The first rumble of it came the very next day.

Sydney and I had been for our usual two hours in the tree, and we were standing at the top of the bank, close to the end of the drawbridge, saying good-bye, when a man on horseback came suddenly into sight, trotting briskly up the hill from the direction of the Plain. It was Uncle Guy. Sydney and I stood like statues. I don't think at first my uncle saw who it was. He came trotting up with his broad red face smiling good-humouredly, and I thought what a perfect type he looked of an English country gentleman. He was short-sighted without his glasses, and he was close on to us before he realised who we were. Then he pulled up with a jerk, and sat there staring with his mouth wide open. I was prepared for a lecture, but I was not in the least ashamed; in fact, I was rather proud, to tell the truth, that he should see me with the man whose love I had gained. So I waited, with the smile on my face of a person who has been caught out in an innocent fraud. But the smile did not last long. Uncle Guy looked as if he had seen a ghost; his jolly face went as white as a cloth, and he clutched with one hand at the pommel of his saddle.

"What's all this?" he said.

The words came out very quick and faint, as though he were short of breath.

"This is Mr. Grayle, uncle," I said, smiling as well as I could.

"Yes, I know Mr. Grayle," he said. His voice was stronger, and the colour was slowly coming back to his face. "And may I ask to what I owe the pleasure of Mr. Grayle's presence in my park?"

I gave a start, and looked up in horror. It was not so much the words, as the tone of voice. He was speaking through his teeth, and in a slow and strained voice that sounded dreadful. His eyes seemed to have got quite close together and very small, and on his forehead there stood out the great V-shaped vein that I remembered noticing that terrible luncheon after I had been to Mrs. Beddington's.

"I was not aware that you excluded people from your park, Mr. de Metrier," Sydney said, quietly.

"No, sir; but I exclude *poachers!*" His voice was raised now, almost to a shout, and the look on his face was appalling.

"Certainly," said Sydney, laughing; "that is customary in most parks."

His self-control was beautiful. He looked so splendidly calm beside the other. Uncle Guy pulled out a bandanna and mopped his face.

"Ha! ha!" he laughed. "Very good, very good—customary in most parks—so it is—so it is! No doubt you are bothered at Ashby just the same as we are here; damnable country for poachers—worst in England."

He went on holding his handkerchief to his head till I thought he must be ill; then suddenly he said:

"By the way, let me introduce my niece to you."

"Thank you," said Sydney, pleasantly, "I have made Miss de Metrier's acquaintance."

"Quite so—quite so—almost old friends, no doubt—sorry I must carry her off—luncheon time, you know—mustn't be late, mustn't be late—pitched into hot by her ladyship if one is, you know. Ha! ha!"

His face was quite white again, and looked so ghastly that I was frightened.

"Come along, Josephine; we must trot off now. Good day, Mr. Grayle."

I walked by the side of his horse, and we moved slowly away towards the house. We went in dead silence till we reached the foot of the hill, some quarter of a mile away. Then he stopped his horse and faced me.

"So," he said, speaking through his teeth again, "you dear little unsophisticated thing, you sweet innocent babe, you artless child of nature, you shameless abandoned jade, this is the way you spend your mornings, is it?—running about after men in the woods?"

"I hope I haven't done anything wrong, uncle," I said. I was perfectly terrified by his manner. He looked like a madman. *

"Oh, dear, no, sweet Miss Innocence! nothing the least wrong—lying to your aunt and me day after day— telling us you were exploring the woods and what not— and all the while you were carrying on with this man. You worthless little baggage, you—you want whipping, that's what you want! How long have you known this fellow?"

"Oh, several weeks."

"Several weeks! Several weeks! Lord of mercy! Several weeks! And this is your return for all our kindness to you, is it? This is the sort of girl I have brought here as a companion to my daughter, is it? Oh! you— you damned little viper!"

I thought he was going to hit me. He flourished the cane in his hand over my head and back, and once I actually shut my eyes and crouched, expecting the blow. But it never came. I was spared that. The man was clearly out of his mind, and he had to hit something, so he hit the poor horse. It was a beautiful thoroughbred—one that had come from his racing-stables—and at this strange treatment it bounded forward, with its head in the air, and broke into a gallop. Again and again he hit it till the cane broke in his hand, and he was carried out of my sight. The next minute I saw him again, galloping like a mad thing across the Plain.

Uncle Guy did not appear at luncheon that day; he had some taken to his own room. As for me, I was still so frightened, and shaken, and miserable, that I could neither eat nor talk. What had I done that was so dreadful? I would have given anything to know. For that I *had* done something which was very bad indeed I had not the slightest doubt. Uncle Guy would never have gone on the way he did about nothing.

So I sat and puzzled over it, with a white, miserable face, and got not an inch nearer the truth for all my puzzling. I felt perfectly wretched at having so annoyed my uncle. It was quite true what he had said—that they had given me nothing but kindness ever since I had been at Selworth, and the only return I had made for all this was to do something which had displeased him so dreadfully that he was unable to come to luncheon. What could it be? As to the names he had called me, I troubled myself not a rap. I felt certain I deserved them all, and more. If I had not done something very bad he would certainly not have been so angry. None of the others at luncheon knew anything about it. I told them I had a headache and felt sick, which was perfectly true. Aunt Harriet wanted to send for the doctor, and when I wouldn't have that, insisted on my going to bed at once, which I was very glad to do. So in bed I stayed all that day and the next. The doctor came, of course, and looked very wise, and said I had got a chill from getting wet feet; and that afternoon sent up three bottles of medicine, which I emptied out of the window.

On the afternoon of the second day, to my amazement, Uncle Guy came to see me. Poor man! he looked

quite sheepish and ashamed. I longed to tell him how
sorry I was for being so ungrateful and annoying him
so, but he never gave me the chance. He talked incessantly from the moment he came in, and seemed so
anxious to make it up, and make friends, and forget all
about what had happened the day before, that after the
first five minutes I couldn't have said anything about it
to save my life.

"Not much amiss, little Joe?" he said. "That's right,
that's right. Couldn't do without you downstairs, you
know—couldn't do without you, damme no—miss that
bonnie face of yours terribly. We'll send you up some
champagne to-night—nothing like champagne to put any
one on their feet again. Can't take it myself—gout, you
know—plays the very dickens with me—so does port,
worse luck! so does port—temper goes wrong, you
know—damnably wrong—always had the worst temper
in Europe—means nothing, you know—soon over and all
that, but the very devil while it lasts—got me into many
a tight place—ha! ha! ha! many a tight place—Gad!
yes. Nobody minds it, though, who knows me—not a
rap! 'Poor, peppery old devil!' they say. 'All bark, no
bite; not a bad-hearted old chap at bottom—always sorry
after he has broken out.' Well, well, little niece, I must
be trotting off—glad to see you looking so well—does
one good to see you—does us all good to see you, Gad!
yes—don't know what we should do without you—
brighten up the whole place. As to Norman, blest if I
don't believe the boy would stand on his head for a week
to please you; never saw any one so gone—never; quite
comical it is. Norman, too, of all people! Ha! ha! ha!
Norman, that all the girls in London have been setting
their caps at these last five years! Never would look at

them—never cared a snap of his fingers for any girl that
lived—and now to be bowled over neck and heels by a
little minx of a cousin. Ha! ha! ha! Gad! though, I
don't blame him—not I. Well, good-bye, little girl;
pitch into that champagne well, and come down as soon
as ever you can—place don't seem the same without
you—all the brightness gone—dull as ditch-water now—
dull as ditch-water!''

He waved his hand, and went shuffling out with a nod
and a smile. Poor old uncle! he was like a big child
with his roundabout apology. I felt so touched I almost
cried; but I didn't. I did something far more sensible,
for I rang the bell, and told Griffiths I was quite well,
and going to get up at once. Griffiths looked relieved.
She was not fond of waiting on me, and, goodness
knows, I didn't trouble her much when I was well. Of
course, when I was in bed it was different; she had to be
there more or less.

"When will you have your hot water, miss?" she
asked.

"Oh, now, please," I said; 'I shall get up at once.''

"Very good, miss," she said, looking more like an
old vinegar pot than usual. I forgot till afterwards that
it was just the servants' tea-time. However, I needn't
have worried. She took pretty good care to have her
tea comfortably, and without hurrying, before she
thought of bringing me my things. I wished to goodness Aunt Harriet would have let one of the housemaids
look after me, or even Sophie's maid; I couldn't stand
old Griffiths. I had tried hard to like her at first, but it
was no good. She seemed to be thinking the whole time
she was with me what a hardship it was, and how unin-
teresting a person I was to look after, with my few poor

dresses, and my one crystal locket as my entire stock of jewellery. I suppose she thought I was too poor to tip her well at the end, which, of course, I was.

So Griffiths and I didn't quite hit it off. I am sure she thought me a heathen, too, for not going to chapel in the mornings; she told me as much a dozen times. Well, if she was a type of Christian, I would sooner be a heathen any day. However, enough of old Griffiths.

They were all so pleased to see me down, and so kind and nice, and Uncle Guy gave us all champagne at dinner—which, by the way, he was not over fond of doing unless there were visitors—and Father Terence got extremely convivial, and Aunt Harriet made at least two jokes, and altogether it was one of the pleasantest evenings we had had since I came.

CHAPTER XII

I HAVE A BIRTHDAY

THE twelfth of December was my birthday. I had said nothing about it myself, and had no idea the others knew. So when I came down to breakfast, and was greeted with a chorus of "Many happy returns!" and with much kissing, and many little packets done up in silver paper and tied round with blue ribbon, it quite took my breath away. Norman gave me nothing, but was not behind with the rest, I remember.

It was a glorious day, still and bright and frosty. From the dining-room windows one could see a thin mist still hanging over the Plain, and the deer moving about in it like ghosts. Over the top of the mist, and standing out clear and crisp in the sunshine were the Flexham Woods on the hill, a mile away; and higher still, a huge procession of rooks were slowly plodding across the sky, filling the still, silent air with their cries. A grand day for a birthday, I thought; a grand day to be alive at all, at any age, but a particularly grand day at nineteen.

There were two long letters with the Chelmsford postmark—two dear, sweet letters, telling of two little presents laboriously worked by four loving old hands, which presents, alas! had not come. And there was a large white cake in the middle of the table, with nineteen candles round it (not to be lighted till tea-time), and "Joe" on top, in twisted pink letters. I knew as soon as I saw it who had given orders about that cake; no one but Uncle Guy would have had "Joe" put on it.

I wondered what Norman was going to give me, and why he was keeping his present back. Of course, I knew he was going to give me something; he was wonderfully generous at all times, and had already given me more that one present; so that on a birthday it was a certainty; but why keep it back?

"Will you come for a walk, Joe?" he asked after breakfast.

"Of course, I will," I said. "Where shall we go— the 'Marsh'?"

"No; I want to take you *my* way to-day; you have done leader often enough. I believe there's at least half of the park that you know nothing about."

"All right," I said. "I don't care where we go, as long as we go somewhere. It's a sin to stay indoors on a day like this. I'll go and put on my hat."

"All right," he said; "no hurry."

He took me across the Plain, but bearing away to the left. Flexham Wood and Inversnaid and the old Manor House all lay away to the right. He was quite right; I hardly ever came that way—why, I don't know. I suppose I preferred sticking to old friends. He took me round the shoulder of the hill, and up the glen beyond— the narrow glen that cuts the wood in two. After we had gone for a quarter of a mile up this, we turned to the left up the hill into the wood. I had never been near this part of the park before; it was too far away for comfort. I remember thinking, as we walked, that the entrance to Dante's Inferno ought certainly to have been here, instead of in prosy little Marigold Marsh. It was a huge, gloomy, silent beech wood, the trunks of the trees white and shiny with age, and towering up into the very sky; underneath, of course, bare of anything but the red carpet of leaves. Here and there among the trees were strange little ponds of black rain-water, choked up with leaves.

We climbed and climbed, and then quite suddenly came upon a place the existence of which I had never even dreamt of. This was a kind of knob or mound bulging up in the middle of the wood; the trees formed a clean circle round it, and seven avenues starred outwards, showing far-off glimpses of the park. It simply took my breath away, it was so beautiful! One looked through long dark lanes of trees down on to the sunlit plains beyond. One of them pointed straight to the house itself, two miles away; another showed the whole length of the lake shimmering in the sun, and beyond, again, the double towers of the Greystoke Lodge; and another pointed to the chalk pit up by the Welham Lodge; and another to the ups and downs of woodland that rose beyond the old Manor House.

It was a glorious scene, only to be seen in its full beauty in midwinter, when the trees were naked. The mound itself was covered with long, coarse yellow grass—partridge grass, I think, they call it—and on this we flung ourselves down in the warm sunshine, and revelled in the beauty of the scene before us. There was not a sound of any sort to break the silence and stillness of the day except the distant cawing of some rooks down towards the lake. We neither of us spoke for some time; then Norman said:

"It's a fine view, isn't it?"

"Heavenly!" I said.

After another long pause, he said:

"It's nice to think that all this will be mine as long as I live."

"I should think so, indeed," I said; "you lucky fellow! I don't believe you half appreciate it."

"You think you'd appreciate it better, do you?"

"I know I should," I said, laughing, "*infinitely*. I'm quite certain I'm a thousand times fonder of the place than any of you are. People never half value the things they've got."

"Would you like to live here, Joe, for the rest of your life?"

"Well, naturally, I should. What a question!"

"You can if you like," he said, looking at me.

"What on earth do you mean, Norman?" said I, knowing perfectly well, of course.

"Little Joe," he said, taking no notice of my question, "I have got a present for you here; I do hope you will like it."

He pulled a small round parcel from his pocket, and put it in my hand.

"O Norman," I said, "it *is* good of you to think of my birthday. I really didn't want anything. Oh! how *lovely! ! !*"

It was a diamond and ruby half-loop bracelet, with a true lover's knot in the middle. I gasped, and looked at Norman, who was smiling up at me from the grass.

"It is not for *me*, Norman?"

"Yes, for you, my sweet little cousin, and not nearly good enough, either."

"O Norman, I can't take it."

"Why not?"

"Oh, it's too much—far too much for me! It must have cost a fortune."

"Nonsense!" he said; "it's nothing to what I should like to give you. I should like to see half a jeweller's shop on your arms and neck, and glittering on the top of that sweet little head of yours. Will you let me get them, Joe?"

He had hold of my hand, and was drawing me towards him.

"Joe," he said, "dear little Joe, let me do this. I will make a queen of you, and crown you with diamonds, and you shall reign over Selworth—the Selworth you are so fond of—for ever and ever, as long as we live. Say you will, Joe; I will be so good to you, and make you happier than anybody ever was before."

I felt perfectly miserable. It would be nonsense, of course, to pretend that I didn't know Norman liked me, but that he should want to marry me had never for one moment entered into my head; the idea was too preposterous—why *should* he?

"Norman," I said, "you can't mean this; you are not serious."

I knew, of course, he was, poor fellow! One had only to look at his face; it was all white and drawn.

"Not serious!" he laughed. "Not serious! Heavens above! I wish I was not. I'm sick with love of you, Joe—positively *sick* with love."

"No, no," I cried, "you can't be; it's impossible! What is there in me to be in love with?"

"Joe, Joe!" he said, clutching at my hand, "say it's all right! For God's sake, say it's all right!"

"But it's all wrong, Norman—dreadfully wrong! Oh! what in the world has put this madness into your head?"

"Madness!" he cried, "there's no madness about it. Nobody but a stone could live in the same house with you, and not fall head over ears in love. Joe, you will marry me, won't you?"

"I can't, Norman," I said. "I'm dreadfully sorry, but I can't."

He let go my hand, and sat bolt upright, looking straight before him. I stared away over at the lake, feeling more miserable than I can say; it all seemed so brutal and ungrateful; but what could I do?

"Joe," he said, after a little, speaking very slowly and looking the other way, "if you only knew all that this meant to me, and others, I think you would give a different answer—I am sure you would. You don't dislike me, do you?"

"Of course I don't," I said; "you must know that, Norman. I like you ever so much."

"Then, why won't you marry me?"

I was silent. What could I say?

"Is it that fellow Grayle?"

"Yes, it is Mr. Grayle."

There was a long pause. Then he said:

"Do you know, Joe, that Grayle is practically a beggar—that he has no right to ask any girl to marry him? I call it a selfish, cowardly thing for a man to drag a girl he pretends to like into a life of starvation and drudgery —infernally selfish! He ought to be ashamed of himself!"

At this I am afraid I forgot to be sorry for Norman any more. I think I got very red, and I know my voice shook.

"I don't care a bit," I said, "if he hasn't a penny in the world. I would sooner black his boots than wear every diamond you could buy in London."

"You think yourself in love with him, then?" he asked, quietly.

"I would die for him," I said, "willingly. I would wash for him, and cook for him, and scrub the steps, and think myself the happiest girl on earth."

"Pooh!" he said; "it's easy talking like that beforehand. Wait till you try a week of it."

"I am not afraid," I said, a little defiantly.

"Joe," he said, turning to me once more, and catching my hand, "you are very young, and a mere child in experience; for Heaven's sake, think well over what you are doing! What I am going to say sounds vulgar and snobbish and horrible, but there is no help for it. One must speak plainly. Look here! I can give you everything in the world you can wish for—horses, carriages, jewels, one of the finest places in England, a house in London, balls, operas, everything, in short, that you can imagine, and the passionate, devoted love of a man that almost any girl in England would be glad to marry. I know it's a horrible thing to say, but I must put things plainly—there's too much at stake to mince matters. And what can this other fellow give you? A miserable pittance derived from an agency which may come to an end any day, and leave him and you absolute beggars. Will your love stand such a test as that? Think of the years to come! Think of your children! Will *his* love stand such a test, do you think? Love soon languishes when the fight for existence begins. O Joe, darling little Joe! my love for you is just as strong as his. Don't you believe in my love for you, Joe?"

"Yes, Norman, I do. You would never have asked me to marry you unless you loved me, of course. Why should you? I can't tell you how dreadfully sorry I am

about the whole thing.   You must think me such a *brute*,
and so ungrateful, and all.   But, you see, I love him,
and I can't help myself."

"No, I suppose not," he said.

I should never have thought Norman could have felt
anything so deeply.   I always looked on him as one of
those light-hearted, easy-going sort of fellows who take
nothing particularly serious.   But here he was, looking haggard and ghastly as a ghost, and with a deep line
between his eyes; it was terrible!

"Dear Norman," I said, taking his hand, "I am so
sorry.   You have all been so good to me; it makes me
wretched to see you like this."

"Don't touch me!" he snapped, shaking me off
roughly.   "If you won't marry me, leave me alone.
None of your cursed wheedling tricks!"

"I'm sorry," I said, miserably.

"No, no, Joe; I beg your pardon; I didn't mean
that—honestly I didn't; but I'm pretty near off my
head, and really don't know what I'm saying, and that's
the truth."

I felt like a murderess.

"Oh, dear! oh, dear!" I said.   "Why in the world
should you go and fall in love with *me*, of all people,
when there are such hundreds of infinitely nicer and
prettier girls all over the place?"   It seemed such a pity.

"O Joe, Joe!" he wailed, "you don't know—you
don't know what utter nonsense you're talking.   There's
not a girl I've ever seen can hold a candle to you."

"Oh, that's absurd!" I said; "think of all the beautiful girls you must have seen in London!"

"You are more beautiful than any of them, Joe—a
hundred times more beautiful!"

"But I'm *not!*" I cried, half angrily. "It's ridiculous talking like that. Everybody knows I am not pretty. Aunt Harriet has told me so a dozen times."

"Pooh!" he said, laughing scornfully; "mother, indeed! Ask a man, Joe—ask *any* man. What does Grayle say, for instance?"

"Oh, he's prejudiced, you see. A man in love doesn't count."

"Joe," he said, rising on to his knees, and looking me straight in the face, "are you absolutely sure of your own mind, do you think?"

"Yes, Norman, quite sure; I shall never change."

"Very well, then, there's nothing more to be said. Shall we make a move?"

We walked for a long way in silence; what was there to talk about? I kept thinking what a wretched thing this was to have happened on my birthday, and how nice it would be if one could wipe out the last hour, and go on just as we had done before. But, of course, that was hopeless; things could never be the same again now.

Suddenly Norman said:

"You will keep this little bracelet and wear it, Joe, won't you? It's the least you can do for me."

"I don't think I ought," I said; "it's too much. And, besides—there's that thing in the middle."

"Oh, bother the thing in the middle; why, even bridesmaids get that on their lockets and things. It won't hurt you."

"I think it would look odd, don't you?"

"No, not a bit. I think it's the least you can do for me under the circumstances."

"Well, if you put it that way, I suppose I must," I said, trying to get up a laugh.

"That's right."

There seemed a kind of gloom over us all that day at luncheon; only Sophie and Aunt Harriet were in the usual spirits. Norman was very silent, and ate next to nothing, and I was not hilarious. I caught Uncle Guy once or twice looking at us curiously; he, too, I thought, seemed ill at ease and fidgety. He got up before luncheon was over and went to his room, to write letters, as he said. Later on I saw him go out for a ride with Norman. Sophie and I rode, too, but we saw nothing of the other two. However, we had a good gallop, which did us a world of good.

CHAPTER XIII

ANOTHER SHOOTING PARTY, A SURPRISE AND A PUZZLE

THE week before Christmas there was a second shooting party. They were to shoot the other side of the park. I was not excited at the thoughts of it, remembering the last one. I only wondered mildly whether the United Kingdom could produce a second batch of antediluvians as prehistoric as the last. I suppose, as a matter of fact, it could not, for the present party turned out to be babes in arms by comparison. They were also, for the most part, delightfully frivolous and unpolitical! The bulk of the visitors only arrived just before dinner, and went straight up to their rooms to dress. For my own part, I dressed with considerable care that night, putting on my very best dress—the yellow satin—and finished up by clasping Norman's bracelet on my left arm. I flattered myself I really looked quite presentable. As a rule, I was the last down, being one of those people who are never in time for anything; but to-night, for a wonder, I was early, and the drawing-room was almost empty when I got there. There was a man bending down over the papers on the table; I suppose he heard the rustle of my dress—it did make an appalling noise!—for he straightened himself and looked round. It was Sydney!

I don't suppose I have ever been so surprised in my

life. Sydney Grayle an invited guest to Selworth, of all
places! I could hardly believe my eyes.

"Good evening, Miss de Metrier," he said, with the
old mocking smile: "you don't appear overjoyed to see
me."

"Sydney!" I gasped, "you here! Did they ask you?"

"Oh, no," he said, "of course not. But I managed
to get in, after a bit of a fight with the butler and three
footmen."

"No; but isn't it an extraordinary thing?"

"I don't see anything extraordinary about it. Am I
too great a yahoo for any one to have inside their house?"

"Sydney, they know all about it!"

"Well, let them. I don't care—do you?"

"No, but you know they all hate the idea of my marrying you."

"Do they? Who particularly?"

"Oh, Uncle Guy and Norman, I think. But I don't
know. I never talk about it, nor do they."

"And who gave you that pretty bracelet, little Miss
Dryad?"

"Norman gave it me on my birthday."

"Oh, Norman gave it you, did he?—true-lovers' knot
and all?"

"Oh, that's nothing!"

Across the polished floor of the hall we could hear
the sweep of many skirts. A whole army of people
began trooping in, with the slow, uncertain march of new
arrivals and strangers. We pecked and bobbed at one
another for a couple of minutes, and smirked amiably,
and made inane little remarks; and then Aunt Harriet
arrived, and we were all introduced and told one another's
names, which we forgot next moment. A certain Lord

Grannet took me in to dinner. He was very nice, and quite young, and had a very pretty wife, who was simply blazing with jewels. I never got a word with Sydney the whole night. Father Terence, of course, sang after dinner, and Sophie played, and every one seemed pleased. There were no songsters among the visitors.

When the time came for the lighting of bedroom candles, the men, as usual, gathered round in force at the foot of the stairs. When I said good-night to Norman, to my very intense surprise, he stepped forward and kissed me before them all. He had never done this, or attempted to, since the first night of my arrival. I held out my hand to Sydney, but he barely touched it, and turned away. I could see he was very angry.

Sophie came to my room, and sat there some time, discussing the various people, and then she went to bed, and I lay awake for hours puzzling over the mystery of Sydney being there. The more I thought it over, the more inexplicable it seemed—so inexplicable, in fact, that after a time I gave up bothering about it; there was no possible explanation that I could see. However, it was very nice having him there, I thought, only I wished Norman hadn't kissed me. It was very tiresome of him— and stupid, too, before all those people. And then I turned over and went to sleep, and dreamt that Sydney and I were wandering about looking for Inversnaid, which we couldn't find. As we were looking in the passages of Selworth, this was perhaps not surprising.

I was down very early next morning. I wanted, if possible, to have a word with Sydney, and explain about Norman the night before. But the lazy fellow never came down till breakfast was half over, and then, of course, we wretched females were dragged off to the morning-room to do polite conversation, and he went off shooting with the others; so the chance never came. I should have loved, of course, to have gone out with the shooters, but this was not allowed.

However, my early rise was not absolutely barren of results. I overheard a conversation, or part of a conversation, between Norman and Father Terence that set me thinking for some time. It happened this way. Selworth is a house that has probably more staircases than any other house in Europe. I suppose it comes from having been built at so many different periods. Not one of them run from top to bottom of the house; they all stop short half-way, and then begin again somewhere else! Some of them are not more than a dozen steps high—ridiculous little things springing out of places like cupboards, where no one would ever dream of looking for a staircase. Others are double or treble this height, according to what is required of them; for the floors are just as irregular in their way as the staircases, and equally unconventional—rising and falling and twisting about from right to left for no possible reason that one can see except to puzzle people, and give them exercise. It took me more than a month to find my way about. After that I used to amuse myself by trying to get from my room to the drawing-room by as many different ways as possible. Sophie had a different form of amusement. Whenever Aunt Harriet asked her to take a visitor to her room, instead of going the plain, straightforward way, she used to drag the wretched woman upstairs and downstairs, round corners, and down twisting dark passages, then up another stair, and down another, with more passages and more corners, till finally, after walking half a mile, she landed her, breathless and bewil-

dered, at the door of her room.   There she would leave
her, hoping, with a sweet smile, that she would find her
way down again all right.

Well, this particular morning it happened that I
went down from the first floor to the long passage below,
by a little dark staircase known to Sophie and me as the
"red stairs."   This staircase really connects the robbers' passage above with the little corridor that leads to
the chapel.   The robbers' passage, by the way, was in
reality the place where the men-servants slept; but it
was not on this account that we gave it the name, but
because, as children, we were firmly convinced that it
was the chosen home of several bands of robbers.   No
power on earth would have taken us down it after dark.
At the bottom of the red stairs there is a sort of lobby,
apparently devised by the architect for the purpose of
wasting space.   As I went down, I heard voices below,
and looking over the banisters, saw Norman and Father
Terence in earnest conversation.   I thought nothing of
this at the time, and stood there for a minute watching
them, and wishing I had something to drop on their
heads.

"Me dear boy," the priest was saying, "it often happens in this world that we have to do certain things
which are repugnant to our natures, especially to the
emotional side of our natures.   But when such actions
are the only means of averting a very grave calamity,
they become not only justifiable, but a positive duty.
There can be no question of that."

"You think so?" Norman said, doubtfully.

"Me dear boy, I'm sure of it.   Don't have any fear."

At this moment I suddenly appeared on the bottom
flight of steps.

"Ah! Miss Joe," he said, "now don't you agree with me? I have been telling Norman that in all questions of obvious duty personal feeling should be put on one side. What do you say, now?"

"Oh, I don't know, I'm sure," I said; "I think duty's always a bore."

Father Terence went off towards the chapel, and Norman and I strolled along towards the morning-room to wait for breakfast.

"What is this very disagreeable duty you have to perform?" I asked.

"Oh, nothing in particular," he said; "he was generalising, you know—preaching a sermon, in fact; he's rather fond of it."

I felt pretty certain this was not true. People don't talk in the earnest, decisive tones that Father Terence was using if they are only generalising, nor do they look so particularly disconcerted at being overheard. There was something behind; I felt sure of that.

Norman was absent and dejected, and I didn't press him. He had been in terribly low spirits ever since my refusal of him the week before—quite a different man, in fact—haggard, silent, and cross. I had no idea he could have taken anything so to heart—especially the mere loss of so valueless an article as myself. Whether he had told the others I had no idea—I thought not. Why should he? Of course, *I* had said nothing about it, even to Sophie; I was much too sorry for Norman, and besides, it seemed so conceited.

So I and my love affairs were left alone by the rest of the family. Everybody was the same to me as before—cheerful and kind and thoughtful. Father Terence went on telling his anecdotes, and laughing at them louder

than any one else, and Uncle Guy went on swearing his
mild, amiable oaths, and patting me on the head, and
paying me his funny, old-fashioned compliments, just
exactly the same as before.   Still, for all this, there *was*
a change.   It was nothing that one can describe, or put
into words; it was far too slight and indefinite for that;
but there it was—quite unmistakable—and it made me
very unhappy.   It had started from the day that Uncle
Guy had found me with Sydney, and it had not become
less after Norman had asked me to marry him.   Sophie,
of course, was just the same as ever; there was no
change in her, or in Aunt Harriet, either, for that matter; but, then, I don't think Aunt Harriet ever *really*
liked me, so that, even if she was angry with me, it was
not likely to make any great difference in her manner.

I put it all down to their pride.   The De Metriers
were immensely proud, and always had been—proud of
their long descent, of their name, of their place, and—a
little, I think—of their wealth.   I had no pride.   Ten
years of Chelmsford, and white cotton stockings, and tea
and shrimps, had made away with any original pride I
might have inherited; I don't suppose I ever had any.
I was not the least *distinguée*—as Aunt Harriet was so
fond of impressing upon me—either in appearance or
manners.

Still, I did bear the family name, and I thought they
were annoyed at the idea of a De Metrier wishing to
marry a penniless land-agent, even though he was a
peer's son; and still more annoyed at the idea of a
homeless charity-girl presuming to refuse the heir and
hope of the family.

During this, to me, intensely memorable shooting
party, there occurred one little incident which, in view

of after events, I must mention.   I was coming downstairs 'from my room just before dressing-time when I
met Norman's valet coming up the turret stairs carrying clothes and hot water.   He was a man named Frenetzi, a flashy-looking Italian, that I rather disliked, but
that Norman swore by.   I stopped and stared at him.

"Why, where are you going?" I said, "you can't get
to Mr. Norman's room that way."

"These are Meestare Grayle's clothes," he said,
with a bow and a flourish.   "Meestare Grayle he bring
no *valet-de-chambre*, and Meestare Norman say I wait on
him; he has what they call the Blue Room."

"Oh, I see," I said, and passed on.   I thought nothing of this at the time, but a great deal a little later on.

CHAPTER XIV

A NIGHTMARE

IT was the 22nd of December—a day that I shudder at even now. The shooting finished that day, and the guests were all going off next morning. The party had been an immense success from every point of view—social, sporting, climatic. Every one seemed to enjoy themselves, even poor, dejected Norman. There was a certain Miss Fortescue among the guests, an heiress, and a bit of a beauty, to whom he made desperate love; and she, for her part, I must confess, seemed more than content that he should—in fact, all the women flocked round Norman, morning and evening, making a regular hero of him. They stood behind him out shooting; they talked across the table to him at dinner, and left their proper partners sulky and neglected; they sat in a circle round him after dinner, or disappeared with him to the billiard-room; there was no end to it. And from time to time I would catch him shooting a quick glance at me, to see if I was taking it all in, and noticing what a fine fellow all these smart ladies thought him. Of course, I noticed it, but it made no difference to me; he was welcome to them all, as far as I was concerned.

For Sydney and I had made it up—made it up, I mean, about Norman and his bracelet, and that first good-night. The bracelet I had put away out of sight, with many a sore pang of regret, it must be owned; and as to the other thing, I had explained to him that it was not my fault, that Norman had taken me by surprise, and that what had happened was by no means a practice—very much the opposite, in fact. I told him that he was a real old stupid not to see that the whole thing was an open and transparent attempt on Norman's part to stir up bad blood between us. And Sydney, being just as anxious, I think, as I was to see things in a reasonable and satisfactory light, admitted that this was more than probable.

So that little cloud passed away in sunshine; and the sunshine shone out brightly and merrily—though at very long intervals, alas!—till the end of the last day's shooting. After that there was no more sun for many a day.

The shooting was finished, and they were all going off next morning after breakfast. The great ceremony of candle-lighting and separating for the night was over, and Sophie and I were sitting in my room discussing people in general, and Sydney in particular. Sophie went so far as to allow that she was quite in love with Sydney herself, but qualified this admission by saying that girls that let their feelings get away with them, so far as to wish to marry penniless younger sons, ought to be shut up as a danger to the state.

"Pooh!" said I, "don't be priggish! Really, Sophie, you are getting to talk exactly like old General Borrodaile."

"I don't care; you ought to be shut up! He's very nice, but you ought to be shut up; you *both* ought to be shut up—silly young nooks!"

"Well," I said, laughing, "it's high time we were both shut up for this night, anyhow. Do you know it's past twelve o'clock?"

"Goodness!" she said, "I had no idea it was so late. I hope I shan't meet any of the men. Good-night."

I watched her scuttling down the stairs, candle in hand, till she was out of sight, and then locked the door, tore off my dressing-gown, and hopped into bed. I was just comfortably tired, and at peace with all men, and all women, too, and I expect I was asleep before Sophie got to her room.

In the middle of the night I woke quite suddenly, and without warning, and lay still, listening. I had not the faintest idea of what had wakened me, but in a second I was awake, and fearfully conscious of some vague terror in the atmosphere. My heart thumped madly against my ribs, and my mouth felt dry and parched. What was it? Not a sound broke the stillness of the night. The fire was out, and the darkness was intense. With every nerve at full stretch, I lay still, waiting for the sound of that which I *felt* was near. After what seemed an age it came, a faint, insignificant noise, but one that literally stopped my heart with a jerk, for it told me as plain as words that there was some one in the room. I would have screamed, only that I was too frightened. My feeling was that if I made the slightest sound, the unknown presence would hurl itself at my throat. I remember now wondering vaguely—even in the middle of the cold agony I was in—how any one or any thing *could* have got into the room. I always locked my door, and the windows were little diamond-paned slits that nobody could have squeezed through. Then there came another noise—a sort of stealthy creak and the sound of breathing; I could hear the breathing now quite plainly. Why my hair was not snow-white next morning is a marvel to me! I put my head under the clothes, and lay there in a shaking ague beside which death must be a mere joke. Like a flash, all the murders I had ever read of shot through my mind, vivid, horrible, appalling! I longed for death—for anything to put an end to it. I brought my head out very slowly from under the clothes. There was that ghastly breathing as plain as ever—sounding closer if anything than before. A strange kind of reckless courage came over me—the sort of courage that people must have who commit suicide. I put out my hand very, very softly, and felt for my matches. They stood by the side of my candle, and my hand found them after a short moment's groping. Very carefully I brought out my left hand, too, and felt for the place to strike on. My great terror now was that the match might not light at the first strike. If it was damp, after the manner of matches, and simply gave out a tell-tale scratch while refusing to light, I felt that my brain would crack, and I should go stark, staring mad that very moment. Holding my breath, I dragged the match madly across the rough, and it lit—blazed up at the very first attempt. I think that was the most terrible moment of all. God knows what I expected to see! I held the match up high, and glared across the foot of the bed with my teeth chattering like castanets. The next moment I sank back on the pillows with a sigh of such relief that I think I nearly fainted. I had just strength and presence of mind enough to light the candle, and no more.

Norman was standing with his back to the fireplace. He had on a gorgeous red and gold dressing-gown, and his hands were in his pockets.

The relief I felt at first was so immense—so indescribably immense—that I quite forgot to wonder what he was doing there—or how he got in. I felt like a person who has just been snatched from the jaws of some awful death. I felt almost as if Norman was the person who had rescued me. For a minute or two I lay back with closed eyes and gasped.

Then I began slowly to recover my senses. It was Norman who helped me principally to do this. He began walking towards me, and I opened my eyes, and looked at him. He looked very odd. His face was red and flushed, his eyes were very bright, and he wore a foolish sort of smile. He looked to me like a man who had been drinking.

"Norman," I said, "what are you doing here?"

"Oh, I just came to have a little talk," he said with a foolish leer.

"Talk!" I cried. "What do you mean? What do you want to talk about? Do you know what time it is? Go away! How did you get in?"

"Oh, love can always find a way," he said, grinning.

"Go away this very minute," I said; "I believe you're drunk."

"No, Joe, only desperately in love," he said.

I sat up in bed and faced him. I was not in the least afraid now. If it hadn't been for the terror before I might have been, but after that it seemed nothing.

"What—do—you—want?" I said, very slowly and distinctly.

He gave a silly little laugh. His manner was half-sheepish and half-defiant, and quite unlike himself.

"What do I want?" he said. "Well, Joe, in the first place, I want a kiss."

He began coming my way, and in one second I was out of bed. On the right of my bed was a washing-stand, and between that and the bed was the bell. I seized the rope with my right hand, and faced him.

"Norman," I said, "this bell rings in Griffiths' room. If you come one step nearer, I'll ring."

"Oh, no, little Joe," he said; "you wouldn't do that, I know."

He came shuffling on in his slippers, and I pulled the bell three times, with all my strength. At the third pull the rope came down with a clatter. I was really frightened now, terrified; but to my amazement, Norman spun on his heel, and went into peals of laughter. He took a match-box off the table at the foot of the bed, and lighting a cigarette, threw himself into the armchair by the fireplace. I stood perfectly still and watched him.

"Are you quite mad?" I said.

"No," he answered, "method, you know—a certain amount of method."

"Will you have the goodness to GO," I said; "Griffiths will be here in a minute."

"Oh, bother old Griffiths! Who cares for her?"

"Do you mean to say you are not going?"

"No, Joe, dear; it's so beastly lonely in my room, and this chair is awfully comfortable."

"And you call yourself a gentleman?" I said.

"Sometimes I do. Not just now."

He looked at me again over his shoulder, and laughed loud and inanely.

"Well, for goodness' sake, don't make such a noise," I cried.

"All right, Joe," he said, and lit another cigarette.

For five minutes by the clock we stayed so, in dead silence—I standing shivering by the broken bell-rope, Norman lazily smoking in the armchair. I was trying all the time to think of the best thing to do, and couldn't. My brain refused to work—everything was in a kind of haze. All I knew was that the situation was becoming intolerable. In the distance, through the silence of the night, I heard the sound of a door shutting. I turned to Norman and ground my teeth.

"*Will* you go?" I cried, stamping my bare foot.

"Not just yet," he said, carelessly; "all in good time, you know."

"But she's *coming!*"

"What? Old Griffiths? Oh, never mind the old girl; let her come."

I could hear her footsteps on the stairs now. All sounds seemed plain to me that night; every sense was at high pressure Higher and higher they came on the stone, uncarpeted steps—the dragging steps of a tired elderly woman. There was a knock at the door; I never moved; to tell the truth, I didn't know what to do. I heard her try the handle, but the door was locked; then, quite distinctly, I heard her sniffing outside, exactly like a dog who thinks he has found a suspicious smell. I was not surprised; the room was full of smoke.

She tried the handle again, shaking the door this time.

"Miss Josephine."

"Yes," I answered, trying to put on a sleepy voice.

"Did you ring? Your bell rang in my room as though the house was on fire."

"Yes, Griffiths, I did ring. I thought I heard burglars, and was frightened; but I think it was nothing. I am so sorry for disturbing you. Good-night."

"You had better let me come in, miss, and look about; there might be something."

There was half a minute's silence while I racked my
brains for the best thing to do. Then, to my unspeakable horror, Norman's voice came across the room to
me in an extremely clear stage-whisper:

"Get rid of the old girl somehow, Joe, for goodness'
sake! We don't want her in here."

I heard a regular gasp from outside the door—the
catch of the breath a person might give if they saw a ghost.

"It was really nothing, thank you, Griffiths," I said;
"please go to bed. I am very sorry about it."

"Oh, certainly, miss," she said, in a tight, acrid voice.

We heard her clicking down the stairs, and Norman
burst into a loud peal of laughter.

"Well done, Joe!" he cried out; "you managed that
splendidly!"

"You *devil!*" I said. "Hold your tongue."

He laughed again, quietly this time.

"By Jove!" he said, "how splendid you look when
you are angry; and what splendid hair you've got! You
ought always to have it down like that!"

"Get out of my room!" I said.

"Yes, I'll go now, Joe, but I must have that kiss first.
You've no bell to ring now, you know."

He got up quite slowly from the chair, and began
coming my way. I think all fear had vanished now before the overpowering rage that boiled within me. I
took a step towards the washing-stand, and seized the
water-bottle by the neck.

"I swear I'll break this over your head if you do," I
said.

"All right, Joe, don't get so excited. No one's going
to eat you."

I stood eyeing him, and balancing the bottle in my

right hand; I even emptied half the water into the jug
to prevent wetting myself. I felt I should have loved
to have had one clear sweep at his head. He evidently
didn't like the look of the bottle.

"I'm going," he said, shortly. "I think you are
very disagreeable; give me a light."

He held out a bedroom candle, one of those with a
long glass on them. I had not noticed it before.

"No," I said. "You've got matches."

He shrugged his shoulders, and began to whistle
softly; but he lit the candle with a match, and placed
it on the far edge of the chimney-piece. I watched him
with intense curiosity. He pulled a chair opposite the
fireplace and climbed from this on to the chimney-
piece. Then he ran his hand quickly up the inside of the
picture frame above, paused for a second at a particular
spot, and fumbled about with his fingers. The next
moment great grandfather Maurice swung noiselessly out
of the wall, leaving a black, cave-like space where he had
been. Norman took his candle and stepped in. By the
light I got a glimpse of stone steps. Then Norman
turned round to me, nodded and kissed his hand, and
slowly pulled the picture after him.

"Good-night, little cousin," he said. "Sorry I had to
bother you—beastly sorry, 'pon my word!—but needs
must, you know, when the devil drives. See you at
breakfast."

The picture closed with a snap, and he was gone. By
the faint light of my one candle I could see Maurice
looking down at me with his old, supercilious smile, and
to my excited fancy, the smile seemed more of a sneer
than ever. I shook my fist at him frantically for a
minute, and then I fell on my knees and burst into tears,
with my head buried in the pillows.

CHAPTER XV

A LECTURE FROM AUNT HARRIET

I BELIEVE I did sleep for about two hours towards morning. When I got up, and looked at my face in the glass, I almost laughed, it was so ghastly. All my colour was gone, and my face looked quite drawn. However, there was no use making a fuss over things, so I dressed quietly and went down in good time for breakfast. I wanted to see Sydney before he went. Norman was not down; he often had breakfast in bed, like a woman. I was thankful for that much.

It appeared to me, before I had been down long, that I must look worse even than I had thought, people stared at me so. Several times I caught both Uncle Guy and Father Terence looking at me slyly, out of the "tail of their eye." Aunt Harriet stared at me openly, with a cold, unsympathetic stare; but the worst of all was Sydney. When I first came into the room, he looked at me as if I had been a ghost—looked at me with the eyes with which I should fancy people watch a bull-fight. I smiled across at him, but he looked away, pretending not to see. He, too, looked old and haggard, I thought.

The guests chattered away gaily, but over the house-party there seemed to hang a settled gloom. Even Father Terence, the irrepressible, looked anxious and uneasy; I saw him watching the door as each fresh per-

son came into the room, as though expecting some one.
I never was more glad when a meal was over.

Sydney's dog-cart came to the door about ten, and I
stood about outside under the portico, patting the horse,
and waiting to say good-bye. It was a dull, grey morning, and there was a slight drizzle falling. The deer,
browsing on the Plain, looked blurred and misty. He
came out at last, very quickly, in a long overcoat, and
began climbing in, without looking to the right or left.
Frenetzi followed close at his heels, carrying a dressing-
bag, which he handed in after him. I ran forward, and
with my hand on the horse's quarters, looked up at him
and smiled. I wished Frenetzi was not there; the groom
on the back seat didn't matter—he was looking the
other way. But as it turned out, neither the groom nor
Frenetzi, nor any one else, would have been the least
in the way. Sydney just stared down at me with a hard
glassy stare, and raised his hat.

"I think we are going to have rain," he remarked.

"Oh, I hope not," I said, "at least not before you
get home. But, anyhow, you have not far to go."

"No, only four miles or so. Good-morning!"

He tightened the reins, and drove off. I jumped back
quickly to avoid the wheel, and stood watching him till
he swept out of sight round the corner. He never once
looked back. A load like lead settled round my heart,
and I felt that the end of life had come to me. It was
not so much what he had said—or rather left unsaid—it
was his manner, and the look in his eyes. Slowly and
miserably I turned to go into the house. Frenetzi still
stood at the door, and, as I passed, he bowed low, with
hands outspread, and smiled at me sardonically—at least
so it seemed to me.

I passed down the little passage that runs by the side
of the great hall, and gaining the long corridor, made
my way by unfrequented routes to the schoolroom. I
heard them all gabbling like geese as I passed the morning-room, and I felt I hated the whole pack of them.
What right had they to froth and bubble when I was so
abjectly miserable?

There was a big fire blazing in the schoolroom, and
I felt glad of it, for misery is the chilliest thing on earth.
I threw myself into a big chair and sobbed unrestrainedly
for ten minutes. No one has ever felt quite so utterly
wretched as I did then. I felt that every soul at Selworth was my enemy—excepting, of course, Sophie; not
dear, gentle Sophie—but every one else—even the servants.

There was a conspiracy against me, I felt—a vile,
mean, cowardly conspiracy! It was a shame—a cruel
shame!

What had I done to deserve it? Why should they all
set on a miserable, defenceless girl! I could have borne
it all except for Sydney. If he had remained friendly
and loving and loyal, I would cheerfully have snapped
my fingers at the rest; but there it was—some *brutes* had
been poisoning his mind with villainous lies, and he
wouldn't look at me—never would look at me again,
never, never, never!

I buried my face in the back of the chair, and shook
the room with my sobs. I was not by any means a
"crying girl," but all my nerves were unstrung, and it
did me good.

Sophie came in after a little, and kissed me, and
stroked my hair, and asked me what it was all about,
and was altogether very nice and sweet and kind. But,

of course, I couldn't tell her—how could I? I said
Sydney and I had had a quarrel, and she was very sym-
pathetic, and said it would come all right in the end, and
I must not fret, and that Sydney had told her in confidence one night at dinner that he was so madly in love
with me he could hardly sleep at night. I laughed hys-
terically at this, and said he would sleep soundly enough
now.

Poor Sophie! I am afraid I was cross to her. I
always was cross when things upset me. But she didn't
mind; she had an angelic temper—not the least like
mine—and the crosser I was, the more she tried to comfort me.

Then, about twelve, there came a knock at the door,
and Mercer, the groom of the chambers, came in.

"Her ladyship," he said, "would like to see Miss
Josephine in her sitting-room."

"That's Griffiths," I thought; "the old cat! I should
like to shake her."

I ran to my room, and with the help of a sponge and
brush, made myself look as respectable as I could, and
then marched defiantly downstairs, past the long gallery,
to Aunt Harriet's sitting-room. After all, what had I
got to be ashamed of?

I knocked boldly.

"Come in," said the stiff, prim voice I knew so well.

Aunt Harriet was sitting at her writing-table, facing
the window. Why do people always sit at a writing-table
when they mean to lecture one?

"Oh, it's you, Josephine, is it?" she said, looking up.
"Sit down for a minute; I want to speak to you."

She went on writing for some time, while I drummed
with my fingers on the arm of the chair, and stared dis-

mally into the fire. Then, very deliberately, she half turned her chair round and faced me.

"Josephine, this is a very extraordinary story I hear from Griffiths."

I found no need to make any comment.

"She assures me that Norman was in your room, with the door locked, between three and four in the morning."

"Yes," I said, calmly; "it's perfectly true."

She looked at me hard over her spectacles, and coughed nervously.

"You take it very quietly," she said; "but do you realise what it means?"

"I realise nothing," I answered, sullenly. "It was not my fault. I couldn't help it."

"Hush, Josephine; no one has yet said it was; *qui s'excuse s'accuse*, remember; but this is not exactly the point. The point is—What are you going to do?"

"What am I going to do?" I cried. "What is there to be done?"

She coughed again. She seemed far more nervous than I was, I thought.

"My dear child, there is no need to take up that defiant tone. I am not blaming you, understand; I merely desire to discuss with you what had best be done in your own interest, having due regard to *les convenances*."

"Nothing can undo it," I said.

"No, nothing can undo it—true; but the sting may be taken out of the *esclandre*. I am afraid the story is not only all over the house by now, but has been carried away by the majority of the visitors."

"That's dear old Griffiths!" I said.

"Griffiths is an excellent woman, and a first-rate maid, but her tongue unfortunately is apt to run away with her.   It is her only fault; she is a little inclined to be *babillarde*."

"Which means, I suppose, that she has told every one in the house?"

"Well, in this case it's possible she *may* have been a little indiscreet; but I imagine the person that really did the mischief was not Griffiths, but that dreadful servant of Norman's."

"Frenetzi?"

"Yes, Frenetzi. I understand he is a confirmed *mauvaise langue*, and makes a practice of retailing all the scandal and gossip he can pick up downstairs to Norman, and—*any one else he happens to be waiting on.*"

There was a silence; both of us stared hard into the fire. I could see Aunt Harriet's fingers twitching as though she had an ague.

"Well," I said, desperately, "I think the best thing I can do is to go away—back to Chelmsford; nobody wants me here. I am only in the way, and now I have become a disgrace and a scandal to everybody as well."

"My dear child, you *can't* go back; have you not heard? Your Aunts Fielding have gone to Cannes. Maria Fielding's cough was worse, and your uncle sent them a cheque for £100 to help expenses, if they cared to go abroad while you were here. They started last week."

A few days earlier I should have received this news with the greatest joy—glad that my dear old aunts had at last fulfilled the dream of their lives; but now it filled me with nothing but dread and foreboding.

Why should Uncle Guy have sent them £100? He was not particularly fond of them, and to my certain knowledge had never sent them a penny before. Why now, of all times? The surface reason was, of course, that they could move more easily and cheaply, now that they were relieved of my burden, but somehow this failed to satisfy me. It was so unlike Uncle Guy to send them that £100. It was so unlike him to bother himself at all about the welfare of two poor threadbare old maids vegetating at Chelmsford.

The effect of Aunt Harriet's announcement on me was indescribable. I felt that the only two people in the world who loved me, and whom I could really trust, were a thousand miles away, with a cruel stretch of sea between.

"In that case," I said, "I think I shall drown myself. I am only a nuisance and a trouble to every one."

"My dear Josephine," said my aunt, "you must not allow yourself to be so easily depressed and dispirited. You must understand that none of us attach the slightest blame to you for last night's—ahem!—*contretemps*. I have seen Norman, and he takes the whole blame upon himself."

"Does he?" I said, laughing miserably; "that *is* generous of him."

"Hush, my dear; pray control yourself. No, we are not blaming you, but we are very much concerned about your future. You see, unhappily, a story like this sticks to a girl for life. However much a man may be attracted to a girl, he naturally fights shy of her when she has once *tombée en discredit*. Of course, Norman is very greatly to blame—inexcusably, in fact—but he is a gentleman at heart, and he is prepared to make the only reparation in his power."

"Yes?" I said, dully. "What reparation?"

"Norman is prepared, and indeed even anxious, to

marry you as soon as possible. He is, as you perhaps know, extremely attached to you, and though I had other hopes for him, and though I cannot say I personally approve of first cousins marrying, still, on the whole, I think it is the only thing possible for either of you—certainly the only thing for you."

"Why the only thing for me?"

"My dear child, you must surely see that you are to a certain extent *souillée* by what has happened. These things are not easily forgotten, and they make it very difficult sometimes for a girl to marry."

"Why should I want to marry?" I cried. "I should make a splendid old maid; I'm so methodical."

"Hush, Josephine; you are excited and overwrought, and I hardly wonder at it; but try and look at things sensibly. For a girl like you, penniless, and practically homeless, it is of paramount importance that you should marry. If anything were to happen to your aunts, you would be thrown on the world."

"Oh, I suppose I could go out as a governess or something," I said.

"No, my dear, indeed you could not! You are so lamentably ignorant! You cannot even play the piano decently."

"Well, then, I *will* drown myself!" I said; "nobody would care."

"But there is not the slightest need for anything so tragic and senseless. You can marry Norman, and have everything in the world that a girl can want."

"I can't marry Norman, Aunt Harriet!"

"But why not?"

"Oh, a hundred reasons!"

"I suppose it's that Mr. Grayle, is it?"

"Mr. Grayle doesn't care about me, Aunt Harriet; so he can make no possible difference."

"Mr. Grayle undoubtedly heard the whole story from Frenetzi. There can be no possible question about that; and having heard it, it is extremely improbable that he would care to marry you. What can you expect?"

"Oh, I expect nothing," I said, "and I wish I was dead!"

For the second time that morning I burst into tears, and sobbed madly, with my face buried in the silk cushions. Aunt Harriet knelt by me and kissed me gently.

"Poor child!" she said, "you must not take this so much to heart. It will all come right in the end, I hope."

I looked up in amazement, tear-stained eyes and all. Aunt Harriet, the austere and unapproachable, was actually crying, too!

"Could you never care for Norman?" she asked, plaintively. "He is *so* handsome, and so attractive, and—and the advantages to you would be so great."

I rose, and flung my arms round her neck, kissing her passionately, and blubbering freely on her grey silk dress.

"Dear, dear Aunt Harriet," I sobbed, "I love you very much, and Uncle Guy, too—and you have all been so kind to me—so kind and good—but I *can't* marry Norman—I really can't!"

"There, there, my dear," she said; "don't fret—don't fret. If you can't, you can't, and there's an end of it; but it was for your own sake. Norman, of course, can marry any one he likes; he has only to pick and choose."

She drew herself up, as though ashamed of the glimpse of human kindness she had shown; I suppose, too, she was offended at my not jumping at Norman—naturally she would be.

"I know it's all for my sake, Aunt Harriet," I said, "and I know that I'm not worth it, but the truth is, I don't want to marry any one—I only want to be left in peace."

"Very well, then, my dear, you *shall* be left in peace; but if you think that Mr. Grayle will marry you, you are making a very serious mistake. He knows the whole story, and he will never look at you again, you may be sure of that—no man would. And now I think you had better go and get ready for luncheon; the gong will ring in a minute."

I went off with the uncomfortable feeling that I had added Aunt Harriet to the list of those who were against me. I felt, too, that there had been one moment when I might easily have turned the scale the other way; but my presumption in not jumping at Norman was a thing she clearly could not forgive.

Outside the library door I came suddenly upon Uncle Guy, Norman, and Father Terence. They were standing in a cluster, and talking earnestly—pitching into poor Norman, it seemed to me.

"You fool!" I heard Father Terence say, in a hissing kind of voice between his teeth. "You poor, faint-hearted fool!"

His back was to me, but Uncle Guy saw me coming along the passage, and called out, hurriedly: "Hullo! little Joe, where do you spring from? Been exploring the old gallery, eh? Come along to luncheon."

He passed his arm into mine, and led me along, speaking volubly. Norman slipped sheepishly into the library, and the priest bustled off in the direction of the chapel. I caught a glimpse of his face as he brushed past me; it was black with fury.

Luncheon that day was a miserable meal. I sat between Aunt Harriet and Sophie, and tried to talk about the people who had left that morning. I was *afraid* of the men—afraid of them all, even Uncle Guy. He talked as cheerily as ever, but his face looked pale and drawn, and his eye was shifty. Norman never spoke at all, nor did the priest. I had never seen Father Terence look as he did that day. His face was black as thunder, and by no means pleasant to look upon. His eyes never left his plate or his glass, which latter he filled repeatedly from the port decanter.

"Coming for a ride, Joe?" my uncle asked. "No? Well, one can hardly blame you—damme, no—old Pasha is a bit of a bone-shaker, there's no doubt about it—not a lady's hack—not a lady's hack! We must try and find you something better now—something with a little more quality, eh? You'll come, Norman?" he went on; "I want to ride over and see old Fothergill about those dogs."

· "All right," Norman said, shortly.

"Shall I come, too, papa?" Sophie asked.

"No, no, my dear, best not—bore you to death— what does a girl know about dogs?—sporting dogs, that is. No, no, you stay at home."

"All right, Joe," she said, laughing; "you and I will go for a walk."

I saw them start off about three, and then I did something that I had been longing to do all day. I ran up to my room, and carefully wrapped up Norman's bracelet in paper, sealing both ends, and addressed it to him in my big, sprawling hand. Then I locked the door, and getting a chair, scrambled on to the broad marble mantelpiece. The inside of Maurice's frame was elab-

orately carved, and I struck a match, and ran it up and
down the left side of the frame, where I had seen Norman press.

There was nothing much to be seen except a succession of little circular festoons. I remembered distinctly
whereabouts it was that Norman's hand had rested when
he pressed the spring; so I lighted a candle and poked
about with my fingers till I felt something give. I
pressed harder, and the frame swung slowly and noiselessly outwards. It struck me as an extraordinary thing
that a secret entrance of this kind should open so
smoothly after all these years of disuse. As a matter of
curiosity, I held the candle to the hinges, and saw that
they had been freshly oiled. No words can describe the
horror with which this discovery filled me. I think it
appalled me more than anything that had gone before.
I felt suddenly faint and dizzy, and almost fell upon the
narrow stone steps within. So there *was* a deliberate
conspiracy!

The horrible business of the night before had been
coolly and calmly planned. Who could tell what hideous schemes might not be brewing for the future? I
shuddered and shook, and for some minutes closed my
eyes, and leant limply against the cold, dust-shrouded
stone.

Then, remembering Sophie, I pulled myself together,
and took up my candle. The place where I was was
extraordinarily narrow. It was simply a miniature stone
spiral staircase, with very steep steps, not more than
eighteen inches long. I am certain no fat person could
possibly have got up or down. It was inches deep in
dust.

I picked up my skirts as high as I could, and began

climbing.   Every now and then there were irregular sort
of openings to the left of me—that is, to the outside of
the stairs.   They appeared to have no particular object,
but to be just blank spaces in the thickness of the wall.
Some of them were as much as six or eight feet deep.
After mounting about twenty steps, I came to a door. It
was a very palpable door, with no attempt at disguise,
and with an ordinary handle.   I turned the handle and
pushed, and the door opened slowly and heavily, as
though there was a weight against it.   I found I was
pushing a bookcase into the room—a regular tall bookcase filled with books.   The room was empty, and I
slipped in through the narrow opening, and laid my
packet on the table.   It was a big room—as big as mine,
only not nearly so high, and not directly above mine, as
I had imagined—for my room looked over the east garden—but the windows of this gave one a splendid view
across the Plain.   For the rest, it was bare and old-fash-
ioned-looking, with no attempt at smartness; there were
two oak bookcases reaching nearly to the ceiling, one of
which I had pushed into the room, a worn, faded carpet,
white dimity curtains, fringed with pink, and a white
wall-paper with a skeleton diamond pattern in pale green.
However, for all this, it was a cheerful, comfortable-
looking room, fresh and airy, and as I have said, with
a splendid view.

Sophie, I knew, would be waiting for me to go out,
so, without stopping to make further observations, I
crept down my little stairs and through the open frame
of wicked, supercilious Maurice.   I was beginning to
believe in his wickedness now.

For all my care I was one mass of dust, so I changed

my skirt, and took the old one out on to the stairs to brush it (this for fear of Griffiths).

Then I called for Sophie, and we went out.

That evening I borrowed a screw-driver from Mercer, and took off the handle that opened Maurice's frame from the staircase.

CHAPTER XVI

A CHRISTMAS PRESENT

WHAT a Christmas! We all gave and took our little presents, and kissed one another, and said, "How pretty!" but there was no life in it at all. I honestly tried to enjoy myself, and forget all about everything, but it was more than I could manage; gloom was in the atmosphere. It was a mild Christmas—no snow, or anything of that sort—but for all that, huge fires blazed in every room, and mistletoe hung from the ceilings and banisters, and forests of holly were stuck about the place, trying to cheer us up.

We ate mince-pies and plum-pudding, and we went and stared at the sideboard, on which every conceivable form of cold meat that a cook's mind could devise was marshalled in long rows, and we drank the loving-cup, though that was not till dinner, and in fact, did everything that people ought to do on Christmas Day, except being merry, and that we could not manage. Father Terence tried hard, with the help of port and champagne, but his merriness was not amusing, and fell flat.

Two things happened that day—two noteworthy things, I mean.

After breakfast Uncle Guy called me up.

"Joe, little lady," he said, "I've got a present for you—a Christmas present, in return for that delightful paper-weight you gave me. Will you come and see it? It's outside."

"Outside!" I said. "Why, what is it?"

"Come and see, come and see, and don't ask so many questions."

We passed through the great hall to the entrance door, and out under the portico. Away to the left, along the broad, straight, gravel drive, a stable-boy was leading a chestnut horse—such a beauty!

"Hi!" shouted uncle. "Bring her here! Come along, boy; run her up smartly!"

The boy ran as fast as his tight breeches and gaiters would let him, round the broad sweep of gravel before the door; and the horse trotted behind, snorting, with ears flicking backwards and forwards, and head raised and staring from side to side. It was a lovely creature, bright chestnut, and with the most perfect little head and neck ever seen. It could hardly be said to step high when it trotted, but shot its legs out straight to the front, and hardly seemed to touch the ground with its feet. I couldn't believe my senses; was this glorious beast really for *me?* For my very own? I looked up doubtfully at my uncle's face; he couldn't mean it—it was a joke!

Uncle Guy was smiling at me sideways, as though to see how I took it.

"Well," he said, "do you think she'll do?"

"What is it?" I said; "I don't remember seeing it in the stables."

"No, I daresay not, I daresay not," he said, with a chuckle; "odd if you had, considering she only arrived from Newmarket last night. What is she, do you say? Well, we call her Maid Marion, and she is the present property of Miss Josephine de Metrier."

I laughed loudly, as if he had made an excellent joke; I thought it the best thing to do.

"Gad!" he said, "I mean it. She's yours to do as you like with."

"Do you mean to say that I can ride her as often as I like, as long as I am here?"

"No, Miss Joe," he said, "I do not; never do things by halves, you know—never do things by halves. What I mean is, that she's yours—neck, body, and heels—now and for ever."

"Do you mean to say that you give her to me—absolutely?"

"I mean to say that I give her to you absolutely—and unconditionally."

"Oh!" I said, "it *is* good of you! I really don't know how to thank you!"

"No thanks, little girl, no thanks. Thanks enough for me if you like her."

"Like her!" I said; "I shall *love* her. Is she a racer?"

"Well, she was a racer, but she is not quite fast enough; and she's such a splendid hack that I thought I'd have her here."

"But all racers pull so dreadfully, don't they?"

"Pull! not a bit—mouth like velvet. Here, Bob, jump on her back, and give her a spin down the approach. Never mind the grass. Come here, and I'll put you up."

The boy had been leading her by a snaffle, but now he threw the reins over her neck, and led her up, snorting and sidling, to where we stood. She had no saddle on.

"Now, up with you!" said my uncle, hoisting him on to her back by the leg, "and let's see what sort of hands you've got. Canter her up to the iron gate, and then let her extend herself coming back, d'you understand? Off you go now!"

Bob grinned from ear to ear, and kicking his heels

most irreverently into the mare's satin sides, went lollop-
ping away up the gravel. As he neared the iron gate he
swung round on to the grass, and shaking her up a bit,
came back at a good smart gallop. The mare went like
an angel. She arched her neck and played with the bit
like a kitten, swinging along so smoothly that the boy
never moved on her shiny bare back.

"You *darling!*" I said, trying to kiss her soft muzzle,
and getting a bump on the nose, and a shower of foam
on my dress in return. "Can I ride her to-day, Uncle
Guy?"

"Better not to-day, little Joe, better not to-day;
she's only just come, you see, and wants to settle down
a bit. Better wait till Monday."

This was Saturday, and Monday seemed a long way
off, but there was no help for it. When Uncle Guy said
a thing, he meant it, as all of us had learnt by this
time.

"I think I shall go and sleep in the stable with her,"
I said.

"Yes, and get that pretty little head of yours kicked
open. No, no, Joe, even the panelled room's better
than that, I think—even the panelled room's better than
that."

I stared at him, wondering what he meant, but I
found nothing in his face; it was the picture of good-
nature and kindliness.

This was the first event of the day; the second was
not so cheerful.

We were sitting at luncheon, eating mince-pies, covered with blazing brandy, and trying to be merry, when
we saw a groom riding at full gallop across the Plain.

"Looks like some one from Ashby," said Uncle Guy.

The man galloped straight up to the road, and then slanted off in the direction of the stables.

"H'm! don't mean to honour *us*, anyway."

We thought no more about the matter till Mercer presently entered the room with an air of more than usual pomp and melancholy, and whispered in my uncle's ear.

"Good God!" he exclaimed, pushing back his chair; "Good God! you don't say so! The Duke is dead!"

We all stared at Mercer rather than at Uncle Guy, and he, responding readily to the appeal, said:

"Yes, a groom has just left word that His Grace died this morning at eleven o'clock. *Hangela pectoris*, they think it was."

"How truly shocking!" moaned Aunt Harriet, with uplifted hands. "Poor dear man! And on such a day, too! It's too dreadful!"

"I thought him a bit shaky the other day when he was here," Uncle Guy said. "Shot badly, too—devilish bad!"

The rest of us stared at one another helplessly; it was not easy to volunteer appropriate remarks.

"Well, this will be a finisher for young Grayle," Father Terence remarked. "Lord Barham can't stand him—always away hunting, he says, or shooting, or something."

"Yes," agreed my uncle; "he'll bundle him out pretty quick now—hates a gentleman agent—always did—always did!"

I had little doubt that this was all for my benefit—all this about Sydney, I mean—but I finished my mince-pie with an unmoved face—at least I think so.

This bit of news gave an immense stimulus to the

conversation. Every one cheered up at once—every one, that is, except poor me—for Father Terence's shot had told heavily. Not that I saw with any great clearness all that this possible dismissal of Sydney's might mean for me; I don't think I troubled myself to look close into the details of the thing at all; I was too dazed, what with one thing and another, and too callous perhaps. Everything was combining so against me that there seemed no use in worrying over anything, or in fighting any more against fate. All I knew was that it was another blow, and I bent my head to it meekly and sullenly.

That evening Norman tried to make it up with me. I was sitting at the far end of the library, reading, when he came in. He walked straight up to the fire, and stood with his back to it.

"Joe," he said, "will you forgive me, and make friends?"

"Why, of course I will, Norman—only too thankfully; I'm sure I don't want to play cat and dog."

"It was only a joke, you know—a practical joke."

"A poor sort of joke for me," I said. "Jokes that ruin girls' lives are not very gentlemanly, are they?"

"Joe," he said, dropping on his knees by the side of my chair, "it was a brutal, caddish thing to do, I know; but, on my honour, it was only done for love of you."

"Well, Heaven save me from such love as that!" I said, earnestly.

"No, no, you don't understand. I thought it might force you to marry me, that's the real truth; and to get you to marry me I think I'd do anything in the world."

"However low and base?"

"Yes, I think so."

I looked at him with a kind of wonder. There was no doubt about his earnestness; his face was all drawn and pale, and I think he was trembling. He held my hand, and nubbled it between his own two.

"O Joe, you can't understand such love as mine—how could one expect you to? I would walk barefoot to London to win you, and will, too, for a word from you."

"And yet, with all this great love, you could do what you did the other night!"

"Yes. I thought, you see, you would *have* to marry me after that. And, then, Joe, there are other things behind that you know nothing about. I am not my own master. I am being driven and bullied and sworn at. Oh, you don't know—you don't know all that's going on."

"What is it, Norman?" I whispered, bending forward; "I have felt all along that there *is* something."

"Oh, I can't tell you, Joe; it's an old, old story—fifty years old and more—a sort of family ghost, you know," he said with a laugh.

"And you won't tell me what it is?"

"No, I can't. I'm sworn to secrecy. You wouldn't have me break my word?"

"Oh, no," I said, shrugging my shoulders; "no one wants you to do that. After all, it doesn't matter to me."

"Then you'll make friends, Joe?"

"Yes."

"And you'll forget all about the other night?"

"Yes."

"But you won't marry me? O Joe, don't say you won't, for God's sake, don't say you won't!"

He clutched my hand, and covered it with kisses.

"Don't!" I cried, angrily; "what's the use of that? How can we possibly be friends if you do that sort of thing? It's stupid."

"All right," he said, jumping to his feet; "I won't bother you any more, if that's the way of it. Let's be friends, and friends only. But whatever we are, Sydney Grayle's no go now, I can tell you that much."

"Thanks to you."

"Yes, thanks to me. Why should I help another fellow to get you?"

"I like that," I said, scornfully. "Much help he wanted from you, indeed! He has got me, thank you, and always will have, what's more."

"Joe," he said, seriously, "if you only knew what a lot of trouble it would save if you would only marry me."

"Now, look here, Norman," I said, jumping up, "if we're going to be friends, there must be an end to this sort of thing. You may just as well understand, once and for all, that I shall never marry you—never, *never*, NEVER—not if Mr. Grayle were to marry half a dozen other people."

"Thank you," said Norman. "I quite understand. It is by no means necessary to emphasise it so; besides, from what I know of him, Grayle is the very last person to put himself within reach of the law by marrying six people at once."

"Oh, well, if he married only one it would be just the same," I said, idiotically.

"Yes," said Norman, and stared up at the fire-flecked ceiling. After a minute or so he came up to me, and held out his hand.

"Well, little Joe," he said, smiling, "we're to be friends, then, in spite of everything that's gone."

"Yes," I said with emphasis, "*friends*."

"Oh, I quite understand," he said. "Well, being friends, I shall now perform my first act of friendship."

"What's that?" I asked, staring up at him.

He walked to the far end of the room, and tried the door. Then, coming back, he leant over me and whispered, "Don't you ride that chestnut mare, Joe."

"What do you mean?" I cried. "Not ride it!"

"No, don't ride it. Take my advice."

"But why not?"

"Oh, I don't know; but these thoroughbred mares are shifty, unreliable brutes, especially when they are chestnuts; and you have not had very much practice in riding, you know."

"But she's as quiet as a lamb, Norman," I said. "I saw Bob cantering her about, bare-backed, in front of the house; a child could ride her."

"Don't you get on her," said Norman, doggedly.

"Why? Is she vicious? Do you *know* anything about her?" I asked.

"No, I know absolutely nothing about her; but I am afraid—horribly afraid."

He looked straight before him, and avoided meeting my eye.

"You are very mysterious," I said.

"Yes, possibly I am. But I know what I am talking about. Don't you get on her, at any price."

"It seems to me you have either said too much or too little."

"Perhaps I have; but that's all I'm going to say. It's quite enough for your purpose."

"Do you mean to say that Uncle Guy would let me ride a horse that was dangerous?"

"I mean nothing," he said, looking dreadfully frightened; "you have had my advice, take it or leave it."

"In that case," I said, "I am very much obliged to you, but I shall certainly leave it. I never heard such a preposterous idea."

"All right," he said, shrugging his shoulders; "please yourself, only don't say I didn't warn you. Well, good-bye, Joe, I must be off now; I'm glad we're friends, anyhow."

He strolled slowly away, and I sat alone and brooded.

CHAPTER XVII

AN AFTERNOON RIDE

O N Monday morning I got a letter.

I found Father Terence examining the envelope as it lay on the marble table outside the breakfast room.

"Ah! Miss Joe," he exclaimed, cheerily, "how are you this morning? But, indeed, I needn't ask; you're looking grand—fresh as a summer rose, be Gad!"

"Thank you," I said; "I'm very well."

"I think I saw a letter for you somehere here. Ah, yes, here it is."

He handed it me, with a smirk and a bow, and I rammed it hastily into my pocket, to be read, at leisure, after breakfast. I had recognised the writing.

The moment breakfast was over, I rushed off to the schoolroom, and tore my letter open. How much depended on the contents none but myself could ever dream. The first line was enough for me. I sank back limply in my chair, and closed my eyes. So it was all over; all over for ever and ever and ever!

"DEAR MISS DE METRIER," I read, "owing to the Duke's death, I have lost my position here as agent, and am now, to all intents and purposes, a beggar. Under these circumstances, I hasten to set you free from an engagement which I have every reason to believe was not a necessary condition of your happiness. As soon as I can get things in order, I shall first visit my mother in Scotland, and then sail for America, where I hope to succeed in making a living for myself. Thanking you for the share of your favour with which you have honoured me in the past.—I am, yours very truly, SYDNEY GRAYLE."

I wasted no time in thought when I had once read this. I dashed at the writing-table, and seized the nearest pen.

"DEAR MR. GRAYLE," I wrote, "I am truly sorry to hear that you have lost the agency at Ashby, and that it will be necessary for you to go to America. However, it will be a great blessing for you having no one to look after except yourself. Perhaps you will marry some one out there—a negress, perhaps, or a millionairess; a penniless wife is a terrible drag around anybody's neck; remember, please, that they are always things to be avoided, and shunted, and thrown over. Wishing you all prosperity and good luck with the negress.—I am, yours very truly,

"JOSEPHINE DE METRIER."

I sealed and posted it then and there, dropping it into the letter-box outside the dining-room. How any self-respecting girl out of Hanwell could have written such a letter, I don't know; it was neither logical, witty, nor grammatical. But I never stopped to think; I just dashed at it, and dropped it into the box, and half an hour later the box was cleared, and repentance was useless.

So I whistled loudly down the passage, and ran up to the stable to see Maid Marion and give her a carrot; and I gave one, too, to old Pasha, and told him I was sorry not to ride him any more (which was not strictly true), and that he was an old dear, and I loved him (which was quite true), and that I was not going to ride Maid Marion because she was younger and faster, but because I was afraid Uncle Guy would be offended if I didn't. To all of which the Pasha listened sedately, with pricked ears and open nostril. Then I ran down to the house again, whistling and singing, and feeling quite sure I didn't care tuppence if Sydney Grayle went to the North Pole or to Timbuctoo.

Every one remarked what good spirits I was in that day at luncheon.   I said it was because I was going to ride the mare.   I came down in my habit, and we were to start directly after luncheon, so as to get a good long ride before dark.   Sophie was coming, and Uncle Guy, too; he was anxious to see how the mare went the first day.

"I do hope," said Aunt Harriet, "she won't kick or pull or run away, or anything.   I can't bear new horses myself, they are so horribly uncertain."

"Oh, nonsense, nonsense!" said my uncle, gruffly. "Don't get frightening the child with your silly notions. Nothing makes any horse run away except the rider himself."

Aunt Harriet shook her head doubtfully.   She was always nervous, and saw foolhardiness in any venture outside the glass case that surrounded her own life.

Uncle Guy talked incessantly during luncheon, but I thought he looked pale and worried.   I had an idea money matters had been bothering him lately.   Father Terence, on the other hand was, for him, extraordinarily silent.

They all came out to see us start.   Maid Marion looked lovely as the groom led her up and down the gravel sweep.   I gave her a piece of sugar, and then Uncle Guy put me up, and as Sophie was not down yet, I trotted her to the iron gate, and then cantered her back along the grass.   She went like an angel!   I had never been on a thoroughbred before, and the difference from dear old Pasha was something perfectly astonishing. She arched her neck, and swept over the ground like oil, without pulling or fussing or jolting one about in the way Pasha used to do if one ever took him out of a slow canter. They all praised her, and patted her, and even Aunt Harriet allowed that she seemed "a nice, gentle creature."

"Indeed, you just seem made for one another," Father Terence said.

Sophie came running down, full of apologies, and we started.

Uncle Guy proposed riding out at the Slade Lodge, and on to Ashby Park. This, of course, took us across the Plain, and when one went across the Plain the obvious thing to do was to gallop. However, uncle wouldn't have this.

"No, no," he said. "Too soon after luncheon—play the deuce with me if I were to start galloping for another ten minutes yet. Must take your pace from the old 'un, you know."

So we walked across the Plain, Maid Marion dancing a little, and flicking her ears backwards and forwards as though she saw as well as we did that the place was literally made for a gallop.

When we were about half-way across I turned to Uncle Guy.

"Now," I said, "surely we can go now? We shall be at the other side before we start if we don't take care."

Uncle Guy was a little behind, and I had to turn half round to see him. When I caught sight of his face I was perfectly horrified. He was as white as death, and had the look on his face of a man in terrible pain.

"Good gracious!" I cried, "are you ill?"

"No, no," he said; "nothing at all, nothing at all that's to say; slight pain in the side; be all right directly. Yes, may as well have a gallop now; do me good, do me good."

So we started off, Sophie and I side by side, and my uncle just behind, pounding along on his big brown horse. The mare pulled more than I liked, but not more than I could manage with a little attention. I was an inexperienced rider, and I have little doubt a bad one, but I was not nervous. In fact, I preferred an animal that occupied one's attention to one that moved along like a cow. It was so much more interesting. So at first I exulted wildly in the tosses of Maid Marion's head, and her wild snatches at the bridle, but not for long. For suddenly, when we had gone a couple of hundred yards or so, without the slightest vestige of warning, she bolted. There was no intermediate stage; the whole thing was done in a second. One moment she was cantering along contentedly and sanely, the next she was dashing wildly through the air with all the mad clatter of a runaway.

No one who has never been run away with can have an idea of the utter misery of the feeling. You are at the absolute mercy of a mad, irresponsible beast of twenty times your own strength. It is horrible! The part of the Plain where we first started galloping was slightly up hill, and remained so for nearly half a mile. Here, if ever, was my only chance of stopping the mare, and I tugged and hauled till my arms were numb, but I might as well have hauled at a steam engine. Like a whirlwind we raced up the incline, with the wind blinding my eyes and whistling madly past my ears. It was all plain sailing, and there was nothing to fear as far as the crest. But afterwards! The very thought of afterwards turned me sick. I knew the ground so well—the slope downwards, covered with dead bracken, and simply riddled with rabbit holes, and beyond again a stretch of park forest still sloping downwards for a quarter of a mile, till it reached the glen running up to the Slade Lodge. Quicker than it takes to tell, we were over the crest, and plunging headlong down the slope beyond. I had no idea a horse *could* go so fast. I gave up trying to stop her now; I should have been pulled over her head if I had tried; I just sat still and tried to steer.

Straight ahead of us lay a huge rabbit burrow—a perfect honeycomb in sand. There was no thought of steering here. I leant back and waited numbly for the crash. But there was no crash then—nothing but a frightful stumble that shot me with a crash right on to the mare's neck, and a lightning recovery that shot me back again with a big bump over my left eye, and we were racing down the hill again as madly as ever. Through the long, dead bracken we crashed, tearing it out by the roots in bushels as though it had been groundsel; the stuff clung round the mare's legs like long stockings, but she kept her feet. Beyond I could see another burrow, and beyond that again the trees! I remember craning forward and wondering vaguely which of them would be the one to dash my brains out. But I was not frightened, not even excited, though I hadn't the faintest hope in my own mind of ever coming through alive. The thing seemed a sheer impossibility, and I think, perhaps, it was this utter absence of hope that made me so callous and unmoved. My chief feeling, I remember, was one of dull curiosity as to what this sort of death would feel like; also, I wondered, like a flash, if Sydney would be a little sorry when he heard of it, and whether he would come to the funeral, and wear mourning afterwards.

I hoped rather he would.

Then we came to the second burrow. There was another appalling stumble—a stumble that would have sent old Pasha head over heels like a shot hare—and another amazing scramble and recovery, and we were among the trees—great antediluvian giants stretching out their long, twisted limbs to tear me from the saddle. I bent level with the mare's neck, and let her go her own way. Where she could go, I could go, I thought, but the question, of course, was, could she go? Was there room between or under the spread of those branches for any horse, tearing along at that breakneck pace, to pass? Thought is quick, but scarcely quicker than the beat of the mare's legs as she plunged into that wilderness of trees. The answer would soon come now. I shut my eyes, and clasped my arms round the mare's neck, pressing my head close down against her shoulder. A fearful blow across my legs made me think the end had come at the beginning; it sent the little mare reeling to the right, but our pace was not checked. Other blows followed, quick as a shower of hail. My hat was torn off, my hair dragged down and pulled out in handfuls. I was bruised, battered, and bleeding, faint and sick, but the blow that was to dash me broken-backed and senseless to the ground had not yet come. I wondered why not.

A long wooden arm clutched me round the waist, and with hard, spiky fingers tried to drag me from the saddle. I tightened my grip round the mare's neck till I thought I should be torn in two. I think I screamed out with the pain. And then there was a crack of splintering wood, the clutch of the wooden arm gave way, and we burst out into the open. Three hundred yards of bracken stretched before us, and beyond again trees— cruel, death-dealing trees!—but in the centre of the bracken lay the smooth green ride that led up to the Slade Lodge. If I could get into that I might be safe! I clenched my teeth, and leant back, and with both hands hauled with all my strength at the left rein. I knew the danger of it—the awful danger!—the all but certainty of a crushing, murderous fall. But then beyond were the trees, and my strength was nearly gone, and there was no other way.

The mare's head came round to my knees, but she still went boring on, crashing at the same breakneck pace through the long fern. I thought she *must* fall.

I still believe any horse in the world except Maid Marion must have fallen. But she—she just went on galloping like a crab, with her head round at my knees, and her legs the other way, pecking and stumbling fearfully, but never falling.

And all the while, slowly but surely, she was little by little edging to the left.

We were within five yards of the ride, and I threw back the whole of my weight, and gave one final desperate tug. There was no question about it now; she must either come round or go over like a rabbit. And she came round—only about a quarter of a point, but it was enough. We were in the ride, and I was practically safe.

And now that the great and glaring danger was past, there came upon me for the first time fear, real, genuine fear, and an overwhelming wish to live. It was still nearly a mile to the Slade Lodge, and the ride ran the whole way, and the whole way it was uphill. Surely, I thought, this should stop her! My own strength was gone—it had gone with a snap in that last desperate pull—and I was as weak as a child. But still, a mile uphill, after tearing through all that long, clinging bracken, surely that must be enough!

I knew nothing, you see, of the endurance of thoroughbreds, especially of thoroughbreds that had been in training. And so, when I found the mare galloping on, strong as ever, and breasting the hill without an effort, I thought I was on a steed possessed of the devil. Pasha would have been dead long ago if he had come the pace we had. And yet on we went, a little slower, perhaps, as the incline got steeper, but still full of go. I gathered myself together, and hauled upon the reins, and the mare slowed down a bit, there was no doubt of it, she did slow down, distinctly; but the moment I let go to take a fresh pull she bounded forward again as fast as ever.

And so we went on, I getting weaker and weaker, and the mare going on as if she meant to gallop for a week; and then we came to the final steep pitch that leads to the lodge. I looked ahead, and saw the great iron gates were shut. Of course they were—they always were kept shut. I wondered whether Maid Marion would charge them, or swerve to the left and fling me off against the wall. Any swerve would have shot me off now; I was regularly reeling in the saddle.

She was going ever so much slower up the pitch, and with my ordinary strength I think I could have stopped her, but not now. I was done.

I vaguely remember sending up a wild prayer for one second of the strength I had had five minutes before; I remember the quick, short breathing of the mare, and

my own feeling of utter, hopeless misery; I remember
the sudden apparition of Sydney's stalwart form standing in the ride, and waving his arms like a couple of
windmills; I remember, in a very feeble voice crying
out, "Stop her, Sydney, stop her!" I remember what
the old books call a "mortal sickness" coming over me,
and my falling in a limp, helpless mass, into something
that held me very tight, and then, for about a minute, I
remembered no more.

When at the end of it I recovered consciousness,
I found that Sydney was kissing me with immense
vigour.

"What do you mean by kissing me, Mr. Grayle?" I
exclaimed, faintly; "you have absolutely no right to,
and I call it mean and cowardly."

I tried hard to summon up a certain show of dignity,
but it is not easy when you are lying on your back on the
grass, panting like a dog.

"Quite true!" he said, "it is!" And did it again.
"Are you hurt, Joe?" he added.

I smiled inwardly at the name. He had picked that
up at Selworth.

"No," I said, "I think not—a bit bruised and battered. No, you really *must not* kiss me, Mr. Grayle!"

"Why not?"

"Because—you know perfectly well why not."

"No. Tell me."

"Well, for one thing, you believed horrid stories
about me."

In a moment his manner changed; the mocking mood
passed away like a flash.

"I did, God forgive me!" he said. "But not now,
Joe, not now."

"Why," I exclaimed, "has anything happened? Has any one told you?"

"Nothing has happened, and no one has told me any-thing; but it is impossible for any one to hold you in his arms, as I am doing, and look into your eyes, and not know that you are as true as gold."

"Thank you!" I said, with rather a derisive laugh.

"Joe," he said, very earnestly, "I see the others are coming up. Tell me before they come, for God's sake, that you are true, and that you still love me."

"Both!" I said, with a nod.

"Thank God!" he said. "And will you come with me to America?"

"I will go with you to the end of the world, and be-yond, if you like."

"Really and truly?"

"Yes, really and truly."

"I have no money, you know—not a penny."

"Oh, bother the money! We shall get along some-how. I will dig potatoes, or make shirts, or something. I am as strong as a horse."

"Come to the tree to-morrow," he whispered, "and we will talk it over."

I heard the close thud of hoofs on the grass ride, and the next moment my uncle's voice calling out wildly, "Is she hurt, Grayle, is she hurt?"

"No," Sydney answered, "I think not. Only shaken and rather exhausted."

"Thank God!" he cried; "thank God! thank God!"

He flung himself off his horse and came and knelt at my side. His face was white and drawn, and he seemed quite unnerved. He took up my hand, and began strok-ing it feverishly. "Thank God!" he kept saying over and over again. "Poor little girl! Poor little Joe! Quite sure you're not hurt?"

I had never seen him so moved; there were tears in his eyes, and he was trembling like a leaf—much more upset, in fact, than I was. Sophie stood on the other side, white and terrified, and Sydney held the two horses.

"I'll gallop back and send the carriage up for you," he said; "and the doctor, too—best have the doctor. O good Lord! good Lord! if you had been killed!"

"Oh, I'm all right," I said; "I can ride back perfectly well."

I rose to my feet rather shakily, and began looking about for Maid Marion. There she was, wicked thing! with the reins dangling about her feet, munching the coarse grass as peacefully as a Jersey calf.

"You are surely not going to ride that mare again?" Sydney said, starting forward.

"Yes; why not?"

"Mr. de Metrier," he said, turning to my uncle, "you positively cannot allow your niece to get on that dangerous brute again. She ought never to have ridden it in the first instance."

"You must allow me to be the best judge of that," said my uncle, getting rather red. "The mare is as quiet as a lamb."

"Mares that are as quiet as lambs are not in the habit of running away," Sydney answered, quietly. "She is evidently quite unsafe for any lady to ride."

"Damme, sir!" cried uncle, fuming and puffing a good deal, "will you have the goodness to mind your own business? What the devil has it got to do with you?"

"Nothing, I suppose," said Sydney; "but every, one has a right to express an opinion, and I say emphatically that that mare is not safe for a lady to ride."

"And I say she is, sir, as safe as any horse in my stables."

Sydney shrugged his shoulders.

"And you are actually going to make your niece ride her home?"

"My niece shall do exactly as she likes, Mr. Grayle; and that without consulting you in the matter."

"Oh, I'm quite ready to ride her, Uncle Guy," I said. "I am sure she wouldn't do it again."

"Don't you get on her, Joe," Sydney said, decisively; "she's a vicious brute!"

Whether it was the name, or whether it was the remark or what, I don't know, but Uncle Guy's face turned positively purple with rage, and I saw the same look come over it as on that terrible day when I had first told him of my visit to Mrs. Beddington. He seemed to find it hard to speak; his hands opened and shut, and his mouth worked like a man's in a fit.

"What the devil do you mean, sir? What are you insinuating?"

"I am insinuating nothing, Mr. de Metrier. Why should I? I simply state a fact, and that is, that the mare is vicious, and dangerous for a lady to ride."

I thought for a moment Uncle Guy would have hit him with his hunting-crop; there is not much doubt he would have liked to; his face was distorted with passion. Suddenly he spun round to where Sophie stood looking very scared.

"Sophie," he said, "get on the chestnut; Josephine shall ride Norah home."

Poor Sophie turned as white as a sheet, looking help-lessly from one to the other of us.

"Do you hear me, girl?" he shouted, stamping his foot; "don't stand there staring like an idiot."

She picked up the skirt of her habit; and in her long, polished boots began tramping through the dead bracken to where Maid Marion stood peacefully cropping the grass. She looked scared to death, poor Sophie! No wonder; courage was not her strong point.

"Do let me ride her, Uncle Guy," I pleaded; "I'm quite right again now."

"Nonsense!" he said; "you're shaken and tired. You get on Norah here; I will put you up if you are ready."

To tell the truth, I was pretty glad of a quiet mount home. When I got on my feet I found that I could hardly stand. My uncle put me up on Norah, and then strode away to where Sophie was fumbling with Maid Marion's reins.

"Up you get!" he said; "the sooner we're off the better."

"Mr. de Metrier," Sydney said, coming forward, "will you let me lead the mare home for you? I shall be delighted to do it."

"No, sir, I will not, and I shall be obliged if you will mind your own business. I tell you the mare is perfectly quiet; my daughter could ride her with a thread. The Lord only knows what it was made her bolt before."

So poor Sophie was put up, trembling, Uncle Guy climbed on to old Admiral, and we started slowly down the ride. Sydney stood watching us for a minute, and then turned away in the direction of the Lodge.

Never shall I forget that ride home. It was a grizzly

performance! None of us spoke—no one ever spoke to
Uncle Guy when he was in one of his rages—it was not
safe. We rode in dead silence, and at a foot's pace,
towards the Plain, through the dead bracken, and between the great spreading oaks that had clutched at me
as I raced through. I followed the track of my mad
career with interest; the ragged furrow torn through the
fern, the uprooted plants flung to right and left, and the
long slides ploughing up the sand of the rabbit-burrows.
I saw the broken end of that last wicked branch that
had gripped me so murderously round the waist, and
wondered how in the world my backbone had managed
to prove the stronger of the two.

Maid Marion apparently troubled herself with none
of these things. She stepped lightly and delicately over
the pits and trenches her hoofs had scored in the ground
twenty minutes before, with no signs about her of any
such breakneck madness beyond the dried lather on her
smooth arched neck. Sophie was still nervous, I could
see, but gaining a little confidence, I thought, from the
mare's quiet, unexcited behaviour. Poor Sophie! her
nerves were to be tried before we got home in a way that
neither of us expected.

What the idea was I don't know, but I think it was
simple obstinacy. Uncle Guy was still brooding, I
think, over Sydney and his remarks—I could tell that
from his silence; and I suppose he wanted to prove to
all of us, including himself, that the mare was perfectly
quiet to ride. However, whether that was so or not,
what happened was this. When we were down on the
level of the Plain he turned suddenly to my cousin and
said:

"Just canter home, Sophie, and tell your mother that

Josephine has been run away with. Tell her she is not hurt, you know, but a little bit shaken, and ask her to have a hot bath ready, and some brandy—nothing like brandy for shaken nerves.''

Sophie looked as though she had been ordered to sudden execution. Her jaw dropped an inch, and her poor eyes got at least twice their common size. I think at first she thought her father was joking.

"Now, off you go," he said, roughly. "What are you gaping at?''

I saw her look hopelessly to right and left, as though for some means of escape. All the colour slowly left her face, and I could see her hands shaking. She never said a word, but her face begged for mercy as plainly as though she were on her knees. It was pathetic.

"Now then, don't you hear?" Uncle Guy said once more.

"I really don't want any bath or brandy, either," I said; "I'm perfectly well, and brandy always makes me sick.''

"Nonsense, nonsense!" he said; "can't have you laid up, you know; little girls must do as they are told. Hurry up now, Sophie; we'll follow slowly.''

He lifted his crop and rode at the mare as though to hit her on the quarters.

"All right, papa; don't touch her!" Sophie cried, in a voice that was almost a shriek. She shook the reins and pressed the mare into a canter. I saw her lean forward, and I knew she was whispering soothing sounds in the mare's long, flicking ears—those soothing sounds that were in this case almost a prayer for mercy. As for me, I was simply boiling over with indignation. I thought what Uncle Guy had done was one of the most

brutal things I had ever seen. I was also in mortal terror
for my poor Sophie. If the mare had bolted going away
from home, what was she likely to do now?

I was so angry, and so frightened, that I think I was
on the point of saying something to Uncle Guy; anyhow,
I turned towards him with anger against him raging
within me. But when I saw his face I thought better of
it. He looked twice as frightened as I did! His eyes
were following Sophie's retreating form with such a look
of anxious agony in them as I have never seen before or
since. She—Sophie, that is—was lolloping away like
a hare—or rather the mare was—going as easily and
quietly as though running away was a thing that had
never entered her head since the day she was foaled.
To say that I was surprised is to put my feelings in very
mild terms; but, of course, my prevailing feeling at the
moment was one of immense relief—relief with a faint
background of humiliation. It was clearly a case of my
bad hands, and Uncle Guy was right after all; the mare
was quiet—quiet as a sheep, with proper riding.

Aunt Harriet met us at the front door with an anxious, scared face, and loud exclamations of thanksgiving
for my escape. She had sent off for the doctor, she
said, and in the mean while I must have a warm bath
and some sal volatile, and go straight to bed. Dear,
kind soul! In vain I told her I wanted none of these
things—especially the first. What earthly good could
the poor man do? There was nothing in the world the
matter with me beyond a few bruises and scratches.
However, short of open rebellion there was no escape
from her persistency, so, rather sulkily, I am afraid, I
yielded to the whole programme—bed, brandy, sal volatile, doctor, and all, and even drank the inoffensive mix-

ture which the poor man thought it necessary to send up. To tell the truth, I was rather glad to be alone and think. I wanted to think over my hardly-to-be-believed reconciliation with Sydney, and his plan about going to America, and our scheme for meeting at Inversnaid next day; all these things had to be thought over and hugged and gloated over as altogether too good on the face of them to be true, and yet things that absolutely and literally *were*.

CHAPTER XVIII

MYSTERY AND SUSPICION

I WOKE next morning as stiff as a board. Unsuspected bruises discovered themselves in various colours all over my body. My head smarted and tingled where stray wisps of hair had been torn out by the roots; there was a long scratch on my left cheek, and another over my eye. And yet, for all these things, I doubt if on any day at any time in my life I have jumped out of bed with such pure joy of soul as I did that morning. I threw open the little latticed windows as wide as they would go, and craned out my rumpled head into the morning air. It was a still, dull day, with little patches of blue showing here and there among the grey clouds. Not the faintest breath of air stirred the naked limbs of the mighty trees beyond the balustrade. From the ground rose up the fresh, damp smell of dead leaves—very pleasant to my nostrils—a real homy English smell. My friend, the robin, was piping plaintively among the holly bushes, and my other friends, the cock-pheasants, were swaggering gallantly about, picking up—whatever pheasants do pick up—worms, I suppose. I was glad they had not been shot.

Eighty yards away, by the steps to the lower terrace, a gardener was tickling the path with a broom. He took no notice whatever of me; why should he? He was used by this time to such unkempt apparitions. I expect he had long ago put me down as a harmless lunatic.

I looked up at the dull sky with satisfaction. The clouds were not heavy, only the grey Shetland-shawl sort of clouds that one expects at the end of the year. "No rain to-day," I thought; "Sydney will come all right." I wished I hadn't got that long scratch down the left cheek; it made me look such an object. Then I thought of Inversnaid and the "drawbridge." The very thought of wriggling my poor, battered body up that long, spiky branch was positive agony to me. How in the world was I to do it, and not fill the very welkin with my shrieks?

I dressed at my leisure that day, beguiling the weary hour, by way of a change, with singing. It was not often I did this, and when I did, I always did it out of tune. Whistling was more in my line; nobody expects one to whistle in tune. But that morning somehow I felt full of song. The gardener left off tickling the path, and stared up with open mouth. This was a form of lunacy he was not used to. But what did it matter? The musical ear of my uncle's gardener is not over-critical, as Ollendorf would have said. So I went on:

> "And though the wild fir trees were creaking,
>   And ghosts were in every part,
> I found what I long had been seeking,
>   A heart I could take to my heart."

The clang of the chapel bell put a stop at last to my singing, and told me that there was half an hour still to breakfast; so I went out and prowled about the garden, and found nothing particular to do, and wished with all my heart it was two hours later.

"Well, Joe, what are your plans for this morning?" Uncle Guy enquired at breakfast, with a broad, cheery smile.

"Oh, I don't know—poke about, I suppose," I answered, carelessly. After I had said it, it suddenly dawned upon me that I was growing into an appalling liar. The idea horrified me; I had always been rather the other way, and hated liars as I hated the Evil One.

"May I come and poke about, too?" Norman asked.

"Of course," I said, wishing him at the other end of the world, "if it won't bore you."

It was really too maddening, just this one morning of all others, when I so particularly wanted to be left free! I could have thrown something at him; however, I knew that several pairs of eyes were watching me; so I did my best to look happy (more lying! but there was no help for it).

So Norman and I went and rowed about on the lake, and fished for pike, and caught nothing but one small but gluttonous perch. And I was rather sulky, I am afraid, and snubbed Norman, and made rather a fool of myself generally.

Then we came home to luncheon, and Aunt Harriet said she would take me out for a drive, as I was on no account to be allowed to ride Maid Marion again. She had scolded poor Uncle Guy most desperately for letting me ride her at all, and still more for letting Sophie ride her home.

This was all madly annoying, of course, but still I consoled myself with the thought that Sydney would understand, and would in all probability come to Inversnaid next day on the chance. But when the next day came, and exactly the same thing happened, and the next, and the next after that, it became pretty clear to me that I was not meant to do as I pleased. It was impossible it could be accident. I was being watched, guarded, escorted, sometimes by one member of the family, sometimes by another. Even Sophie was made use of to watch and report upon my movements—quite innocently and unconsciously, of course, poor thing! but that only made it all the worse. I felt, in fact, that I was a prisoner, never allowed to move without a warder at my side. I was afraid even to confide in Sophie—dear, gentle Sophie! I knew, of course, that she was absolutely devoted to me, and that she would sooner die than do anything that would knowingly injure me, but then there was Father Terence, and he had a way of worming things out of people that I had already experienced, to my cost.

So I kept my own counsel, and grew sullen and suspicious, and as a consequence, cunning and deceitful; it was really dreadful, but what was I to do? Every one's hand was against me, even down to the servants.

Griffiths was a spy, and Frenetzi—as far as his opportunities went—was worse. The family were, of course, friendly and polite on the surface, but even from them the mask would at times fall off. Not that I mean to imply that I ever caught them off their guard, scowling demoniacal glances at me; but they were different from what they had been; they were different from what they were when I came. Uncle Guy, when I first came, had been as cheery and jolly a specimen of a country gentleman as one may meet in a lifetime. With his round, red face, clear grey eye, and short aquiline nose, it would have been hard to conceive a more perfect type of the jovial squire of the sporting school. Norman, for his part, had been frivolous, light-hearted, and irresponsible—what the books call *debonnaire*. Both of them had been the picture of health. Now, however, all this was changed.   Uncle Guy looked white, haggard, and pinched, while Norman stalked about like a ghost, with drooping head and hands in pockets.   What was the meaning of it all?   What was this horrible mystery, this gloomy spectre, that had worked so astonishing a change?   Why, too, was I watched and guarded as though I were a felon?

For my own part, I connected the whole thing in some way with Father Terence.   Not that I had the slightest ground for this, beyond the fact that I was perpetually coming upon him in the byways and passages of the house, whispering with Norman or my uncle.   There never was such a place as Selworth for tumbling on people unawares!   And every time, whenever I did find them, it always seemed to be Father Terence who was laying down the law, and the others who were listening. Of course, all this might well have been pure imagination on my part, for I never overheard a word they were saying, and for all I *knew* to the contrary, they might have been talking of food or weather or the chants for the following Sunday.   But Father Terence frightened me; I never had cared for him, and now he positively frightened me.   I used to catch him sometimes staring at me with the oddest look you ever saw in a man's face—a look in which horror and curiosity seemed struggling for the mastery.   What did the man *mean* by looking at me in that way?   I felt instinctively that, for some extraordinary, un-get-at-able reason, he was my enemy.   He was always civil—far too civil, in fact—full of silly, idiotic compliments that made me sick; but for all that, I knew, as surely as a pigeon knows a hawk, that the whole being of the man was hostile to me, and dangerous.

And I began to get very frightened.

The thing got on my nerves, and kept me awake at night—kept me awake for hours, while I stared into the darkness and tried to find some clue to the mystery. My face—like Norman's and Uncle Guy's—began to get white and pinched, and I noticed a scared, strained look in the eyes that faced me from the looking-glass. The worst of it all was there was no single, solitary soul in the whole place, except Sydney, that I could confide in, and ask advice from. And Sydney was out of reach— kept out of reach, I knew, by intention.

One night, about a week after the Maid Marion business, I lay awake, feeling utterly miserable, and wishing I was dead, when a thought flashed across my brain in the sudden, unaccountable way that things do come across one in the small hours of the morning. I thought of old Mrs. Beddington, and of the words she had twice used at parting, "Come to me if you are ever in need of a friend." Surely, if ever I was in need of a friend, it was now! I would go. I made up my mind on the instant. The moment it was daylight I would slip out of the glass door, and take her at her word. The thought was an immense comfort to me—the thought of *doing* something, instead of sitting still day after day among all these mysteries and whisperings and white, gloomy faces.

The moment the first streak of grey began to show through my blinds I jumped out of bed and began to dress, and long before it was light enough to read, and long before the housemaids had started prowling about the passages, I had slipped out of the little turret door, and over the stone balustrade, into the shelter of the trees. I went boldly across the Plain; I knew no one would be up at that hour. And besides, I could see that every blind in the great house was down; only in some of the little dormer windows at the top the glow of candles told me that the housemaids were beginning to stir.

I almost ran across the thick, sopping grass, for I knew that on this day of all others I must be punctual for breakfast. The deer were still lying down, dotted about like huge toad-stools, but they got up and shook themselves as I came near, leaving bright green marks in the white wetness of the grass. They stared at me haughtily for a minute or two, as though asking what I meant by disturbing them at such an hour, and then trotted lightly away with head and tail in air.

I went first to Inversnaid, for I had something to do there.

I climbed up, and just over the fireplace, where it would be shielded from the rain, I pinned a bit of paper I had brought with me. On it was written:

"Cannot get away except before breakfast; try and come some morning about half past eight. I want to see you badly.—J."

He might find it, or he might not. Anyhow, no one else would find it, for, thank Heaven, no living soul, except us two, knew of Inversnaid and all its hidden glories. I looked round at all the old nooks and corners with a feeling of such immense love as it is quite beyond me to describe. I felt that this old tree had remained faithful and true when all else had failed me. Selworth House, from being the dream of my childhood, had grown to be a nightmare; the park—the glorious and peerless park—had all but proved my death, and my lovely panelled room had turned out to be nothing more or less than a treacherous trap. But Inversnaid was still true to me; Inversnaid was on my side—my only ally—against all the forces that were assailing me, a very tower of strength and secrecy, with its mighty limbs and unknown hiding-places; and over and above all, Inversnaid it was that had brought me Sydney. This was enough in itself.

I would have loved to have stayed there, and lit some sticks in the charred, blackened fireplace, but I remembered what time meant to me that morning. So I slipped down and ran across the valley to the Manor House. Henry Beddington was just leaving for the Abbey as I came to the door. He stared at me open-mouthed.

"Is your mother up yet?" I asked. "I want particularly to see her."

"Oh, yes, miss," he said; "she be up, right enough. I reckon you'll find her in the kitchen."

I hammered at the door, and Mrs. Beddington herself opened it.

"So you've come," she said instantly, looking me full in the face with her dark, piercing eyes.

"Yes, I've come."

"Well, step in, child, and sit down. You look as white as a ghost, to be sure. What have they been doing to you?"

"Oh, nothing!" I said, sinking into a chair. I felt half-dead, I was so tired.

"Nothing! and you to look like that! Well, well, sit quiet a minute while I make you a cup of tea."

"Then you won't marry Norman! I suppose that's where the trouble lies?" she added, suddenly and sharply, as she bustled about with the kettle.

"No, I can't marry Norman," I said.

"And why not, pray? Isn't he good enough for you?"

She spoke so sharply that I looked up at her in surprise. She was positively scowling at me from under her thick eyebrows. Was this the friend, I thought, that I had taken such trouble to come and see? My heart sank with a feeling of utter hopelessness. Here, then, was another one against me!

"I don't care for him enough to marry him," I said, weakly.

"And whom do you care for well enough to marry?"

I made no answer, but sat and stared into the crackling fire.

"Is it that young Sydney Grayle?"

"Yes; I would marry Mr. Grayle."

"Well, well, to think of any girl preferring a beggarly young fortune-hunter like that to a man like Norman de Metrier!"

"Norman isn't fit to black his boots!" I cried, rising to my feet, "and I don't think I want your tea, thanks, Mrs. Beddington; I must be getting home."

I was very angry, and on the verge of tears. It was so hard to find this old woman against me after all.

"So that's the way of it, is it?" she said. "Well, well, I've nothing more to say, then. The Lord's will be done."

I had my hand already on the door-latch, but at her last words I turned round and faced her   What did she mean by the Lord's will being done? I remembered Father Terence using those very words some time back when I had overheard him talking to Uncle Guy in the great hall.

"What do you mean?" I said.

"Come here, my dear," she said, "and sit down, and

drink your tea. You've come to me, as I told you to, because you want a friend?"

"I did come because I wanted a friend, but I'm afraid I've wasted my time," I said, bitterly.

"Nonsense!" she said, sharply; "sit down, like a sensible girl. I am your friend, and a good one, as you'll find."

"So you love this young Grayle?" she asked, after a pause.

"Yes, I do," I said, defiantly.

"And you would marry him, beggar as he is, and beggar as you are?"

"Yes," I said, "I would, and I wish for nothing better."

She took my two hands in hers, and stared into my face as though she would read my very soul.

"Then," she said, "I will help you, though it prove my death."

"Prove your death!" I exclaimed. "What do you mean? Why should it prove any one's death? Surely I can marry any one I choose."

She took no notice of my questions.

"I would have given everything I have in the world for you to have married Norman," she said, solemnly; "but as it is, I bow my head to the will of God. It is a just punishment for my sins."

"I don't know the least what you mean," I said. "I came to you because I am in terrible need of a friend, and you told me to come if I wanted one. I thought you might advise me."

"And so I will, my dear, so I will, and more than that. There are very few things I would not do for Guy de Metrier's daughter."

"Guy de Metrier's daughter! Do you mean Sophie?"

"No, my dear, not Sophie. However, never mind that now. Tell me what they are doing to you up at the Abbey."

"Oh! what are they not doing?" I cried, wringing my hands in a way I should have been ashamed of two months before. "What are they not doing? They are watching me, and spying on me, and guarding me as though I were a prisoner. Even the servants are leagued against me. There is not a soul in the place I can trust. I am frightened, Mrs. Beddington — horribly frightened!—what of I don't know. I couldn't tell you to save my life—but there is something, I am sure of that."

"Poor lamb!" the old lady said, "is it as bad as that? Well, well, they are bad to cross, these De Metriers, and always have been—gentlemen all, and smooth as milk as long as things go straight, but any that crosses them must bend and break unless they are the stronger, as I myself should know as well as most, God help me!"

"What is it all about?" I said piteously. "What have I done to offend them? Is it about Norman?"

"There, you have said it," she replied, "and in three words; it is about Norman, and nothing else. If you married him there would be no more trouble for any of us."

"I can't do it," I cried, "I can't really. I would sooner die!"

"Hush! my dear," she said; "don't talk like that, for Heaven's sake!"

She raised her hands, as though to shut out some evil sight, and shuffled across to the far end of the room. I rose to my feet.

"I must be going now," I said; "it is getting late, and I *must* be in time for breakfast."

I was miserably disappointed. She had told me nothing, advised me nothing; and she was my one last hope of friendship.

"Must you really?" she said. "Well, well, I am sorry; but come again, my dear, come again soon, for I want to have a long talk with you."

"How in the world can I come again soon?" I cried, irritably. "Haven't I told you that I am watched and spied on and guarded from morning till night? What nonsense you do talk. I don't suppose I shall ever get another chance. Ten to one they will find out that I have been here this morning, and there will be a fine to-do. Uncle Guy has expressly forbidden me to see you."

"Yes," she said, thoughtfully; "he would naturally do that." Then, quite suddenly, she cried out: "'In the midst of life we are in death,' and I may as well do it now. Wait here one minute, my dear, and I will give you something to take home."

She climbed toilfully up the little wooden staircase, and I stood at the open door, with curiosity slightly aroused. What was she going to give me?—a talisman?—a love-philtre?—or what?

She was barely gone a minute, and came down with a scarlet leather box in her hand. She carried it by a handle attached to the top, and from the handle, on a piece of white tape, hung the key.

"Miss Josephine," she said, very seriously, "take this box, and guard it as you would your own life. Let no one see it, and hide it where no single soul within the four walls of Selworth will be able to find it. The moment I am dead, open it, and read what is inside. While I am alive you are on no account to open it till I give you leave. Do you promise me this solemnly?''

"Yes," I said, feeling rather awed.

"That is good. You are to be trusted, or I would not give it you. But the moment you hear of my death, open it—if possible in company with Mr. Grayle.''

"Why do you talk of dying?" I asked. "You look quite well; is anything the matter?''

" 'In the midst of life we are in death,' " she repeated, shaking her head. "I have grievous sins that must be expiated here or hereafter; God grant it may be here.''

I took the box, and held it limply in my hand, waiting for her to say more. I was far too impressed myself to speak. The old woman stood shaking her head and muttering to herself. Then suddenly she turned to me, and seized my hand.

"In the meanwhile," she said, "I will give you advice. Trust no one at Selworth, least of all the priest. Whatever he advises you to do, do the opposite. Be secret and watchful, and keep your own counsel. Write no letters, and, above all things, show no signs of distrust — remember that.''

I nodded silently.

"There is one thing more," she went on, "but it may be difficult. Get Lady Harriet, if possible, to change your room.''

"Why?" I said. "Do you mean the picture?''

I have never seen anyone look so astonished. It almost made me laugh, miserable as I was.

"What do you know of the picture?" she asked, sharply.

"I know all about it," I said, with some triumph,

"and especially this, that nobody will open it from the staircase side again in a hurry."

"They have tried, then?" she asked in a horrified whisper.

"Never you mind," I said, laughing; "it's all right now, anyhow. And now I must really be off. Good-bye, Mrs. Beddington, and a thousand thanks."

"Mind the box well," she said, shaking a finger at me, "and let no one see it on any account, except Mr. Grayle. And since you're set on him—young Grayle, I mean—I'll give you both an old woman's blessing, and that with all my heart. He's a fine young fellow, and worth a dozen ramshackle De Metriers when all's said and done. God bless you both!"

She turned into the house, and I went dancing off down the track.

It was wonderful how my spirits had risen during the last ten minutes. I think it was the box or perhaps the tea, or the discovery that there was one person at any rate in the world who would turn a smiling eye upon my marriage with Sydney Grayle. Anyhow, whatever it was, the result was astonishing. I had not been in such spirits for days, almost weeks. A pale sun was up now, slanting through the bare branches of the trees opposite, and flecking the bracken with streaks and stars of light. I had just three-quarters of an hour to get home, and I knew it was none too much.

I was just rounding the bend in the track that shows one the bottom of the broader valley below, with the green ride running up its centre, when my heart gave one immense bound, and then stood stock still. I darted like a rabbit behind the roots of a big fir-tree that had been blown down, and flung myself full length on the wet, stony earth on which it had once stood. And there I lay, hardly daring so much as to breathe; for what I had caught sight of in that one wild moment was nothing less than Uncle Guy himself riding slowly up the track towards the Manor House. He had not seen me yet; I was sure of that; and the upturned root, though only three yards from the track, shielded me well enough so long as nothing prompted him to look back when he had once passed. If he did that, I was lost—absolutely and irretrievably lost—for on that side there was no shelter at all. Oh, those awful moments! Did ever mortal man ride so slow before? I heard the slow, regular beat of the horse's hoofs drawing nearer and nearer as they climbed the hill. I heard the old horse softly blowing his nose, and the smack of Uncle Guy's cane against his gaiters. Would they *never* pass?

Uncle Guy gave a loud sneeze, and it sounded so appallingly close that I almost jumped out of my skin. A horrible dread came over me that from the top of his horse he might be able to see my feet sticking out behind the root. However, movement of any sort would be absolutely fatal, so I lay still, and trusted vaguely to Providence. Next moment horse and rider burst out into full view. He was kicking his heels loosely, and smacking his leg with his cane, and his head turned quickly from side to side as though taking stock of his property. Once he rested his hand on the horse's quarters, and turned squarely round to the right, looking straight over my head towards the Abbey. An insane inclination came into my head to kick both my legs straight up into the air, and give a wild view-halloa; it would have made him jump so. However, thank

Heaven! I resisted it. The next moment his head turned to the front again, and I was safe.

He rode round into the yard, whistling and calling for some one to take his horse, and I picked myself up, and scurried madly down the track.

I had to go a long round home to keep out of sight of the bedroom windows—along the edge of Flexham Wood, then down under the dip in which the Home Farm lay, through the straggling oak-trees between the house and the lake, and then for two or three hundred yards across the open, till I reached the shelter of the trees outside the garden balustrade. After that it was all plain sailing.

I got in five minutes before the bell rang, and hid my box in the drawer at the bottom of my wardrobe, and spent the rest of the time in washing my face in cold water, and brushing my clothes and my hair, and generally making myself look as though I had not been out of the house for weeks.

Uncle Guy was down as soon as I was; *he* looked very much as though he had been out of the house—hot and pale and dishevelled, and very cross. He clattered the dishes about in an awful fashion, and broke two plates, and swore a good deal under his breath. No one dared speak to him. I wondered what Mrs. Beddington had been saying to him.

No one asked me any questions, and I took it for granted that my walk would pass down as one of the unrecorded incidents of history; but before twenty-four hours had passed I had reason to change my mind. And for this reason.

I got up early next morning to go to Inversnaid; I

thought it just possible that Sydney might have found my paper. Anyhow, it was worth going on the off chance. But to my utter amazement, when I got to the glass door, I found it locked, and the key nowhere to be seen.

"Officious housemaids," I thought. "However, it doesn't much matter, luckily." I passed on to the door into the garden by Aunt Harriet's room, but here again I found the same thing—door locked, key gone! This time I did not say "officious housemaids." I said nothing, but I thought a good deal, like the parrot. I have never seen a house where there are so many outlets as there are at Selworth. I tried them all, including the front door. They were all the same—locked and barred. There were, of course, windows out of which I could have climbed, but it was not worth while. In the first place, I should probably have been seen by a housemaid, and in the second place the locked doors told a story with a very plain moral—so plain a moral, in fact, that I went straight back to my room, and threw myself sulkily on the sofa at the foot of the bed.

I had lain for twenty minutes brooding rather miserably, when a sudden, startling thought flashed across me. My box! My precious red box! What an idiot I was! I had clean forgotten all about it.

I flew to the drawer where I had hidden it, full of terror and self-reproaches. What if it were gone? What if old Griffiths had found it, and studied its contents?

It was hidden under one of the poor old sadly despised Chelmsford frocks that I had worn when I came. That was why I had put it there, because I knew full well that Griffiths would have died sooner than soil her fingers with such trash. I had, however, in a sudden impulse of extraordinary caution, arranged the key and the string that it hung from in a particular pattern, so that I should know in a moment if any one had tampered with it.

It was all right. I need not have worried myself. I ought to have known that I might have left the thing there for a year in perfect safety. The key and the string and the pattern were just as I had left them, and with a sigh of immense relief, I took the box and sat down to consider.

I had long ago made up my mind where I would hide it; the only question was whether the moment was not a little dangerous. However, something must be risked, I thought. Over-caution is as bad as none; and after all, the risk was not much greater than that of leaving the box where it might be found.

I made up my mind to chance it.

I locked the door, and lit a candle, and put the candle and the box in the middle of the chimney-piece. Then I took off my shoes, and getting a chair, climbed on to the left end of the chimney-piece, and ran my fingers up the left side of the frame till I came to the tenth knob from the bottom. I knew exactly where to look for it by now. I pressed the spring, and with one last supercilious smile at me, Maurice swung back out of sight.

Now came the nervous part. For all I knew the staircase might act as a kind of speaking-tube into Norman's room. I knew, of course, that he was there—probably still in bed. Fancy if he pounced upon me, box in hand!

I took the box in one hand and the candle in the other, and crept softly up. Half-way to the top there was a kind of deep niche in the wall—a kind of place

that looked as if it had been meant for one of those narrow slits of windows one sees in old castles.   It was an
irregular wedge in shape, and ended in a sort of point.
So far this was of no great use for my purpose, but just
short of the end, and about four feet from the staircase,
there was a deep hole as though some big stone had
fallen from its place.   This was the place I had my eye
on.   I crawled on my knees along the dust-covered
stones, and stretching out my left arm, pushed the box
as far as it would go into the hole.   It was magnificent!
My hand followed the box as far as the wrist, leaving it
absolutely invisible to any evil-minded person prowling
up and down the stairs.   Nothing, in short, could have
been better.   The place seemed positively to have been
made for my purpose.

I crept down again, closed Maurice with great caution, and brushed my knees, and put on my boots, with
the satisfactory feeling of having done a good morning's
work in spite of all the machinations of evilly disposed
people.

CHAPTER XIX

MORE MYSTERY

THAT week Uncle Guy went to London, and stayed there till Saturday night. Sophie said he had gone to see his lawyers about money matters. I don't know how she knew, but she was generally right. She told me she thought he was very hard up for money, as he had given orders to have all his race-horses sold at New-market, which was really an extraordinary thing to do, as the De Metriers had owned race-horses for over half a century.

"That's what has been making him look so worried and ill lately, I expect," she said; "he was immensely proud of his horses."

To me all this was a revelation, and a cause of much wonder. I had always looked upon my uncle as a man into whose pocket money poured in such boundless quantities that he found it difficult to know what to do with it all. The horses, the carriages, the servants in their powder and their liveries, the masses of gold and silver plate, everything, in fact, about the place gave one the idea of unlimited money. And that the owner of all this should actually have to sell his horses and borrow money—as Sophie said he was doing—seemed a thing almost beyond the bounds of possibility.

Of course, if this was true, it accounted for a great deal that had puzzled me before. It accounted for the whisperings and the consultations, and the pale, harassed faces, and for a great deal of the mystery that had seemed to hang about the place lately.   But it accounted in no way that I could see for my being locked into the house, and sent out every day under escort.   Unless it was that Sydney, as the Duke's agent, knew all about Uncle Guy's money difficulties, and they were afraid he would tell me.   That might possibly be it.   I wondered.

Sophie and I talked over all these things by the hour. We came to the conclusion that he had been speculating, or betting on horse-races, and had lost more money than he could pay.

One day Sophie and I were walking about down by the lake when we met a long string of horses—ten or twelve of them—in hoods and rugs and knee-caps, going in the direction of the Greystoke Lodge.   We ran up in great excitement, and Sophie asked one of the grooms where they were going.

"Going to Lunnon, miss," he said, touching his cap.

"London!' she said.   "Why, what for?"

"Don't know, miss, I'm sure—Mr. Clarke's orders."

We thought this the most extraordinary thing of all, but there was more to come.   Next day there were three huge vans in the yard outside the back door, and Mercer and Gedge, and half a dozen men, were hoisting in any number of great wooden cases.

"What's all this, Mercer?" Sophie asked.   She was just as inquisitive about it all as I was.

"Some things we are sending up to London, miss," he answered.   "Plate mostly, and china, and one or two pictures and pieces of furniture."

"But why on earth are they going to London?" she asked.

"Well, I fancy, from what I hear, the family will be going up to town next week, and I suppose these things will be wanted there—dinner-parties and receptions, perhaps."

"Oh, what fun!" cried Sophie; "I do hope we are! But why have we heard nothing about it?"

"Can't say, I'm sure, miss. Likely as not the Squire's only settled it lately."

My uncle was always "the Squire" with the servants. It was a fancy of his. Mordaunt had been "the Squire" before him, and Maurice again before that, and possibly Roger before Maurice. It always sounded funny to me, for he was not my idea of a squire somehow. He seemed too big a swell to fit the name.

Sophie and I went in, and made all sorts of discoveries about the house. Four of the best pictures in the long gallery were gone, and the Vandyck in the passage outside Aunt Harriet's room, and almost every picture out of the drawing-room. The drawing-room, in fact, was swept bare. There were three large cabinets that had been full of Sèvres china—quite priceless, I believe; these were empty now. And three marble statues that stood between the windows were gone, too. We had not been using the drawing-room since the last shooting party, so we had not the slightest idea of what had been going on. We were speechless with amazement. How had they managed to do it so quietly and without any noise?—and why? In the name of all that was reasonable, why?

"Is the London house very empty?" I asked Sophie.

"No, I don't think it is. I have never thought much about it, but it has always seemed to me much the same as this. The pictures, I believe, are better."

"Then, why take all these things up?"

"Goodness knows!"

"Perhaps he's going to sell them," I whispered, "like the horses."

"Oh, not likely," she said; "in the first place, he is not allowed to by law without Norman's consent; and, besides, it's ridiculous, of course, to suppose that he's as hard up as all that.   He can always raise any amount on mortgage."

At luncheon we propounded the question to Aunt Harriet—at least Sophie did—I don't think I should have had the courage.

"I really don't know, child," she answered, plaintively.   "Your father does not think it necessary to consult me every time he moves a picture or a plate. *Ce ne vaut pas la peine.*"

"No, but he is sending up such huge quantities of things.   The poor old drawing-room looks like a barn."

"I fancy, Sophie," Father Terence put in sonorously, "that your father contemplates some changes.   Some of the London things are coming here, and some from here going to London.   The idea is, I should say, to get things more suitably grouped than they are at present. But really I know very little about the matter."

"And are the horses going to be more suitably grouped, too?"

"My dear child," said Aunt Harriet, "don't ask such very foolish questions.   *Je ne m'occupe pas des écuries.* Why don't you ask Clarke?"

Poor Sophie collapsed.   I never knew any one so easily put down.   From the end of the table Norman looked up, and said, carelessly:

"I expect the Squire will sell some of the horses, and

a good thing, too. They're more or less of a three-cornered lot, what with one thing and another."

"Not Norah, I hope?" said Sophie.

"Oh, no, not Norah, of course, but some of the other old crocks; and Maid Marion, of course, he'll sell—nobody would care to ride her again after her bolting with Joe."

It occurred to me casually that Maid Marion had been given me for my own, and that if any one had the right to sell her it would be myself, but naturally I kept these thoughts to myself.

"Is is true we are going to London next week?" I asked, rather nervously, looking at Aunt Harriet.

"I really don't know, my dear; there was some talk of it, but it depends a good deal on your uncle's arrangements. If he can get through his business by Saturday we shall probably stay here. I can tell you nothing definite till he comes back."

"I hope to goodness we do go up!" said Sophie, with emphasis. "What fun it will be! Won't it, Joe?"

"Won't it?" I echoed, with as much spirit as I could summon up. To tell the truth, I was not sure that it would be fun at all—for me.

Uncle Guy came back late on Saturday night. We had all gone to bed—Sophie, that is, and Aunt Harriet, and myself—but I could hear his loud, cheery voice talking and laughing downstairs, and I jumped to the conclusion that his business, as far as it had gone, was satisfactory. I hoped it would cheer things up a bit at Selworth. There was need of it.

The next day, Sunday, Norman proposed to me again. He positively frightened me, he was so wild and odd. He rolled on the floor, and grovelled, and seized my hand, and kissed it, and slobbered over it, till I honestly thought the boy must be mad. To tell the truth, it had entered into my head more than once that both Norman and Uncle Guy were a little mad; they were so strange at times, and unexpected, and unaccountable. They both, too, had an odd look in the eye at times—a kind of excited glitter. As to Norman, on this particular day he was beyond anything.

"For God's sake, Joe!" he cried, gripping my hand till he hurt me; "for all our sakes, for your own sake, don't say no!"

"But, Norman," I said, "how can you talk like that? You know I am engaged to Mr. Grayle."

"Would you marry me if it was not for him?" he asked.

"How can I tell? How can any one tell what they would do if everything was different?"

"No; but what I mean is, if you had never seen him, do you like me well enough to marry me?"

"What *is* the use of asking riddles?" I said. "I really don't know. I *have* seen him, and that settles it."

We were in the morning-room, and every moment I expected some one would come in, and find him on the floor. We should have looked such awful fools. I wished he would get up.

"Joe!" he whispered, glancing nervously round the room over his shoulder, "if you knew that by marrying me you would avert some great family misfortune—a terrible danger that threatens all of us, including yourself—yourself more than any, in fact—wouldn't you do this for the sake of all we have done for you? Joe, darling little Joe, for God's sake, think it all over! Is it such a very dreadful thing that I am asking you to do? Do you hate me so much that you cannot even marry me to save the whole family from—from a horrible, hideous curse? O my God! My God! if you only knew!"

He sprang to his feet, and walked wildly up and down the room, his brows knit, his hands clenched tightly behind his back.

"What is this terrible thing that I could avert?" I asked. "You are all so dreadfully mysterious."

I felt quite ashamed of myself for being so calm; it seemed so unfeeling.

"Don't ask me what it is, Joe, for I can't possibly tell you; but I give you my word of honour that there is such a thing, and that it is very real and very dreadful— far more dreadful than you can ever dream of. And you can save us all—Sophie and my mother and all—if you will only marry me. I would be so good to you, Joe."

Why was I not more moved by his pleading, agonised face? The plain passion in his eyes ought to have melted a stone; but I remained icily calm and indifferent. I can't say why. I don't think, for one thing, I quite believed what he was telling me. All the time he was talking, Mrs. Beddington's warning words kept running in my head, "Trust no one at Selworth; keep your own counsel, and be watchful and secret." What right had they and their mystery to come between me and my love? The thing was a plot from the beginning—a mean plot of the whole family to get me to marry Norman just to suit their own convenience. I had felt honestly sorry for Norman before, because I thought he really did care for me; but now I saw the whole thing was just put on in order to help their nasty, underhand plans. Another thought, too, flashed across my mind, and helped to keep me calm—the thought of that ghastly night when soft footsteps had creaked about my room in the marrow-curdling darkness. I tightened my lips and steeled my heart.

"So all your love-making and pretence of affection has just been a sham?" I said. "You just wanted to marry me for business reasons?"

"Before God, Joe," he said, kneeling down beside my chair, "there was no sham about it. I love you as I never thought I could love any one in the world. I am a selfish, easy-going sort of chap, as you know, and it never entered into my head that I *could* fall very much in love with any one. But you—you simply knocked me head over heels from the first moment I saw you. Look at me, Joe—look at me! Can you look at me and not see that I am almost out of my mind for love of you?"

"I see that you are very much excited about this terrible disaster which will overtake you if I don't marry you," I said, slowly.

"No, no, no!" he cried, "it is not that, Joe—before God, it is not that! I only said that because I thought it might—help!"

"Help what?"

"Help to persuade you to marry me. But it is you that I want, Joe—you and only you, my sweet, beautiful darling! It is the others that are thinking so much about the—expediency of the thing."

"What others?"

"Oh, all the others," he said, vaguely.

I could see that he already regretted what he had said.

"But I don't understand," I said. "Five minutes ago you asked me to marry you to avert some mysterious curse; now you ask me to marry you because you love me? Which do you mean? You contradict yourself so."

"No, I don't, Joe; can't you understand? There is this mysterious curse, as you call it, and if you married me you would put an absolute end to it, and it was in reality for this that you were asked here; and I made up my mind to sacrifice myself and marry this dowdy little Chelmsford cousin that no one had ever seen, for the sake of the family. But before you had been here a week I knew that this dowdy little Chelmsford cousin was the one and only girl in the whole world that I could ever care to marry—absolutely the only one. So there you have the whole history of it in a nutshell. And now what do you say, Joe?"

"Nothing that I have not said before," I answered, rather miserably. "I am dreadfully sorry about it all, Norman, but no one can force their own heart, and— there's nothing to be said that I can see."

"You won't marry me? Not even now that you know all?"

"No, Norman; I really can't."

He stood still, looking at me with such a miserable face that I felt like a murderess. I felt, too, that it was dreadfully mean and selfish and ungrateful of me not to do what they all wanted so badly. I hated myself for it, but there it was—there was no help for it.

Norman came quite close to me, and said: "Very well, Joe, I will accept that as final, and I will not bother you any more; but there is one thing more I must say to you now; I know it will make no difference to your decision, but all the same I must say it."

"Well?" I said.

"You are in danger, Joe—in awful danger! Get Sydney Grayle to take you away from here at once— instantly—this very day, if you can. Run away across the park to his house, and tell him to keep you there, and hide you and lock you up.''

He nodded at me fiercely.

''My dear Norman,'' I said, laughing, ''you must be mad. How on earth can I do a thing of that sort?''

''Never mind how you can do it, but do it. What do custom and convention and propriety matter in a case of life and death? I tell you, you are in mortal danger here.''

''Who is this talking about danger?'' said a loud, musical voice at the door. ''Faith! there's danger enough for all poor men with your bright eyes going about the house, Miss Joe. What has Norman been saying to you? Making love, the rascal, I'll be bound, and small blame to him, either!''

We were both silent. Norman seemed to shrink into nothing, and with a white face and trembling hands, took up a book. I was too horrified by his last words to make any pretence of seeming otherwise than in the depths of gloom. Father Terence seemed to notice nothing.

''I came to look for that copy of 'Giraldus Cambrensis,' '' he said, ''lying thief of the world that he was! I hope you've not been studying him, Miss Joe.''

''No, I've not seen it,'' I answered, quite seriously. To tell the truth, I had hardly heard his question.

''No, indeed, I suppose not,'' he said, with a fat laugh. ''Why would you? Love sonnets are more in your line, just as musty old Latin tomes, written by court liars, are in mine.''

''I hate love sonnets!'' I said, rather crossly; ''silly, mawkish things!''

''Ah, well!'' he said, ''the mere reflection may well

seem silly in presence of the reality. We only cherish portraits when the original is absent. Well, well, that villain Giraldus must be in the library, and poor, fat Terence Boyle must go puffing and blowing after him. Gad! these passages grow longer every year. They'll be the death of me some day. Norman, me dear boy, be a good Christian, and give an old man an arm as far as the library. Miss Joe'll give you leave of absence for five minutes, I make no doubt."

Norman went up without a word and offered his arm; he looked exactly as if he was going to be hung. They passed out together, Father Terence doing all the talking, and I was left alone with my thoughts.

CHAPTER XX

FLICKERS ON THE RAFTERS

IT turned out that I was not to go to London with them, after all.

"You see, my dear," Aunt Harriet explained, "you have no suitable dresses, and, I think, altogether you would be rather miserable. And we shall be very quiet—no balls, no entertainments, nothing in the least amusing."

She peered at me over her glasses rather nervously, I thought, as though expecting me to fly into a wild passion.

"Then, what am I to do?" I asked. "Am I to stay here all alone?"

"No, my dear, we could hardly ask you to do that," she said, with a little awkward laugh. "You see, for one thing, we are going to have a regular cleaning in the house here—it is needing it terribly—and so, if the housemaids are to have a fair chance, we cannot well have any one living in the house. And so your uncle thought that perhaps you would not mind staying for ten days or so at the old Manor House with Mrs. Beddington. There is a very charming room there that you could have, and the old woman is really an excellent cook. Do you think you would be terribly *embêtée?* Sophie, I know, would die of *ennui* in six hours, but you are so different, so fond of roaming about the woods by yourself, so independent and strong, that we thought perhaps you would not dislike it very much. What do you say, child? Of course, if you object, we could try and make some other arrangements.''

Aunt Harriet blinked at me, and I stared back at her in such utter amazement of mind that I could find no words. Stay at the Manor House with Mrs. Beddington, the forbidden! And at Uncle Guy's suggestion, too! It was too bewildering!

I shall remember that scene to my dying day—the last evening I was ever to spend under Uncle Guy's roof. We were sitting in the great hall, after dinner on Sunday night. Both the huge fireplaces were piled up with blazing logs, for it was a cold, frosty night, and the red flicker of them went fitfully up into the darkness above. Father Terence sat at the piano singing ''He Shall Feed His Flock Like a Shepherd,'' in the soft voice that I liked so much better than the bellowing that he sometimes was inclined to. Sophie and Norman were playing chess on the far side of the fireplace, and Aunt Harriet and I sat facing each other on the huge bed-like sofa that faced the drawing-room door. My uncle had disappeared to his room—he often did after dinner—went there to write letters, I suppose, or to go to sleep in a chair perhaps.

I remember as though it were yesterday the reflection of the dancing firelight on Aunt Harriet's spectacles, and the quick, nervous jerking of her crochet-needles. I can see the expression of Father Terence's face now, as, with upturned eyes and rolling head, he sang the glorious words of ''The Messiah.'' I remember thinking how like a pig he looked, and how I wished he would not keep turning his eyes on me, when they were not searching the gloom of the vaulted roof.

Ah well! such is the perverseness of human nature, that the recollection of that scene brings with it still the faint shadow of a regret—in spite of all that happened afterwards, and in spite of the knowledge of what was then below the surface—simply because of the ridiculous fact that I was then nineteen, and am now—well, rather more.

And all the actors in the tragedy that was then brewing—Father Terence, bloated and effusive; Aunt Harriet with her tight, silky, iron-grey curls, and thin, anxious face; Norman, handsome, dashing, and *debonnaire;* and Sophie, beautiful, gentle Sophie, all these come back to me now as pleasant ghosts, in spite of all their mean, wicked plottings, and forgiven even their one crimson crime for the sake of Auld Lang Syne.

But of this crime and these plottings Aunt Harriet knew nothing, absolutely nothing, nor of course did my own sweet Sophie; let me hasten to make this clear while I may. They were both puppets, utterly unconscious puppets, in the hands of—well, the Instigator. Facts I must record, but God save me from judging any man, or from dwelling more than is necessary on sins that have been read out before this at the steps of the Judgment Throne! God have mercy on that man's soul, I say with all my heart, Protestant as I am. So now no more of this, and back to plain facts.

It is the simple truth that I was so overjoyed at what my aunt had just told me that, for decency's sake, I had to bite my lips and frown furiously into the fire to prevent breaking out into open smiles of unseemly joy. To be alone with Mrs. Beddington, and have unlimited time to ask her the thousand and one questions I was dying to have answered, to get away from the gloom and mystery of Selworth, and above all, to be within a mile and a half of Sydney Grayle's house, with no one to interfere with our walking together, or sitting in Inversnaid all day long, seemed such an impossible combination of delights that the prospect fairly dazzled me.

Aunt Harriet looked at me hard, with a sort of frightened, apologetic look.

"Of course, if you dislike the idea, Josephine, we could perhaps arrange things some other way."

"But, dear Aunt Harriet, I don't dislike it at all," I said, truthfully, and yet with only half the truth. "I should love to sleep in that dear old Manor House; and then, as you say, I am always quite happy climbing trees and poking about in the woods alone."

O deceitful Josephine! was that last word *quite* honest?

My aunt's face brightened in a wonderful way.

"You are a dear, good, adaptable child!" she said, patting my hand. "To tell the honest truth, I was a little ashamed of asking you. It seemed almost shabby. You are quite sure you don't mind?"

"Quite, dear aunt," I said, kissing her. "I shall really like it much better than stuffy old London."

Father Terence's voice rose and swelled in a pæan of thanksgiving, and Aunt Harriet, rising and shaking her stiff skirts, called out:

"Well, you young people, have you finished your game? It's half-past ten, and quite time for bed; remember we have an early breakfast to-morrow."

"Oh, I'm ready," Sophie cried, jumping up. "I'll give you the game, Norman; you're quite sure to win, you know; you always do."

Sophie's cheeks were rather redder than usual.

"Temper, temper!" Norman said, playfully.   "Little girls ought to learn to have more self-control."

"Rubbish!" said Sophie, sweeping past disdainfully.

"Good-night, mamma" (kiss).

"Good-night, Aunt Harriet" (kiss).

"Good-night, Sophie dear" (kiss, kiss).

"Good-night, Norman."

"Good-night, Father Terence."

CHAPTER XXI

AN EXODUS FROM SELWORTH

HOW am I to set about recording all the events that crowded themselves into the following day—Monday, the seventeenth day of January? It would take a book to contain all that happened during that long, endless day—all the joys, surprises, fears, horrors—horrors, fears, surprises, and joys. My day began very early, for I had something to do. I got up at daybreak and slipped out at my little glass door. To my astonishment, it was not locked. I supposed they no longer thought it worth while. I ran down, through the garden, to the keeper's house, and found there what I wanted, which was Tom Beddington.

"Tom," I panted, "do you think you could manage to take this note to 'Mr. Grayle's house this morning? It is important!"

"Of course I can, miss," he said, with a grin of intelligence. I suppose they all knew about me and Sydney. "I'll take it this very minute."

"Thank you, Tom," I said, "so much; it would be good of you."

I had nothing to give him, and I felt terribly ashamed. I had a sort of idea keepers always expected something. But I had literally not a penny in the world. It was a curious thing that though my uncle and aunt gave me everything in the world I wanted in the way of clothes, besides countless other presents, they had never given me any money at all. So I had none—literally none.

Tom, however, looked quite content, and I ran home, and got back to my room without meeting any one, and felt glad that at any rate I should see Sydney some time that day.

At ten o'clock the clarence and the omnibus stood under the portico, and I kissed and hugged them all, even poor Norman, he looked so utterly wretched, and I cried a little, and waved my hand as they disappeared round the bend towards the Greystoke Lodge. Every soul was gone, even Father Terence—no one left in the house except the housekeeper and the housemaids. Already they were busy taking down curtains and rolling up carpets in the front rooms.

I felt horribly depressed.

It was a lovely day, still, cloudless, and sunny, with a faint breeze from the east.

A stableman appeared from round the corner of the portico, and touched his cap.

"What time would you like the dog-cart round, miss?" he asked.

"Oh, soon, please!" I said. "In about half an hour."

So in half an hour my modest box was hoisted on to the back of the dog-cart, and off we went. Our way lay at first along the road to the Welham Lodge, but at the bottom of the hill we turned off to the left over the grass, and followed the green ride that eventually finds itself at the Slade Lodge. My spirits rose like magic as we bumped and jolted along the grass ride that ran so smoothly under a horse but so roughly under heels. The day was glorious, with sun and calm and clearness; and the rabbits, who knew this as well as we did, were sitting out in hundreds along the edge of the bracken, hardly deigning to move as we lumbered by, up the incline.

Sam and I were not talkative.   On such a day it is a sin to waste time and energy on mere words; thoughts are so infinitely quicker and so much more beautiful. My thoughts that morning were very beautiful, and very happy, too, but I might as well attempt to put them into words as to paint the landscape that smiled on me from either side.   Both the one and the other would be a desecration, and even in the hands of a master a mere flimsy shadow of the reality.

What Sam's thoughts were I don't know—probably beer. The only view that calls up emotions in the breast of his class is the view of homely buildings with square boards hanging over the door. However, away with satire! If we had all spent our lives hitting horses with linen rubbers, and polishing stirrups, we should perhaps be less given to the unpractical reflections which are the privilege of leisure, and which in reality do good to no one.

When we turned off the ride up the track to the Manor House, I got out and walked, the jolting was *too* awful.   Mrs. Beddington had her best cap and gown on, and looked such an old sweet, standing in the porch, that I couldn't help kissing her, then and there, at which Sam in the dog-cart stared his eyes out.

My room upstairs was so utterly delightful that when we got there I had to kiss her again.   The panelled room at Selworth was not to be compared to it.   It was very low, with a moulded ceiling and dark oak panelling right up to it.   The bed was small and white, and all the furniture of white painted wood with a green line running

round—the manufacture, I take it, of Henry Beddington, the carpenter. There was a wood fire blazing in
the old-fashioned grate, and the window was wide open
to the sun; altogether a most heavenly little room. And
the view from it was a thing beyond words! My window
looked out from the end of the house that faced the
park—the only window on that side, as I afterwards
found—and from it I could see up and down the valley
that crossed below, and beyond it again to where the
edge of Flexham Wood stretched down to the Plain.

"Isn't it glorious!" I murmured, with my head thrust
out to take stock of what lay close at hand. The garden ran round below the window, bleak now and bare of
flowers, but marvellously neat and old-fashioned and
delightful. There was an old yew arbour just opposite,
cut out of a single tree, I think, and a high box hedge,
trimmed perfectly square, dividing the garden from the
park beyond. On the right, between the garden and
the road track, was a low, green-painted, wooden fence,
and a little gate, with an iron latch, stood in the corner,
just where the hedge and the fence met. I wondered
why there was a second gate there, so very near the principal one.

"Yes," said Susan Beddington the practical, "it's
nice and airy."

We went down to the old parlour, and sat in the two
tall-backed elbow chairs, with wings for the head, that
stood one on each side of the fire. A kind of awkwardness came over us, I can't exactly say why. I noticed
for the first time, so taken up had I been with the house
and my room and everything, that the old woman looked
ill and worn. She seemed very nervous, poor old thing!
Her hands and her lips were never still, and on her face

was a look that I had never seen there before—the look,
it seemed to me, of a person in physical fear.   I noticed
that there was an open Bible on the table by her side.

Was this just nervousness on account of the arrival of
a guest, I wondered?   It seemed hardly possible, and
such a guest, too!   And yet, what else could it be?

"I have hidden the box all right," I said, nodding
across at her.

"Yes," she said, smiling a feeble, twisted little smile.

"What is it, Susan?" I said, dropping on my knees
beside her chair.   "Are you feeling ill?"

I felt horribly familiar calling her Susan, but the other
was such a mouthful.

"No, I am quite well, my dear," she said; "please
get up off the floor."

"Then what is it?" I said; "there is something—I
am sure there is!"

For a minute or two she sat silent, staring hard into
the red, dancing flames.   Then she said, turning her
spectacles full on to me:

"Has it never struck you that it was a very extraordinary thing of the Squire to send you here?"

"Well, yes," I said, "perhaps, but there was nothing
else they could do with me, you see."

She shook her head mournfully.

"Everything that they do is carefully thought out,"
she said; "nothing is left to chance."

"But what possible object could they have in sending
me here?"

"We shall find out before long, I make little doubt.
In the meanwhile, we must just watch and pray, my
dear; what more can two weak, helpless women do?"

She frightened me dreadfully by her manner.   Like a

flash, Norman's warning words came back to me, "You are in mortal danger!" What did it all mean? I had tried all Sunday evening and the following morning to get a word with Norman, and make him explain himself, but he had avoided me; there was not a doubt about it, he had avoided me purposely, so in the end I gave it up.

"Tell me what you mean?" I said, gripping the arms of the chair and leaning forward. "Do you think they would—hurt us?"

She nodded at me gloomily.

"But why? What have we done? What have *I* done that they should hurt me?"

"My dear, we are both standing dangers to them, and we should be well out of the way; and I am afraid."

"Tell me all about it," I said; "you *must!* I am sick of all this mystery. Why can"t you speak out plainly?"

"Because, till Wednesday night my lips are sealed. I have given my word, and I will not break it—not even to save my poor, worthless life. On Thursday I will tell you everything, and till then we must just trust in God and be patient."

"And—you think we are in danger?"

"I do, my dear. In very great danger."

"But do you mean to say," I cried, in horror, "that Uncle Guy would lend himself to any scheme that would—be dangerous to me—his own niece?"

"I have known three generations of De Metriers," she said, quietly, "and I heard plenty about Maurice when I was a girl, and from all accounts they change little from one generation to another. Any that stand in their way they crush with as little compunction as a horse crushes a worm. And you, my dear, stand in their way."

"How?" I asked.

"That is what you will learn on Thursday, but not before."

"But," I argued, "have I always stood in their way all these nineteen years, or has it only just begun?"

"That, my dear, I cannot tell you, and I should take it kindly if you would not press me with questions which I am not allowed to answer."

I felt rebuked, and fell back in my chair thinking. Strange as it may appear, I was not particularly frightened. I could not bring myself to believe all that she said. I thought that she was probably ill and nervous, and that her mind was full of fancies and imaginations, as old people's often are. But when I looked out at the peaceful, silent woods, smiling in the clear, bright sunshine, I felt that the idea of danger—real danger, that is—was ludicrous. Of course there must be something— I knew that—something that would be affected by my marrying Sydney; and I did thoroughly believe that they would plot and scheme day and night to prevent my doing that—in fact, they had done so already—but anything beyond that I put down as a mere fairy-tale. However, that was bad enough, and would have been quite sufficient to make me share old Susan's low spirits, if it had not been for the fact that I was going to see Sydney that very afternoon, and would be able to tell him everything, and ask his advice. With him so near— only a mile and a half off—and with no one to prevent our seeing each other as often as we liked, and for as long as we liked, it was really impossible to feel afraid; I couldn't manage it.

At half-past twelve Mrs. Beddington and I had our luncheon together, or dinner, as she called it. It was the funniest meal! She had got in a girl from the village who waited on us in the most comical fashion ever seen. I suppose the girl had cooked it, too; certainly Mrs. Beddington had not, for she had been with me. It was not an immense success from a cooking point of view. However, as was usually the case, I was hungry enough to overlook defects that would have made Aunt Harriet turn faint. Mrs. Beddington ate nothing, and I think she looked at me with astonishment. That any one could eat so much with such a load of mysterious danger hanging over her head must, I suppose, have seemed to her a thing beyond all understanding.

We talked no more about the mystery; that was dropped by common consent. Besides, there was no sense in it; she wouldn't answer questions, and the subject was not a lively one. So we talked of Sydney instead, which was much better in every way—and of what a splendid fellow he was, and what a shame it was that the Duke—the present one, that was—had turned him off.

And then, about half-past one, I went out down the track and across the valley to Inversnaid. Sydney, as I had foreseen, was not there, but it was early yet, and there was no hurry—no tiresome luncheon to be back for, or anything of that sort. So I climbed up to the top of "my branch," and sat there watching the wood away to the north, till I saw him coming through the trees. I knew he would come, of course, and I shouted out from the top of my branch with all the voice I had. Who was afraid of a little noise now?—now that he and I had the whole park to ourselves? I came tumbling down hand over hand, with more speed than elegance, I

am afraid, and plumped with a splash into the leaves at
his feet.   I had no idea of spending the afternoon in a
tree.   I wanted to take him across, and show him all my
favourite corners in the gardens, and the window of my
room, and my "bolt-hole," as I called the little glass
door at the foot of the stairs, and a host of other things.
It was too fine to potter about the wood all day.

Sydney said he didn't care a brass farthing what we
did, so long as we did it together, which was nice of him.
As we went I told him about Norman's strange speech,
and about the red box, and Mrs. Beddington's warning,
and also about her having called me Guy de Metrier's
daughter.   He looked extraordinarily grave when I had
done.

"What do you think it all means?" I asked.

"It means very clearly," he said, "that they either
want you married to Norman, or else—out of the way.
Which again probably means that in some way you stand
between them and some money."

"How can I possibly stand between them and any
money?"

"There may be some legacy that we have never heard
of, or there may be a condition attached to some will
that unless Norman marries you he loses something—
property or money—which would revert to you.   There
are often mad conditions of that sort in a will."

"But whose will?"

"I don't know; how can one tell?   But there must
be something of that sort; it is the only possible explanation."

"And then, what did she mean by calling me Guy de
Metrier's daughter—Mrs. Beddington, I mean?"

"Are you quite sure she did? As far as I can make
out, she only said she would like to help Guy de Metrier's
daughter; she didn't say it was you."

"No, but who else could she mean?"

"And, then, if you were Guy de Metrier's daughter,
they could not possibly want you to marry Norman."

"Perhaps Norman isn't his son!"

Sydney shook his head.

"There's not the slightest use in bothering about that
part of it," he said; "apparently we shall know all about
it on Thursday, whatever it is. What does trouble me
is the other part."

"What?"

"Why all these warnings, or threats, or whatever they
are, and this vague suggestion of danger that is hanging about? I don't like it. I wish I could come and
stay at the Manor House, too, and keep guard over
you!"

"Oh, do!" I said; "that would be splendid. I
shouldn't be afraid of anything with you near."

"I'm afraid it wouldn't do," he said, shaking his
head.

"Why not?"

"Well, what Lady Harriet would call *les convenances*,
you know."

"Oh, bother *les convenances!* What nonsense it is!
Do come, Sydney!"

"I'll tell you what I will do," he said. "I've got a
sister in London I could get to come and stay with me,
and then you could come to my house. You would be
safe enough there, I'll undertake."

"That would be nice!" I said, feeling a little doubtful about the sister.

We were almost across the Plain by now, and straight opposite the front of the house. It seemed *too* extraordinary that Sydney and I should be walking together right in front of the windows, and in broad daylight—so extraordinary, in fact, that I felt almost distrustful of the many windows, blinded and shuttered as they were. Those windows were so associated in my mind with danger. It had become such a second nature with me to dodge them, and hide away along the hollows towards the lake, that this open flaunting about with the forbidden Sydney, in full sight of them, made me feel horribly guilty and wicked. I think I half expected them to burst open, like the ports of a ship, and wither us with hidden lightnings.

We were across the road now, and opposite the belt of chestnuts and beeches that run between the house and the stables—the same belt of trees that fringed the balustrade outside my window. I wanted to show Sydney my window, and the place where I dropped down out of the garden, and the other place, near the corner, where the gutter-pipe helped me to climb up again. The ground under the trees was six feet below the level of the garden, so that one couldn't see in without first climbing up.

I scrambled up first, and then turned round to watch Sydney and see how he did it; and then we both sidled along the balustrade towards the place behind the holly bush where I generally got over. I was just putting up my foot to vault over, when I felt Sydney tug me by the sleeve.

"Keep down!" he whispered.

I was all too used to hiding and dodging, and dropped down like a hare. We crouched side by side, with our eyes just above the parapet, and then I saw a sight that for the first time during all these days sent a thrill of genuine terror creeping down my spine.

Father Terence and Norman were talking just outside my little glass door! Father Terence and Norman!—both of whom I had seen start for London that very morning! What did it mean? I could hardly believe my eyes.

I turned round and looked at Sydney. His face had a look on it I had never seen there before. As a rule, his face wore a careless, laughing expression, as that of a man who finds it hard to take things seriously. But now it looked grim and stern, even to fierceness; his brows were bent and his teeth forced tightly together.

"Hush!" he said; "listen!"

Father Terence was talking earnestly—almost angrily, in fact. He stood in the doorway, and was emphasizing his words by banging one hand into the other. His manner was that of a masterful man issuing orders. Norman stood about six feet off on the path, with his hands deep in his pockets; he was kicking the gravel with his toe, and now and then I saw him shrug his shoulders. He was looking down sulkily, and his whole figure was limp.

It was quite clear they were having a disagreement, but what it was about, and what they were saying, we could not hear; the leaves rustled so in our ears. Father Terence seemed to be using his powers of persuasion without effect, for Norman kept shaking his head with an appearance of some decision. Suddenly he lifted his head, and spoke rapidly for some minutes, while the priest stood and glowered at him heavily. In the end, with a sharp nod of the head, he spun on his heel and strode away. Then at last we heard Father Terence's words, for he lifted his great voice, and bellowed after him:

"So, you poor calf-headed dolt, you would sacrifice your faith and your family, your Church and your kin, for the sake of a smooth, silly baby-face! Bah! you fairly sicken me!"

He stood for an instant scowling after Norman's retreating figure, and then turned into the house, and slammed the door.

CHAPTER XXII

MRS. BEDDINGTON SPEAKS

SYDNEY and I, without a word, dropped down again among the leaves, and crept out into the open. Sydney was very white, and I was trembling like a leaf. In dead, unbroken silence we strode best pace across the Plain—thinking. They were not pleasant thoughts; at least I can answer for my own, and judging from Sydney's face, his were little better. I think it was the uncertainty—the underhand secrecy of the whole thing, that frightened me so. A man—and even a woman—can face an open danger bravely enough so long as they can see it, but a terror that creeps in the dark is a horrible thing for any one. I know this sight of Father Terence frightened me more than all the vague warnings I had had from Norman and Mrs. Beddington—*far* more. I felt completely stunned and bewildered.

We must have walked half-way across the Plain before either of us spoke. Then I said:

"What on earth does it mean, Sydney? I *saw* them drive off to the station this morning."

"I don't know," he said; "some infernal scheming and plotting, you may bet your life. But what does it matter? I don't know why we should bother ourselves about them after all. To-morrow I'll telegraph to my sister to come down, and we'll have you out of this, and into my house; and then they may plot away till they're black in the face for all we shall care. Eh, Joe?"

He spoke brightly and cheerfully, but I was not in the least taken in. 'I saw perfectly well that he was just as frightened as I was myself. His hand kept gripping his stick till the knuckles stood out quite white and hard, and he slashed viciously at the bents and ferns.

"Are you coming back to have some tea?" I said. "*Do!* Mrs. Beddington wants to see you, I know."

"Yes, I'll come," he said, shortly.

Down in the bottom we saw Henry Beddington in front of us limping up to the Manor House, with a carpenter's bag over his shoulder. He must have gone round by the green ride, along the hollow, or we should have seen him before. I think Uncle Guy objected to any one walking across the Plain—except, of course, the family and visitors—they could be seen so plainly from the windows.

"Is *he* all right?" Sydney asked, nodding at him.

"What, Henry Beddington? Good gracious, Sydney, of course he is; all the Beddingtons are all right. What a question to ask!"

"And you are quite sure of your friend, the old lady?"

"Absolutely sure—as sure as I am of myself."

"H'm! She has not got a very clean record, you know."

"Why, what is there against her?"

"Oh, there are plenty of stories about her; but, of course, they are all very old ones, and I daresay not true."

"Tell me what they are; I have never heard of them."

"Well, if you have never heard of them, don't ask. Take her as she is, and never mind about what she was."

"Now *you* are getting mysterious," I said. "Goodness gracious! there's no end to it!"

"I don't think there's much mystery about me," he said, laughing. "I am a very plain, commonplace sort of person."

"But why don't you *tell* me?" I cried, almost angrily. "Why be so secret?"

"Because there's no good in raking up old scandals. I am sorry I said anything about it. Come, little girl, let's go in and have some tea, and not bother about what happened a thousand years ago."

It was quite dusk when we got in, and the sitting-room looked wonderfully bright and cheerful. Mrs. Beddington was sitting by the fire with her back towards the door.

"Susan," I said, "I have brought you a visitor."

'Ah!" she said, without turning round, "you've brought him, have you? Well, I'm glad."

She dragged herself up out of the chair, and stood facing us.

"Mr. Grayle," she said, "you have got a great treasure here. Mind you take care of her."

"I have not got her yet," he said, laughing, "and as far as I can make out, people don't mean that I shall."

"Bah!" she said, contemptuously, "I don't know what you young men are made of nowadays. Fifty years ago if a lad was in love with a winsome maid, and she with him, he married her first, and thought about the trouble afterwards—and that in spite of father, mother, uncle, or priest."

"What do you mean?" he said, doubtfully.

"What do I mean? Why, that you should take and marry her to-morrow. What's to hinder you?"

There was a long silence. Old Susan fixed her piercing eyes on Sydney, Sydney looked at me, and I looked at the hearthrug.

"It is very unusual," he said at length.

"Unusual!" she echoed; "you will find more unusual things than that happen if you are not quick. Goodness me! in my day lovers didn't bother about trifles of that kind."

"Possibly not," he said, a little coldly. "It might have been better if they had, sometimes. You see, Mrs. Beddington, I am not the only person to be considered; and I tell you plainly that I would sooner not marry this young lady at all than marry her in a way that would get her talked about."

"Ah, well!" said Mrs. Beddington, "every one to their own fashion of wooing. But, for my own part, give me the man who marries first and thinks about it afterwards."

"Or who doesn't marry at all?" suggested Sydney.

The old woman laughed shrilly.

"Sydney Grayle," she said, "I am an old woman, and I am not going to quarrel with you; besides, I am your friend in this business, not so much for your sake, of course, as for Miss Josephine's, but still your friend because of her."

Sydney bowed.

"And a very valuable friend, too, I am sure," he said.

"You may well say that, Sydney Grayle," the old woman said, nodding; "and if you think what you say, you will act upon my advice, like a sensible lad, and marry the girl while you can. I know what I'm talking about, mind you."

"Why is there such a great hurry?" Sydney asked, smiling. I think Mrs. Beddington amused him.

'O good lack!   Good lack!'' she cried.   "Was there
ever such a poor, wishy-washy lover as this?   It was the
girls used to ask that question, not the men.   Sydney
Grayle, I think nothing of you; and with a bride fit for a
prince waiting for you, too!   Well, well, the girls
always are a world too good for the men they throw
themselves away upon.''

She turned away with uplifted hands and a shrug of
her thin shoulders, and Sydney and I both laughed outright.   She was so serious over it.

"What do you think we saw at Selworth this afternoon?'' I said, wishing to change the conversation.

She looked at me enquiringly.

"How should I know?'' she said, sharply.   "I know
what *I* should have seen if I had been there—a poor
noodle of a young man mooning about with his lass.''

"Well, what *we* saw,'' I said, "was Father Terence
and Norman in the garden.''

Her hand went up and caught the edge of the chimney-piece, and her face turned quite slowly to a dead
white.   She staggered along the front of the fire, and
with a sigh sank back into her chair, staring fixedly
before her at the wall.

"Norman   and   Father   Boyle?''   she   said.   "No
others?''

"No, we saw no one else.''

"Ah!'' she said, dully.   Then, after a little: "You
or me, my dear, you or me—one or the other, and very
soon now.''

Sydney and I glanced at each other.

"What do you mean, Mrs. Beddington?'' he asked,
in a clear, loud voice.   "Do you attach any particular—
importance to these two having come back?''

She seemed not to hear him. In a dazed kind of way she went on muttering to herself:

"God help us all! God have mercy on me, a miserable sinner! I thought the Lord might have turned the Squire's heart—not the priest's, of course, but the Squire's—but it was not to be."

It was ghastly to hear her; she spoke like a woman walking in her sleep, in a dull monotone, and with glazed eyes.

"So the end has come," she went on, "the end has come at last!"

"What do you mean, Susan?" I cried, roughly, for I was dreadfully frightened. "What are you talking about? What end? The end of what?"

I caught her by the shoulder, and shook her, but she took no notice. She just kept rocking backwards and forwards, muttering vague prayers and lamentations.

"Stay here a minute," I said to Sydney. "I will be back directly."

I ran into the dining-room, where I knew there was a bottle of brandy standing in the cupboard. Pouring out half a tumbler, I hurried back and placed it in her hand.

"Drink it," I said; "it will do you good."

She held it for a minute or two, staring at it vacantly; then she put it to her lips and drained it to the last drop. The effect was magical. A faint colour sprang to her cheeks, her eye became human once more, and she glanced round at us nervously.

"What have I been saying?" she asked.

"Nothing, Mrs. Beddington," Sydney answered. "I wish you had."

"Well, I will say something now," she said. "Come here, both of you."

We went forward and stood before her, and I slipped
my hand into Sydney's. She stared at us for an age
through her spectacles before she spoke. Then she said,
slowly:

"Sydney Grayle, the air is full of danger for this little
maid who has given you her heart. Take her away and
marry her—at once—to-morrow—this very evening, if
you can. Do you hear me? This is no time for fooling
about over fashions and customs, and what people will
say, and what people will not say. It is life or death, I
tell you—life or death. Marry her to-morrow, I say, and
let all the world know you have married her, and you
may save her yet. But leave her here, and she is lost!"

"Lost!" he said. "What do you mean by 'lost'?"

"I mean what I say," she cried. "And unless you
are a fool, you will do what I tell you, and waste no time
asking foolish questions."

"What do *you* say, Joe?" Sydney asked, turning to
me. I said nothing, but pressed his hand.

"Very well," he said, stoutly; "I will do it. I will
be round here by eleven o'clock to-morrow morning,
and we will drive straight off to Ashby Church and be
married. And in the meanwhile, what of to-night?"

"To-night we are in the Lord's hands," Mrs. Beddington answered, resignedly.

"What is it you are afraid of?" Sydney asked with
some impatience. "Can't you tell us right out?"

"No, I cannot, Mr. Grayle, and what is more I will
not. I have warned you, and I can do no more. Get
her away, and marry her, and she will be safe enough."

"Yes, she will be safe enough with me," Sydney
answered. "But what about yourself, Mrs. Beddington?"

"I am an old woman," she said, "and my time is short in any case. They will kill me."

"Kill you!" we exclaimed together.

"Yes," she said, calmly, "they will kill me—kill me to silence my tongue. If I spoke out I could save my life, but I will not, and the Squire knows that—not at least before Thursday. He knows that I will die before I will break my word, and die I will. I am a great sinner—God knows! an awful sinner—but I will not go before the Judgment Throne with perjury on my lips to spin out a year or two more of my useless old life. So never mind about me," she added, flourishing her hands excitedly in the air; "see to yourselves, and remember the red box, for whatever does come will come between this and Thursday."

"Does your son sleep here?" Sydney asked.

"Yes, Henry sleeps here."

"Has he a gun?"

"Oh, yes, he has a gun. But what is the use of that?"

"It may be of every use. Make him sleep here on the sofa, with the gun loaded by his side."

"Well, for Miss Josephine's sake, I will, just for to-night. But you may be sure that one poor man and a gun are not much use against the wiles of the Devil."

"Never mind; you make him do it. And now I must be off. I must go and make arrangements for our marriage to-morrow; I hardly like to call it a wedding. Will you come to the gate with me, Joe?"

He shook hands cordially, and with a great show of cheerfulness, with Mrs. Beddington, and then we went out together into the still, frosty evening. It was quite dark now, with a clear starlit sky, and a faint light away to the East that told that the moon would be up before many hours.

"Joe," he said, "which is your room?"

I took him round, and pointed up to my window staring with its single eye out of the blank wall.

"Do you sleep with it shut?"

"No, open—always."

"Well, shut it to-night, and bolt it, and lock your door.   Do you promise?"

-   "It will be so stuffy, Sydney," I said.

"Never mind that for one night; do it."

"All right," I said, "but I think it's nonsense."

"Little girl," he said, taking me by the shoulders, "it is horrible having to leave you like this.   I would give the world to be able to stay with you, and guard you.   But it is only for one night, and I shall not be far off, you may be sure of that.   If I sleep at all, it will be with one eye open."

"Like a dear old watch-dog," I said.

"Yes, like a watch-dog.   And now, good-bye, little Joe, and God bless and guard you!"

He hugged me so tight that I almost screamed; then, without another word, he turned away and strode down the track.   In about a minute he came running back.

"Joe," he whispered, "before you go to bed put your hand on the ledge outside the sitting-room window. You will find a present for you there.   Good-bye!"

I stood as still as stone till the last sound of his footsteps had died away, and then slowly went back into the house.   Mrs. Beddington was sitting by the fire staring at an open Bible on her knee, and without a word I dropped into the chair opposite, and sat there thinking.

Strange, mixed thoughts they were that came crowding into my brain—thoughts principally of Sydney, and of his dear, strong face and cheery voice; but also thoughts of Chelmsford, and of the kind old aunts that the name brought back to me, and of what they would think of this helter-skelter marriage; and lastly, thoughts of Selworth, and of the silent, creeping danger that seemed to be hanging over our heads.

Our supper that night was not a cheerful one. We spoke little and ate less. Not a word passed our lips on the subject that must have been in both our minds. What was the good of it? There was nothing to be gained, and it only depressed one. Only, when we rose to go to bed, old Susan took me by the hand and said, gravely:

"Miss Josephine, I wonder whether you will ever forgive me for all the trouble I have brought upon you. I have done you a terrible wrong, as you will find out some day, and I am suffering for it now—suffering as I deserve to suffer. But remember this, my dear, that the greatest happiness sometimes springs out of troubles of this kind; and when you have found that happiness—as God willing! you will find it—perhaps you will think less hardly of old Susan and her many sins."

There were tears in her poor old eyes, and I took and kissed her as I might my own mother.

"Whatever happens," I said, "I will always think of you as the dearest, kindest old thing that ever lived."

She went labouring up the narrow wooden stairs, and I slipped out of the door into the night, to see if Sydney had been back and left his present for me. I found it—on the window-ledge where he said he would put it. It was a revolver, very small and brightly polished, and

I took it in my hand, and crept back into the house. What a wedding present, I thought!

I dragged myself miserably upstairs, and laid the thing on the table. I had no notion of how to use it, but had an idea that if I touched the trigger it would go off. Down on the ground floor I heard Henry Bedding-ton bolting and barring the doors and shutters, and stumping about in the room below. I knew he was mak-ing preparations for his night upon the sofa. I remem-ber hoping that his gun wouldn't go off and shoot me through the ceiling; and then I laughed—actually laughed! It seemed so absurd—a carpenter and a girl in her teens sleeping with loaded guns and revolvers by their sides. If they shot anything, it would probably be each other.

I sat down by the window and looked out. Good-ness! what a long day it had been! The twinkling stars blinked peacefully down from a cloudless sky, and away to the left the rising moon threw a faint silver light over the tops of the dense, silent woods. In an hour, I thought, the place would be as light as day. I wished they had a dog; a dog would have made me feel quite safe; it was ridiculous not to have a dog in a house like this. The grandfather clock at the foot of the stairs struck eleven; time I was in bed and asleep, I thought. I bolted the window, and locked the door as I had prom-ised Sydney, and threw myself on my bed, clothes and all. Next moment I jumped up and blew out the can-dle; it was impossible to sleep with a candle blazing in one's eyes. There was a red patchwork eider-down quilt on the bed, and I drew this up to my chin, and kicking off my shoes, curled myself up like a whiting. I think I fell asleep at once.

CHAPTER XXIII

THE END OF THE OLD MANOR HOUSE

WHEN I woke up, the moon was showing plainly through the blind and the white dimity curtains that covered the blind. I wondered what o'clock it was, and why I was suddenly so wide awake. And then, next moment, while I was in the very act of wondering, I knew. For outside my window 1 heard quite plainly a scraping, grating noise, like the noise of stones rubbing together. My heart gave one huge thump, and then stood stock still. So it had come, I thought, this creeping horror—it had come at last! I thought of the sensation it would make in the papers: "Horrible murder at the old Manor House, Selworth! Young lady found with her throat cut! Supposed clue! Activity of the police!"

I wondered if they would give any description of me, and how they would describe me if they did. I thought of Sydney, in deep black, with a sad, white face, putting flowers on my grave. That was rather a nice thought, and I dwelt on it. I wondered where they would bury me—Ashby, perhaps—I hoped it would be Ashby—it would be so near Sydney. But then Sydney was leaving; he was going to America. He would probably marry some one else, and forget all about me. And perhaps in twenty or thirty or forty years he would come back, very grey and tired, and would go and stand over

my grave, and remember all about the old days at Selworth, and perhaps put a few primroses or violets on the
green mound with the plain headstone.   It would be
quite green then, and grown over, and the stone would
be stained grey and brown and yellow, and the letters
on it would be quite indistinct.   He would have to stoop
down to read them, and perhaps to wipe his glasses.

JOSEPHINE DE METRIER
AGED 19 YEARS
MURDERED ON THE 17TH JANUARY 1858 AT
THE OLD MANOR HOUSE, SELWORTH

Did they put it on the tombstone when people were
murdered?   I was not quite sure.

What had happened to that noise outside?   It had
stopped.   Perhaps it was nothing—Henry Beddington
going round to see that all was clear, perhaps.   His
mother must have told him to be on the look-out.   What
a fool I was!   Frightened of everything and nothing, and
imagining all these idiotic things!

How cold it was!   My feet were like ice; that was
why I couldn't sleep, of course.   I drew my feet up, and
got inside the bed, pulling up the clothes to my chin.   I
might just as well be warm, even if they were going to
murder me.

Ah! that was better.

My eyes grew heavy, and I felt very comfortable, and
forgot all about the noises of the night.   At last I even
began to think that I had not heard them—that I had
dreamt them—or imagined them, and that in any case it
was no use bothering about it.   I had so often been
frightened by noises before in the night, and they had
always turned out to be nothing.   How I should laugh

over the whole thing in the morning! And how Sydney would laugh when I told him! Dear old Sydney!

I have no idea how long I slept—it may have been one hour, or two, or three—I had no means of judging. I woke quite suddenly, after a host of horrid dreams, and for a time the sounds of life and the thoughts of sleep were still mixed up in a hopeless jumble. I heard sounds, and distinct sounds, but attached no particular meaning to them. Then, at last, in an instant as it were, I was wide awake, and sitting up in bed with every sense at its full stretch. What had happened? The room was full of smoke, and below me was a dull, cease-less roar. The heat, too, was intense. Fire! fire! fire!

I leapt out of bed, and made a dash at my shoes. Thank goodness! I had my clothes on! I laced them up with feverish, clumsy fingers. There was plenty of light—the light of a full moon shining through the win-dow, and mingling with it, a red, lurid glow that seemed to fill the whole atmosphere. Heavens! what a horrid crackling! and what a sickening heat! The floor seemed to be curling up under my feet. Susan! I thought—poor old Susan! Where was she? Was she awake? Had she escaped? Or was she in her room, prisoned and helpless? At any cost she must be saved!

I rushed to the door, unlocked it, and flung it open. Next instant I stumbled back appalled. A huge fountain of flame was spouting up the staircase, filling it from side to side as water fills a pipe—red, angry, murderous flame that licked and lapped and darted with long, fierce tongues down the short little passage that ran to my room. I was doomed, imprisoned — hopelessly, horribly imprisoned. To have advanced six feet would have been certain and instant death.

"Susan!" I screamed, "Susan! Fire! fire! fire!"

Was it possible she was still sleeping? Or had Henry Beddington rescued her at the beginning? A long, vicious flame shot out of the red, glowing mass to within a foot of my face. I staggered back into my room, shrieking, with my hands over my eyes; I thought I was blinded.

The window! I thought; I must throw myself out; better any number of broken limbs than this ghastly, grilling death. I coughed and choked and spluttered as I plunged with outstretched hands at the curtains, and tore them apart. Merciful heavens! how the smoke had thickened in the last minute! The soles of my shoes were hot, too—burning my feet. I dived under the blind and flung open the window. It opened on a hinge, like my window at Selworth, and the thing was done in a second.

The smoke dashed out in a thick black column that absolutely blinded me for a time. I stretched out my hands, and groped blindly before me in the dark—groped for air and breath and coolness—and as I groped, my hands struck against something that projected above the window-ledge. I opened my agonised eyes, and peered down through the murk. It was a ladder! Thank God! a ladder!

In one instant I was on the window-ledge, and astride it. I had learnt the trick years before in Tom Jeffery's yard at Chelmsford. I hooked my legs round the uprights, and slid—slid without any attempt at check— just letting myself go. At the bottom I came with tremendous force against something heavy and soft. I heard a hideous oath in a gruff man's voice, and the next moment found myself standing on my feet. It was in the little yew-clipped arbour that faced my window; the end of the ladder had been run right into it, and now partly filled the entrance. On the ground I saw—as well as my smarting, blinded eyes could see—the struggling figure of a man. I thought it must be Henry Beddington, and as I stooped down to make sure, a hand came up and clutched me roughly by the skirt.

"Curse you! you cat-witted trull!" said the same voice, "you've 'most bruk my back with your sliding tricks! Damned if I wouldn't have let you burn, for my part. Here, none of that! You've got to come along of me, and come quietly, too. Ah, would you? you little she-devil! Hi! Pete, hurry up here and collar this baggage of yours, if you don't want her knived. I ain't a-goin' to be clawed and scratched for no one."

As may be gathered from this speech, I was engaged in a fierce struggle with the man I had overturned in my descent. He had clutched my skirt as he lay on the ground, and gradually struggling to his feet, was trying to increase his hold, while I dragged myself away from him with all my might. I was very strong for a girl, and mercifully the foot of the ladder stretched between us, right to the back of the arbour, and he had to lean across this to keep his hold of me. The man was on his feet now, and in the red glow from the burning house I recognised, with a shudder, the elder of the Morrises—the father, in fact, of the two others. He was lame, I thought—thank Heaven! he was lame! If I could once get away he would never catch me. The man knew that well enough, I fancy; his evil face scowled darkly at me across the ladder. I was tugging at my dress in a frenzy, and hammering at his hand with my own.

"Softly, my lamb, softly!" he said, with a vicious grin; "that's fine thanks to give a cove for savin' you from frizzling, blessed if it ain't!"

He made an effort to skip across the ladder and get my side, but by the mercy of Providence his foot caught, and he fell full length on the gravel. With one tremendous tug I wrenched myself free, and dashed at the little gate in the corner. I heard a torrent of horrible oaths from the arbour, and next moment the man yelling for Pete to come and catch me; then more oaths—in Pete's voice this time—and then the clang of the little gate that told me he was on my track; and then for a time I heard nothing more but my own panting and the thud of my feet as I flew down the incline.

I was a good runner, and had little doubt that for a short distance I could hold my own with Pete or any other heavy-booted clod; but that I should not last very long I knew well. I was three parts exhausted by my struggle with the elder Morris, and I think the smoke and heat in the house had got into my lungs, and sapped my strength—perhaps it was the fright, or one thing on the top of the other, but anyhow, whatever it was, I felt faint and weak and exhausted before I had reached the foot of the hill. My breath came in short, quick sobs, and my legs seemed to bend under me. The bottom of the hollow was in darkness, for the moon was very low by now, and I felt infinitely thankful that it was so, for there was no shelter there except from knee-deep bracken. And I had a long way to go yet! Merciful God, give me strength to get as far as Inversnaid! If I once got there, with sufficient start to let me get up, I knew I should be safe. I pressed up the hill, with elbows squared and head thrown back, and a pain like a knife in my tired heart—up and up, tripping and stumbling over the bracken, and dragging my feet along at a pace that was hardly better than a walk, but still always getting nearer and nearer.

I was among the beech-trees now, and knew I must be out of sight of any one pursuing. Had he seen the way I went, this horrible Pete? What were they going to do to me? Kill me? Torture me?

Through the naked branches ahead I could see the moonbeams glancing on a huge, dark, symmetrical mass that loomed up into the sky. It was Inversnaid! Ah, if only I had not been seen! If only my heart would hold out till I was up!

I grabbed at the drawbridge and dragged myself up. Tired as I was, exhausted, *dead* with terror and fatigue, I believe I did the ascent quicker than I had ever done it before. I tore my hands, I scratched my face, I lost a shoe that flopped down into the leaves below, but I got up, over the base of Sydney's branch, and down into the sheltering hollow beyond.

I dropped on the soft earthen floor, and lay back against a branch with my head on Arthur's Seat. I closed my eyes and offered up silent thanksgiving to Heaven. Was I safe, though? Was it not possible that they might have seen me? My own panting had been so loud that it would have drowned any footsteps pursuing me, however close they might have been. I raised my head and listened. There was not a sound. An owl hooted somewhere away towards Flexham Wood, and from the east there came a dull, roaring sound that I knew must be the fire at the poor old Manor House; but close at

hand there was nothing but intense stillness—the stillness of a frosty winter's night.

Oh, for Sydney! I thought. If only I could get my
strength again, I would crawl as far as Elmhurst and
hammer at the door until he let me in. It was dreadful
out here in the wood, so lonely and silent, and so cold,
too! A minute before I had been burning hot, but now
I was cold—cold as ice. I wished I had some matches
with me; I would have lit a fire. There was a host of
fuel at hand, collected by Sydney and me some time back,
and piled beside the fireplace for future use.

Hark! what was that? A stick cracked in the distance—no such very great distance, either, and again,
closer at hand this time. O Heaven above! if it were
they—those awful Morrises! I could hear footsteps now,
and voices—cautious, whispering voices, and the crunching of dead leaves under heavy feet.

They were coming nearer, there was no question
about it now—coming straight for where I lay. It *must*
be the Morrises—who else could it be? They must
have seen me, after all.

I sat up and listened. My breathing was quieter
now, and I was not so faint.

"I tell you, I seed her legging it straight for the
wood 'ere," said a voice. "I'll bet she ain't a mile
away now."

"A mile away! yer blasted fool!" said another. "'Ow
in 'ell are we to find her fifty yards away on a night like
this?"

It was old Morris. I recognised his horrible, growling, brutal voice. And the other must be Pete. I leant
my head against the tree and prayed.

"A blooming fine runner you are, to be beat by a

girl! Gar! I'd as soon 'ave a couple of women with me
on a job as you and the old 'un, blessed if I wouldn't!"

"You shut your jaw, Mike; I'll run you for a pot any
bloody when!"

Mike!—so there were three of them! Good Lord
deliver me!

"It's all along of Pete, and this blasted job of 'is and
Norman's," said the old man. "If it 'adn't been for
that, the pair of 'em would have been dead as herrings
by now, and fifty blooming pound in our pockets."

"Well, and ain't we a-going to make fifty more over
my job, yer silly old beggar? What are yer growling at?"

"A darned sight more likely lose the 'ole lot. You
bet the governor won't pay if the gal gets loose, not he.
'Both of 'em snug in kingdom come, and there's fifty
blooming sovereigns in your pocket, Joe Morris,' says
he."

" 'And you bring the gal safe to Selworth, and there's
another cool fifty from me,' says Norman."

"And now we ain't done either the one or the other,
thanks to you! You been and jolly well botched the
'ole show, that's what you 'ave."

"Rubbish!" said Pete, "she ain't far off. Hiding in
one of these 'ere trees as like as not—maybe in this very
blooming tree what we're standing under."

I saw the rays of a lantern shoot here and there
among the branches.

"Thick as 'ell up there. Might be twenty of 'em up
there for all we could see. I've a blamed good mind to
get up and 'ave a squint round."

"Rot!" said old Morris. "You've botched the job
for us, and we may as well go 'ome before we're nabbed.
There'll be plenty about the place before long."

"And what's to hinder us from coming with the others to see what the fire's about, eh, you old silly? Nobody'll nab us for 'elping to put the bloody flames out, will they?"

"'Ere, what's this?" said the third voice, that I took to be Mike's. "Gor blimme! if it ain't a shoe—and a gal's shoe, too, by God! Well, if so be as this is your gal's shoe, Pete, she bain't far away, you may bet your life on that."

"'Ere, I'm a-going up," said Pete, with the ring of a sudden energy in his voice. "It's worth a bit of climbing to nab this bird. Fifty pound don't tumble down from the sky every day of the week."

I heard the cracking and creaking of the branches as he began hauling himself up, and with a sickening fear in my heart, I jumped up and rushed past the fireplace to the foot of "my branch." At the same moment, the light of the dark lantern shot right across me, and I knew that I was discovered.

"By God! we've got her!" cried the old man in wild excitement. "Hurry up, Pete, the sooner we finish with this job the better. Lord! what a bit of luck!"

I heard no more at the time, for faster than I had ever climbed in my life, I clambered up the branch—my own particular branch of days gone by. I knew every turn and twist and off-shoot of that branch. I knew where to put each foot and hand so as to make the best use of the shape Nature had given it. Scores of times I had gone up that branch for no other reason in the world than a pure love of climbing; but never, in all the efforts of imagination that had been brought to bear on that particular tree, had it entered into my head that a day would come when I should actually fly up it for my very life.

The rays of the lantern followed me at every step, and foul, coarse jokes were bandied about from one to the other. They were in great good spirits now, these horrible wretches! I shut my ears to them, and struggled on, with teeth clenched, and the terror of desperation hammering at my heart. Pete was on my branch now; I could hear the creaking of the twigs plainly. But I never looked down. I fixed my eyes on the highest point that experience had taught me could be reached, and made for it desperately. I had no particular plan in my head, only a fixed determination that I would fling myself off the tree sooner than be taken. But, then, there were two more of them below! Oh! it was awful!

I reached the end of the branch, where it was no bigger than a man's arm, and sat astride it, facing the way I had come. Pete was coming up like a monkey, twenty feet below. I looked round desperately for some loophole of escape. There was none. The other branches ended far away to right and left. Below me was nothing but black, impenetrable darkness. The terror was awful, and before I knew what I was doing, I had sent three piercing shrieks out on the still night air. A chorus of the vilest oaths came up from below.

"By God! missy," said Pete, between his quick short gasps for breath, "if you squeak like that again, I'll stick you like a pig, by God, I will!"

He pulled out a long clasp-knife, and opening it, held it between his teeth, and crept up nearer and nearer. I could see his horrid eyes fixed on me like a cat's. From below muttered cheers of encouragement came hoarsely through the branches.

"Chuck her down, Pete, if she won't come quietly.

We'll get the governor's fifty that way, anyhow; and Norman's can go to the devil. Besides, she knows too much now, damned if she don't."

"Now, missy, are you coming quietly?" said Pete, with the knife still between his teeth. He was astride the branch now, and was dragging himself forward inch by inch. The branch swayed and bent fearfully under the double weight, for we were near the extreme end of it, and I had to tuck my heels close under me to keep my balance. There was nothing to hold on to. I looked round wildly for some weapon of defence, but there was none—nothing but thin twigs and darkness. Then a thought came into my head—a mad, desperate thought. I slipped down my hand, and pulled off my remaining shoe, holding it by the toe. Pete came nearer and nearer, with a devilish grin upon his evil face. We were facing each other now, each astride the branch, and not more than three feet apart.

Suddenly he drew the knife from his teeth and flourished it within an inch of my face.

"Gurrr!" he yelled, mouthing at me hideously, like a maniac.

And then a very dreadful thing happened. I think I was half mad with terror. No words that ever were written could give an idea of the *awfulness* of the position up there, perched as I was on a dancing, swaying little branch, with black darkness below, and facing me as villainous a looking ruffian as the world could produce, with under jaw thrust out, murder gleaming from his eyes, and a long, glistening knife in his hand. The wonder is I didn't turn into a driveling idiot on the spot.

Well, what happened was this. It was when he flourished the knife at me that I did it—and only from sheer, stupefying terror. I hit at him with all my might with the shoe, and the heel struck him fair and square to the side of the eye, and toppled him over like a ninepin.

It was all done in a second, and long before I could realise what had happened I heard him go crash, crash, crashing through the branches, and then hit the ground with a sickening thud right below me. I all but fell myself. The effort of reaching out overbalanced me, and the leap of the branch as he fell from it all but shot me after him, but I managed to hold on somehow, with feet and hands, and chin and elbows; and I lay along it trembling in every limb, and peering down into the darkness to catch the whispers of the men below. God grant I hadn't killed him. What an awful thought!

I could see the light of the lantern playing on to a white, upturned face, and the other two crouching over the fallen man and whispering excitedly.

"Is he hurt?" I called out, craning my head forward.

"Hurt! yer——! Not so hurt as you'll be before we've done with you! You wait a minute!"

I began slowly coming down the branch. I felt I simply *must* see how the poor fellow was, even if the others killed me. Perhaps I could help him in some way—bandage him up, or set a bone perhaps, if one was broken. I suppose they saw or heard me, for old Morris called out:

"You keep your eye on her, Mike; she'll slip us if we don't mind. What's that? Listen!"

I saw them both raise their heads and stare into the trees, and the next moment the lantern was turned off, and everything was in darkness. What was it? I listened, too, and heard distinctly the sound of feet running, as it seemed, over the crackling leaves. The men below lay in perfect silence; not a sound broke the stillness except the footsteps coming nearer and nearer.

Suddenly they too stopped. For at least a minute the whole wood was still as death. Then a loud, clear voice called out:

"Joe, Joe!"

It was Sydney.

"Here!" I cried; "Sydney, help, help!"

I heard muttered oaths below, and the lantern once more flashed searchingly among the tree trunks.

"Take care! they have knives!" I called out; "they will kill you!"

"Sooner me than you," he answered. "Never mind their dirty knives; I have something better than that here."

I saw him striding towards us through the trees, with the lantern turned full upon his face. He looked very stern and very splendid, I thought, and he had a thick stick in his right hand. I knew how the light must blind him, and I called out again.

"Take care, Sydney; there are two of them."

He made no answer, but I saw him grip his stick, and give a sort of loose hitch to his shoulders.

And then, when he was about six yards off, they rushed at him, both at once. The lantern rested on the ground and lit up the whole scene plainly enough. Sydney jumped back a yard or two, and then I saw the stick come round like lightning, and Mike went head over heels into the leaves. At the same moment I screamed out aloud, for old Morris's knife rose in the air, and seemed to bury itself in Sydney's side. Down the branch I went, scrambling, slithering, sliding, till I reached the platform, and from there swung myself down

into the leaves by the first branch that came to hand.
I fell all in a heap on my face, but I was up in a moment,
and running forward to where I had last seen Sydney.

When I got there he was kneeling on old Morris's
chest, with a dripping knife in his hand. Mike lay
upon his face a few yards off, groaning.

"Are you hurt, Sydney?" I gasped.

"No, no, little girl; I'm all right. Are *you?*"

"Yes, yes, but I saw him stab you."

"Oh, that was nothing. He didn't quite bring it off.
Now, Joe, do you think you could run down to the
Manor House and bring two or three of the Beddingtons? or anybody else would do quite as well. You see
that rogue on his face there might come round any moment, and make it a bit awkward."

"Of course I can," I said; "wait till I find my
shoes."

The shoes were lying close together by the side of
poor Pete. I had only time to give him one glance as I
ran off through the trees. He looked horribly still, poor
fellow!

I ran like a hare this time. The thought of Sydney
alone with those three men gave me strength, and I covered the whole distance without stopping once; and it
must be quite half a mile.

George Beddington and his two boys were the first
people I ran against.

"Quick, quick!" I panted. "Mr. Grayle is alone
with the three Morrises, and if you are not quick they
will murder him!"

"Where, miss?" they all asked in-the same breath.

"At Inversnaid," I said.

"Inversnaid! Where is that, miss?"

"Oh, don't be so stupid! The big pollard beech, of course, towards Flexham Wood. Run, run!"

We were walking fast down the incline. I had no more run left in me, and it maddened me not to be able to make them understand.

"Now, straight forward in that direction," I said, "about half a mile on. Holloa, and he'll be sure to hear you; but for goodness' sake, be quick!"

The men went off in a trot, and I followed as well as I could. I heard them holloaing among the trees beyond, and I thought I heard Sydney's answering shout, but I was not sure.

I struggled on, and in ten minutes or so came to the tree. Old Morris and Mike were sitting on the ground with their hands bound behind their backs, and the three Beddingtons and Sydney were bending over Pete's prostrate form.

"Is he dead?" I asked in a horrified whisper.

"Lor' bless you no, miss," the keeper said with a laugh; "vermin such as him ain't so easy killed. Leg broke, I think, and knocked out of time by the fall, but nothing else. You see these 'ere leaves are 'most like a feather-bed to fall on—a foot thick if they're an inch."

"Poor fellow!" I said, looking with horrible remorse at a swelling on the left side of his head, just to the side of the eye. "What are you going to do with him?"

"Well, we must just leave him here and go back for a hurdle to carry him on. There ain't nothing else to be done."

"Yes," I said, eagerly; "I'll stay with him while you are away."

"Indeed, you'll do nothing of the sort," Sydney said with a short laugh. "You'll just come straight home with me to Elmhurst. You've done quite enough for one night, and I don't mean letting you out of my sight again.''

"But you can't leave him here all alone?" I said.

"Oh, never fear, miss; he can't get away—leg's broke right enough," put in Tom Beddington, gravely.

Sydney and I both laughed; it was impossible to help it.

"Yes, I wasn't thinking of that," I said. "I was thinking how horrible it was leaving him all alone in the wood here with a broken leg."

"Oh, he'll be all right, miss," Tom said, cheerily, "we shan't be long gone. Here, you two beauties, march!"

Old Morris and Mike rose sulkily to their feet, and the five men disappeared in the direction of the keeper's house.

"Send for the doctor at once!" I shouted after them.

"All right, miss; we'll look after him, never fear!"

Sydney and I were left alone with the fallen man.

"We *can't* leave him like this," I said, "can we, Sydney?"

"We must, little girl," he said. "We can't do the poor chap any good, and the Beddingtons 'll be back in half an hour. Besides, I must get home soon, or I shan't get there at all."

"What do you mean?" I said.

"Well, I think I've lost a good deal of blood, and I'm beginning to feel rather weak."

"Blood!" I cried. "Then he *did* stab you?"

"Yes, he struck me in the left arm. It's nothing to hurt, but it bled a good deal, and is getting very stiff."

"You poor darling!" I said. "Let me bandage it up for you."

"No, no, I daren't touch it till I get to the house. I've stopped the bleeding to a certain extent with a handkerchief tied round, and we had best leave it like that for the present."

"Come on, then!" I said; "let's get to your house, quick! Take my arm."

He laughed, and said that was no use, but that if he put his arm round my neck it might help him a bit. So, of course, I had to agree, poor fellow! and we went the rest of the way like that. He didn't seem so *very* bad after all, I thought—at least as far as spirits went. He really seemed to enjoy having a bad arm.

As for me, considering what I had gone through, I was extraordinarily calm. I couldn't understand it myself. I had a host of questions to ask as we went along—questions about the fire, and old Mrs. Beddington, and as to how he had found me, and any number of other things. And of course he had plenty to ask me.

Mrs. Beddington, he said, was dead—not burnt, or even so much as hurt, but dead—dead of fright and failure of the heart. Henry Beddington had been the first to take the alarm about the fire, and he was in time to rush upstairs and carry out his mother in his arms. Then he thought of me, and had tried to get in again, but it was an utter impossibility. The house was mostly of wood, and very old, and the fire had spread with extraordinary quickness. He had run round to the shed where the ladder was kept, but to his amazement it was gone. After hunting about for a minute or two, he dashed round to my window, and there found the missing

ladder, my window wide open, and sheets of flame dart-
ing out.

That was all, as far as the Beddingtons were concerned. Martha, the girl, had got out easily enough.
She slept beyond the kitchen, on the ground floor, where
the fire had scarcely reached.

Sydney's own story was this: He had been on the
look-out all night, fearing he scarcely knew what—but
still fearing something. He had slept for a time in a
chair, and then feeling uneasy, had wandered out in the
direction of the Manor House. Before he had been
walking five minutes he noticed the red glow in the sky,
and fearing the truth, ran the whole distance at top
speed, and arrived just as the roof crashed in. It was
the quickest fire, every one said, that had ever been
seen; the wonder was that any one escaped at all.

Well, Sydney found Henry Beddington bending over
the body of his mother, and from him learnt that I had
probably escaped by the ladder, but that no one knew
where I had disappeared to. He had rushed blindly
down the track, full of every conceivable terror, but
never for a moment thinking of Inversnaid; why should
he have? And then suddenly he heard my screams, and
in an instant knew where he must look for me. The rest,
of course, I knew.

"Poor old Susan!" I said. "What a horrible thing!"

"Yes, but it might have been worse, of course."

"How?"

"Well, she might have been burnt, poor old lady! As
it was, let us hope her end was painless. And then, you
know, it might have been you, Joe."

"Would you have minded so *very* much?" I asked.

"Minded!" he said. "My God! my God! don't talk of it! You don't know what you are to me, Joe. I wouldn't give a brass farthing for life without you!"

I felt a great shudder run through him, and I was glad to feel it.

"You old darling!" I said.

And then he said several things not nearly so true, but I was very glad to hear them all the same. And I told him all about the terrible night I had had, and asked him if my hair was white.

We had so much to say to each other that I almost forgot all about his arm till we got to Elmhurst, and he had turned the lights up and taken his coat off, and then I think I nearly fainted, for his sleeve was drenched in blood from shoulder to wrist. I never saw anything like it. He rang all the servants up, and made them heat some water, and bring up some food, and get ready a bed for me. And then I cut off his sleeve with a pair of scissors and washed away the part that was sticking to the wound, and then washed the wound itself. It was a horrid-looking place, with black, bulging lips, and I am afraid I must have hurt him dreadfully, but he didn't seem to mind. He said I was a splendid hospital nurse, and he wouldn't mind being stabbed every day if I would only be his doctor.

I don't know what the servants thought. I saw his man staring the eyes out of his head, and the old house-maid looked as sour as vinegar. I suppose she thought it all dreadfully improper.

CHAPTER XXIV

FROM ELMHURST TO ASHBY

I BELIEVE I slept till nearly twelve next morning. Anyhow it was half-past twelve by the time I got down. Sydney was out; his man—who still looked at me with suspicion—said he had started about ten o'clock in the dog-cart, but had left no message as to when he would be back. So I sat in his room, and looked over all his things—regular man's things—pipes and sticks and choppers, fishing-rods and photographs — and I thought what a particularly ugly, dreary room it was, and of how I should have altered it if I was going to live there. And that made me think, of course, of our marriage, and of what Sydney had settled about it. We were to have been married, of course, this very morning. Perhaps that was what he had gone out about. I wondered.

There seemed something rather horrible, to my mind, in getting married the very day after poor old Susan Beddington's death; still, of course, if Sydney wished it, I would do it. And then I began to think over, one after another, all the events of the night before—that awful, never-to-be-forgotten night! I had had no time to think till then. Events had chased one another so quickly that thought of what had gone before had been impossible. But now I sat in the worn, shabby leather chair by the fire and tried to think it all out. What did it all mean? Had the fire been accidental, or had it anything to do with those Morrises? And then, what were the Morrises doing there at all? What did they want with me? And who was "the governor"?

The whole thing seemed to me now like a nightmare; I could hardly realise that it had all actually happened— that I, Josephine de Metrier, had gone through all these things only a few hours before. I got up and looked at myself in the glass over the chimney-piece. There ought to have been some extraordinary change in my face; it ought to have looked old and drawn and haggard, but it did not. It was exactly the same as ever. I felt almost ashamed of myself; it seemed so indecent and unfeeling.

And then I thought of Pete—poor Pete! I wondered how he was getting on down at the keeper's, and what they had done with the other two. I had a good mind to walk down and see; I should be back in time for luncheon. The only thing was I had no hat; I had come away, of course, without one, and my others were all at Selworth. However, there were plenty of Sydney's—shooting-caps of all sizes and shapes—and I took one of these, doubled it up behind, and pinned it on. It did splendidly.

I had just got as far as the gate when I met Sydney himself, driving full tilt up the road.

"My dear child," he called out, "where on earth are you off to?"

"I was going down to the Beddingtons to see after that poor man with the broken leg."

"Good Lord!" he said, "are you mad? Haven't you had enough yet of Selworth and its people? Thank goodness, I caught you in time!"

"Why?" I said; "what's the objection to going?"

"Well, if you don't see, it's no use telling you," he said. "But I want you to come with me this morning."

"What?—to get married?"

"Well, no," he said, looking rather shamefaced. "The fact is, Joe, I don't think we had better get married to-day, if you don't mind."

"Mind!" I cried. "Good gracious! don't think *I* mind. I had much rather not."

He was leaning forward in the dog-cart, playing with the lash of the whip. He didn't look at me, but answered quite quietly:

"Of course. I didn't suppose you were in a hurry; that's why I thought we had better not. I am in a hurry, but there are several reasons why I think it had better be put off for a week or two."

"A month or two, if you like," I said.

He gave me one quick, enquiring glance.

"Joe, dear," he said, gently, "I don't like it at all, but I think perhaps it is best."

"Why?" I asked, simply for curiosity. "Last evening you wanted to get married to-day. I thought it was all settled. Not that *I* care."

"Yes," he said; "yesterday I thought that would be best for you; now I think the other will be best for you."

"All right," I said; "then perhaps you will drive me back to Selworth."

"God forbid!" he answered. "I want you to come with me to Ashby. I have just been there, and they will be delighted to have you. I have got a note for you from the Duchess."

"But I have got no clothes."

"Oh, that will be all right. The girls will lend you

any amount of clothes. Lady Beatrice is just about your size, I should think.''

I stood for a minute in doubt. Of course it was obviously the best thing to be done, and the idea of a cheerful, healthy household where there was no mystery appealed to me strongly. But, on the other hand, I was not at all happy about clothes. I read the Duchess's note; it was very kind and pressing. ''You positively *must* come,'' she wrote, underlined several times.

''All right,'' I said.

''Then jump in! You have left nothing behind, have you?''

''No; but the cap, Sydney!''

''Oh, the cap's all right. You look ripping in it. Jump up!''

I did jump up, and Sydney made me drive, as he said he was not very safe with only one arm. The other he had in a sling. It seemed he had already been to the doctor and had it properly looked to.

''You *have* been energetic,'' I said. ''And I am only just out of bed.''

''Did they give you breakfast all right?'' he asked. ''I told them not to disturb you.''

''Oh, yes, I had it in bed. Sydney, are they very terrible, these Ashby people? I don't know any of them, you see.''

''Not a bit; they are as jolly as possible. You will get on splendidly with them; Lady Beatrice is a ripper!''

''Is she?'' I said. ''You seem pretty full of Lady Beatrice.''

''And so will you be in a couple of days, see if you're not,'' he said, laughing.

''Sydney,'' I said, ''I've been thinking of something.''

"Of me, I hope."

"Of you! No, not likely," I said. "No; I have been thinking about that red box. Do you remember what Mrs. Beddington said?"

"Yes, I do."

"She said that the moment she was dead we were to open it."

"I remember. I have been thinking about it, too. That is one reason why I thought our marriage had better be put off."

"Why?"

"Well, I thought you had perhaps better see what was inside first."

"But how can we get it? You know it is in the secret staircase out of my room."

"I think I could get it, if I only knew the way to your room, and the way to open the picture."

"I could tell you how to open the picture, but you would never find your way to my room. It is rather complicated."

"Then you will have to come and show me," he said.

"But, good gracious! they will see us. You know Norman and Father Terence are in the house. And besides, all the doors are sure to be locked."

"Then, we must break in," he said.

"What, at night?"

"Yes, at night."

"Oh, how glorious! But do you think we can do it?"

"Yes, I think so. I am rather an expert burglar—not professionally, you know, but in an amateur kind of way."

"Shall we try to-night, Sydney?"

"No, certainly not, you little adventuress; you must

have at least one good night's rest first, and so must I,
for that matter. It'll be no child's play when we do try
it.''

As he spoke we drove through the Ashby Lodge. The
park was not nearly so big as Selworth, but very pretty.
The house was big and modern, ugly and comfortable.
I had often seen it, of course, from the outside, as one of
Uncle Guy's favourite rides had been through the park,
but the inside was unknown to me. The Duke never
came there except for the winter months; his principal
place was in the North.

I confess to feeling very uncomfortable as we drove
up to the door. I was unhappy about my cap, and still
more unhappy about my clothes for the evening and for
dinner. I had absolutely nothing except what I carried
on my back. However, before I had been five minutes
in the house I felt as much at home as though I had
lived there all my life. Sydney was right; Lady Beatrice
took me by storm. I fell in love with her from the first
moment that she caught me round the neck and gave
me a loud, smacking kiss. The other girls, Mary and
Alice, were very nice, too, and the Duchess was far
from formidable. Poor woman! she was still in the
deepest mourning for her husband, of course.

I need not have worried myself about dresses. The
girls simply piled up my room with things. They kept
coming in, one after the other, panting under enormous
armfuls of clothes, which they flung in heaps on the bed
and sofa. Each one wanted me, of course, to wear her
own particular things, and I got perfectly bewildered in
trying to divide my choice equally. After tea they all
came up to my room, and made me try on things till dinner time, dancing round me and clapping their hands,

and pulling me about, and all talking at once and at the
top of their voices.   They were extraordinarily gushing
kind of girls, never out of temper or spirits, and what
Sydney called always working in triplets—that is to say,
what one did the other two did as well.   If one came to
my room, they all three came.   One hardly ever saw
them singly.

I was half dead by dinner time, but they all said I
looked all right in a white dress of Beatrice's.   I think
it did suit me pretty well.   The Duke took me in to dinner, as I was the only stranger.   I had never seen him
before, but had always hated him ever since I had heard
he had turned Sydney off.   However, he was pleasant
enough to talk to—rather a good-looking man.   I talked
to him a great deal about Sophie, to try and find out if
he was in love with her, but he was distinctly disappointing.   I don't believe he was.

"Isn't she *lovely?*" I said.

"Oh, yes," he answered, lightly; "very nice looking,
perhaps a little too like a Paris fashion-plate."

"I think it's horrid of you to say that," I said.   "I
think she's the prettiest girl I've ever seen."

"Yes, but then you haven't the advantage that I
have," he said, laughing.

"What's that?"

"Well, I've seen some one that you never have—
except perhaps inverted."

"I don't know the least what you mean, but I'm quite
sure you've never seen any one prettier than Sophie."

"And I'm quite sure I have."

"All right," I said, "we won't fight over it; but I
think you've very bad taste."

I was bitterly disappointed.   Here was a plain end of

poor Sophie's chance of being a Duchess. I wondered who the other girl was. I felt sure she was a pig, whoever she was.

After dinner I asked Beatrice if the Duke was in love with any one. They were all three in my pocket, of course, and they all three went into fits of laughter.

"Not that we know of," they cried in chorus. "There's a chance for you, if you like to try. I think he seemed rather taken with you at dinner."

"Thank you," I said, coldly, "but I'm engaged already."

"Engaged!" they shouted out. "Who to? Tell us all about it."

I was sorry I had spoken, then, but there was no help for it.

"I am engaged to Sydney Grayle," I said.

"To Sydney!" they cried. "Goodness gracious! Think of that!"

And then they all must needs kiss me, and wish me all manner of joy, and descant for twenty minutes on Sydney's innumerable virtues and graces.

At the end of that time Sydney and the Duke came into the room, whereupon they all three set up a howl of congratulation, and charged him in line.

"Sydney!" they cried, "*why* didn't you tell us of your engagement?"

"Engagement!" he said. "What engagement?"

"Good gracious!" Beatrice said, "the man talks as if he had a dozen. Why, your engagement to Miss de Metrier, of course."

I saw his face contract with a quick little frown.

"Because," he said, "I have not the privilege of being engaged to Miss de Metrier."

"Oh, yes, you have! she has told us all about it," said the chorus.

Sydney turned away, and began talking to the Duchess about something. The girls, seeing that something was wrong, stopped short with blank faces; and as for me, I felt ready to sink into the floor with shame and anger. What did he mean?

Beatrice, with ready tact, changed the conversation, and began asking me about the fire, and my adventures of the night before. I was quite a heroine in a small way, but of course nothing was known by the world in general of the real facts. All they knew was that a fire had broken out in the middle of the night, and that I had escaped by a ladder providentially found under my window. Sydney was very reticent about his part of the business, and the wound in his arm. His story was that he had seen the fire, and was hurrying through the woods to see if he could be of any help, when he fell in with some poachers, who wounded him in the arm. One of the poachers seemed to have fallen from a tree and broken his leg—presumably in attempting to noose roosting pheasants—and the others he was able to defend himself against, till the keepers came up and captured the whole three.

"Then where did you find Miss de Metrier?" the Duchess had asked.

"Oh, I found her wandering about, homeless and houseless, in the woods," Sydney said, laughing.

"But I don't understand what Miss de Metrier was doing in the woods; was she poaching, too?"

The Duchess looked at me with puzzled eyes.

"No, not poaching. I suppose she was scared by the

fire, and her own narrow escape and had run away from the very sight of the blazing house.''

I said nothing. I was a bad hand at lying; and it struck me Sydney was not much better. The Duchess did not look completely satisfied with Sydney's explanation; it would have been odd if she had been. But I imagine she thought the mystery was connected in some way or other with our love affairs, and discreetly forbore to press us further.

CHAPTER XXV

A DEEP LAID PLOT

I SLEPT that night as I had never slept before—nine hours or so straight on end. They all wanted me to have breakfast in bed, but that was a thing I hated beyond anything, and, besides it was absurd after sleeping all that while. So I came down to half-past nine breakfast, and found two letters waiting for me on the big marble table in the hall—one from Uncle Guy and the other from Aunt Harriet. I also noticed a letter in Uncle Guy's writing addressed to "The Honourable Sydney Grayle." What did he want with him, I wondered? I opened my uncle's letter first, and read it standing by the window.

"My Dearest Little Joe," it began, "I cannot say how thankful I am to have heard of your merciful escape from that dreadful fire at the old Manor House. What a horrible thing it was! It has upset us all here dreadfully, especially poor old Mrs. Beddington's death. However, one must be thankful after all that the poor old lady was not burnt. That old house was such a regular tinder-box, it is a wonder any one had time to get out. We are all so delighted to hear you have found an asylum at Ashby. They are very nice people, and I think you will like them. They will, of course, let you stay there till we come back, which will probably be in about a fortnight, but our plans are still a little uncertain. Of course, we should have been delighted for you to have gone to Selworth, only, as Norman is the only person in the house, of course it is impossible at present. He was determined to go back to see after some alterations to his rooms. However, it will be much livelier and nicer for you at Ashby just now. When we get back to Selworth, of course we shall claim you at once, and you will have to stay with us until we go up to town for the season.

"Write me a line to say you are none the worse for your terrible experience. We are all so anxious to hear from you. Ever your affectionate old uncle,

"GUY DE METRIER."

Aunt Harriet's letter was much in the same strain, only longer. She hoped I was not terribly *éffarouchée* by the shocking catastrophe of the Manor House; and I must remember that Selworth would always be my home for as long as I liked to stay. Sophie sent her best love. It was a nice, kind letter.

Just as I finished reading it, the Duke came down.

"Good-morning," he said. "I see you are first down, after all. Those sisters of mine are the laziest girls in the world; they never can get out of bed. Come in and have some breakfast."

We had finished our breakfast before they came down. They came in, all three together, of course, and talking loudly. There was five minutes' kissing, and a host of enquiries after my health, which really was not in need of any enquiries, before they finally settled down to their breakfast. The Duke walked out with his hands in his pockets. He said all this cackling was bad for his digestion. Beatrice hit him on the back of the head with a roll as he was disappearing through the door, but he took no notice, and stalked out with dignity.

"What shall we do to-day?" they all said at once, bouncing up in their chairs.

I didn't want to do anything. I wanted to wait about till Sydney came, as I knew he would do some time in the course of the morning. I had told him the day before he positively must go down and make enquiries about that poor Morris boy with the broken leg, and I knew he would come up to report.

I told them I was tired, and would like to keep quiet, and sit about and read.

"Of course," they said. "How stupid of us! You must be *dead!* We'll all sit and read."

And then came a chorus of questions. Had I read this? And had I read that? And did I care for Anthony Trollope's books? They did not. And had I read "Misunderstood," by Florence Montgomery? Such a love of a book! It would be sure to make me cry.

I said I had read hardly anything, and was a miserably ignorant person in every way, but thought I liked Ernest Grizet's books better than any others, which they thought an extraordinary good joke. They laughed for about five minutes.

"What?—the 'Hatchet Throwers'?" they said, "and 'Bear Island'? and those other ridiculous books? You don't mean to say you like *them?* We like sentimental books."

I said I was afraid I did not, which they seemed to think extraordinary.

"We *love* them!" they said; "Italian stories especially, about Venice and Naples."

"Oh, I know," I said. "Silly things out of *Forget-me-not*, where people are called Beppo and Giacomo and Guiseppina, and other ridiculous names."

They laughed loudly.

"We will give you 'The Settlers at Home'," they said. "You will like that."

Then, flying off at a tangent, "Did I sing?"

"No," I said, "I did not sing, or play, either. I had no accomplishments, and was very uneducated."

They *all* sang a little. Would I like to hear them?
Yes? Come along, then, we would go to their own sitting-room, where there was no one to hear. John hated
music.

I don't think any of them sang very well, but they
seemed to enjoy it. They sang a number of Italian
songs, which I neither understood nor cared for.
Didn't I like Italian songs? Oh, well, they knew plenty
of English ones. They sang "Clochette" and "A
Bridge of Fancies," and then Alice and Beatrice sang a
duet called "Wilt Thou Tempt the Waves with Me?"—
a thing that began like a funeral march, and ended like
a jig. And lastly Mary sang "The Bridge," which I
liked better than any of them, and made her sing again.

They were really very nice girls, but there was no
getting rid of them. They stuck to me like leeches. I
think they had taken a fancy to me, for they never left
me alone for a minute, and never stopped talking to me,
even when I was reading.

I said I thought I would go outside and stroll about,
and of course they said they would come too. I went
straight out of the door without a hat, and in my thin
house-shoes; I thought they might go and change theirs,
but not a bit of it. They pursued me just the same—
hatless and shoeless.

I must really come to the stables, they said, and see
the horses—such darlings! We must have a ride in the
afternoon. Molly would carry me splendidly. So we
went and used up at least a bushel of carrots, which a
helper, walking behind us, carried in a basket. And
then, when we had patted the last smooth, glossy neck,
we strolled back again towards the front.

I saw Sydney walking up and down with the Duke; I

supposed they were talking business. Beatrice and the other two waved good-morning to him as we passed, and I looked the other way, and pretended to be examining the front of the house. I had no idea of making him too happy after the way he had talked the night before. If he wanted to see me, he could come in and find me in the drawing-room. If he did not come, I never wanted to speak to him again.

He *did* come, after we had been there about five minutes, and shook hands with the other girls. I pretended to be very much interested in my book. Presently he walked straight up to me, and said, "Can I speak to you for a minute?"

"Oh, certainly," I said, looking up, and laying the book face downwards on my knee.

"I should like to speak to you outside, if possible."

"Is that necessary? Surely we can say what we have to say here. I have only thin shoes on."

"We can walk on the gravel," he said. "I should be very glad if you could manage to come."

"Oh, very well," I said, jumping up. "Come on, and let's get it over."

He followed me out in silence. We walked down the gravel road for about a hundred yards, and then he said, "I wanted to talk to you about that red box."

"Yes?"

"I think we ought to get possession of it without delay."

"Why do you think so?" I asked, contradictiously. Of course I knew quite well.

"Because Mrs. Beddington's strict injunctions were to open the box and read the contents the moment she was dead. She was not the kind of woman to say that without a very good reason."

"It can't possibly affect her now."

"How do we know? It may very easily affect her family."

"Well, how are we to get hold of it?" I asked, sulkily. His manner annoyed me; he talked to me as if I were a stranger, and I noticed he never once called me by my name.

"I thought if you were not too tired, we might go to-night and get it."

"What! before dinner?"

"No, in the middle of the night—do a little midnight house-breaking, in fact."

"Do you think we could get in?" I asked, forgetting for the moment my wounded pride in the excitement of the idea.

"I have very little doubt of it," he said. "I am rather good at that sort of thing."

"I must say I should like to see what's inside that mysterious box," I said, doubtfully. As a matter of fact, I was mad with curiosity to open it.

"Well, look here," he said, "I'll come up here at one o'clock to-night. There's a little room on the ground floor, at the end of the house, that you could get out of easily enough. I'll show it you now. It will take us about an hour and a half to walk to Selworth; then I calculate about an hour to get into the house and get the box, and another hour and a half back. That will get you here by five o'clock. It will be very hard work, I am afraid."

"Oh, I don't mind that," I said. "I'll come—of course I will."

"Here's the window," he said, pointing it out to me. "You see, there's no difficulty about getting out or in again. I only wish we had as easy a job before us at Selworth."

"Yes, this part of it will be simple enough," I agreed.

"They will all be in bed by one o'clock, and you can slip downstairs, with your shoes in your hand, and let yourself out. I will be waiting just outside."

"Oh! won't it be splendid?" I cried; "a real, genuine burglary!"

"Yes," he said, with a faint smile, "it will be very splendid."

I thought he was looking ill and rather miserable. I suspected it must be at the idea of leaving Ashby and going out to America. Perhaps the Duke had been disagreeable to him that morning, or perhaps it was his poor arm. I felt a great wave of pity, and perhaps something more came over me, and without thinking, I forgot all my pride, and just blurted out what was in my mind.

"Why did you say we were not engaged last night?"

"Because," he said, "I was not sure that you knew your own mind. What right has a penniless beggar like me to be engaged to any girl?"

"So you want to be off with it?" I said, coldly. "Enough for one, but not enough for two; I suppose that's the idea."

"I know very well there's not half enough for one," he said, laughing rather bitterly.

"Oh, I see! So I should only be in the way?"

"What nonsense!" he said, angrily. "Can't you understand that I'm thinking of you, and not of myself?"

"Some people are altogether *too* considerate," I suggested.

Sydney got very red, and I thought for a moment he

was going to lose his temper, but he recovered himself
and said, quietly:

"I want you to make me a promise."

"Yes?" I said.

"Will you think the whole thing well over, and write
to me after luncheon to-morrow, and say whether you
really wish our engagement to hold good or not?"

"I could tell you that much now," I said.

"Yes, but I want you to think it well over in the
meanwhile.   It is only a fad of mine, of course, but I
should like you to do it if you would."

"All right," I said, laughing, "if it amuses you, I'll
do it, of course."

"Thanks," he said, gravely; "then that's settled.
And so is the other matter about the box, I think.   You
quite understand?   One o'clock outside this window."

"Yes, I quite understand."

"Good-bye, then, I must be off."

He turned and walked quickly away without once
looking back.   I stared after him in amazement.   What
was the matter with him?   Why was he so different?—
so grave and solemn and generally disagreeable?   Was
it possible that he was jealous of the Duke?   If so, I
would have some fun with him when he next came to
luncheon or dinner; that I would.   I would pay him out
for being so high and mighty.

CHAPTER XXVI

A DARING BURGLARY

I THOUGHT that day would never pass. I was half wild with excitement and expectation. But in the end dinner was over, and the dreary talkee-talkee that followed, and the girls had at last consented to leave my bedroom, and I was alone.

I sat in a pink wrapper of Mary's, with my feet before the fire, and thought. It was just twelve, and in an hour the time would have come. I got up, and shook myself, and began to dress. I had worn Alice's house-shoes all day, so that my own thick ones shouldn't be taken down to be cleaned. Of course, I had about ten pairs belonging to the other girls, but they didn't fit the same as my own, and I hardly fancied a ten-mile walk in any of them.

At ten minutes to one I took my shoes in one hand and a bedroom candle in the other, and began creeping down the passage. It would be an awful thing, I thought, if any one popped out and caught me, for I was dressed in my own day frock, and the shoes in the hand had a distinctly criminal look. However, nothing so appalling happened. I got safely down to the little unused room, unfastened the shutters, threw up the window, and looked out.

It was a fine night, still and dry, but darkish. The moon had shrunk away to nothing, and was hidden for

the most part behind thick clouds. I heard the stable
clock strike one, and sat down to put on my shoes. At
the same moment there came a low whistle from the
bushes opposite. I blew out the candle, and swung myself lightly down.

"You are wonderfully punctual," Sydney said, emerg-
ing from the darkness.

"Yes," I answered, laughing, "and so are you. I
wasn't quite sure that you would come at all. Men
don't, you know, sometimes."

"Well, now we are here, we had better get on," he
said, prosaically. "We shall have to step out, you
know, if you are to be back by five. You had better
follow me. I know all the short cuts."

He turned and strode away down the walk. I felt
more chilled and mortified than I can say. What kind
of a lover was this, who could not even take the trouble
to shake hands? What about all our vows of everlasting
love and constancy? and all *his* protestations of passionate affection? Here was a mere practical business man
on a practical business undertaking—a man who, under
conditions that tended in quite an opposite direction,
talked to me as a lawyer might to a judge!

However, there was no use in worrying one's self over
causes, so I resigned myself sulkily to the effect, and
followed dumbly at his heels. We walked at a good
four miles an hour, and in absolute silence. Under the
park wall Sydney stopped to pick up a bag and a
lantern.

"Can you manage the lantern?" he asked. "You see
I have only one arm."

"Of course I can," I said; after which silence reigned
once more.

He had a key that let us through a little wooden gate in the wall, and we found ourselves in the high road.

The way into Selworth was not quite so simple, but there was no great difficulty even about that. The park wall ends, for some reason, at the Slade Lodge; I suppose because the high road turns off at right angles there and ceases skirting the wall. The whole way from the Greystoke Lodge to the Slade Lodge the road runs just outside the wall, but at the Slade Lodge it turns sharp off towards Hexham, and beyond is nothing but a big cover bounded by a hedge. We scrambled through this hedge, and at the end of a narrow ride, over another, and we were in the park. Then came a three-mile tramp through the Flexham Woods and across the Plain. It was dreary work. Sydney's extraordinary surliness took all the life and excitement out of what we were doing; otherwise, I should have wished for nothing better. We just tramped along side by side in silence, I swinging my lantern and he his bag.

When we got to the road, we bore away a little to the right. Sydney, of course, with his wounded arm, was not up to climbing the balustrade, so we had to go round by the gate. There is a little path running through the belt, that lets one into the garden by a small iron gate. It is a gate that squeaks cheerfully on its hinges, and swings to with a prolonged rattle of the latch. However, on this occasion we suppressed the rattle, though the hinge squeaked bravely, giving out the little tune I had heard such scores of times from my window. I loved that little tune; it made me feel at home at once, and does still.

We marched up the gravel path straight for the little glass door at the foot of the turret stairs. The house loomed up huge and black before us. Not a glimmer of light showed anywhere; not a sound broke the stillness of the night. For some extraordinary reason the moment we were in the garden Sydney became more like his old self. I suppose the excitement of housebreaking made him forget the part he was playing—for of course he *was* playing a part, I knew that. Anyhow, he became a different being, brisk, animated, and strange to say, cheerful. I even heard him whistling softly to himself.

"You are sure nobody sleeps this side?" he said.

"Certain; these are all visitors' rooms."

"That old priest doesn't sleep here?"

"Oh, no; he sleeps miles away, at the other end of the house. Of course Norman's room is not far off, but then his window looks out to the front."

"That's all right," he said; "he won't bother us."

At the door we stopped. Sydney lit the lantern and began rummaging about in his bag. I looked on with interest, and an insane desire to help. He produced a thing like an ordinary pencil, with which he cut quickly round one of the middle panes of glass. It made a harsh, grating sound, and I guessed there was a diamond in it. Twice he followed the same lines, and then with his one hand in a thick hedger's glove smeared with putty, pushed in the bottom of the pane and brought the whole thing out on the palm of his hand. It was the neatest thing ever seen.

"I believe you are a professional burglar," I whispered.

"I should like to be," he said, laughing. "Don't I do it well?"

He put in his hand, unbolted the window, and told

me to open it quietly. When the window was up, the little wooden door at the bottom, of course, opened easily enough. We were now face to face with the shutters.

Sydney produced a hand-drill, and told me to bore little holes in a circle as high up in the middle of the shutter as I could reach. Of course he couldn't manage it with his one hand. It was horribly tiring work—the stretching up made it so bad—and I had to stop and rest half a dozen times. But at last the circle was made, and he pulled out a very thin little saw, and began sawing from one hole to the other. After the first start off, this was easy enough, and in five minutes he had a neat little hole in the middle of the shutter. His first care was to put his hand through and bring out the bell, held firmly by the tongue.

"That's a good job over," he said with a sigh; "now for the bar. We must cut another hole in the left-hand bottom corner."

So I knelt down and set to work again. This was ever so much easier than the first hole, as it was far more get-at-able; besides, I was getting more used to the instrument. We had another hole cut in no time.

"Now," said Sydney, "you put your left hand through the middle hole, and keep the bar from swinging, while I undo the fastening."

I had to stand on tip-toe to do this, and held the bar till I felt the weight of it fall upon my hand. Then I stretched my wrist through, and kept my hold of it till it got beyond my reach, when I let it go, and it dropped against the wall with a sullen clang. The shutters swung open, and we were inside the house!

"Not bad for an amateur burglar?" Sydney whispered.

"I should think not," I said. "Shall I take the lantern?"

"Yes, take the lantern. We will leave the bag till we come back."

My heart was thumping like a steam-engine, and I felt an insane desire to laugh, but fortunately suppressed it. Sydney was very serious.

I led the way—the way I had travelled such scores of times before—up the turret stairs, through the swing door at the top, and along the stone passage till we came to my own special staircase, the staircase that leads to nowhere except the panelled room.

The door was locked, but the key was on the outside. This we soon altered, changing it to the inside, and locking the door again.

"It is just as well to be prepared for a siege, if necessary," Sydney remarked. "We should, anyhow, have time to master the contents of the box before they could force the door."

My poor old room looked most dejected and bare, with its dust-sheet coverings and recumbent jugs. It smelt stuffy and airless, too, with the airlessness of days.

I turned the lantern on to Maurice, to see what he thought of our enterprise, but there was no reading those features. The curled lip and supercilious eye might mean either pity, scorn, or defiance.

"Hadn't you better get the box?" Sydney suggested, mildly. "We are behind time as it is."

"I must take the lantern," I said. "Have you got a candle?"

"No, but it doesn't matter; you can leave me in the dark; I am not nervous."

I climbed on to the chimney-piece in the old way, with

the chair, and swung Maurice back into the room. Then, picking up the lantern, I crept quietly up.

The place where I had put the box was nearer the top than the bottom of the stairs. It was, as may be remembered, a deep, wedge-shaped recess in the wall. I put the lantern on the floor of this recess, and wriggled myself forward on my hands and knees.

It was a good stretch to where I had hidden the box— very near to the point of the wedge, in fact—and just as I had got my fingers on the end of the box a very dreadful thing happened.

I had jammed the box in so tight that it was not easy to get it out. My fingers could just stretch sufficiently to grip the end of it, but I could get no purchase, and the box refused obstinately to move. I suppose in my efforts I forgot to look after my feet as I should have done. Anyhow, the long and short of it is, that I kicked the lantern over, right down the stairs.

I shall never to my dying day forget the appalling clatter that lantern made as it went dribbling down the stone steps. I made up my mind on the spot that it *must* wake every soul sleeping in the house. As to Norman, the noise must have given him a perfect fit. Of course, the stupid thing, not content with making enough noise to wake the dead, had gone out as well, and I was in absolute darkness. However, I suppose I am obstinate by nature, not to say pig-headed, for instead of groping my way downstairs into safety, I ground my teeth and held on to my red box like grim death. I knew Norman would wake, and I knew the chances were he would come down to see what was going on, but for all that I was not going without my box. I had come to get it, and get it I would.

So I tugged and tugged till my fingers all but cracked, but the box refused to budge. I changed my grip, and pulled in a rather different manner, and to my unspeakable joy I felt the box yielding. But at the very same moment I heard the door at the top open, and a ray of light shot across the dusty stones. Norman was coming down!

The box was half-way out by now, and I was wriggling it up and down, and drawing it out inch by inch. I could see the reflection of the candle coming nearer and nearer with every second. I remember quite distinctly thinking how brave it was of Norman facing the unknown dangers that clattering lantern might have meant for him.

With one frantic final effort I wrenched the box clear, and grabbing it by the handle, backed myself on to the stairs. I thought to slip quietly down into the panelled room, while Norman was still standing undecided; but he was too quick for me. As my feet touched the steps I felt myself seized by the wrist.

"No, no, my sweet little cousin," he said; "since you have done me this great and unexpected honour, I really cannot allow you to make off in this unceremonious manner. It would be too great a slur on the hospitality of Selworth."

I said nothing, but made desperate efforts to get clear. If he had had both hands free, I should of course have had no ghost of a chance with him; but as it was the candle in his left hand prevented him from holding on to anything, and I was at a distinct advantage. I pulled him down step by step, and for my own part I wanted nothing better. My one idea, of course, was to get to Sydney. With his bad arm it was a sheer impossibility for him to come to me, poor fellow! I knew that.

I think Norman must have tried to put down the candle on the ledge where I had been kneeling. Anyhow, he half turned his back on me for a moment, and I, seeing my opportunity, gave one desperate tug, and brought him tumbling down a-top of me, candle and all. The candle, of course, went out, and we both rolled to the bottom of the stairs in pitch darkness. I could hear Norman's quick, short breathing as he grabbed wildly at me in the dark.

"Let me go!" I gasped, "or we shall both break our necks. I'll talk to you in the room below."

"You must let me get down first, then," he said. "I wouldn't trust you else."

"All right," I agreed. "You get down first." I chuckled to myself to think of the surprise waiting for him below.

He let me go, and we both struggled to our feet panting. Then, slowly and cautiously, I heard him let himself down into the room. Next moment there was a scuffle below, followed by a loud oath, and the sound of a volley of blows given in quick succession.

"Damn you, whoever you are!" I heard Norman say. "Why the devil can't you show yourself?" There was no answer, but the sound of a couple of smacking blows, and then Norman's voice again, "Take that anyhow, you damned, sneaking burglar!"

There was no doubt the De Metriers had pluck, whatever faults they might have on the other side.

I was sitting on the chimney-piece ready to drop down, but afraid of tumbling on the top of the two below; but suddenly Sydney's voice called out, "Come here, Joe, and strike a match; you will find the box in my pocket."

His voice told me where he was, and I dropped down

behind him and got my hand into his pocket. It was not easy, for he was swaying about the room like a tree in the wind, but I managed it in the end, and lighting a match, held it high above my head in my left hand. The light flickered feebly round the room, casting weird, ghostly shadows upon the walls. Between the fireplace and the dressing-table Sydney and Norman were fighting like wild beasts. Sydney had his left shoulder turned away from the other, to protect his bad arm I supposed, and with his right was driving Norman backwards, towards the window. The first thing I saw with any clearness was Sydney's fist strike Norman full under the chin with a soft, pulpy noise. Norman spun half round, and next moment Sydney had seized him by the back of the neck, and held him at arm's length, kicking frantically. How splendidly strong he was, I thought!

"Joe," he called out, "unlock the door, take out the key, and put it on the outside of the door. Have you done that?"

"Yes," I said. His back was turned to me.

"Now, light a fresh match, and get outside into the passage."

"All right!" I cried.

I saw him hurl Norman with all his force towards the window, and next second he was outside with me, and we had the door locked. Norman rushed at the door and rattled it furiously, using the while words that were not pleasant to hear. Then we heard him stumble to the bedside and tear at the bell. We could hear the strained wires creaking in the woodwork over our heads.

"Ring away, my friend," Sydney laughed. "You won't hurt us."

We tumbled post haste down the stairs by the light of

the matches. The third one was just burning down to my fingers as we dashed out into the garden.

"Come along!" said Sydney. "He's capable of shooting us from the window if he gets the chance."

We ran till we were clear of the trees, and across the road on to the open Plain. The big clock behind us chimed a quarter past four; we were at least half an hour later than we should have been, but what did we care? We had the box, and that was the great thing. They were not likely to hang me, even if I was caught making a burglarious entrance into Ashby. I laughed aloud at the thought of breaking into *two* distinct houses in one night! Jack Sheppard was not in it with me! It would seem quite tame after this, going into houses by the ordinary, matter-of-fact methods!

Sydney thawed considerably on the way back, especially at first. He was excited, I expect, by his struggle with Norman, and quite forgot for a time to be stiff and stand-offish. Later on, however, when we were near home, he dropped back into the old way again, and was perfectly odious. At first we talked a good deal. Norman, he said, had hit him in the face three or four times. He quite expected to have a couple of black eyes in the morning.

"I shall certainly be too unpresentable to appear at Ashby," he said. "You will have to send for me if you want me."

I laughed, and said I was not likely to do that; it would simply be giving myself away.

"Yes, I suppose so," he said, shortly; and after that came the old dreary silence, and tramp, tramp, tramp across the wet, spongy grass.

He came with me as far as my open window; he

insisted on doing that. It had a terribly criminal effect, that black, gaping window.

"Fancy, if a real genuine burglar has been getting through it in the meanwhile!" I suggested.

"Not likely," he said; "burglars don't grow in the garden, that I know of."

I turned to him and held out my hand.

"Good-night!"

"Good-night!" he said, shook hands limply, and walked away.

It must certainly be the Duke, I thought.

CHAPTER XXVII

MY HEADACHE, AND WHAT CAME OF IT

I SUPPOSE it was twelve o'clock before I awoke next morning. I was getting quite into the habit of sleeping on into the middle of the day. I had pinned a paper on to my door telling the world that I had a headache, and wished not to be disturbed, and consequently I had been allowed to sleep the sleep of the just burglar. I had been so utterly dog-tired the night before that I had not even had the curiosity to open my box, or rather my exhaustion had been greater even than my curiosity, and I had tumbled straight into bed, leaving the box unopened on the sofa. Thank Heaven, there was no need to hide things away in this house!

When I awoke it was some time before I could collect my thoughts. I rubbed my eyes, and yawned, and wondered why the girls' maid hadn't called me, and then suddenly, like a flash, the whole thing came back to me.

Good gracious! What time was it? I wondered. I jumped out of bed and opened the curtains and shutters. It was very broad daylight, indeed. The winter sun was well up in the sky, and there was an indescribable feel in the air that told me as plain as a clock that it was nearer luncheon time than breakfast. So I jumped into bed again and rang the bell. My watch— one of Uncle Guy's many presents—I had of course forgotten to wind up; and the ancient French clock on the chimney-piece was equally, of course, not going, so that I had nothing but my own senses to trust to.   In five minutes the maid arrived.   •

"What time is it, Cécile?" I asked.

"Half-past twelve, miss," she said.

"Oh! my hot water, please, then, Cécile."

"Yes, miss. And will you have anything before luncheon?"

"No," I said, laughing, "I think not.   I can't come down to a one-o'clock breakfast at my age."

I was ravenously hungry, it is true, but then I had the box, which would feed my curiosity if not my material frame, and the hunger of the first was if anything greater than the second.   So I dashed into my bath, and dashed out of it, and into my clothes in a feverish state of hurry and excitement.   By a quarter past one I was clothed and in my right mind, and flung myself on the sofa in a state of such eagerness as has never been equalled by the most ravenous devourers of new and stimulating novels. What hidden mystery of a past generation was I not about to unravel?   What unrevealed tragedies and crimes might not be hidden inside that little red box?   I turned the key, and the box opened with a readiness that was almost disappointing in its simplicity.   I should have preferred a refractory lock, and key rusted and crusted with age, and hinges that creaked and groaned with the lifting of the lid.   It would have been more exciting, more suggestive of some ancient, jealously guarded secret.   But of all this there was nothing; the box opened easily and simply at the first time of asking. Within lay several papers, some tied together with tape, others separate.   The topmost paper was the bulkiest, a long, thickly folded document, written in big, bold manuscript. On the outside I read, "The confession of Susan Beddington, a great sinner before God and man."

The other papers were without description. Poor old Susan's, I thought, was the one to start on; hers was probably a *résumé* of the rest—the gist and kernel of the whole thing.

I opened it with the slow deliberation which is often the outward and visible sign of a feverish impatience within; and the next moment I had folded it again, flung it into the box, slammed down the lid, locked it, and rammed the whole thing under the chintz valance of the sofa.

For coming along the passage was the sound of voices—happy, healthy, laughing, tiresome, irritating, *maddening* voices. There was a knock at the door, and the next moment, without waiting for an answer, they trooped in, the three inseparable sisters.

"You poor darling!" said Alice, falling on my neck, "how are you now?"

"Oh! she *does* look pale, doesn't she, Beatrice?" cried Mary, with face and voice agonised with sympathy.

"It was those truffles, you know, Josephine," said Beatrice, shaking her head in mournful reproof. "I was afraid when I saw you eating them; they always disagree with me."

Their hands were packed with bottles and phials and boxes.

"I have brought you my ether spray," Beatrice said; "it is the most marvellous thing in the world for a headache."

"Splendid!" assented Alice, hurriedly; "and if you will take one of these powders before luncheon, you will

be as right as a trivet before three o'clock.   Dr. Watson
gave them to me last year.   They are *wonderful!*"

"Well, I will back hot sal volatile and water against
anything in the world," put in Mary from the background.   "And you can put a lump of sugar in it if you
like.   *Do* try it!"

"And mother wants to know if you would like the
doctor sent for."

"And she hopes you will not on any account leave
your room unless you feel quite up to it."

"And she is having some white-wine-whey made, and
some barley-water.   It will be up here directly.   She
says there is nothing like it."

"And what would you like sent up for your luncheon?"

"And Cécile will bring you a hot-water bottle in a few
minutes."

"And mother has given orders that no one is on any
account to come down this passage except Cécile."

"And you have got no fire!"

"And your window is open!"

"And you are sitting in a thorough draught!"

"But I am all right," I cried, laughing in spite of
myself.   "There is nothing in the world the matter with
me now.   I was just going out."

"Your headache is gone?" they cried in chorus, and in
open disappointment.

"Yes, quite gone.   I slept it off."

"Well, take some sal volatile anyhow," pleaded
Alice, not to be baulked.   "It will do you a lot of
good."

"Thanks," I said, laughing.   "I don't want any
good doing to me.   Let's go out."

I knew I should never get rid of them otherwise.

There was no help for it. `Susan's confessions must wait.

"Yes, let's go out." They all assented with one voice. They were always ready for anything one proposed.

"Put on your shoes," said Beatrice. "Why, good gracious! they're all wet!"

"Oh, I'll put on another pair," I said, hurriedly. "A pair of yours, Beatrice, I think; they seem to fit me best."

"But how disgraceful of Cécile not taking them down! I'll ring the bell and pitch into her."

"Oh, please don't!" I said, in a whirl of terror. "What does it matter after all? Let's go out while we can. There's not much time."

So the episode of the shoes was overlooked, and in five minutes clean forgotten, and we went out and strolled about the garden till the outside bell went for luncheon.

"We were quite alarmed about you, Miss de Metrier," said the Duke. "You narrowly escaped having Gull sent for to see you."

"I think she still looks a little pale," said Alice, concernedly. "Make her have some port, mother!"

"I found some property of yours in the garden this morning," the Duke said, suddenly.

"Of mine?" I cried, feeling I was growing scarlet.

"Yes, in the bushes under the octagon room."

"Oh, yes," I said, inanely, diving under the table to hunt for my napkin. I was bound to provide *some* explanation for my apoplectic colour.

"From the place in which I found it, and from the signs, I should say you had been making burglarious entrances into the house," he went on, smiling.

"Ha! ha!" I said.

"I hope you girls have not been climbing in at that window," the Duchess put in plaintively. "You know I have begged you not to, repeatedly. It simply ruins the woodwork and paint."

"Oh, no, mother!" cried the chorus.

"Some one has," said the Duke, "and has dropped that in doing so. Perhaps it was the housekeeper."

The housekeeper weighed nineteen stone.

He laid a handkerchief on the table, very clearly marked in red cotton, *J. de Metrier*.

"Why, you weren't in the garden yesterday," Mary said.

"The footprints are very fresh," said the Duke, looking at me with much amusement in his eye, "and not very large."

Every one looked at me, and I suppose my face was like a frosty sunset, for the Duchess called out suddenly:

"Good gracious! I had almost forgotten about driving into Greystoke this afternoon. Which of you girls is coming with me?"

I felt I could have hugged her, dear old thing! I suppose the others saw her intention, and followed her lead, for no one said any more about my handkerchief, or the footprints under the octagon room. Only afterwards, when we were alone, Beatrice whispered:

"Did you really climb in at the octagon window?"

"Yes, I really did."

"Oh, what fun! It drives mother wild, but of course it saves a lot of trouble if one is that side of the house. They ought to make a door there if they don't want one to climb in at the window."

"When did you do it?" Alice asked.

"Oh, some time yesterday; I forget the exact time."

"Fancy your thinking of it! I suppose it was a natural inspiration."

"It proves conclusively to my mind," said Beatrice, "that the window was made expressly to climb in at. What else could possibly have put it into Josephine's head?"

Alice drove into Greystoke with the Duchess, and I went out riding with the other two in Alice's habit. We had a long ride, and when we got in there was tea, and it was very difficult to get away, for their mother not yet being back made the two girls cling to me more than ever.

"I am going up to my room," I said presently.

"Oh, all right. May we come, too?"

"Well, I have got some papers to read, and I don't think I should understand them very well if you were there talking."

"We won't talk. We will read, too, if you like."

"There are not enough comfortable chairs."

"Oh, yes; we'll manage somehow. Come along."

So, with their arms encircling me, they dragged me off; and seeing no way out of it, I made the best of a bad job, and consented with as good a grace as I could. After all, there was no reason I should not read the things with them in the room.

"You must be very quiet," I said, when we had lit all the candles, and I had got the red box on my knee. "These are family documents, and require deep thought."

"They look splendidly mysterious," Mary said, "the box alone is worthy of a Prime Minister."

"Hush!" I said, "I'm going to read."

CHAPTER XXVIII

SUSAN CROSSLEY'S CONFESSION

I TOOK out the thickest paper, the Confession of Susan Beddington, and spread it open on my knee. On the inner sheet was written, "To Miss Josephine de Metrier," and below it:

"If ever this writing should come to your eyes, it will in all probability be when the poor sinner who writes it has passed away. I have never seen you since you were eight years old. In those days you promised to be the dead picture of your glorious mother, the grandest creature I ever saw, and the best, from all accounts; and if you are like her in mind as well as in body, you will perhaps forgive me the immense injury I have done you, as I hope the great God above will forgive me the greater sins I have sinned against Him. This poor attempt at atonement, this miserably late endeavour to undo in some part the wrong I have done, comes, I know, only from the fear of death and of the Great Judgment. As long as I was strong and young, and death seemed a faint, far-off thing in the distance, I cared for nothing but the vanities and pleasures of this world, and beyond these never looked. But now that a cold hand grips my heart, and the grave gapes close before me, I do look beyond, as well as back, and I see the red horror of my sins, and trusting in the infinite mercy of God, I write this confession in the hope of undoing the wrong I have done, and of making, if may be, my peace with Heaven."

I turned over a fresh sheet and read:

"The Confession of Susan Beddington of the sins of Susan Crossley.

"It was in April, 1806, that the evil began. I was standing outside the door of Croft's Farm when a groom rode up the lane, and waved to me over the gate of the garden. I took no manner of notice at first, thinking the man was merely bent on fooling, but after a little he called out from his horse, 'Mistress Susan, Mistress Susan, I have a letter for you from the Squire.'

"He waved a white square in the air, and the sun fell on it, and painted it whiter still, and thinking he was lying, but still full of idle curiosity, I strolled slowly towards the gate, swinging my sun-bonnet in one hand by the ribbons.

"It was for me, sure enough—addressed to Miss Susan Crossley, and bearing the De Metrier arms. I opened it carelessly, and with a fine show of carelessness read:

"'Mr. and Mrs. de Metrier would be very pleased if Miss Crossley would undertake the care of their child at the Abbey. If she is willing to do this, she will be so kind as to come up to the Abbey at once. A cart will be sent to bring up any things Miss Crossley wishes to have with her. Mr. de Metrier is prepared to give £30 a year if Miss Crossley will act as nurse.'

"'Thank you,' I said, as haughty as possible, and trying to look as if I was not ready to jump out of my skin with joy at this extraordinary honour; 'will you say that I will be up in an hour?'

"I had no fear of what father and mother would say. I knew they would be just as proud and honoured as I was, as indeed they were, and even more so. The only thing that puzzled them was why in the world they had hit upon me, a mere slip of a girl with no experience, to undertake such a precious charge. However, there it was, there was no question about that, so I dressed myself out in all my Sunday finery—and pretty good finery it was for a girl in my situation; too good, father always would say—and up I tripped to the Abbey, first across the fields, and then through the park, singing and carolling like the silly, empty-headed young fool I was.

"The. Squire saw me first in his study, and then the housekeeper took me up to the nursery.

" 'Haven't you got a decent black dress or a plain print?' she asked, with a touch of scorn, I thought. 'I never did see such a figure for a gentleman's servant.'

"I was more than a little surprised at this, for my dress was thought a deal of in the village, but I said nothing, thinking perhaps she was ignorant or jealous.

"In the nursery we found a housemaid trying to rock the baby to sleep, and making but a poor hand of it, for the child was screaming fit to take the roof off.

" 'The monthly nurse left to-day,' the housekeeper explained, 'and he misses her, poor mite!'

"Well, to make a long story short, I stayed with the child from that day on, and got to love it as though it were my very own. It was a poor little misery of a thing, with one leg two inches short of the other, and cross-eyed as a weasel. I often think it was a wonder that it lived at all, for the child was never well, and no one but its mother and myself seemed to care if it lived or died.   I begged Mrs. de Metrier time without end to send for the doctor for it, but she said I must ask the Squire, and that if he said no, we must just nurse it as best we could between us.   I think that poor woman forgave me everything, and even loved me in spite of everything, just because of the love I had for her child. But when I talked to the Squire of a doctor he just flew into a rage, and told me not to be a fool, and that the child was well enough, and at all events, as well as it ever would be, doctor or no doctor.   So, after a bit, I gave up asking.   I am as sure now as I am of death, that one of the reasons the Squire chose me as a nurse for the child was because he thought that I was young and careless and ignorant, and would as like as not let the child die of neglect.   I was barely eighteen at the time, and had a name for giddiness and folly and vanity for many a mile round.   But in this he made a very great mistake indeed, for giddy and foolish though I was, and with my silly head full of my own good looks and what not, I was not downright wicked at that time. That came after.   And, thank God! I can say truthfully, and with a clear conscience, that no mother could have loved and cared for that child more than I did. But as to Mordaunt—the Squire, that is—he simply loathed the sight of it, though, if he and Mrs. de Metrier chanced to be in the nursery at the same time, he would make a pretence of playing with it, and taking it on his knee, and the rest of it, just to keep her quiet, and hinder her from thinking other things.

"The boy was christened Guy, and a proper name for him, too, every one said; for a more woeful little Guy was never held to a font.

"Well, exactly ten months after Guy was born there

came another baby, a boy, too, and this time as bonny a babe as man or wife might wish to see, but with no little finger on the left hand, only a little bit of a stump with no nail on it. They got another nurse for it, a Mrs. Graham from somewhere in Scotland, and it was put in the old nursery at the other end of the house. The day after it was born, Mordaunt came up into my nursery. - I have never seen a man so changed; his face was beaming from ear to ear, and his spirits were more like a boy's let loose from school than a grown-up man's.

" 'Susan,' he said presently, 'I want you to pay particular attention to what I am going to tell you. In the first place, you are never to take this child to the east of the door at the foot of your stairs. When you take him out, you are invariably to turn to the left, and keep in the shrubberies that side. In the second place, you are never, under any pretence, to speak to Mrs. Graham, the new nurse; and in the third place, you are always to take the child out with a thick white veil over its face. Do you see?'

" 'Yes,' I said, 'but why? The poor child will choke on a hot day!'

" 'Nonsense!' he said; 'show me some of its veils.

"I brought out a number from a drawer, and he selected one, and held it out to me.

" 'Never anything thinner than this,' he said, nodding his head at me, 'remember that. Order as many more as you want. And one thing more, never let any one see this child, in the house or out. You understand?'

" 'Perfectly,' I said, 'there's no difficulty about it, if you insist upon it, but it all seems to me very extraordinary.'

" 'Never mind what it seems to you,' he said, laughing. 'I do insist upon it very strongly; so do what I tell you, like a good girl, and don't bother your little head about reasons.'

"I did it, of course—Mordaunt could make me do what he liked—and I saw no particular harm in it, though, of course, it did seem strange and unnatural. Twice I did meet Mrs. Graham. The first time was in the long west passage. I was going to borrow a book from the second housemaid—a thrilling book she had promised to lend me—and on the way back I met Mrs. Graham. I had never seen her before, nor she me, but of course we both guessed who the other was. She was a tall, handsome woman of about forty, with a strong, kind face. We passed one another without a word. She had clearly had her orders as well as me.

'The next time was about a month later, and that time we did speak. It was on the back stairs that lead from the first floor to the basement, about ten o'clock at night. I was coming up, and she was going down. I can't say what prompted me to speak. I suppose it was just because I had orders not to. Anyhow I smiled across at her and said:

" 'Baby quite well?'

" 'Quite well, thank you, and yours?'

" 'Getting on nicely, thank you.'

" 'Good-night!'

" 'Good-night!'

"That was all; but little as it was, it led to great results, as you will presently see.

"A month after the new baby was born Mrs. de Metrier died. She had never got over it properly, they said, and in fact, she never really left her bed. Every one was sorry, for she was a sweet, kind lady, and I fancy had no easy time of it with Mordaunt; what wife would have had?

"Mordaunt made a great show of grief, but in his heart I knew he cared nothing. He never had cared for her—married her for her money and not for herself—and after she had brought poor little Guy into the world, I believe he positively hated her. He put the whole blame of it on her, and perhaps rightly, poor thing! As to the new baby—Gerard, as they called him—he simply raved about him. He used to come into my nursery and talk by the hour, telling me what a strong, handsome little fellow he was, and how like himself and the old line of De Metriers, till it used to make me sick with anger and disgust. For I used to think of the poor, white, crooked little mite asleep in his cot in the next room, and wonder who would be found to take his part, and say a good word for him, in the days that were to come.

"Mordaunt, I knew, would always hate him. He was extraordinarily vain and proud of his beauty, and of his father's and grandfather's before him; and his one idea in life was to have an heir who would keep up the traditions of the family, and not disgrace him.

"However, nothing happened till Guy was two years old, and Gerard ten months less. Then something did happen, though no one thought anything of it at the time.

"Mrs. Graham was found dead in her bed in the old nursery. The doctor came and gave a certificate, and there was no fuss at all, and the poor woman was buried in Benton Churchyard and forgotten. Mordaunt came to me with Gerard in his arms early in the morning. The child was muffled up in shawls and veils, and he came and laid it gently on my knee.

"'Mrs. Graham is dead,' he said. 'We will have another nurse here to-morrow, and in the meanwhile you must look after both. And I wish no one to come into this room on any account except myself. All the milk and things must be put in the next room and left there. You and the children are to stay here, and let no one come in. Lock the door, do you understand? Lock the door, and open it to no one.'

"He was quite excited for him; his eyes were glittering, and he spoke very fast.

"'I understand perfectly,' I said, looking at him hard. 'What did Mrs. Graham die of?'

"'Oh, nobody knows yet,' he said, carelessly; 'but we have sent for a doctor, and he will soon find out.'

"I said nothing, but stared at him with a kind of horrid curiosity, for I believed then, truly and honestly, that he had murdered her. Afterwards I changed my mind, but to this day I am not sure about it. God grant he was innocent! He had plenty against him without that. It seemed to me later on that it was absurd to think he would have murdered the woman; it would have been so much simpler to have sent her away. But what put it into my head was this: Two days before I had had a note from Mrs. Graham brought me by one of the housemaids. This note is in the box with the other papers marked A."

Here my curiosity got so much the better of me that I turned up the letter in question and read it. It was written in a spidery hand, and in very faded ink, but was quite legible.

"DEAR MISS CROSSLEY,—I was horrified and amazed yesterday by a proposal that was made to me by the Squire. He actually suggested changing our two babies, and turning mine into the eldest and yours into the youngest. He had the effrontery to offer me £100 down if I would consent to this, and swear myself to secrecy. Of course I told him I could never agree to do such a wicked, dishonest thing, and he then flew into a towering rage, and said there was nothing dishonest about it, and it would hurt nobody, and he would give me a day to think it over. Of course he will send me away, for no money will induce me to have part in such a wicked scheme; and I write to you to implore you to have nothing to do with it either, for of course he will make the same proposal to you. Miss Crossley, don't do it. You are very young, and he will try hard to persuade you, but believe me, nothing but harm can come of flying in such a way in the face of the Lord's will.

"MARGARET GRAHAM."

I replaced the letter in the box, and turned again to the Confession.

"This letter I received on the evening before the poor woman's death. It might, of course, be accident, but I thought it looked odd, and I stared very hard at Mordaunt as he stood swaggering in front of the fire.

" 'Well,' he said, roughly, 'what are you looking at?'

"I answered nothing, for I was dumb with the horror of my thoughts.

" 'Don't you like having the two of them to look after?' he said. 'Is that why you look so glum? Well, it's only for one day, Susan. You needn't make such a to-do over it.'

"I was making no to-do at all; I was just silent and thoughtful. But this was clearly what he didn't like, for he shrugged his shoulders, and turned up his eyes, and walked out of the room whistling.

"In the evening he came again. The doctor had been, and the certificate was made out, and everything was as it should be. Then he told me of his plan.

"A new nurse would be coming the next day. She should take my poor little weakling, believing that it was Gerard, the youngest. And I was to take the child that had been with Mrs. Graham, and it was to be called Guy, the first-born. In fact, the two were to be changed, names and all. There was no difficulty about it, for the real Guy was very small for his age, and the other a splendid big child, who might readily have passed for the elder. And no one had seen either of them—except at the christenings—and then there was not much to be seen beyond the point of a little nose sticking out of a bundle of lace. So that the plan was simplicity itself, if I would only agree. And of course I did agree, God forgive me! Mordaunt could make me do anything. What was I to stand against him? I was only a silly, vain child, and he coaxed me into it in five minutes. I was to go to the old nursery with my new charge, and the new nurse was to stay in the nurseries where I had been before. I say now, honestly, before God, that at the time I consented, I had persuaded myself that it was impossible and absurd and against all reason, that Mordaunt should have murdered Mrs. Graham. The doctor said it was heart; everybody in the house seemed quite satisfied that it was heart; why shouldn't it be heart? Of course it was. I felt mean and despicable for ever having suspected anything else. Mordaunt had his faults, without doubt; he was far from spotless, but he was not a murderer.

"So, like many another before me and since, I persuaded myself easily of that which I wished in my heart to believe. Later on, when I learnt of the staircase in the wall that connected Maurice's room, where Mordaunt then slept, with the old nursery, I became doubtful once more, but it was too late then. Murderer or no murderer, it was all the same then.

"The new nurse came next day in the afternoon. I had begged Mordaunt to let me stay with the two children till she came. For my heart was very sore at leaving the little sickly thing I had learnt to love so; I wanted to tell the new woman all about his food, and what he liked, and what he did not like, and a hundred other little things that no one knew of but myself. I wanted to get a sight of the woman, too, and see what she was like, for though I would have stood on my head at any time for Mordaunt, I had no trust in him. I knew him to be selfish, vain, and headstrong, and a man, too, that would stick at nothing to gain his purpose; and so, you see, I was afraid for the child, afraid of the sort of woman he might have got. For I knew he hated the child, hated the very sight of it, and would have been glad enough if any nurse that had it had starved it to death, or killed it with gin or brandy, or with the neglect that in this case would have done equally well. And so I wanted to see the woman and talk to her.

She came in about five—a fat woman with a hard, red face. I took a dislike to her the moment I saw her, and she to me, I think, for she sniffed at me with her nose very high. The housekeeper showed her in, and introduced her as Mrs. Grace, and after a little left us together with the children.

" 'Are we all going to live together here? A kind of happy family?' she asked with a snort, as she laid her bonnet on the chest of drawers.

" 'Oh, no,' I said. 'I and little—Guy are going to the old nursery at the other end of the house.'

" 'Then, what are you doing here, pray?' she asked, as sharp as vinegar.

" 'I was looking after Gerard till you came.'

" 'I see,' she said, 'and now that I have come, perhaps you will leave me to put the room to rights.'

" 'Oh, certainly,' I said, stiffly; 'I have no wish to stay here.'

"I caught up the child, and was moving out when she stopped me.

" 'So you are to be head nurse, and I the underling,' she said. 'H'm! a pretty state of things, indeed!'

" 'There is no head nurse,' I explained; 'we each have our own child to look after.'

" 'Yes,' she snorted, 'you takes the eldest one, while a respectable woman like me has to put up with a half-fledged brat of a thing like this!'

" 'I have always had the eldest one,' I said, with perfect truth.

" 'Well, off you go, you and your eldest one, and, leave me to mine.   Lord! what a little wretch it is!'

"It made me miserable to hear the woman talk like this, for I feared it boded no good for the poor little thing I was leaving with her; so at the door I stopped, and half turned back.

" 'Mrs. Grace,' I said, timidly, for the woman's manner frightened me. 'I should like to tell you one or two things about little—Gerard's food. You see, he is so dreadfully delicate that the least thing upsets him.'

" 'Hoity-toity!' she cried, flaring up as red as fire all in a moment; 'so you're beginning the head-nurse business already! Let me tell you this, my fine miss, I was a nurse before ever you were born, and a better one than you will ever be, if you live to be a hundred.   The idea, indeed!   Teaching your betters their business!'

" 'I had no idea of teaching you anything,' I said, 'not even manners.   But, of course, I know the child better than you can, though you are sixty years old.'

"She was not more than five-and-forty at the outside, and she flew into a perfect fury.

" 'Get out of my nursery, you hussy!' she cried, 'you and your ribbons and frills and furbelows.   It's easy seeing there's no mistress in this house, with the likes of you about!'

"I waited to hear no more, but caught up the new Guy and passed out into the passage.

"We were not great friends after that, as may be imagined, and kept clear of one another on our own account, for there were no longer any orders to keep apart.   We were allowed to go where we liked, and to talk to whom we liked, without question from any.   And there were no more veils.   The children went out with their natural faces to the air, and folks came and looked at them, and passed remarks after their kind.   And these remarks were always to the same tune: what a splendid, handsome young fellow Master Guy was, and so like his father, and what a poor, miserable-looking wretch the other was; and what a mercy it was that Master Guy was heir to the place and property, and not the little cross-eyed atomy with the white face.   And Mordaunt loved to hear them talk so, and would smile and strut and hoist the boy on to his shoulders, and walk about the room with him, while the child crowed with joy.

" 'A proper De Metrier in face and limb, thank God!' he would say, piously.   But at the other he never looked.

"But as to Mrs. Grace, the new nurse, I am bound to

say this, that little Gerard—that is the one that had been Guy—grew and flourished properly under her; and I felt sorry for the wicked things I had thought about her when she came, and tried to make friends, and wipe out the memory of our first falling out.   But she, poor woman! hated the sight of me from first to last, so that after a time I gave up trying, and just left her alone.

"Six months after the coming of Mrs. Grace, Mordaunt came up one day to the nursery, and said quite quick and sudden:

" 'Susan, I have got a husband for you.'

"And I, a poor fool, went straight down on the floor, and clutched him by the knees, and prayed him, for the love of God, not to send me away.

" 'What do I want with a husband?' I moaned.

" 'Everything,' he said, shortly. 'Come, Susan, don't be a fool.   Many a girl in your place would think herself pretty lucky to get one.'

" 'And am I to go away?' I asked, feeling that I might as well die at once.

" 'Not a bit of it,' said he; 'at least not far.   I am going to let you have the Manor House at the other end of the park.   It is well furnished and a good house, and you can have as much firewood as you want, and as much farm produce—eggs, butter, and milk—as either of you can carry from the Home Farm each day.   And besides this, I will go on paying you your present wages as long as I live.   What more can any girl want?'

"I said nothing, but sat looking miserably out of the window, for I knew very well what I wanted more.

" 'Well,' he said, turning my face round so that I had to look at him, 'haven't you anything to say?'

" 'No,' I answered, dully, 'nothing. When have I got to go?'

" 'Well, the sooner the better, I think,' he said; 'but you don't even ask who the man is. Did any one ever see such a girl?'

"As if it made any difference to me who it was!

" 'Who is it?' I asked, seeing he expected me to ask it.

" 'It is Henry Beddington, the house carpenter. He is a capital fellow, steady and respectable, and getting good wages; and I doubt not but he will make you a very excellent husband.'

" 'And I will make him a very excellent wife, I suppose,' I said, bitterly.

" 'Yes,' he said, 'I see no reason in the world why you should not.'

" 'No, Mordaunt, no,' I cried, going down all in a heap on the floor once more. 'I can't do it, I really can't! Don't send me away! For God's sake, don't send me away!'

"He had been laughing and very merry up to this, but now, at the sight of my tears, his face hardened, and three straight lines came out between his eyes.

" 'My dear girl,' he said, slowly, with a pause between each word, 'you are talking like a fool. It has to be done, as you yourself must see, and there's an end of it.'

"Of course he got his way; he always did. We were married that week, and drove up to our new home in one of the new farm carts—a bright blue one, with bright red wheels, I remember—amid a deal of cheering and holloaing. But as to myself, I felt like going to my grave.

"However, I was strong, and strength and youth will live down most things; and after a time I got used to it, and to Henry Beddington, too, after a fashion. · And one of us would fetch the farm stuff every morning in a basket, as much as we could carry in a single journey, and did so till Mordaunt's death, and afterwards, too, in Guy's time.

"There were four children, and they came as quick as quick; and two months after the last was born, Beddington died. He was never strong—a poor little fellow with a weak chest, and always coughing, but a true man and honest, and with a heart of pure gold. He was a world too good for me from first to last, and every one knew it, too, except himself. But I honestly believe the poor fellow loved me so blindly that he thought that in my hands wrong *must* turn to right, whether it would or no.

"However, he died, and I was left with the four boys, and there I lived for twenty years. And at the end of twenty years Mordaunt sent for me to be house-keeper at the Abbey. George, the eldest boy, was underkeeper now, and living in the Manor House; and Bill and John, the two next, the Squire had sent out to India, and started them well in life; and the youngest, Henry, was carpenter now at the house in his father's place.

"So I went, not very willingly, for I had no knowl-edge of housekeeping, but the Squire wished it, and that was enough.

"The Squire was failing fast, so all men said. Free living and overmuch claret and port had brought him to a very evil state, and all men foretold a new Squire before the years were many more. He was not an old man, either, only fifty-two, and as merry and jolly and handsome in face as ever; but he walked with two sticks, and his back was bent, and for days at a time he would lie in his bed and groan, for the touch of the past was in his joints.

"In those days I had not yet found the Lord, and my mind was still full of wickedness and deceit, and I began to think of the days to come, and of how I should fare under the reign of Master Guy.

"So, when I had been three years at the Abbey, and the old Squire—as we called him afterwards—began to be oftener in his bed than out of it, I set myself to think hard how I could make my position firm, and put the seal of truth upon the tale I had to tell. And after a week of thinking I found a way, or at least what I took to be a way.

"Mrs. de Metrier had had different doctors when Guy and Gerard were born. For Guy she had had Dr. Benson, and for the other Dr. McCullum. They were both Greystoke men, and Benson had the name of being the best; but he had a rough kind of knock-me-down manner, and the mistress being a bit frail, and quick to feel the harshness of a loud voice, took a feeling against him, and when Gerard came sent for Dr. McCullum.

"At the time I am talking of we had a doctor of our own at Benton, and the Greystoke men came no more to Selworth. As to Benson and McCullum, they had both long since moved to London, where they were said to have fine practices. I found their addresses out of a Medical Directory in the library, and wrote to each of them the self-same letter, saying that the Squire was ill and fidgety about trifles, and moreover, not in a state to put pen to paper; and that as I had been nurse to both

his sons, he had told me to write and find out certain
things that were a trouble to his memory. He wanted
to know what body marks the boys had when they were
born, and nothing else would give him peace; and that
if they would write to me their recollections of the child
they had helped into the world, it would take a load of
worry off his mind.

"They both wrote back next day, and their letters
are in the box with the other papers, marked B and C.
I flattered myself that with their letters and Mrs. Graham's I was fairly safe, and so in the end it proved. My
first care was to copy all three, and put away the real
ones safely; and having done that, I sat down and
waited for Mordaunt to die.

"It was curious to mark how the old pride held him
to the end. He sent for me on his death-bed, when his
breath was short and quick, and speaking a sheer pain,
and he sat up against his pillows and took my hand, and
said, 'Susan, swear by all that's holy, to hide the truth
about the boys.'

"And I said—God forgive me for my hard, wicked
heart!—'I swear, so long, that is, as I am not disturbed.
But if they meddle with me I must see to myself.'

"He seemed well satisfied with this, and nodded his
head and closed his eyes, waving me to go away. And
I take it afterwards he put his word upon Guy to leave
me in peace for my life.

"So Mordaunt died, and for a while things went on as
before, only that Guy made great changes in the servants,
as folks do when they step into the shoes that have been
before them. To me he said nothing, but I knew he
wished me away, and for my own part I was much of the
same mind; so one morning I went to him in his room,

and asked to go back to the Manor House. This was not more than a month after the old Squire's death, and with the dead man's wishes still in his ears, he could but say 'yes' with a fair grace. Besides, he was very young at the time, not more than twenty-five, and he knew I had been his nurse, and 'no' would have been a hard word to say.

"So back I went to the Manor House, and well enough pleased to be there, too. George and Henry had lived there all along, while I was up at the Abbey. And for a time things went smoothly enough, and the three letters lay harmless and unheeded in my box. But the trouble came before long, as I knew full well it would. During the old Squire's lifetime I had always had £30 a year paid me quarterly by Mr. Quayle, the agent. When I went as housekeeper, of course, this stopped, and I got regular wages of £50 a year. But now when the first quarter came round, I looked in vain for my money, and so, after waiting a week, wrote to Mr. Quayle to let me have it. I got no answer for two or three days, and then a stiff business letter asking what money I referred to. I wrote back and said it was the £30 I had had every year for the last twenty years, and would he send me the first quarter at once. There was a wait of three more days, and then another letter, saying he had had no instructions from Mr. de Metrier to pay me £30 a year, but that if I would put the matter right with the young Squire, he would, of course, send me the money at once. Then I saw that the letters would have to come out of my box, but for a month or two more I did nothing, not wishing to make trouble before it was due. And the Lord knows it came due quite quickly enough!

"It began about the farm stuff. There was a new bailiff since the old Squire's death, and though he allowed George or Henry or myself to take away our basketful every morning, I could see it went sorely against the grain with him. And one morning, when I went as usual with my basket in my hand, he told me straight that I could have no more without direct orders from the Squire. I said never a word, but marched straight away home, and looked up the copies of my three letters. And that afternoon I was up at the house asking for a word with the Squire.

"I knew well enough how it had all come about. The priest at the Abbey at that time was Father Harris, a decent man enough, I make no doubt, and for all I know a good one. But on me he never looked kindly, partly because I was a Protestant, and partly because of what he thought he knew about my past. With the old Squire, Father Harris had had no more weight than a raindrop has with an oak, but with the young one it was very different. He told him—as I heard afterwards—that I was a standing reproach to the family; and that it was a scandalous thing that I should be allowed to live in ease and comfort inside the park as the price of my past iniquities, when there were plenty of good, respectable Catholics who were far more deserving of the food and house and money that were wasted upon me. And that this was not only the priest's opinion, I knew well enough; almost every one about the place thought the same, not knowing the *real* cause of the old Squire having allowed me all these things, but going off with a wholly wrong idea from the start.

"So I stood outside the door of Master Guy's study, waiting to put these things right.

" 'Good evening, Mrs. Beddington,' says he, looking not over comfortable, I thought. 'You wished to see me, I believe.'

" 'Yes, sir,' says I, coming straight to the point. 'Do I understand that I am to have no more allowance, and no more farm produce?'

"He fidgeted queerly with the paper-weights on his writing-table, and without looking up, said:

" 'I can see no real reason why you *should* continue to have these things, Mrs. Beddington. If you come to think of it, you have only been six years in all in the service of the family, while for twenty years you have been entirely supported by the estate. I think the balance of debt lies with you.'

"He looked up with a smile, with his handsome head cocked a little on one side. I looked straight into his smiling eyes, and said:

" 'I have as much right to all the things I've had as you have to be here, sir.'

"He laughed outright at this, but with a touch of awkwardness, and said:

" 'Perhaps it would be just as well for all parties not to go into that question.'

" 'Why not, sir?' I asked, coldly.

" 'Because,' says he, with another little awkward laugh, 'the grounds on which your rights are based are scarcely such as will bear scrutiny.'

"The moment for which I had been waiting had come. I looked at him straight, and said:

" 'No more will yours, sir.'

" 'What *do* you mean?' he asked, in a puzzled way. I think he thought me mad.

" 'I mean,' I said, 'that this place, Selworth Abbey, belongs to Guy de Metrier.'

" 'Yes,' he said, pityingly, 'I was aware of that.'

" 'And you, sir, were christened Gerard St. Clair de Metrier.'

"He went quite white, but beyond that not a muscle of his face changed. He smiled up at me the same superior smile as before, and said, calmly:

" 'Pray explain yourself, Mrs. Beddington. You are rather mysterious.'

"I said nothing, but pulled out letter No. 1—Mrs. Graham's, that is—and laid it on the table before him. He read it through without a word, and at the end tossed it across the table to me contemptuously.

" 'Pooh!' he said, is that all?'

" 'No, sir,' says I, 'not quite,' and gives him No. 2—Dr. Benson's.

" 'Any more?' he said, quietly, when he had finished. I gave him Dr. McCullum's, and he read that, too, as he had read the others, calmly and without a word.

" 'Well?' he said, looking up.

" 'Well, sir,' said I, 'those letters are copies. I have the originals in a safe place. As to the change of babies, I did it myself. There is no doubt about that part of it; you are Gerard and your brother is Guy.'

"For at least five minutes after that there was not a word spoken on either side. He sat fingering the pens and things, and I stood bolt upright before him. From the picture on the wall behind Guy's shoulder, Mordaunt's clear grey eyes looked straight into mine. In the days that were long past I had learned to read those eyes like an open book, and it seemed to me now that they frowned upon me angrily.   Presently Guy cleared his throat and looked up.

" 'These letters,' he said, 'may be genuine, or they may be forgeries; your statement again may be true, or it may be false.   We will not go into that question now. I imagine you have brought these matters forward because of the stoppage of your allowance, and your supply of farm produce?'

"I bowed.

" 'And if everything was continued as before, you would be satisfied?'

" 'Perfectly, sir,' I said; 'that is all I ask.'

" 'In that case,' he said, rising, 'we will, if you please, consider that this interview has never taken place.   I will give orders for everything to be continued as it was in my father's time.'

"Guy was as good as his word, as indeed he was bound to be.   I went back to the Manor House for another twenty-five years, and the world went round as usual.   Guy married, and the children were born, and eight years or so afterwards Gerard married.   A glorious creature was his wife, but she died, poor thing! soon after her little girl was born.   And Gerard followed her a few years later.

"So there was a new rightful owner to the property —a little, penniless, orphan girl that no one had ever seen.   Gerard had left her all he had to leave, which was in truth nothing, for he had fooled away all that had ever been his, and was to all ends a beggar.   When he died, his wife's two maiden sisters took the child, and no one at Selworth bothered their heads any more about her.

"Then at last, when I was seventy years old, and the

grave and judgment in plain sight, the sins of the past began to take hold of me, and I saw all my awful wickedness in its true light. And sometimes, for hours at a time, I would writhe upon my knees, and cry out to the Lord for forgiveness. And all the while I was doing it, I would feel what a pitiful hypocrite I was, for though many of my sins were past recalling, there was one which could be put right by a word from me. I knew Guy well enough by this time to know that he was as bad to cross as Mordaunt had been; and that I should be turned out of house and home was as sure as death. This is a hard thing for an old woman near the grave, who wishes to end her days in peace, and the struggle with myself and with the old wicked love of ease was not won in a day. I thought, too, in all honesty, that he might kill me. I remembered Mrs. Graham, and my horrid doubts about her end, and here would I be a greater danger and harder to overcome than ever poor Mrs. Graham had been.

"However, one day the little good that was in me got the upper hand, for my heart had been very bad that day, and I felt that any moment I might find myself face to face with God, bearing the full load of my sins upon my head; so I sent a note by Henry to the Squire, asking him to come up and see me. It was summer time, when the days were long, and he came riding up that very same evening, whistling and humming as gay and chirpy as a linnet. But he neither whistled nor hummed when he rode away; there were three deep lines between his eyes, and he spurred his big horse cruelly down the track. For I told him, as plain as words can speak, that I would hide the truth no longer, not if I died in the workhouse for it. I had nothing put by; all that I might have saved had gone out, bit by bit, to the two boys in India, and to be turned off meant the workhouse, sure enough. For I knew right well that Henry, and George with his wife and children, would go out of Selworth by the self-same gate as shut behind me. There would be no mercy shown. Mercy was never a strong point with the De Metriers. And I knew all this, and for all I knew it, faced the Squire bravely, while he stormed and thundered and stamped about the room.

"There was one chance left for both of us. If Norman married this orphan girl, I said, I would be content, and hold my peace; and till the year's end, I said, I would give them to bring this about by hook or crook.

"I thought at one time Guy would have struck me down, and killed my secret with me then and there, but just when his rage was at its hottest, he spun on his heel and flung out of the house, leaving me sitting by the table, white and trembling.

"And what will be the end of it, God knows! I am terribly afraid for my life; and for fear of what may overtake me, I have written this confession, which, with the letters, I will lock up in a box and entrust to my son Henry, to be given with his own hands to Miss Josephine de Metrier in the case of my death. The Lord have mercy on my soul and save me from the wrath to come!"

This was the end of the Confession, which was signed "Susan Beddington," and below this was written:

"Signed by Susan Beddington, this day, in my presence, September 12th, 1857,

"GEORGE HOLLAIRE,
"Rector of Benton."

There was another short paper with the others in the box, which took up the story, and ended it in a fashion. It began:

"Miss Josephine,—Now that I have seen and known you, I must add a few lines to pray your forgiveness for the terrible wrong I have done you. God grant it may yet come right! Time after time I have given the Squire another week to bring about the marriage between you and Norman. He tells me each time it is all but settled, but I have my doubts.

"Be good to my sons, who have never known anything of this, and do not judge Guy too hardly. The sin was his father's, not his. Lady Harriet knows nothing, nor yet Claud or Sophie. Norman did not at first, but I think he has been told. The priest, I know, has been told all. It is of him I am afraid. If you were a Catholic, he could be got over to our side, but, as it is, he will fight to the death before Selworth goes to a Protestant. Beware of him, he is a dangerous man, and can twist Guy round his fingers. God bless you, my dear! and do not think too ungently of a wicked old woman who will be dead before this can ever meet your eyes."

The only other two papers were the letters marked B and C.

The first was from Dr. Benson.

"Dear Madam,—In response to your enquiries, I can satisfy the Squire's mind on each of the points as to which his memory is doubtful. Guy, the eldest boy, had no distinguishing marks on his body. His left leg was of course, considerably shorter than the other, and even at that early age there was a very pronounced squint in his eyes. Both hands were perfect.

"I remain, dear madam, yours to command,
"Joseph Benson."

The other was very similar.

"Madam,—My memory is perfectly clear as to the condition of Mrs. de Metrier's second child at the time of birth. He was as fine a baby as I have ever seen, and perfectly formed, with the exception of a little finger missing on the left hand. The finger was not absolutely missing, but was only a stump as far as the first joint, and nailless. As to the eldest child, I can say nothing, as you will remember it was Dr. Benson who attended Mrs. de Metrier in her first confinement.

"I am, madam, your obedient servant,
"JAMES McCULLUM."

I slipped the papers gently back into the box, turned the key, and put the box upon the chest of drawers. Then I got up, and stared down into the red, glowing embers of the fire.

"Well?" said Beatrice, with a stretch and a mighty yawn. "Do you know all about it now?"

"Yes," I said, "I know all about it now."

"You look dreadfully solemn over it all; what's it all about?"

"Mostly about my father when he was young," I said.

"Oh, that sounds rather interesting. I suppose we must go and dress now. I heard the gong a long time ago."

They strolled off down the long passage to their rooms, and I was left alone.

My first feeling, and my strongest at that time, was undoubtedly one of intense pity for my Uncle Guy and all his family. If I had acted on the impulse of the moment, I should have written off to him then and there, saying that the whole thing was wrong and a mistake, and that as far as I was concerned I wanted nothing, and would much rather that everything went on just as it always had gone. I thought of all the numberless kindnesses I had received from them, of my aunt with her frail, feeble health, and the little old-world airs and affectations she loved so well, of Sophie turned out of her home by one on whom she had showered all the love and kindness of her nature, and I felt that of all the mean wretches that lived, I should be the meanest if I was the cause of bringing such things upon them. And then I thought of Sydney, and of how nice it would be not to be a drag and a burden to him, but to come to him with something in my hand that might make up in part for my own unworthiness. But then again, did he really want to marry me? He had been so strangely stiff and stand-offish lately, and then there was that extraordinary remark of his about our not being engaged! Was it simply that he was tired of me, or liked some one else better, or was it only jealousy about the Duke? I looked into the red-hot coals for an answer, but found none; but I found there the outline of an idea, and as it grew and flourished in my head I smiled to myself, well pleased.

My watch pointed to eight, but no one minded one being late at Ashby, so I dashed at my writing-table, and scribbled off a line to Sydney:

"Come up to-morrow: I want to see you particularly."

Then I dressed, and tore down to dinner, three steps at a time, slipping my note into the letter-box as I passed through the hall. The post went out at eight, but there were usually a few minutes' law given for the sake of late, eccentric people like myself.

CHAPTER XXIX

WHAT CAME OF THE CONFESSION

NEXT morning the whole world was white with snow—three inches of it at least—the first real winter we had had. Great fires blazed in all the grates, and the robins—bound, I suppose, by the laws of custom and of Christmas cards—came hopping round outside the dining-room window in search of hospitality, which—poor things!—they got without stint.

Sydney came up about twelve, trudging through the snow in thick shooting boots and gaiters. I waylaid him in the hall, and beckoned to him to hold his tongue and follow me into the library, for I knew the others would all rush garrulously out at the sound of his voice, and upset all my deep-laid plot. Sydney, looking rather mystified, and very solemn, shook himself clear of snow like a wet dog, and followed me meekly. In the library we were likely to be left in peace, for the whole family was essentially gregarious, and hated nothing more than solitude, except silence. At the present moment I knew them to be safely collected in the drawing-room, working feverishly for the Greystoke bazaar, and as usual, talking in chorus. I suppose I ought to have been doing the same, and for that very reason, of course, I was not. It was most unusual for me at any time to be doing what I ought.

"You wanted to see me about something?" Sydney

said, after we had both selected comfortable chairs.
There was a certain out-of-the-way look on his face, I
thought. Was it anxiety or curiosity, or what? Was it
hope, or was it fear?

"Yes," I said, rubbing my chin, and looking up at
the ceiling reflectively. There was a long pause. "I
wanted to ask you," I said, slowly, "whether you
thought it would be right for me to write to Uncle Guy
for some money. You see I must tip the servants here,
and I literally have not got a penny."

He looked very surprised.

"Oh, is that all!" he said, with an odd little laugh.
"No, I should certainly not write. You must let me
advance you whatever you want."

"But you are not a relation," I said. "I certainly
can't let you do that. I might as well ask the Duke."

"Hardly that," he muttered. "You do know me a
little better than you know him."

"Oh, I don't see much difference."

"Don't you?" he said, shortly. "No, I daresay not."
Then, after a moment, he added:

"Then your message had nothing to do with the contents of the red box?"

"Oh, no," I said, in great surprise. "Why should
it?"

"What was inside it?" There was open curiosity in
his voice now.

"Oh, a long rigmarole, all about Mrs. Beddington's
younger days. Nothing that you would care to know."

"Then there was nothing in it that affects you in any
way?"

"Good gracious, no! What an extraordinary idea!
Why should there be?"

"Oh, I don't know. But I can't quite see the object of giving you the box if there was nothing in it of interest to you."

"I don't say there wasn't. I say there was nothing that affects me in any way."

"Nothing that will make any difference to your life?"

"No, nothing."

Sydney got up, and for a minute or two stood with his back to the fire, looking straight before him. Then suddenly, before I knew what he was up to, he had slipped into my chair by the side of me, and had his arm round my waist.

"Joe, my little darling," he said, "I am so glad!"

"Not so fast," I cried, jumping up; "you take too much for granted, my friend."

Poor fellow! he looked dreadfully crestfallen.

"What do I take for granted?" he asked, sheepishly.

"Why, everything. In the first place, I am not your darling, and in the second place, you have no business to put your arm round my waist. We are not engaged!"

"Joe," he said, simply, "will you marry me?"

"I am not at all sure that I will," I said. "You have been extremely disagreeable lately, not to say horrid!"

"I have been worried," he said, "and anxious about several things. It was not my fault, Joe, honestly it was not."

"But you told the Duchess we were not engaged."

"I had a reason for doing that; I will tell you about it some day. But it was not because I didn't want to be. I can tell you that much now."

"Are you really sure you love me?" I asked, doubtfully.

For a minute or so he made no answer. When he

did, it was so emphatic a one that it was some moments before I could get my breath again. As soon as I could speak, I put exactly the same question to him again, for no particular reason that I know of, except to prove the perversity of woman.

"But do you *really* love me?"

"Well," he said, laughing, "if you still have any doubts, I can only repeat—"

"No, no," I said. "Sit down quietly, for goodness sake! What I want to know is, would you marry me whatever I had done?"

"Yes," he answered, "I will marry you whatever ghastly crime you may have committed."

"Even if I have deceived you?"

"Even if your hair is a wig, and your complexion put on with a brush, and your figure stuffed with sawdust."

"Then," I said, solemnly, "I *have* deceived you."

He did not look the least alarmed.

"Really?" he said. "Will you undeceive me now, then?"

"Yes, I will. There *was* something in the box that affected me."

"What?"

"Well, Mrs. Beddington says my father was the eldest son, and the place really belongs to me."

"Josephine," he said, looking as solemn as twenty-four judges, "you should have told me this before."

"No, I should not," I said, putting my two hands on his shoulders; "and don't call me Josephine; it's rude."

"What are you going to do?"

"Marry you," I said, "first. You know you promised you would; you can't back out now. After that, I shall think."

For at least five minutes Sydney paced up and down the room like a wild beast, then he said, suddenly:

"Do you think it's true?"

"Yes," I said; "I don't think there's the slightest doubt about it!"

"Let me see the papers, will you?"

"Yes, I will get the box."

For the rest of the morning he sat poring over all the papers I had read the night before.   That brought us on to luncheon time.   Just before we went in I whispered to him: "Will you tell them about our engagement?   It will look so odd unless you do."

"All right!" he said, "if you like."

So, in the middle of luncheon, after the servants had left the room, Sydney, looking remarkably foolish, said: "Duchess, I have an announcement to make to you. Miss de Metrier and I are going to get married."   Upon which the whole family rose from their apple-tart, and kissed me without ceasing for five minutes—all except the Duke, and he couldn't very well, poor man.   And then such a chorus of questions as arose.   Did Mr. de Metrier know of it?   And wouldn't he be pleased?   And what would poor Mr. Norman think?   They were afraid he would not be quite so pleased, from what they had heard.   All of which questions I cunningly avoided by means of convenient blushes.   And then more questions: When was it to be?   And where?   And who were to be my bridesmaids?   They would positively never speak to · me again till the day I died if I didn't ask all three of them to be bridesmaids.

I was very glad when it was all over.

And now, knowing the state of things, the girls were just as openly anxious to leave Sydney and me alone as before they had been to do the opposite. So, instead of asking me what I was going to do, and suggesting half a dozen different plans at once, as generally happened after luncheon, they bustled out of the drawing-room with much meaning, one after the other, leaving us alone in our glory.

"I will walk back with you, Sydney," I said.

"Yes," he said, "I wish you would. There are several things we must talk over."

Out in the park it was better. We could talk openly there and freely, without fear of screens and portières and soft-footed servants.

"Have you thought what you are going to do?" Sydney asked, when we were clear of the garden.

"I have thought what I am not going to do," I answered, "and that is anything which will in the slightest degree interfere with Uncle Guy's possession of Selworth. It has been his home for over fifty years now, and I should be a *pig* to try and turn him out because of a crack-brained fancy of his father's."

Sydney laughed. "That is rather woman's logic," he said. "But apart from that, do you really think that he and his deserve much consideration at your hands?"

"Yes, I do," I answered, stoutly. "He has always been kindness itself to me."

"H'm!" he said; "how about that chestnut mare, and the burning of the Manor House, and one or two things that Master Norman had a hand in?"

"I don't believe for a minute that Uncle Guy knew anything at all about the fire at the Manor House; and as to Maid Marion bolting, it was a pure accident, owing to my bad hands. She was as quiet as a lamb, really."

"I took the trouble," said Sydney, slowly, "to make

some enquiries through a friend of mine at Newmarket, and I heard from him that the mare invariably bolted if there was anything behind her, and had always to be exercised alone in consequence."

"I don't believe a word of it," I said. "Anyhow, Uncle Guy knew nothing about it. Why, he let Sophie ride her home."

"Yes, but alone."

"Oh, that's all nonsense. The whole thing was entirely my bad riding."

"Very well, then," he said, laughing; "we won't quarrel about it. But in the meantime, what are you going to do?"

"Well, I thought that I might ask Uncle Guy to allow me so much a year—just enough for us to live on, and in return I would give him the papers."

"Yes," he said; "that's not a bad idea. It would be a blessing to have enough to let us live in the old country. America is right enough for a man, even though he goes there with an empty pocket, but it is altogether a different matter when he proposes taking a poor little Dryad with him. It is a bit rough on the Dryad."

"Is that why you have been behaving in this extraordinary way lately?"

"No; I have been behaving in this extraordinary way, as you call it, for quite a different reason."

"Were you jealous of the Duke?"

"No, I was not even jealous of the Duke, don't you flatter yourself," he said, laughing.

"Then, what was it?"

"I think you know pretty well without my telling you."

"Yes, I know, you old stupid! It was because you guessed what was inside that box."

"Yes," he said; "I was afraid my little Dryad might think I was a fortune-hunter instead of being merely a Dryad-hunter. But now that you are going to give it all up, it's all right, and I'm not a bit afraid of you any more."

We were leaning over a rough-shaped oak rail, bordering one of the woods that fringed the park. It was a typical Christmas evening—long past Christmas, it is true, but still redolent of peace and good-will to all men. The freshly fallen snow lay white and clean as a new-washed sheet, the sky was pure and cloudless, and not the faintest breath of wind stirred the frosty air. The silence was intense—vast and limitless—and I think the witchery of the moment took hold of both our souls. We wasted nothing in words—words would have been an outrage, a desecration of the glories of those moments. And for my own part, no words that ever were framed by poet could have given shape to the immense happiness that was welling up in my heart on that evening. Words are cumbersome, pompous, inadequate; how can they cope with the divinity of thought? What words could draw the shadowiest picture of our feelings that night as we walked home together over the smooth, crunching snow with the "myriad eyes of Heaven" specking the inky sky overhead. And if there were such words, would any one care to write them for the inspection of the world? Such things are sacred—sacred to the library of the mind, where, among the dusty volumes of memory, sweetness and melancholy rub shoulders so strangely on every shelf.

CHAPTER XXX

UNCLE GUY MAKES A MOVE

IT was arranged that Sydney should write to my uncle, telling him of the papers in my possession, and asking him what he proposed doing in the matter. He was also going to arrange that the Morrises should not be brought up before the magistrates for another week, as the fear of what disclosures they might make would be likely to help Uncle Guy towards a reasonable frame of mind. Norman and Father Boyle, we learnt, had left Selworth for London.

It was nearly a week before he received an answer, and then it was only half an answer. My uncle said that the allegations contained in Sydney's letter were so extraordinary that time must be given him to think the matter over. Would Sydney send him the papers or copies of them?

Sydney wrote back and said that he feared it was impossible at present to procure copies of the papers, but that there appeared to be no shadow of doubt that they were in perfect order, and so complete a chain of evidence as could scarcely fail to ensure the result of any appeal to law.

To this there was no reply, and after a few days, Sydney wrote again, begging for a definite proposal of some sort, as Miss de Metrier's position was naturally an uncomfortable one. On the second day Uncle Guy

replied that at the end of a week he would make a proposal which he had little doubt would satisfy all parties
concerned.

In the meanwhile the Morrises were had up before the
magistrates, charged with trespassing in Selworth Park
in search of game, and with feloniously assaulting and
wounding the Honourable Sydney Grayle, and lastly with
arson and attempted murder, in that they did, on the
seventeenth day of January, wilfully and maliciously set
fire to the premises known as the old Manor House, Selworth Park. I had the whole thing from Sydney.. My
name was kept entirely out of the business, but Sydney,
of course, had to give evidence. The charge of arson
was unsupported by direct evidence, but undeterred by
this, the magistrates remanded all three Morrises to take
their trial at the Greystoke Quarter-Sessions.

Still there came no answer from Uncle Guy, and when
a second letter was equally ignored, Sydney made up his
mind to go up to London and beard my uncle in his very
den. What success awaited him there may be best
judged from his own letter:

"MY DARLING LITTLE DRYAD—I arrived in London yesterday about noon, and at once went to your uncle's house in Curzon
Street. Judge of my absolute amazement when I was told by the
grimy old caretaker who answered the bell, that Mr. and Mrs. de
Metrier and their son and daughter, accompanied by the Rever-
end Father Boyle, had sailed from Liverpool for America on the
Saturday previous. I asked if there were any servants in the
house, and was told that they had all been dismissed. A sudden
inspiration dawned upon me, and I bribed the old woman with
half a crown to let me go over the house. It was as I suspected.
The place was literally gutted. Every single plate, picture, chair,
table, and cabinet in the house was gone, as were all the carpets
and curtains. The plate-closet and wine-cellar were both empty!
I dashed off to Wade & Bonny, the family lawyers, and from them

elicited the further information that the property, that for many years had been clear of debt, had lately been mortgaged absolutely up to the hilt, and that all the horses, including the racing stable at Newmarket, had been sold by auction. A great many things of value have also, it appears, been brought up from Selworth and sold. The whole thing has been carried out with extraordinary secrecy and quickness, and the loss on what was sold must be enormous. Old Wade, whom I saw, confessed that he thought the Squire had gone off his head, and thought it his duty to write to Norman. But when Norman wrote back saying that he entirely approved of what his father was doing, of course there was nothing left for him but to carry out the instructions given him. Old Wade estimates that, what with the mortgages and the sales, your uncle must have had at least £200,000 lodged to his credit. This money could of course be attached if you thought fit; but from what I know of you, you probably would not care to do that.

"When I told old Wade of the true state of things, I thought his chin would have dropped off, his mouth opened so wide. His glasses dropped from his nose, and he turned quite pale.

"'God bless my soul!' was all he could say, and this he kept on saying at intervals for ten minutes.

"When he had recovered his senses a little, his professional instincts revived. He explained that your uncle's action was a plain admission of your rights, as well as a distinct felony, so that he would hardly be likely to fight the case. In fact, his going to America proves clearly that he acknowledges defeat. I expect the Morrises having been put back for trial has had something to say to this American trip; but it appears, from what old Wade tells me, that he has been preparing for it for months past. Wade, of course, was all for pouncing down on the money in the Bank before it is transferred to America, but I told him I knew you would not wish this done. The old brute asked if you were eccentric!

"So, dear little Dryad, Selworth is yours, with all the trees within it for you to gambol about in. Of course, the estate will be fearfully crippled for many years to come. Wade suggests selling the London house at once. He also suggests that you should live abroad for ten years or so till you are in a position to open Selworth again. How would that suit you? Not over well, I suspect. However, these are all things which must be talked over. I shall be with you soon after this reaches you. You might walk down to the little gate by the fir wood to meet me—about one o'clock to-morrow.—Ever your loving   SYDNEY.

"*P. S.*—Claud, it appears, is still with his regiment."

CHAPTER XXXI

THE DEFINITION OF A NAME

THERE remains little more to tell. Once more, after many years of pinching, Selworth Abbey has opened its doors to the world as in the days of yore; and Sydney and I have emerged from the three little rooms in the west wing that have hidden us all these years. Uncle Guy is said to be prospering mightily in New York City, and Norman and Sophie have both married on to dollars. Father Boyle became, for a while, a centre of political agitation, but is since said to be dead.

At Selworth itself there is little change, only the changes of detail that go on continuously from generation to generation, and will to the end of the world—changes born of the superiority of youth, and the fidgetiness of ownership.

For Selworth is now mine — glorious, beloved Selworth!—to do as I will with. Only one spot is there in the whole domain that is no longer mine.

For Inversnaid—the centre-piece of my life's romance—is mine no longer; it belongs now to Granville, and only by invitation am I allowed to avail myself of its shelter. And when that rare honour is done me, the proprietor kindly provides a sheep-hurdle to facilitate ascent—*my* ascent only, not his; he and Claire and Stephanie get up by the drawbridge, and would sooner die than make use of any other means.

And the great tree itself, alone of us all, remains unchanged and unchangeable, no larger, no smaller, no younger, no older, but just the same—majestic, silent, inscrutable as ever. Sydney has three grey hairs behind each ear, and I have added an inch perhaps to my circumference—not more; but in the tree there is no change. There are still the same hedgehogs stuck on rolling-pins, the ten-acre field, the drawbridge, the moat, the secret chamber, the potato patch, Arthur's seat, and Lake Superior, and above all, the fireplace, blackened with the ceaseless fires of years. Only in the naming of the branches is there any change. "My branch" has been taken from me, and annexed by Granville, aged ten. It was voted "too difficult for mother." Shades of past memories! Too difficult for mother! Mother, who only the day before yesterday sat wobbling astride the tipmost end of it, and felled Pete Morris with the heel of her shoe! But of course the children know nothing of this. And Norman's branch has become Claire's, and Claud's has become Stephanie's, and I have been apportioned the spare branch, the one that for a short time had been Sophie's, because, forsooth, it is low and easy!

Once in a blue moon Sydney comes up with the rest of us, and then it may be that he makes the children open their round eyes very wide, for he tells them that he would still back me, if need be, to climb against any one of them with one arm tied behind my back, for that I am, and ever will be, the one and only Hamadryad.

And then they all cry in chorus: "But what *is* a hamadryad?"

And he says, "A hamadryad is a young lady who lights fires in trees."